A

COMMON

VIRTUE

A
COMMON
VIRTUE

JAMES A. HAWKINS

NAVAL INSTITUTE PRESS
Annapolis, Maryland

1 8 9 2 4 6 9 2 1

Naval Institute Press
291 Wood Road
Annapolis, MD 21402

Library of Congress Cataloging-in-Publication Data

Hawkins, James A.
  A common virtue : a novel / James A. Hawkins.
    pages cm
  ISBN 978-1-61251-796-4 (hardback) — ISBN 978-1-61251-794-0 (ebook) 1. Marines—Fiction.
2. Vietnam War, 1961–1975—Fiction. 3. Bureaucracy—United States—Fiction. 4. War stories. I. Title.
  PS3608.A8933C66 2014
  813'.6—dc23

                                                                        2014027055

∞ Print editions meet the requirements of ANSI/NISO z39.48-1992 (Permanence of Paper).
Printed in the United States of America.

22 21 20 19 18 17 16 15 14   9 8 7 6 5 4 3 2 1
First printing

Dedicated to:
The 58,269 who didn't return

My beautiful Susan
I miss you with my every breath

Ryanne
My daughter and my life

ACKNOWLEDGMENTS

SO MANY PEOPLE helped me with the writing of this book, and all deserve special recognition. Critical acknowledgment must go to Leona and Jerrold Schecter of the Schecter Literary Agency and K. J. Vigue II, whose perseverance and belief brought my work to fruition. Without them and each of my friends listed below, this book would never have been realized. My apologies to anyone I may have missed.

Sandy Anderson
Tracy Bayne
Nathan Childs
Carlyle Clark
Dagnee
Alan David
Ann Everett
Gregg Fujimoto
John Hamler
Cristina Howard
Frank Mezias
"Mits" Okura
Danny Perry
Wes Saito

Dr. Jordan Samhuri
Wayland Stallard
Nancy Steinkamp
Terry Steinkamp
Maj. Gen. Walter Tagawa, U.S. Army (Ret.)
Susan Thatcher
Amy Chia Torres
Kurt Torres
Ann Walters
Patti Yaeger
Craig Young
Wayne Zurl

AUTHOR'S NOTE

I WAS JUST A SCARED KID, but I walked among heroes—men who expected nothing and gave everything. Every Marine I served with remains, to me, a great American, simply because they stood on those muddy hilltops, flew out of those god-awful LZs, humped through the steaming jungle, and returned to a thankless nation. These very special men, these *Marines,* remain the giants of their time, and I hold them in my heart as true patriots.

While Paul Jackson and Bart Rivers are mythical individuals and Marine Force Recon as portrayed in this book is purely a creation of my mind, the heroism I have tried to illustrate through them is the one constant that runs through the many, many men who have served our Corps. I intend for Jackson and Rivers to embody what I believe about being a Marine: that belonging makes you part of a legacy of unselfish courage, regardless of how small a part you played in it. This sense of comradeship comes alive when I hear Sousa's "Semper Fidelis" and is kept vibrant by the pride I have in knowing I once marched side by side with the very best America could offer.

The word "Marine" wells up in a man. It causes him to accomplish great things in the most adverse circumstances. Such were the actions of every Marine who served in a war that even today America despises. Such are the gifts our difficulties have given: pride, honor, and fraternity of the finest fighting force the world has ever known. I am vastly proud of my service—our Corps—and every person who has worn the uniform. We earned the right to be called *Marine,* and we share more than those who were not there can understand.

Semper Fi!

ONE

Quang Tri Province, Northern I Corps

0230, September 10, 1967

WHEN ADRENALINE POUNDS, a man can see great distances in the dark. The Marines knew they were surrounded. The patrol lay motionless. Captain Rivers' heart was beating so hard he worried the enemy soldiers coming over the hill might hear it. Rivers looked at the team's senior NCO. "We're trapped, Macon."

Sergeant Macon's face reflected his chagrin. "Well, you came to find out why we were losing so many patrols. I guess you're about to learn."

"Yeah, well I still don't know shit. I have to know *how* they knew we were here."

Macon just stared at the big captain. "Yeah, you gonna tell me how we're going to learn that or keep it a friggin' secret?"

At 6 foot 2 and 160 pounds, Bart Rivers was a lean, powerful man—40 pounds lighter than when he graduated from Annapolis 6 years ago. He was serving his second tour of duty in Vietnam. As the intelligence officer of the 3rd Battalion, 26th Marines, he possessed information that should have kept him off any long-range reconnaissance patrol, but nearly 50 percent of the LRRPs were coming back mauled, or not coming back at all, and Colonel MacDonald, commander of the 26th Marine Regiment, had sent him to find out why.

Rivers looked at his big, burly sergeant and let the wiseass comment pass. "They're too damned confident, Macon. They aren't even trying to be quiet."

The platoon sergeant stared at the advancing enemy. "No shit. How many you figure are out there?"

"More than enough to get the job done." Rivers' head twisted in a new direction. "What's that?"

Macon spun his head toward the new noise. "*NVA!* Shit, I've never seen that much of the North Vietnamese Army this far south. Hell if I'm going out like this. We gotta go *now*, Captain."

Rivers raised his right arm to signal the LRRP team forward and tried hard to keep the fear out of his voice when he spoke. "Listen up. We're gonna be overrun, and they won't be taking prisoners. When they hit us, I want every man to look to himself. If we evade separately, some of us will make it back."

Sergeant Macon couldn't believe it. "We're not buggin' out on you, Skipper."

"You'll do as I tell you, Sergeant. Some of us have to get back or the patrol is wasted. Now, spread out and pick yourself a path. Macon, you get as many home as possible."

Private Williams, the youngest man on the team, added hysteria to the organized panic. "Sir, they're going to hear us."

Rivers shot a hard look at him. "Hear us? They'll *see* us if they get any closer. Move out."

The team slid through a stand of elephant grass. The razor-sharp edges slashed arms and faces, but they moved on, each man hiding inside his private terror.

Williams continued to echo everyone's fear. "Oh, Christ. We're all gonna die."

Macon grabbed him by the jacket. "*Shut up!* Get ready to rock and roll. We're outta here as soon as the first shot's fired. We'll only have seconds to cut and run, and we goddamn sure ain't gonna surrender."

The LRRP team heard voices across the road and the sound of rifle bolts sliding home. A Vietnamese voice called out. "O đâu là con hoang?"

"What'd he say?"

"He's asking if anyone knows where we are," Rivers translated. "Called us bastards."

Macon whirled around. "Why, that son of a—" Rivers pushed his sergeant to get him moving. When they reached the bottom of the hill Macon slid ahead to scout. A hysterical Williams grabbed Rivers. "Jesus, sir, if we surrender . . ."

Rivers swept a cloud of mosquitoes off his face. "Shut up, Williams. I told you, they're not taking prisoners."

Macon wiped sweat from his eyes. "Christ. If we only had five more minutes." They paused at a bulky stump at the edge of a rice paddy, and a yellow flare popped overhead to cast weird shadows across the flooded square of seedlings. Macon's asshole slammed shut as he slid on his stomach to the edge of the dike. He raised his head over the rim then pulled it down quickly. "*Son of a bitch!*"

Williams cut his face on a punji stick and tumbled down into the fetid water. As Rivers hauled the nearly hysterical private from the rice paddy, two North Vietnamese soldiers raced out of the darkness and hurled themselves against the patrol. If they'd been sure of the team's exact location, the LRRPs would've been done for, but the NVA misjudged their fire.

Rivers pushed Williams against the dike as bullets tore past the spot where Macon's head had been only seconds before. "Get down."

Macon's eyes showed no fear as he thrust his knife under a Communist's chin and yelled, "Get some!"

"So much for being first into the fray," Rivers yelled.

PFC Brown, the team's automatic rifleman, knelt half-in-half-out of the rice paddy and yelled, "Fuck you, gook," as his knife slid into an enemy neck.

But even as the second NVA went down clutching his throat, another threw himself on Macon. The big sergeant dragged him into the muddy water and tore at the man's flesh with his killing knife. "Bullshit! They ain't made the gook that's gonna kill me. No goddamned way."

A few feet away, Rivers looked for a break in the advancing NVA line. There wasn't one. He motioned the men to scatter, then turned and ran as fast as he could across the rice paddy yelling over his shoulder, "I told you when the shit got bad every man was to escape. There ain't going to be any better time than right now." He feared his men still might follow because of the deep sense of camaraderie within the LRRP unit and was elated to see them sprinting in different directions. He ran like a startled gazelle until he saw the glow of several flashlights ahead and realized that NVA were forming in front of the tree line he'd been running toward.

No longer caring about stealth, he shouted to cover his fear, an old habit that did little to ease a large case of galloping nerves. "Serves you right, Rivers, you dumb bastard. Now there's no one left to cover your six, and you're going to get yours." He slid to a halt and hit the ground to watch the enemy come surging into view. He didn't figure to die quickly. He lay completely still and waited. Slowly he slipped his weapon into his shoulder and aimed at the leader's head, hoping to draw the NVA's attention away from his rapidly disappearing squad. His M14 barked out twenty rounds; he reloaded, then jumped up and ran toward the massed North Vietnamese, stumbling as he ripped each foot from the rice paddy. It was an unsure strategy born of desperation, but it didn't fail entirely. It would have succeeded completely if he had reached concealment before the NVA overcame their momentary fear of a crazed American charging into their midst. But cover didn't exist.

One of the NVA saw Rivers scurrying for the top of the dike and yelled to his brothers, "Ò dó nó là. Giêt nó."

As Rivers mentally translated, he no longer doubted his fate. "Christ, they want to kill, not capture me." With nothing to lose, he ran as if chased by demons. He was holding a short lead when he disappeared into the shadows. There, he leaned against the dank earthen wall, smelled the awful stench of human feces, and watched as the pursuit went by. He remained motionless, eyes burning from the flow of sweat and biting insects, utterly done in by fear and exhaustion. After a few moments he took a cautious peek back toward the paddy, then wheeled about when he heard a noise behind him. Only then did he realize the extent of his predicament. "Oh, my God." At least fifty NVA were standing there, all with flashlights pointing into his eyes. From a dozen different locations small, oval faces regarded him with astonishment. Among them, not three meters away, stood their officer, an NVA colonel. Beside him, screaming with unholy delight, stood the local VC commander, the crazed fanatic named Nguyen—the very man Rivers' team had come to kill.

TWO

NVA Base Camp, Quang Tri Province

0400, September 10, 1967

IT TOOK FIVE soldiers to hold Rivers against the paddy dike and lash his hands and feet together. Afterward they thrust a long wooden pole through the bindings so they could carry him.

Hanging from the pole, Rivers stared intently at Nguyen and watched the Viet Cong commander's fishlike eyes, cold and void of emotion, take his measure. The NVA colonel nodded at one of his men, who struck Rivers with the butt of an AK-47. The blow stunned him but didn't knock him unconscious. He felt himself lifted and almost cried out as the ropes bit hideously into his wrists and ankles. He was too big to be carried by the much shorter Vietnamese, and when his back dragged against the ground, they quickly stopped to move the bonds from his wrists to around his torso.

Taking stock of the situation, Rivers saw that his captors weren't all VC. The large, pale-skinned soldier he could see out of the corner of his eye was clearly a Russian adviser. There were a lot of NVA in the group as well, distinguishable by their green uniforms and light brown sun helmets. There were even a few Chinese officers; one, a colonel, stood next to his NVA and VC counterparts holding Rivers' M14 and .45-caliber pistol.

"Nguyen, you son of a bitch," Rivers shouted, "*donner-moi revenir mes armes.*" He pronounced the name "wing" in the Vietnamese fashion and gave his half-remembered high school French a try.

The Chinese colonel stopped talking to Nguyen and looked toward Rivers, then dismissed him with a glance and continued his discussion with his NVA and VC counterparts, unaware that Rivers could understand him. "We have three dead, seven wounded, comrade. One is your aide, Comrade Tong. The others who hid with this one haven't been found."

"Then stop the search," Nguyen said. "We have what we want. The others are enlisted men, so we save our bullets."

The Chinese officer looked at the men lying on the ground. "And the wounded? What about them?"

"Dispatch them. We can't be slowed by the unfit. Those who can't keep up will be left." Nguyen turned to Rivers. "Speak English, Yankee. Your French is deplorable."

"Fuck you," Rivers answered. "Do you understand that?"

"Your humor is in poor taste. Tell me why you are here or I will kill you right now."

Rivers started his Geneva Convention speech. "I demand treatment as a combatant officer and full treatment as prisoners of war for my men if any were captured." He barely got to the warning about the consequences of assaulting a military officer before the Chinese colonel stopped him short. "The Geneva Convention isn't recognized by the People's Army. You've been caught twenty kilometers behind our lines. You're an assassin at worst, a spy at best."

Rivers didn't hesitate. "I'm a captain in the United States Corps of Marines. Untie me this minute."

Nguyen's eyes blazed and he shook his fist. "A captain of Marines? You claim to be one of those black-hearted assassins? *You are not an officer! You are a hired killer!* You broke into our camp, set mines, and slaughtered more than fifty of my soldiers. You came as a thief, blaspheming the Geneva Convention."

The Chinese colonel added, "We know how to deal with people like you, scum."

Rivers was scared but at the same time elated. The claymores had worked; Nguyen just confirmed it. Fifty VC wouldn't see another dawn. He rubbed his face against his arm to wipe the sweat from his eyes and brought forth his best bravado. "You're a liar, Nguyen. I know it, and so do you. If you call it fifty, I'll bet it's closer to a hundred."

He knew he was antagonizing his enemy, but every minute he delayed them was one more his men could use to escape. He turned to the Chinese colonel. "I demand to be allowed to walk. You've captured me; it's impossible to escape, so there's no need for brutality. Carrying me like this is an insult to all military men . . . and it makes the People's Liberation Army look like cowards. What we did was done against a military target, no more than what you've done a hundred times."

Nguyen, a life-long Communist and a senior officer in the PLA, pulled himself up to his full height. "I am no coward. I have never run to save my skin."

That was a lie and Rivers knew it. Insurgents ran away from every fight they were in.

"When we caught you, you were running to save yourself . . . in the opposite direction of your men," the Chinese colonel shouted. "You're a coward . . . a dog sneaking in the night. You'll be shot as a spy." He sprayed Rivers with spittle as he yelled. "But first we'll find out what you know. You'll tell us, if it takes all night."

Either Rivers hadn't heard right or the colonel was bluffing. He continued to taunt his enemy, buying with each word an additional second for his men. "You don't know why we were here, do you? There's no way you could, and there's no way I'm ever going to tell you." Rivers' defiance remained strong and clear, its strength garnered on the Annapolis parade ground and hardened by months in the jungle. His patrol had come into the valley three days ago, entered Nguyen's camp unseen, and left the same way. No one knew the Marines were there until the claymores detonated. So, how did the NVA find the patrol so fast afterward? Rivers continued his insolence, hoping his fortitude would cover his fear. "You'll learn nothing, Colonel. As a professional officer, you can't condone this sort of thing."

The Chinese officer gave Rivers a long, cold stare but didn't reply. Instead he turned and called out into the night. Three more Chinese soldiers trooped in: a bespectacled, bone-thin man of about forty in a soiled enlisted man's uniform and two immaculately uniformed Chinese officers who stood rigidly next to their commander. They carried handcuffs and leg irons to replace the ropes binding Rivers.

"I appeal to you, Colonel. On my honor. What these men are planning is murder, plain and simple."

The Chinese colonel's mouth twisted into a sneer and he snarled at his men. "Take him to the hut. He'll tell us everything. He's no stronger than the others."

Growls of agreement rose from the assembling Communists, and Rivers practically neighed in panic. "I'm an American officer. If you lay a finger—" Bound as he was, he could only listen as the Chinese colonel ordered the three men to hurry.

★

As the three pushed him inside the hut, they began to discuss who would have the honor of inflicting pain. Rivers just about let go of his bladder but held on long enough to yell, "Get the fuck away from me." The younger-looking of the two officers scared the shit out of Rivers. His scarred face looked as if it had been burned by napalm and someone put it out with a garden rake. Using force of will, Rivers focused his words on the VC commander. "You are a coward, Nguyen. You are the worst kind of bastard. If only half of your reputation is true, you're absolute scum. If it's you my fate's left to, well . . ."

Nguyen just stood there and let the insults bounce off. He glared at his captive with hate-filled eyes before addressing Rivers in perfect English. "You speak of war, Yankee? What do you know of it? Your vaunted military is losing. Our comrades are beating you at every corner. In a few months there will be a general uprising and the entire country will be against you and your puppet government in Saigon. I tell you this so you will understand your position. You are beyond help from your big guns and aircraft now."

Rivers didn't hesitate with his answer. "So, I am a prisoner of war after all. Well, it's better we do this here where the Chinese can watch. At least they won't kill me out of hand."

"Shut your filthy mouth," Nguyen snarled. "It's only a matter of time until we achieve victory. You've been an officer long enough to know that. Your small effort here can't possibly make a difference. But what you might have learned tonight could mean a delay in our timetable and order of march, dispositions, objectives, equipment, and morale." His eyes met Rivers' with murderous intent. "Your one hope, spy, lies in full disclosure . . . immediately!"

"I don't know anything worth all this." Rivers nodded his head in different directions around the small hut. "And even if I did, I'd never tell you."

"You'll tell us everything," the scar-faced officer said. The malevolence in his voice chilled Rivers to the bone.

Nguyen nodded, and a man kicked Rivers in the groin. He went down hard; before he could recover he was kicked savagely in the ribs. A long thin rod, its tip cherry red, was brought in front of Rivers' eyes. Scarface laughed wickedly. "Tell us what you learned or you will never see again."

"Đóng cửa miệng của bạn và ngăn chặn nó," Nguyen raged at the man.

Through his pain Rivers mentally translated. "Stop! He will tell me because I will it. Not because of the evil things you can do." He coughed out the blood in his mouth. "I saw nothing worth reporting. I swear."

Nguyen nodded again and a vicious kick to the ribs put the American back on the floor.

"Why did you run?" Nguyen asked.

Rivers spoke quickly before another kick could land. "Because I needed to protect my men. I saw nothing. I swear it. We came to take out your headquarters. That's all." It sounded thin, as the truth often does, but it drove Nguyen into a frenzy.

The VC commander screamed. "Either you're a fool or you think I am. You'll tell us everything under his persuasion." Once again he nodded to the scar-faced officer, who kicked Rivers in the crotch. Nguyen spat on Rivers. "He's capable of extracting anything . . . everything, and he will deliver unspeakable pain. You have a choice. Tell me what I want to know now and die quickly, or this man will find his vengeance in your pain."

Rivers didn't doubt for a moment what he heard, but kept up his bravado. "You're not serious. You're trying to scare me . . . a cowardly trick at best. You're too much of a soldier to use torture. Now I have a question for you. How did you find us? How did you even know we were here?"

Nguyen screamed, "Again," and more kicks landed. His voice and eyes were flat, unemotional. "We heard you coming for hours. Your equipment makes so much noise a blind man would realize your presence. Besides, you Americans stink of milk and aftershave. We have other ways of finding you too, but I will wait until you are taking your last breath before I divulge those. Now answer me. What have you learned? We are beyond military niceties or the Geneva Convention now. There is too much at stake. What you know could cost the lives of hundreds, perhaps thousands of my comrades. I cannot afford to play games or spare any pain when the fate of my country might depend on keeping what you have learned a secret."

Under Nguyen's cold stare, Rivers knew he'd tell them what they wanted to know . . . everybody does if it gets bad enough. "I will tell you nothing."

Nguyen's voice remained cold and unemotional. "Yes. Yes, you will."

Rivers tried hard to respond without emotion, "You will grow tired of this game, Nguyen. I will tell you nothing."

"I give you an hour before they begin," Nguyen said. "Use it to find reason."

"Loại bỏ các hạn chế," he ordered the guards. "Remove the restraints." Then, shoulders slumping, he turned away and pushed past the junior officers like a long-suffering individual who could think of nothing more to say.

But Rivers wasn't through. "Reason? You're a fool. I don't know a damn thing. Why can't you see I'm not lying?"

Before Rivers finished speaking, his guards opened a small trapdoor cut haphazardly into the ground and thrust him through the opening. He fell down a short flight of stone steps into a small room cut into the moldy dirt below—a dark, dank tomb filled with a choking, acrid stench. Scarface thrust a torch into a holder, and the source of the smell became dreadfully apparent.

The scarred mouth twisted. "When you're ready, Captain Coward, I will be waiting.

I have much to repay." He swiped his hand across his face, and the deformed mouth laughed hideously.

Rivers looked around and almost collapsed in fear. On top of a small table lay inquisitional instruments of pain: nutcrackers, pliers, several large knives, and bolt cutters. A charred set of bedsprings lay against the wall with handcuffs and leg restraints hanging from the corners.

Watching the Marine's face, Scarface hooted with amusement. He moved to the bedsprings and picked up a pair of long, heavy wires.

"Christ," Rivers yelled. "Those are jumper cables. By God, you're not going to use . . . "

Scarface stepped forward and hooked one end of each cable to the posts of a large generator. He switched it on and tapped the cable ends together, generating a great shower of sparks. Once again his burned face twisted into a horrible grin. "Immediate is the pain and permanent the damage. A small spark here, and pain will rush to the brain and burn itself into your memory. You will talk then. After you have shit yourself, you will find it impossible to remain honorable." He tossed the cables aside and turned off the small engine. "Hook him to the bed."

Rivers didn't resist as men flung him against the cold metal. They snapped the handcuffs and leg irons on, and he was unable to do more than twist against the rusting metal.

Scarface picked up the jumper cables again. He attached one to the corner of the bed frame and thrust the other against the inside of Rivers' thigh. The bed springs jerked as Rivers writhed uncontrollably against them. Then Scarface turned, picked up the nutcrackers, and grinned with savage delight. "That is only the beginning. When we return, pig, I'll put these charmers to work on your fingers. Like this." He placed the steel rods around the first knuckle of Rivers' left hand pinky finger and squeezed until he heard the bone break, then he dragged the tool back and forth Until the Marine screamed in agony. He leaned forward and laughed directly into Rivers' face, showering the Marine with bubbles of foam. "I will keep you in horrific pain for hours. You will tell me everything long before I am finished; of this you can be sure. It will be as easy as finding your patrol." He thrust his hand back to the table and grabbed a knife Jim Bowie would have admired and slashed it in front of River's eyes. "If you are one of the rare breed who resists the breaking of bones, I will slice off your manhood."

"Screw you, asshole," Rivers swore. "You're nothing but a one-man freak show." The three Chinese crowed with laughter as Rivers cursed them. He gave no quarter and spat what little phlegm he could conjure from his dry mouth. Which must have struck a nerve, because Scarface came at him in a rush, brandishing the knife before him.

"Dừng," Nguyen called from above. "Stop. I gave him an hour, and I want him to talk. If I wanted him dead I would have killed him myself."

Scarface sneered a last threat. "In an hour's time, American." Rivers' tormentors went up the stairs and shut the trapdoor behind them.

Left alone, Rivers struggled valiantly against his restraints, suffering through what the Spanish Inquisition called the fourth level of torture: the period just before the body's agony begins. He struggled to maintain his focus but fell past the edge as pain ripped through his body. He passed into delirium. In his nightmare he saw his recon team standing before him and screamed, "Get the hell out of here, Macon. I swear I'll shoot you if you don't move now." The giant Marine was holding onto a rifle like it was manna from heaven. "Asking you to leave was even harder on me than what they're about to do, but at least you're safe. I'm in this stinking shithole staring at tools that are going to render me useless as a man. They won't stop until I'm dead. That's what they want. I know I'll tell them. Just gotta hang on long enough to save my honor."

After time had passed—an hour, maybe, he didn't know—he heard a noise. Instantly, he bellowed a curse. "Screw you, dirty gook bastards." He sucked up his fear, steeled himself for more pain, and prayed for someone to hear him . . . *anyone*. "Rivers, Bartholomew H.; Captain, United States Marine Corps; 01165449." He shouted until he was hoarse—screaming profanity at his captors. Rivers knew someone would hear and come to his aid. Marines never left one of their own. They would find him and rescue him. He had to believe that.

Even the stupidest dreams can come true. The screaming saved him. If he'd been brave, they would never have found him. Bellowing obscenities did the trick.

The noise grew louder, but he couldn't place its source . . . a distant explosion? For a moment he believed he had gone around the bend. He held his breath, forcing himself to remain silent. Then he heard it again—definitely explosions. The thundering stopped and was followed by a different sound. For a dreadful moment Rivers knew his time was up. They were coming back to finish their work . . . the explosions were only a figment of his crazed mind. Then in the darkness the man from his nightmare spoke.

"Can you walk, Skipper?" Macon asked. Two more Marines knelt by the bottom of the stairs.

"Hell, yes," he croaked. "Unlock these things, *and I can fuckin' run!*"

Macon removed the handcuffs with the bolt-cutter and pulled the pins holding the ankle bracelets.

Rivers caught his breath, rubbed the sweat from his eyes with the backs of his hands, and staggered to where the other men were kneeling. "Let's move," he said hoarsely.

The two Marines turned and bolted up the stairs. Macon spoke to his captain. "If you're having trouble, Skipper, I'll carry you."

"I may not be fast, Sergeant, but I'll keep up."

The big man laughed as he mounted the stairs. "Just bump and scrape against the stairwell and you'll make it."

It took no small effort to move after what he had been through, but with the fear of being recaptured foremost in his mind, Rivers could have climbed those stairs if he'd had to carry Macon. Up he went, nearly sick with hope. The gate to freedom was a foot in front of him when the door to the hut flew open. Rivers almost let go of his bowels, but even as a yell sounded from outside the doorway, Macon's hand grabbed him by the neck and pulled him forward.

As Rivers' head broke through the trapdoor he saw Nguyen bring a pistol up and point it in his direction. There was a flash and Rivers winced as a bullet struck sparks against the cell door behind him.

Macon's rifle barked. The VC commander grabbed at his face and fell backward.

Rivers yelled, "Get some, Macon," and raced for the door. After two steps into the night he felt a stabbing pain and went down swearing.

The sergeant dropped next to his commander, heaved him over his shoulder, and ran as fast as he could away from the hut. He let out a piercing whistle, and suddenly two more Marines appeared and made a chair with their hands.

There were rifle flashes in the darkness and many voices yelling in Vietnamese. Branches ripped at Rivers' face as the four men staggered forward to where four more Marines were spread out in a hasty defense. Macon stopped behind the team's M60, ripped it from the ground, and heaved it over his shoulder. "Grab the Skipper," he yelled.

Two new sets of arms picked Rivers up and hauled him through the grass, running straight toward a small hill about six hundred meters away. As they broke free of the bushes a helmeted figure appeared raising a weapon to his shoulder. Macon hit him with the barrel of the M60 and sent him rolling into the meadow. Before he could react, one of his team thrust a Ka-Bar under his chin. A vicious twist and the NVA's resistance stopped immediately.

"One down and three thousand to go," Rivers said.

Voices yelled from behind, feet pounded, and beams of light were too close for comfort as the team turned the edge of the hill. Macon urged caution. "Gently does it. They ain't comin' into the meadow until they know what's out here. You okay, Skipper?"

"I'm fine."

"Then let's get the hell outta Dodge."

Rivers looked at his sergeant and made no effort to hide the tears in his eyes. "No matter how you came to be here, you're a godsend, you disobedient bastard."

Left to himself, Rivers would have been caught in minutes. Macon, however, knew where he wanted to go. He led the way up a long path before stopping to look back. "Goddamn it to hell! They're back there. How did they know we were moving this way?"

"Nguyen laughed when I asked him," Rivers said. "He said he'd tell me when I was drawing my last breath."

Macon stared at the captain. "No shit? He was going to kill you?"

"Yup, but first he was going to make me tell them everything I know and—" Beams of light on the trail cut off the conversation. Suddenly all of Rivers' pain, fear, and anxiety disappeared. He felt a blinding rage at what the enemy had done to him. "By God, I'll make you bastards pay. I'll kill every one of you cocksuckers." He reached out and jerked the .357 pistol out of Macon's shoulder holster and turned back toward the trail.

Macon yelled after him. "Just where the fuck are you goin'?"

"I'm gonna kill those murderin' motherfuckers. Threaten to cook my ass? Torture me with a car battery? Take that." Rivers fired until the hammer fell against an empty chamber. He got satisfaction from seeing the flashlight beams scatter but didn't manage to hit anything.

Macon laughed. "You feel better now, Skipper? You're sure you don't wanna go back and burn the fuckin' place down?"

"They'll stop now and assess the damage. Let's go. I learned something tonight, Macon. Nguyen didn't tell me, but I'm sure now they have something that helps them find us."

Macon stared at Rivers. "You shittin' me? You can't believe anything he said."

"They have something, and we'll find out what it is eventually. But I know more now than I knew yesterday. Get me home, Sergeant. I've got work to do."

"You bet, Skipper," Macon said as he moved into the jungle.

THREE

Duc Lo Firebase, Quang Tri Province

0100, December 26, 1967

LCPL. PAUL JACKSON crouched inside the bunker. The tall, thin eighteen-year-old stared through the monsoon night at the perimeter kill zone. All he saw was rain and a sea of red, sticky mud. Visibility to his immediate front was good thanks to a constant flood of aerial flares opening over the firebase. Jackson turned to his machine-gunner. "How'd you catch the early watch?"

The gunner frowned. "What the hell's the matter with you, Jackson? I'm here 'cause the friggin' platoon sergeant wants it." On the line with Jackson and the gunner were a couple of hundred more riflemen.

Jackson chuckled. "Hell, and I thought you were just gung-ho, Watkins. Are you a permanent fixture on Sergeant Daniels' shit list? You were here last night, so why again tonight?"

"Just lucky, I guess. Daniels ain't got nothin' on me."

Jackson nodded as if to say, "yeah, right," then looked out across the wire. He watched for a long time, trying to etch the ground in front of him into his mind. His stomach growled. He'd lost a ton of weight after two bouts of dysentery and malaria. He was always hungry now, and his clothes hung on a frame that usually carried 170 pounds. His bright blue eyes flashed as his thoughts deepened, and he lifted an eyebrow as if amused.

The gunner looked at Jackson, trying to cover the bad case of nerves he always got standing perimeter watch. It was the day after Christmas, and the two men were stuck with the midnight-to-two watch. "What did *you* do to piss off Daniels?"

"Why?"

The gunner laughed. "Well, he's got you sittin' in this shithole from midnight to two. I just figure that isn't a reward for giving him your R&R time."

"Yeah, well, you just pay attention to the perimeter," Jackson snapped. "That's why you're out here."

"I've burnt the terrain into my mind," the gunner replied. "I've counted every uprooted tree, bush, mound of earth, and clump of elephant grass within sight, and there's nothing new. What's your problem, anyway?"

Jackson ignored the gunner and passed his gaze over the terrain again. "What do you see now?"

"I see the kill zone, dumbass," the gunner snapped. "What am I supposed to see—a thousand screamin' gooks out for hair?"

"Well, I see something that shouldn't be there." The tension inside the bunker mounted as both men strained to see motion inside the kill zone. Jackson's voice fell to a whisper. "There's something new out there. The Seabees scraped the kill zone before dark, didn't they?"

"You know damned well they did."

"Well, it ain't clean anymore. There's a large clump of elephant grass sitting about twenty meters this side of the tree line, and it wasn't there ten minutes ago."

"I don't think so. That grass is right next to the friggin' trees. I saw it when I did my first scan. Besides, if it was anything, the bunker directly to its front would've already opened up."

"You're probably right, but remember what Daniels said at the briefing."

The gunner aped the platoon sergeant in response. "Charles has been doing some serious probing the past few days. Mostly small sapper attacks, each fewer than ten men, so be damned careful."

Jackson had a hard time restraining the urge to slap the shit out of the gunner. "That's right, asshole. He also said, 'We're dealing with NVA sappers, Charlie's best soldiers. They got inside the wire last night and ripped the shit outta 2nd Squad.' The skipper's worried. He's got 50 percent of the company out here."

The gunner wasn't impressed. "Okay, so fuckin' what?"

Jackson didn't allow the tension to ebb. "You might be right, but I'm not lettin' down. The gooks threw satchel charges into 2nd Squad's bunker. They got lucky and took out the entire squad. Rumor has it—"

The gunner interrupted. "Yeah, rumors. Grunts are like a bunch of old women."

Jackson ignored him. "Battalion thinks they're lookin' for weak points in the line."

The gunner got serious. "Must be the straight skinny. They made everyone carry extra ammo for the M60 and five additional M14 magazines."

Jackson nodded. "Yeah, and that creeps me out. Christ, everyone on the friggin' line is sittin' on pins and needles. If they come, we'll fuckin' murder 'em."

"How'd the sappers miss you?"

Jackson ignored the veiled implication. "I was on ambush. Buddy of mine wanted to celebrate Christmas and offered to take my next patrol."

The gunner didn't believe it. "You missed a Christmas party to sit in ambush? What the fuck's the matter with you? Rumor must be right."

"I suppose you *would* listen to rumor. You bitch like an old lady."

The gunner braced himself against the back of bunker wall to be ready if Jackson started anything. "Getting into a firefight with an asshole who doesn't want to be a grunt isn't my idea of fun, Jackson. Rumor has it you're constantly whining about getting off the line."

"Before you jump to any wrong conclusion, you ought to know the truth. A man could get hurt makin' accusations like that to the wrong person."

The gunner smiled but kept himself taut. "This is what I worry about, shitbird. On the other side of that hill is the DMZ. This is Indian country, and as they say, 'shit happens.'"

"It's not that I want to get away from this garden spot," Jackson said seriously. It's just . . . oh, fuck it. Why do I need to explain anything to you?"

The gunner didn't relent. "Look Jackson, there's only four hundred of us in this miserable shithole, and more'n ten times as many gooks watchin' everything we do. This place is fucked up beyond all recognition—100 percent FUBAR. How long *have* you been here?"

Jackson wiped his forehead with his sleeve. "Four months. Eight months ago I was in high school."

The gunner wrinkled his brow. "How'd you make lance corporal so fast?"

"PFC in boot camp, then lance a month ago. Don't mean shit, though. Just a step toward corporal."

The gunner nodded. "Ain't that the truth? No one gives a shit about rank out here, not even the zeroes. Everyone knows who's who. Besides, it's not your rank but how long you've been here that counts. What's so fuckin' great about bein' a corporal anyway? Just means you got more to do."

"I'll be an NCO, and that means something back in my hometown."

"Yeah? Where's that?"

"Whitehall, Michigan. Save for the gooks, it's a lot like this place—boring."

"Why'd ya leave?"

"I joined the Crotch, dumbass."

The gunner gave Jackson the finger. "You've got a real attitude Jackson. You better shape up or someone's going to straighten you out."

"I can take care of myself. Why is it you short-timers have it in for me, anyway?"

The gunner looked directly at Jackson. "It's what we hear about you. Scuttlebutt says you're always looking for a transfer. You don't like our little slice of heaven and bug the shit outta Daniels. We don't like yellow assholes who think they're better than the rest of us."

Jackson's hands gripped his M14. "I thought that was it. For your information, shitball, being yellow hasn't got a damned thing to do with my transfer requests. Did Daniels tell you that every time we talk, I'm asking to be sent back to Battalion Recon? When I got here, Battalion didn't care if I could shoot. The first sergeant was only impressed by how much time I had in the bush. To him, I was just another cherry who didn't know his ass from a hole in the ground. He figured I needed to be taught everything necessary to survive, so he sent me to this fuckin' garden spot to get my education humpin' the bush. You tell me why I'm supposed to like that."

The gunner thought Jackson was full of shit and said so. "That's what we're all doing."

"Yeah, but you signed up for it. You're a straight-leg grunt. I'm a sniper, and that's what I want to do."

The gunner now saw Jackson differently. "Okay, I can get behind that. Why won't they let you go? How much experience does the first shirt think you need?"

Jackson laughed softly. "When I first got out here, I stopped the squad from walking into an ambush. Since then, every time I bring up a transfer, the LT kills it. I don't think the first shirt even remembers I'm out here."

"Shit, Jackson, they usually reward guys who do that sorta thing. Sounds like the only thing you're gettin' is the shaft."

Jackson smirked. "Oh, they gave me a reward. They let me walk point as often as they can justify it, which is at least half the time we're outside the wire."

The gunner thought that sucked. "Shit, I hate walking point."

"Yeah, well, what really scared the shit outta me was when they wanted to move me up to squad leader. They said if I took the position I wouldn't have to walk point. I really pissed them off when I turned it down. The LT called me a selfish prick and vowed to never transfer me back to Recon. But I don't give a shit. I didn't join the Crotch to teach basic woodsmanship. It didn't mean nothin' anyway. That asshole bought the farm about a month ago, and his replacement doesn't seem to give a shit."

The gunner shook his head again. "You worried about this new zero?"

"You bet your ass I am. I told Daniels to keep my name out of his conversations with that Boat School prick." Tired of talking, Jackson took his night vision scope out of the medical pouch he carried strapped to his leg.

The surprised gunner stared at the night scope. "Where'd you get that?"

"Picked it up when it fell outta the LT's backpack after he bought the farm. I very carefully forgot to turn it in."

"It doesn't look anything like the scopes the others use."

"I dolled it up some. Wrapped some duct tape around the swivels so they don't rattle and modified the sight so it fits tighter against my eye."

The gunner admired Jackson's handiwork. "How've you been able to keep it hidden from Daniels and the gunny?"

"I carry it with me; strapped to my leg." Jackson picked up the scope and placed the lens against his eye until the duct tape completely closed off any stray light, then removed the front lens cap. He was rewarded with an eerie green light that sharpened details in the landscape around him. Carefully he swept the light across the small clump of elephant grass. What he saw made his hair stand up. "Get on the gun. There's somebody out there."

"What?"

"Behind that clump of grass you said not to worry about. Somebody's there, and he's holdin' a big-ass weapon in his hands. Looks like a B40 rocket launcher. From this angle I can't tell for sure, but whatever it is, the bastard's gettin' ready to use it. Write this in your notebook . . . definitely not American. The uniform's different from regular gooks, though. Light-colored material; fitted, not like VC pajamas. Balloon pockets on the trouser legs, and cloth straps running across the shoulders of the jacket. Damned sure not one of ours."

The gunner was wide-eyed. "Don't make no matter who he is. He ain't supposed to be out there."

When he realized what he was looking at, Jackson was afraid and excited at the same time. "That's an NVA sapper, and he's getting' ready to fire a rocket into our bunker."

Jackson lifted his head high enough to see across the strands of wire immediately in front of him. "What's wrong with everybody? We got hundreds of eyes supposed to be watching the perimeter. Why hasn't anyone opened fire?"

He carefully replaced the night scope in his knapsack and picked up his M14. Reaching over to his left, he tapped the foxhole's third Marine, the only guy who'd been lucky enough to sleep. "Get up, and be damned quiet."

The sleepy-eyed Marine was instantly at full alert. "What is it?"

"Get on your gun. There's a gook about twenty meters to our right and about thirty meters inside the kill zone. Looks like elephant grass, but there ain't supposed to be no friggin' lawn out there. Get a bead on him."

The third man focused his attention on the elephant grass.

Both gunners slowly brought the barrels of their M60s to bear. "Got him," said two voices.

"*Fire!*"

It was a simple command, and the two M60s barked out a dozen .30-caliber rounds apiece. Each gunner slowly walked the fall of his bullets back and forth across the "elephant grass," ripping the sapper behind it into small pieces of bleeding tissue.

A whistle blew, and out of the trees came hundreds of screaming NVA and VC, all firing their weapons. Jackson felt recoil smash into his shoulder as his M14 barked into life.

The rest of the line froze for just a moment, but as the enemy advanced, several other positions opened up. Then the shit hit the fan as the louder crack of AK-47s came from a hundred concealed positions to Jackson's front. Several weapons fired rapidly, their bullets moving up and down along the perimeter.

Jackson aimed carefully and squeezed the trigger softly. The M14 spit out three quick rounds and one of the enemy machine guns stopped firing. He quickly shifted his fire, and this time his rifle barked a dozen times. A movement behind him startled Jackson. He twisted and saw someone standing there looking out toward the tree line. It was the newly assigned lieutenant. The officer just stood there, holding his rifle like he was afraid of it. His eyes bulged, and sweat poured down his face.

A quick look at the lieutenant's rifle told Jackson the shavetail hadn't even loaded it; no magazine protruded from its base. Shaking his head, Jackson returned his attention to his front and fired at a running figure about ten feet away. The M14 barked twice, and the NVA dropped like someone slugged in the stomach with a baseball bat. As he took down two more VC running straight at his position, Jackson yelled at the lieutenant. "Load the friggin' weapon and shoot, for Christ's sake."

The machine gun to his right stopped firing. The gunner fell back with a bullet through his forehead. Jackson dropped his rifle, slid behind the M60, and emptied a belt into NVA running through the kill zone. There wasn't time to aim carefully as NVA streamed over the plowed ground, so he walked his rounds through the enemy's ranks.

Finally, the lieutenant did something. He snatched his rifle up to his shoulder and pulled the trigger. When the hammer fell against an empty chamber, Jackson yelled at him again. "The fucker works a hell of a lot better if you put bullets in it."

Quickly the zero dropped to his knees and grappled for a magazine. By the time he had chambered a round, the NVA had started back toward the tree line.

For some reason, this enraged Jackson. "Relax," he said. "Aim." He pulled the M60's trigger and carefully pumped five-round bursts into what was now a fleeing rabble. When he saw several were going to make it to the tree line, the anger in his belly consumed him. Too angry to control the urge to fire, he held the trigger of the M60 back until the bolt fell on an empty chamber. By then there were a lot more NVA down, some of them sprawled on their faces, others crawling away like worms. One hunched over his knees holding his arms across a gaping wound in his stomach.

Jackson ripped open the breech and dug for the spare belt of ammunition he kept in a musette bag. He snared one end of the belt, but as he pulled it past the canvas flap, the end dropped into the sand at the bottom of the bunker. He yelled at the weapon's loader. "*Give me a new belt, goddamn it!*" The loader jammed a belt into the gun's breech, and Jackson pulled the bolt to the rear and fired.

"Get some!" yelled the loader.

When the M60 stopped, two VC had turned around and rushed his position, one rapid-firing with an AK-47, the other firing a pistol. The bullets tore through the new lieutenant, and he fell across the bunker. Jackson killed the VC with a short burst. One .30-caliber round took the VC officer in the face and blew brains and blood across the carefully plowed killing zone.

Finally it was over. No enemy soldiers were left on their feet. All of the ones Jackson could see to his front were dead . . . except one who was doggedly trying to jam another clip into his rifle. Jackson let go with a three-round burst that ripped the enemy's body savagely.

The weapons loader pointed. "There's more than fifty of the fuckers out there, some no more'n five feet away. Looks like the attack was headed straight for us."

"You're right," Jackson said. "This was where they intended to break through."

The loader grinned. "Well, I guess we taught them a friggin' lesson, eh, Jackson?"

"What might that be?"

"Don't fuck with you and me."

Jackson nodded. The battle cries of the enemy to his front turned into screams of agony as the Marine fire ebbed into silence.

Jackson looked at the machine-gunner lying to his right. The top of his head was torn away, and brain matter was visible inside an amazingly white skull. The cherry lieutenant had also taken a round through the forehead and died before he hit the ground. Jackson felt nauseous but forced it down. "My God," he whispered.

Sergeant Daniels yelled from behind. "What the hell happened?"

Jackson's response to the truly stupid question was, "I guess the gooks don't celebrate Christmas, Sarge."

Daniels looked at the lieutenant's body. "Jesus Christ. What happened to him?"

Jackson shrugged. "Dumbass came up here with an unloaded weapon. Before he got his shit together, the gooks made a canoe out of his head." When he turned toward the center of the camp, Jackson saw the cavalry galloping belatedly to the rescue. Three squads of riflemen poured over the inner perimeter and took positions along the main line of defense.

Another shavetail lieutenant led the charge, furiously blowing on, of all things, a red plastic whistle.

FOUR

Duc Lo Firebase, Quang Tri Province

1030, December 27, 1967

WHEN CAPTAIN RIVERS walked into the large bunker, he saw Lance Corporal Jackson stretched out in the far corner. A Coleman lantern hissed a dull, flickering light around the room, making it just bright enough for Jackson to see the crossword puzzle he labored over.

Jackson watched the officer enter and wondered what he wanted. He didn't move until he saw the zero turn in his direction.

Rivers saw Jackson getting to his feet. "As you were."

Jackson eyed the zero warily. Officers, especially the ones with big reputations, didn't visit enlisted bunkers unless they wanted something. Jackson stayed quiet and waited for the other shoe to drop.

"You're Jackson?"

"Yes, sir."

"I'm told I can get a straight answer from you. Is that right?"

"Yes, sir."

"How'd you know the gooks were outside the wire last night?" Rivers noticed that Jackson thought about his answer before replying.

"I saw him through my night scope, sir."

"*Your* night scope?"

"Yes, sir; *mine.*"

"How did you obtain it? No one below staff sergeant can requisition one."

"I took it off Lieutenant Walker the day he got his and never turned it in."

The captain let the issue drop. "Sergeant Daniels tells me you did a hell of a job last night."

Jackson didn't reply.

"I'm told you're very bright. Intelligent, tough, and someone who knows when to keep his mouth shut."

"Thank you, sir."

"Sergeant Daniels asked several men to write statements regarding your performance last night. They say you took out nearly all of the gooks and several machine-gun positions inside the tree line."

"A lot of people were out there, sir. I didn't do anything everybody else wasn't doing."

"The men I'm referring to are from 3rd Platoon. They were in the bunker next to yours and claim you began firing long before everyone else did. They also said it was your position Charlie was trying to take out. What about that?"

"I don't know, sir. I was too busy to see who was trying to do what."

Rivers shook his head. "That's bullshit, and you know it. Sergeant Daniels told me you gave him a fairly accurate, but extremely brief, after-action report."

"Yes, sir. I told Daniels what I saw. But I don't know anything about what the others said."

"The first thing I thought when I heard about you, Jackson, was you were a hotdog who did a John Wayne routine and got lucky. But Daniels thinks I'm wrong. Off the record, he also told me you don't like 2nd Platoon and that he'd like to get you back to where you think you belong. He feels like he owes you, like you're someone special. That says a lot, because Daniels isn't given to flattery."

"I don't know what to say, sir," Jackson said.

"You think being a grunt is so much bullshit, don't you?"

Jackson's face stayed expressionless. He met the captain's eyes but didn't reply.

"If I were an individual with your skills and someone asked me if I hated the place, I'd think he was an asshole."

"You're an officer, sir."

The implication, Rivers understood, was that all zeroes were assholes. Good officers wondered whether all enlisted men thought so or only the smart ones, like this kid, who already knew he was about to get screwed. "In this case, Jackson, before I spoke to your platoon sergeant I was just what you think I am. I thought you were a prick who wanted to get out of the shit. Daniels straightened me out. He said your reason for wanting to leave is so you can work as a sniper. Is that it?"

"Yes, sir."

"Does that mean you want to leave here? Or are you just saying 'Yes, sir'? It's important I get a straight answer, without any bullshit."

"I never wanted to be here, sir. They sent me to learn the ropes, and I've done that. It's time to leave. That's all there is to it. I don't have anything against the company."

Rivers studied the response for a second. "I guess what I'm asking is whether you'd feel like you were screwed if you weren't sent back to Battalion?"

Jackson looked like he'd been kicked in the stomach and let his bitterness show. "I suppose that's it, then. I'm not going to Recon. Is that why you came down here instead of having me haul my ass up the hill?"

Rivers didn't rise to the jibe. "Pretty close. After Daniels told me about you, I asked Colonel MacDonald to have you reassigned. I told him I thought it was a waste of incredible talent to have you be just another sniper, and he agreed. So, Jackson, unless you can provide a good reason why not, you're stuck with me, but not this company. We're being transferred to a new section. In fact, we're going to be the first two members of a very special unit we're going to call Force Recon."

"I don't understand."

"Daniels said you're a man with talents. And I think anyone with the type of jungle smarts he says you have, a cool head in tight situations, and obvious skill with small arms is wasting the Corps' time and money humpin' patrols for a line company. Therefore, you're now assigned where your talents can be fully utilized. You and I are going to be what amounts to fancied-up LRRPs."

"I still don't understand, sir."

Rivers nodded. "At this point I don't expect you to. More to the point, I don't know enough right now to clear things up. What I do know is the colonel told me to make sure you got what you wanted as sort of payment for last night. I think he feels he owes you a little something."

"He doesn't owe me anything, sir."

"Well, he thinks he does, and that's good enough for me. But there's more. As soon as we can arrange it, we're going to the Philippines; a month to six weeks is my best guess. The school's three weeks long, and I'll do everything possible to get us some significant liberty."

Going to the P.I. was damned enticing. Jackson beamed. "You're going to get us out of the shit? I've heard stories about Subic Bay, and if reassignment means we go, who am I to turn it down?"

Rivers laughed at Jackson's newly found enthusiasm.

"Sir, can I speak freely?"

"Let's get one thing straight right now, Jackson. I expect you to speak straight to me at all times. While we'll maintain proper conduct for the good of the service, it's going to be far more important that we trust one another. I want us to have complete confidence in each other. The best approach to achieving trust is to be honest and straightforward. Got it?"

"Rumor has it you've been looking for someone to accept this assignment for a long time."

"Does that bother you?"

"No, sir. What you say sounds interesting, but I have to know I'm being selected for the right reasons. You aren't just settling because no one else wanted in."

"You can count on it. This will be serious business. We'll work alone, and I'm not about to settle for just anyone. If I didn't think you were the right man, I wouldn't be here. I am not, if nothing else, stupid."

"I didn't think so, sir."

"Are you familiar with the S2 Intelligence section of Headquarters Company?" Rivers asked.

"Not really, sir."

"Intel finds things out about the enemy. What units are operating in specific areas, what their strengths are, what types of equipment they have, and the condition they're in. Things like, are they eating well? Do they have good equipment? Are there signs of preparation? You understand?"

"Yes, sir. You're going to determine the enemy's order of march."

"Exactly. We'll be responsible for keeping Regiment informed of those kinds of things in this section of I Corps. Division has given Colonel MacDonald special authority to do whatever is necessary to reduce the losses the LRRPs have been taking lately and, at the same time, improve the quality of intelligence being received. That's where we come in. We're going to be a sort of special recon force for the colonel's S2 section."

Doubt flashed across Jackson's face. "You're saying the information we're getting now isn't accurate?"

"That's partly it. And it's intermittent. Most of the patrols we send out never really see anything; and those that do don't come back. If Charlie sees them soon enough, he hides. If not, he kills them."

"What you're saying is the colonel needs a special group he can count on."

"The regard the skipper has for the intel he's currently getting isn't our concern. What we're going to be doing goes beyond normal intelligence operations. We'll be alone. Think about that."

Jackson nodded. "I have, sir."

"Did it occur to you to tell me to go fuck myself, and not volunteer for this assignment?"

"It did, but there's always an exception to the no volunteer rule, sir. Like when it might be better than what you're doing now."

"Go on."

"I think I have a better chance with one person who knows what he's doing than with a bunch of inexperienced assholes who don't, sir." Both Marines knew that far too many had died because someone new had made a mistake. "I also think if I stay here much longer, someone's going to have me assigned as a squad leader, and that'll end my chances of ever getting back to Battalion. Seems to me the situation you present has got to be better than having some ignorant son of a bitch get me killed."

Rivers nodded. "There's one more thing. Effective immediately, you're a corporal. The promotion orders will be cut as soon as I get back to headquarters. You're going to be a very young NCO, Jackson. Don't let it go to your head."

"Thank you, sir."

"Don't thank me, Corporal. If you screw up, it'll be taken it away so fast your head will spin. Between now and the time we leave, you're to do nothing out of the ordinary. Understand?"

"Aye, aye, sir. I'm not someone you need to worry about."

"As long as it stays that way."

"Yes, sir."

"Pack your gear and tell your squad leader you're being transferred. We'll leave no later than Wednesday. Until then, you're not to take patrol or stand guard."

"Aye, aye, sir."

"Any questions?"

"Can I keep my night scope, sir?"

"Just as long as you promise to bring it with you." Rivers turned, started to head back toward the bunker's entrance, then stopped. "Just one more thing. Did what happened to Lieutenant Trimble last night bother you?"

"Who, sir?"

"Lieutenant Trimble. The officer killed behind your bunker last night. Did it bother you that he bought the farm after being in-country only one day?"

"Straight answer, sir?"

"There's never to be any other kind between us. I thought I made that clear."

"I've been lying here wondering why I don't feel bad, sir. I'm sorry he's dead, but I don't feel bad about it. We're taught a Marine should always be prepared. The lieutenant wasn't. He showed up on the line with an unloaded weapon, exposed himself needlessly to incoming fire, and got himself killed. I don't feel sorry for anyone that stupid. Now, if his lack of common sense got somebody else killed, I'd feel bad for that guy."

Rivers looked at Jackson for a long moment before he spoke. "I'm not sure you're going to like the assignments we pull, Corporal. But I think I'll be happy you're around. I like the way you think. I believe in being prepared and have no feelings about the lieutenant either. I'm just happy no one else paid for his lack of performance. I think we'll make a good team. Welcome aboard."

"Thank you, sir. What will we do first?"

"We'll find out how Charlie always knows where our LRRPS are."

FIVE

Headquarters 26th Marines, Phu Bai

0830, December 30, 1967

WHEN JACKSON ARRIVED, he saw the ubiquitous sign over the door with the instruction to "knock, remove headgear, and wait." A similar sign hung over the door of every first sergeant in the Corps. The fact this guy brought one to 'Nam made Jackson glad he hadn't screwed around on the way over. Chickenshit was alive and well, even in 'Nam. He checked his uniform. His gig line was straight and his boots were clean. He removed his soft roll-up cover when he entered the building. Marines don't wear headgear inside unless they are armed. He knocked on the door—three strong raps—then waited.

A voice called, "Come."

Jackson pushed the door open. Inside, the office spread out into a room large enough for three desks. Behind one was the PFC who had delivered the summons; the second held a tall, redheaded clerk. A nameplate on the third read: "J. Robinson— First Sergeant—USMC." Behind the nameplate sat the ugliest man Jackson had ever seen, his face so pockmarked from a losing fight with acne the corporal wondered how he shaved.

A gash cut into the blemished face snarled, "You must be Jackson. Didn't the transient pukes tell you to report to me first thing this morning?"

"No."

"Damned air wing pukes. They never act like real Marines. Sit down, Corporal. Want some coffee? Ya know, the Corps is expanding too fast. Christ, we got three infantry divisions and three of them lousy air wings on active duty, and another division with its own set of shitbirds in reserve. But what's worse is headquarters keeps us between them and the gooks. That really sucks, in my book."

The first sergeant's tirade made Jackson nervous. He was pissed, probably because he thought one of his NCOs had been screwing off.

Robinson continued. "I put you on report for failure to be at the appointed place of duty. Now I'll have to do the friggin' thing over."

The redheaded clerk piped up. "We can submit an amendment, First Sergeant."

Robinson didn't even look in the direction of the comment before growling, "If I want your goddamn advice, Johnson, I'll give it to you. Sit down, Corporal. You realize jungle headgear is illegal here?"

"It's all I have, First Sergeant."

"Well, stop at Supply and get yourself a utility cover before some hotshot puts you on report for being out of uniform. This ain't the bush. How about that coffee?"

"Coffee would be good." There was something special about being an NCO. The first shirt wasn't giving him a hard time; it was his job to make sure there was good order and discipline in the battalion, and he was just doing his job.

First Sergeant Robinson picked up a field phone and cranked it. While he waited, he covered the mouthpiece and spoke to the clerk. "You heard the corporal. Get him a cup of coffee, and refill mine. If there's any doughnuts back there, bring 'em up too." The clerk scurried from the room as Robinson growled into the phone, "Jackson's out here. No, sir, he wasn't AWOL. The transient pukes never told him to report. I'll handle it, sir." Whatever the person at the other end of the phone said, it didn't take long. Robinson put the phone down and yelled, "Where the hell's the coffee, Johnson?"

A moment later, the door behind the first sergeant opened and a tall first lieutenant entered.

Jackson jumped to his feet and yelled, "Ten-hut."

"As you were, Corporal," the lieutenant said, sticking his hand out. The motion drew a disapproving shake of the head from the first sergeant. Jackson took the hand and shook it firmly. He was really worried now. Since when did zeroes shake hands with newly minted corporals? Not ever, he bet.

"You must be our not-really-AWOL Jackson," the lieutenant said. "Come with me. You too, First Sergeant."

The coffee forgotten, Jackson fell in behind the first shirt. They walked thirty feet down the hall until they came to another red sign. This one read: "*R. F. MacDonald, Colonel USMC—Commanding.*" The three men entered, and the lieutenant spoke to the regiment's senior enlisted man. "This is Corporal Jackson, Sergeant Major."

"The skipper's expecting you, sir," the sergeant major said. "He's inside with Captain Rivers. Go right in."

"Thank you." Turning to the two men trailing him, the lieutenant said, "Have a seat."

The sergeant major pointed at a well-worn couch. "Sit down, John. You too, Jackson. We need to talk before we see the colonel. "Do you know why you're here, Jackson?"

"No, Sergeant Major."

Instead of explaining, the sergeant major stuck out his hand in greeting.

Jackson's heart started to race. *First a lieutenant and now a sergeant major wants to shake hands? What's going on? Why am I being greased so hard?*

"You're about to become the shortest-term corporal in the history of the Corps."

Before Jackson could speak, the colonel's office door opened and the lieutenant stuck his head out. "We're ready for you, Sergeant Major."

The regiment's senior enlisted Marine looked up and nodded, then turned to Jackson. "Here's the deal, Jackson. You report to the colonel. First Sergeant Robinson and I will be right behind you."

Jackson was concerned about what "the shortest-term corporal in the history of the Marine Corps" meant. He knew he needed to report correctly or his assignment might turn out to be shoveling shit into the South China Sea. He hadn't been a corporal long enough for the ink to dry on his warrant and couldn't remember screwing up badly enough for them to take it away. They couldn't be that pissed over the starlight scope. He took a deep breath and rapped three times on the colonel's door.

"Enter."

Jackson marched forward and carefully centered himself before the colonel's desk, three feet in front of its leading edge. He stared straight above the officer's head, came to rigid attention, and barked, "Sir, Corporal Jackson reporting to the commanding officer as ordered, sir."

The colonel stood and moved around his desk. "Corporal, I've read Captain Rivers' report regarding your actions on the night of Tuesday last rather carefully. I particularly paid close attention to your conduct under fire and its lack of effect on you afterward."

"Yes, sir."

"I've also read another report by your old CO. Both seem to indicate you're something special in this regiment. Stand at ease, Corporal."

Jackson immediately came to the position of parade rest—legs slightly apart, hands locked in the small of his back, eyes fixed straight ahead. Enlisted Marines, especially those who were scared shitless, never stood at ease in their CO's office, regardless of who invited them to do so.

The colonel shifted his attention. "Sergeant Major, have you got those orders?"

"Yes, sir." The sergeant major handed the colonel a piece of paper. The officer nodded his appreciation, turned his attention back to Corporal Jackson, and said, "Attention to orders."

Everyone in the room stood to attention. The movement caused Jackson to notice Captain Rivers at the far end of the room. It was the first time he'd seen him since their conversation in the Duc Lo bunker.

The colonel began to read. "Headquarters, 3rd Marine Division. To: Corporal P. A. Jackson, 2395749, USMC. For your conduct on the night of December 26, 1967, and as outlined in the attached citation, you are hereby awarded the Bronze Star Medal with Combat V for conspicuous gallantry in the face of enemy forces. Additionally, you are meritoriously advanced to the rank of sergeant effective January 1, 1968. Signed, Louis Metzger, Major General, Commanding. Congratulations, Sergeant," the colonel said to the startled Jackson. He held his hand out to Captain Rivers and accepted a blue, felt-lined box. From it he took a bronze medal about two inches long cast in the shape of a star. It hung from a red ribbon with a single dark blue stripe down its center, encased by thinner white stripes. Colonel MacDonald pinned the medal to Jackson's left breast pocket. "The Bronze Star, Sergeant. I'm damned proud of you, son." The officer reached out, grasped the bewildered sergeant's hand, and pumped it up and down.

"Thank you, sir," was all Jackson could say.

The other Marines came forward and shook the hand of the Corps' newest sergeant and offered congratulations.

When the attaboys started to peter out, MacDonald took charge of the room and asked Rivers, "Since we've given him the sugar, shall we lay on the salt?"

Rivers smiled. "Yes, sir. Now's as good a time as any."

First Sergeant Robinson smiled. "Begging the colonel's pardon, sir. May the sergeant major and I take care of one thing before you start?"

"Absolutely, First Sergeant, what's that?"

The acne-scarred Marine produced a small piece of cardboard with a pair of new metal sergeant's chevrons affixed. "It's a small matter of Sergeant Jackson being out of uniform, sir."

"Carry on, First Sergeant."

The older Marines removed the still-new corporal's insignias and replaced them with a brand-new set of sergeant's chevrons. When they finished, each man took a step back and, swinging together, hit him hard on the shoulders with their closed fists. "There. That oughta' keep those chevrons on," the sergeant major stated matter-of-factly.

The entire room burst into laughter . . . everyone except the Corps' newest sergeant, who moved to the sofa, rubbed his shoulders, and wondered what they were going to do to him that warranted this kind of foreplay.

SIX

Headquarters 26th Marines, Phu Bai

0845, December 30, 1967

THE ROOM QUIETED after the venerable sergeants initiated Jackson into their ranks. Colonel MacDonald shook his head. "That exhibition has officially been declared cruel and unusual hazing. While everyone knows the Old Corps keeps the tradition alive, it's still taboo."

The two charter members of the Zebra Club didn't appear the least bit repentant.

MacDonald continued for Jackson's benefit. "The 'Old Breed,' Sergeant, is a group of your fellow NCOs who've been in grade at least one day longer than you, and sadly includes people like these two. The disgusting exhibition they just put on is their simple way of bringing new blood into their ranks. Old traditions, especially stupid ones, die hard in the Corps."

When the laughter died down, Rivers turned serious. "It looks, *Sergeant* Jackson, as if our little jaunt to the P.I. is going to have to wait."

Here it comes, Jackson thought.

Colonel MacDonald interrupted. "Division is in desperate need of some critical intel, and I don't like what I'm getting from the LRRPs. You were briefed, were you not, Sergeant, on your new assignment?"

Jackson didn't let his disappointment regarding the delayed trip to the Philippines show. "Yes, sir."

The colonel's dark gray eyes locked on each man in turn as he talked. "During the last six months we've lost far too many of our long-range reconnaissance patrols. Captain Rivers was part of a patrol that barely got in and out, but he was unable to uncover any information regarding why our casualties have been so high. However, while he was held captive, he overheard conversations that have led me to believe that Charlie's planning something big in the near future. Discovering just what it is has become priority one."

Rivers jumped in. "That's where we come in, Sergeant."

The colonel frowned at Rivers' interruption. "Someone familiar with the area needs to go have a look-see. The good captain has extensive experience, and that gives us an opportunity to introduce new recon tactics we think will reduce casualties significantly. He thinks you're the person to help him."

Jackson stared at the two officers. "May I ask a question, sirs?"

MacDonald spoke first. "What is it?"

"Battalion Recon is a damned good outfit. Why can't they get in, find the information you need, and get out?" The question was straight from the shoulder and uncluttered by the usually appended "sir."

Captain Rivers fielded the question. "You're right. Battalion is a damned good outfit; the best I've ever served with. Under normal circumstances this would be just the type of mission they would be assigned. The trouble is—"

The colonel took his turn at interruption. "Give it to him straight, Bart. He deserves the whole truth, right from the beginning."

Rivers nodded. "The trouble is the gooks are finding our recon teams almost immediately after they're inserted. If he can, Charlie hides, but if he thinks we've seen anything, he kills the team. We don't think we can get a standard LRRP in and out without being discovered, and this time Charlie must not suspect anyone's been there. That means we need a very small unit. The colonel and I have decided just two people will go."

"You and me; right, sir?"

The colonel leaned forward. "A normal ten-man LRRP team just won't work here. Those men are all highly motivated and skilled, but the problem is we've developed those teams to work together, and they have adapted themselves to the strategy. To perform effectively, the LRRP unit needs all ten men."

The sergeant major thought the colonel's comment went over Jackson's head, so he rephrased it in simpler terms. "Currently, a ten-man team is a liability. They leave too many signs of their presence: bent trails, broken grass, footprints; you know the drill. They also talk too much, their equipment rattles, and they smell different than the gooks. Captain Rivers heard those exact words from a senior VC officer recently, and we think this is part of the reason our LRRP teams are being discovered. Under the circumstances, we just can't afford mistakes. We must be absolutely sure Luke never realizes we've been there."

Jackson looked at the sergeant major. "What you're saying is, the captain and I are being ordered to enter an area infested with gooks because it's too dangerous for ten men. Who dreamed this up?"

The sergeant major bristled at Jackson's perceived insubordination. "That's enough, Jackson."

The colonel shook his head. "No, it's okay, Sergeant Major. He's right, and it *is* his ass we're about to hang out. He deserves answers. The truth is, Jackson, I dreamed this up, based on information Captain Rivers obtained directly from a VC commander named Nguyen. I assure you what he learned provided all the justification we need to develop this new recon concept. Beyond that, I gave long and serious consideration to the safety of the men who would go in before the final decision was made."

That makes sense, Jackson thought. *The "old man's" not talking about a suicide mission he dreamed up after a long night with a bottle of Jack. He knows the difficulty of what he's presented, and Rivers, who is one smart son of a bitch, seems totally committed.*

Rivers added to the colonel's plan. "The idea, Jackson, is to carry only the actual gear we'll use, plan a reachable destination each day, and get there without making *any* noise. As you know, Charlie moves at night, and that virtually leaves the bush uncovered during the day." He laid a map on the table in front of Jackson. "This is northern Quang Tri, about half of the province. It will be our primary area of operation, or AO. It starts at Quang Tri in the northeast, goes north to the DMZ, and west to the Laotian border. It contains two large rivers, the Cua Viet and the Quang Tri, but the Ben Hai moves across it as well on its way north. Nearly every inch is Indian country, with the United States and ARVN holding only the larger metropolitan areas and a few isolated firebases. Most of the largest battles we've fought in Vietnam have taken place here."

The colonel pointed at a spot on the map marked by a red circle. "We'll insert you here, about ten klicks east and north of Khe Sanh. Close enough so your walk won't be too difficult, but far enough away that Charlie won't know you're there."

The sergeant major pointed at an area approximately a klick north of the insertion point. "Before you're inserted, we're going to have aircraft bomb and strafe this area."

Captain Rivers saw concern flit across Jackson's face. "The idea is to get us in while Charlie has his head down. If it's done right, we'll get in without being spotted and won't have to elude the patrols they send out."

Jackson was appalled. "Let me get this straight, sir. You're going to stir up a hornet's nest, then ask the captain and me to go in, count bees, and get out without being stung. Is that about it?"

The first sergeant thought Jackson was being insubordinate again. "Goddamn it, Jackson, I told you about conducting yourself properly."

"You wait a minute. It's my ass you're so politely puttin' in deep shit, and I can't say I like your plan. There are too many 'ifs' for me. *If* Charlie keeps his head down, *if* we get there undetected, *if* they don't send out patrols. Just too damned many 'ifs,' First Sergeant."

"You got any suggestions, wiseass?"

"Yes, I do." *Keep your temper, The first sergeant is just doing what's normal for Marines with his background. He's been bowing and scraping for so many years he's lost his better judgment. But it's my ass on the line, and I'm damned sure going to have something to say about how it gets exposed.* Jackson focused on Rivers. "What if we don't use aircraft, sir? The VC know we use them only if there's something serious afoot. If we're going to find Luke, let's leave him with his pants down. No sense having him hide what we're trying to find."

The colonel raised his eyebrows and contemplated Jackson as if seeing him for the first time. "What do you suggest, Sergeant?"

"I recommend a pattern of artillery fire using 155's from Khe Sanh. Begin, say, three days before we go in, continue nightly throughout our visit, and finish up three days after we leave. Nothing out of the ordinary; just harassment fire. That'll keep Charlie's head down without piquing his interest."

The colonel looked at Rivers. "What do you think, Bart? It's your ass too."

"I like it. Makes sense and has the added effect of keeping Charlie's movement at a minimum every night we're in the bush. It works for me, sir."

"Good. I like it too. Good job, Sergeant. You'll get the harassment fire. Anything else?"

Rivers wanted the meeting to end before the first sergeant had apoplexy. "Just equipment, sir. We'll need to draw better gear than what we currently have."

"No problem. The first sergeant will get you what you need. Unless there's something else, I'll see you on the flight line."

SEVEN

Supply Depot, Phu Bai

1420, January 3, 1968

WHILE CAPTAIN RIVERS was at S3 (Operations) arranging the harassment fire, Sergeant Jackson went to Supply to draw the equipment they needed. The depot NCO was a tall, powerfully built blond from Illinois, a short-timer who had served most of his tour with the LRRPs. Wounded three times, he was spending his last few days issuing gear to replacements. He wasn't the typical supply weenie, and he definitely wasn't the type line grunts called a REMF to his face.

Sergeant Macon talked slowly and deliberately. "You're damned lucky to be with Rivers. He was my skipper at the Rock Pile, and he's hell on wheels. The last day I served with him the base was hit by rockets. They came outta nowhere, and it was accurate shit. Over a dozen wounded and two KIA. Through it all, the skipper sat on top of a bunker and directed artillery. He was cool as shit, man. Everyone, and I mean everyone, was grabbin' all the dirt they could find, but not Rivers. He just sat there walking arty into the gook positions. Got some, too. One very cool sumbitch.

"MacDonald has all the administrative and supply Marines spend at least half their tour walking the bush," Macon continued. "Ain't no office pukes in the 26th Marines."

That raised the colonel's stock a few points in Jackson's opinion.

"MacDonald and Rivers are Marines' Marines," Macon said. "Rest of them zeroes are a bunch of pukes." He cited most of the regiment's officers by name, so Jackson knew what he said about Rivers was the straight skinny.

Jackson was encouraged by Macon's clear respect for Rivers. "I'll bet the only reason you know what Rivers was doing during the rocket attack," Jackson said, as a compliment, "is because you were helping him get it done."

Macon shuffled his feet as if embarrassed. "Don't mean nothin'."

After Jackson had spent an hour listening to LRRP exploits Captain Rivers showed up. The supply sergeant's demeanor changed immediately. He drew himself up straight and thrust out his hand in greeting.

"Howdy, Skipper," he said. "It's damned good to see you again, sir. I was afraid I wouldn't have the pleasure before I left country. I'm catching the freedom bird tomorrow."

Rivers clasped the sergeant's hand. "Well I'll be damned. As I live and breathe, if it isn't Sergeant Macon. I thought the gooks got you at the Rock Pile. Damned good to see you, Macon. Even better to hear you're getting your bird home." The two men obviously shared the genuine affection only men who'd been in deep shit together could feel.

"I thought you bought the farm at Lang Vei, sir. Rumor said you were gut-shot."

"Just shows you how pecker-checkers exaggerate, Sergeant," Rivers lied. "It was a scratch they patched up in Da Nang. I spent a couple of weeks down there, and that was that."

"Well, I heard it was bad enough they kept you there for six weeks and the only reason they didn't send you home was 'cause you refused to go. At any rate, it's good to see you, sir. I'd hate to think of you buyin' the farm."

"Not this tour, Macon. This tour, Jackson will keep me fit. Right, Sergeant?"

Jackson nodded. "I'll do my best, sir."

The officer in charge of Supply, 1st Lt. Wayne Mills, saw Rivers and hustled over. "Can I help you, sir?"

"Not necessary, Lieutenant. Macon seems to have our needs under control."

"Yes, sir, very good, sir." The lieutenant turned stiffly and walked toward his office.

Macon spoke to Rivers. "Good man, the lieutenant. He had a platoon at Con Thien last summer. Took a lot of casualties working that Golden Fleece bullshit. Took it real hard."

"I know the feeling."

The room grew solemn. Each man shuffled his feet and alternated glances between the others and the floor. After a few seconds, Jackson interrupted. "Well, Macon, do you think we can get our gear?"

"Sure. When I heard it was you wantin' special things, Skipper, I got 'em my damn self. Most of it's over here." Macon led them to a nondescript warehouse just outside the main building and yelled at an American sitting at a desk reading *Stars and Stripes*. "Goddamn it, Ravat, my old skipper's here. Get your skinny ass movin'."

The clerk started pulling various pieces of equipment from a limitless array of green boxes strewn about the building.

While Jackson observed the hubbub, the short-timer drew Rivers out of earshot. "You really goin' back to the bush with this cherry, Skipper?"

"He's all right, Macon. Colonel MacDonald awarded that 'cherry' the Bronze Star this morning, along with those sergeant's stripes he's wearing."

"No shit? You'd never know it by his manner. Don't say nothin'; just sort of listens is all."

"He's something special. I've never seen anyone who can shoot like he does, and he keeps his shit together. Besides, since when is shooting your mouth off a demonstration you know what you're talking about?"

Taking the last statement as a rebuke, Macon broke off the private huddle and walked over to a tarp-covered box with the word "confidential" stenciled on it in large red letters. He pulled back the tarpaulin and gestured for the two Marines to join him.

Inside the box were eleven Stoner system carbines and several boxes of 5.56-mm ammunition. Macon picked up two rifles and handed them to Rivers and Jackson.

"You familiar with the Stoner, sir?" Macon asked. "The Army's been using them for the past year. It's light, easy to carry, and has tremendous stopping power. These here are second-wave prototypes and, in my opinion, the developer—the gun's named for him—has straightened out the early flaws and added a couple of very sexy features. In fact, I think this is the best weapon available today, anywhere. Maybe even better than the AK."

Rivers eyed the black plastic rifles dubiously. "Nope. Never seen one before."

"Then we'll get you checked out. The colonel requires everyone to fire and zero his weapon before we issue it to 'em. He says he ain't havin' any of his Marines die 'cause their weapons don't work."

Rivers and Jackson didn't respond, just nodded and took the magazines the Vietnamese worker handed them.

Jackson hefted the rifle and expressed his doubts. "This thing's too light, Macon. Feels like a toy."

Sergeant Macon also took a magazine and reached for Jackson's weapon. "This ain't, and I repeat, ain't no toy," he snapped. "This is a by-God gook killer. The rounds are small and the stock is plastic, but this bad boy will stop any rice-eatin', fish-head-chewin', nuoc-mam-fartin' son of a bitch gets in its way. I think you two may need an advantage in the bush, and this baby is just what the doctor ordered."

Rivers looked at the Vietnamese worker squatting some ten meters away. His expression didn't indicate he'd heard the sergeant. If he had, he wasn't bothered. Rivers figured he hated Americans and one more insult wasn't going to make any difference.

Macon took the twenty-round clip and slipped it into Jackson's weapon. It locked with an audible click. Then he explained the fire selector switch. "There are four positions: safe, semi, break, and automatic. Come on outside and see. Try it on semiautomatic first."

He handed the weapon back to Jackson, then stepped behind as they shouldered their weapons and fired at some cans at the far side of the range.

Rivers commented first. "Not much recoil. The muzzle's a little light, but we hit what we aimed at. Good balance and quiet."

Macon held up his hand. "Okay, now let's try a little rock and roll."

Dutifully the two Marines moved their selector switches to auto, raised the weapons, and fired in short, then longer bursts. The cans jumped and bounced around as the rounds struck home.

They stopped firing after their clips were exhausted. Jackson looked past the open bolt into the chamber to make sure the weapon was empty and whistled. "Damn. This is a beast. And the smaller ammunition will allow us to hump more without increasing the weight."

A smiling Sergeant Macon handed them another clip. "You haven't seen the best part yet."

"Okay," Jackson said sarcastically, "what've we missed?"

Macon ignored the brash comment. "The best part of this weapon is the break fire capability."

Rivers' interest was piqued. "If you'll humor me, Sergeant, just what is a 'break' rate of fire? What makes it better than full automatic?"

Macon was enthusiastic in his praise. "The weapon can fire only three rounds each time you pull the trigger. It keeps cherries from using their ammunition too quickly." Jackson and Rivers remained silent, letting Macon talk. "You get the idea," he said catching himself before his excitement boiled over and made him look like a fool. "Let me demonstrate." He chambered a round, took careful aim, and squeezed the trigger. The Stoner banged out three rounds in rapid succession, and cans jumped and twisted in the air. The grin on Macon's face was huge. "See what I mean?" He was thoroughly enjoying himself. "You pick out a target now, sir."

Rivers pointed to a rusted fifty-five-gallon drum that looked like it had taken part in several previous demonstrations. "How about the old oil can in the corner?"

Without hesitating, Macon threw the weapon into his shoulder and ripped off a break. The can rocked and twisted, sporting three new holes in its side, all within an inch of each other. The sergeant roared with laughter. He looked at the captain. "You try it, sir. I'm not close to being the shot you are."

"Let Jackson try. How about the soda can over there to the left?"

The younger sergeant took the weapon and stepped to the edge of the range. He looked in the direction of the can, fell to one knee, and let fly with a break that ripped the coke can to shreds. Sergeant Macon nodded his appreciation of the skill he had just been shown.

After a few more clips were fired, the weapons started to click and each man hit everything he aimed at. Jackson realized he could hold the weapon on any target by using the break cycle and still have firepower enough to bring it down. After they finished firing, each quietly removed the magazine from his weapon and handed the Stoners back to Macon.

"That's some weapon, Macon," the captain said. "We'll take these two."

"Not on your life, Skipper. These are shit; just ordinary issue. For you, I've got something better." He turned, walked back into the supply room, and returned with two different rifles . . . one under each arm, with the muzzles pointed at the ground. He looked like a hunter out for a day in the woods. He handed each man a rifle. "I had the armory pogues match these two. Their tolerances are tighter, and I personally guarantee you'll hit what you aim at."

Jackson looked at Rivers in disbelief.

"I can hear what you're thinking, Jackson," Rivers said. "Matched weapons are rare in the fleet, and I've never seen one in 'Nam."

Macon smiled again. "With these, if you spot a gook, you'll nail him bigger'n shit. Just use the break and he'll go down every time."

Jackson reverently took the weapon and thanked the sergeant.

"Don't mean nothin', Jackson. You just keep the Skipper alive so I can serve with him again. Something happens to him, I'll use the weapon to give you a thirty-inch suppository."

For once Jackson didn't have a smartass comeback. "Gotcha, Sarge. I'll do my best."

After hearing the exchange, the captain asked, "What do you think of the Stoner, Paul?"

Jackson was dumbstruck. It was the first time any officer had ever called him by his first name. "Powerful, sir. And deadly."

Macon shot a quick look at Rivers. "Let's go back inside and get the rest of your gear." He heard the use of Jackson's first name and understood the captain wanted him to know how much he respected the younger man.

Rivers smiled and threw Jackson a look as if to say, "Let's get this thing done and get the hell out of here."

Back inside, Rivers spoke first. "We won't need all the stuff your men laid out, Macon. We're going to avoid Charlie, and trippin' through the jungle like a two-man band won't get it done. The boots are good," he added, "but we'll each need an additional pair. It's wet where we're headed."

The requested extra pairs materialized instantly.

Macon smiled. "It's wet everywhere in this shithole. Getting away from the rain is one of the biggest benefits of going home."

Rivers nodded agreement and pressed on. "The ripstops are great. Can you spare a few more?"

"Sure, Skipper, but in case the colonel asks, you don't know where you got 'em. He ain't got his issue yet."

Two more sets of the valuable utilities went to each man.

Rivers smiled. "I'm the soul of discretion, Sergeant. Lose the cartridge belt. I'd rather have a couple of corpsman kit bags. We can carry those tied to our legs and keep our ammo and water inside. We'll each need two additional claymores, but you keep the smoke grenades; they won't work for what we need, and I don't want to hump the additional weight. Next, get rid of the rucksacks and give us two Green Beret fanny packs."

Macon frowned. "I don't know if I got any of those, sir."

"Can you get some?"

"I can trade for 'em, sir. Couple of snake-eaters I know can get anything, but it'll cost. If you want 'em, you're gonna have to ante up. The doggies will want a couple of fifths of booze."

The captain handed over his ration card. "You take care of it. I like the det cord and the C-4 plastic explosive, but only two frag grenades for each of us. They'll make good booby-traps if we need to didi. Also, get rid of the first-aid packets and find some LRRP kits; we'll need the amphetamines to stay awake."

Jackson didn't like that. "Are you sure, sir? I never needed drugs to stay sharp in the bush."

"I would rather have them and not need them than need them and not have them. So they go."

Macon laughed. "You can always mix 'em with some booze, Skipper. I understand that's what most of the grunts are doing."

"I need to stay awake, Macon, nothing else. You get the LRRP kits and I think we got us a deal."

Jackson interrupted. "Sir."

"Shoot."

"You're not going to take those pots and flak jackets, are you, sir?"

"Not on your life. They're only good for making noise. Macon's just having a little fun, and I'm not about to give him the satisfaction of acknowledging that shit is even here. Right, Sergeant?"

Macon laughed. "Yes, sir. Just trying to see if the captain is still sharp, sir." He enjoyed reminding the captain that Jackson was still a cherry, balls or no balls.

"That's it then, Paul, unless you have something else?" Another silent message that said, "I know he's green, but I trust him."

"That's about it, sir."

"Good. Sergeant Macon, it's been a pleasure doing business with you. You drop those special items off at Jackson's hooch tonight. I wish you good luck on your flight home, and I'll look for you on the next tour."

"Roger that, Skipper." Macon stuck out his hand, but the captain ignored it and hugged him long and hard. When they finally let go, each turned away so the other couldn't see the water in his eyes.

Rivers took a foil packet out of his pocket, removed the prophylactic, and secured it over the muzzle of his rifle with a rubber band. He slipped the Stoner over his shoulder; muzzle down, and went off in the direction of the supply officer's desk. He wanted to pay his respects to Lieutenant Mills before he left, not wanting to add insult to the injuries the young officer was already dealing with.

EIGHT

Transient NCOs' Hooch, Phu Bai

1845, January 3, 1968

THE YOUNG SERGEANT had just started getting his 782 gear ready when Sergeant Macon came boiling through the door. Jackson looked up and said, "Christ, Macon, this shit's going to rub my skin raw."

Macon frowned at the whining. "You can soften it by manipulating the canvas. Pay attention to the seams. Folding is better than rolling; gets it pliable faster."

"Fold it, roll it, what the hell's the difference?"

"Do I look like someone who gives a shit, Jackson? You're going to hump the shit, not me. Do it however you want."

Jackson smiled. "I remember seeing an old gunnery sergeant of mine roll his into balls and then work out the wrinkles as he unwound them."

"That'll probably work. You don't get to be a gunny if you don't know your shit. Give that a shot. I'll be back in a bit. Gotta run over to S1 and pick up my orders."

After half an hour of careful manipulation, the canvas bag was significantly softer and Jackson started packing the material he planned to carry.

Macon returned just as Jackson finished with the last bag. "You still working on that shit?"

Jackson waved his newly camouflaged bag. "Almost done."

Macon held up a pile of paper. "Got 'em. Hot damn, a ticket for the freedom bird. Before I forget, I've got the special gear the skipper wanted and a couple of other things I think you might need."

"Grab a squat and answer some questions."

"Glad to, on two conditions."

"What might those be?"

"First, you stop calling me Macon, Sergeant, or Sergeant Macon. My friends call me John. Besides, it sounds kinda stupid for us to be callin' each other sergeant, sergeant, sergeant."

Jackson chuckled. "Sounds like a plan. I'm Paul."

"Yeah, I heard the skipper. He must hold you in high regard."

"What gives you that idea?"

"He never calls anyone by his given name. Least I never heard him before."

"Surprised the shit outta me too."

"The second thing is," Macon said, "you got any beer stashed in here?"

"Yeah, there's a full refrigerator on the other side of the wet bar," Jackson said sarcastically.

"Shit. You got some mouth on you for a cherry."

"Excuse me, *John*, but I'm no goddamned newbie. I've done some time in the bush."

Macon laughed. "Yeah, sure. I'm catching the freedom bird tomorrow. To me, everybody's a FNG, especially those with a smart mouth."

It was Jackson's turn to laugh. "That's me. It's gotten me in trouble before, and I imagine it will again. Sorry."

"Don't mean nothin'. I'll go to my hooch and get some beer. I wanna see a couple of friends from the Rock Pile before I go. They'll have plenty. I could use a cold brew after all the hard work I did today."

That made Jackson laugh. "Rivers told me you are really something. Too bad you're going home. The captain thinks you're the one to be with in a firefight."

"Just the kind you can sleep next to on watch," Macon laughed and left.

Just as Jackson finished loading the last of ten magazines, the hooch door banged open. Macon was back with two other NCOs. The three sat down next to where Jackson was working. "Paul, I want you to meet Mike Brody and Jim Parker," Macon said. "They're both REMFs over at Regiment, and short-timers like me."

All three short-timers sported a Seagram's VO ribbon in the eyehole of their soft utility cover. Short-timer tradition demanded that before anyone could truly be called "short," he needed to drink an entire bottle of VO and then remove the ribbon from the bottle and tie it to his hat—a task requiring extraordinary skill with a fifth of booze in your veins.

Jackson rose and offered his hand. "Glad to meet you."

"Yeah, us too," said the taller one, Brody. "John tells us you're goin' out with the skipper. That right?"

"That's it. We're working for the colonel."

The other Marine looked serious. "What kind of work?" This one went about two hundred pounds, shorter and stockier than Brody with a strong aura of self-confidence. "The name's Parker," he added.

"Yeah, but his friends call him 'the Beast,'" Macon interjected. "Got the name on R&R in Bangkok after he threw a hooker who'd been hired to give him some head out of a second-story window for biting."

Jackson smiled. "I don't really know. Captain says we're going to sneak up on Charles and have our way with him."

That brought the house down. Bottles of beer mysteriously appeared from out of nowhere, and one was thrust at Jackson along with the command, "Drink up."

Brody, a corporal who was headed home next week, watched Jackson work. "Don't pack that rucksack like a cherry."

Macon pointed at Brody. "Nah, I told you he weren't. If he was cherry, you think I'd be drinking with him? Let alone invite you two assholes over here." Macon had downed beer after beer and was now well past sober. He reached over and cuffed

Brody hard on the back of the head. The blow sent the cover, short-timer's ribbon affixed, skidding across the hooch floor.

Jackson sipped his beer. "Can I ask a question?"

Macon didn't hesitate. "Shoot."

"I'd like to know about the captain. I only know his reputation, and some of what I've heard has to be exaggeration."

Parker straightened up and sat his beer down. "You don't have the right to question the captain, cherry. You ain't been here long enough."

Macon interrupted. "Relax, Beast, I don't think he's questioning Rivers. It's more like he wants to know more about him. That about it, Paul?"

"That's it. I'm going into the bush with just him and I want to know my decision wasn't based on horseshit. To hear people tell it, he's John Wayne incarnate. I don't doubt his courage, but I need to know he reasons well. It'll just be him and me out there, and I need to know he won't go gung-ho."

Parker's eyes glowed. "I'll tell you about Rivers, cherry."

Once again Macon came to Jackson's defense. "Goddamn it, Parker, leave the cherry shit out of it. Ain't his fault he just got here. If half of what the skipper's told me is true, I think he deserves to be called better."

Parker got to his feet and crossed his arms. "Think what you want. I don't know this guy. He may be all you say he is, but to me he's still a friggin' cherry, and I call 'em like I see 'em."

Brody wedged himself between Macon and Parker. Turning on Parker, he growled, "Sit down, Beast. What's the difference what he is? The truth is it's his ass goin' in the bush, and if I was him I'd want to know too. He ain't said anything outta line, and he ain't been disrespectful. Christ you've been a REMF so long you've forgotten what it's like out there. When we were with Rivers, there was always a shitload of us to take care of each other if'n he didn't. Jackson won't have that luxury, man."

Parker glowered at Macon and cast an evil look at Jackson, but sat back down on a footlocker. "Don't mean nothin'," he said and took a long pull on his beer.

Brody turned his attention to Jackson. "It's Paul, right?"

"Yeah."

"I spent a long time as a LRRP humpin' the bush with the skipper and not gettin' caught. So let me share this with you. He's . . . well . . . he's magical."

"That's right; beyond belief," added Parker from the bottom of his beer bottle.

Brody pushed Parker off the footlocker. "Shut your face unless you got something important to add." The menace in his voice got Parker's full attention; he quickly reached for another beer.

"Paul," Brody continued, "we were on a walk in the woods up near the Laotian border. Khe Sanh was getting the shit rocketed out of it nightly, and the old man needed some high-level intel. So he asks the skipper to put together a team and have a look. About three days out, I was walkin' point when we came across a shitload of NVA sitting in the middle of a road. The roadbed was big, wide, and hard enough to drive tanks on. I almost crapped my pants, but not the skipper. He got our shit together, moved us back down the trail into some covering brush, and then got us around the gooks. After he knew we were safe, he called in arty on the gooks' position.

I mean, he had enough balls to get their exact location down by coordinates while the rest of us were shittin' our pants."

Macon chimed in. "Ain't nothin'. I was with the skipper inside the Z when we came across a road wide enough to charge a toll. It was heavily graveled and hard enough to allow a truck to move forty, fifty miles an hour. We followed it north until it disappeared into the Ben Hai and reappeared on the other side. Tracks headin' into the river told us the gooks were puttin' plenty of vehicles past. In fact, we were up to our ass with NVA coming and going when the skipper gets the idea to plant a RAPS unit on the north side so the Air Force could plot the position with an intel bird.

"Couple men volunteered to go, but the skipper wasn't hearing any of that shit. He said it was his decision and he'd go. Besides, if he got caught, he'd get better treatment, him bein' an officer and all. We knew it was bullshit. If he got caught, he'd get a nine-millimeter headache for just being there. Gooks don't take prisoners that deep in the bush. But just after sundown, into the river he goes. Swims across, droppin' down about every twenty feet to check the depth, gets his ass out on the other side, plants the RAPS, then swims back. When he gets out of the water, he looks at us and says, 'Don't think I should've done that.' Balls, Paul. The skipper's got 'em so big I don't know how he can fuckin' walk."

Parker, calmer now, looked at Jackson. "Listen, cherry, I was with the skipper when we got caught in the shit, not just walking in the woods like these two assholes. We'd been out scouting for a battalion sweep when we came across this hill. As we started climbing, Charles opens up from dug-in positions all along the crest. They were deliverin' the shit hot and heavy with machine guns and mortars. We lost the first fire team in the initial exchange and more in the second. I was hunkered down behind this tree when the skipper comes flyin' around me, up and over some big roots in front of my position, and as he passes he says, 'Come on Marine. You wanna live forever?'

"Christ, you'd a thought he was Sergeant Major Daly and we was going over the top in World War I. He took the fear outta most of us and we took the hill away from Charlie with no more casualties. Later, I asked him why he'd done such a damned fool thing, and he said he knew if we stayed where we were, we would've all died, and he'd rather die taken than bein' took. He's not only got balls, but he also thinks deeper than most. He understood we were in an untenable position and that doing something . . . anything, was safer than doing nothing. He saved our asses, bigger than shit."

"You see, Paul, the skipper, well, he's special to us 'cause we each owe him more than we can ever repay," Macon said with more than a little emotion. "Each of us, in our own way, loves the son of a bitch, and we wish it was us goin' with him and not you. Now do you understand?"

"I think so. He'll be there when I need him."

"Just make sure you're there when he needs *you*, Paul," Brody said. "And don't tie those sensors to the side of your pack. First branch scrapes across your back will ruin 'em all. Carry 'em in the balloon pockets on your blouse. They'll be where you can find them at night and won't get ruined."

Parker smiled. "See, I told you he was a fuckin' cherry."

NINE

VMO-6 Flight Line, Phu Bai

0300, January 6, 1968

CAPTAIN RIVERS PICKED UP Jackson at 0300. The temperature was rapidly approaching 100° Fahrenheit with the humidity hovering near 90 percent. After the younger Marine threw his gear in the jeep and climbed in, Rivers handed him some pencil flares and several sheets of paper.

Jackson shook the paper. "What's this?"

"Shackle sheets. They're used to encrypt messages and provide authenticity."

Jackson nodded. "The grunts use something similar called day codes."

"The LRRPs use these, and I prefer them," Rivers said. "They turn the alphabet into numbers, and vice versa. On the face of the sheet, every letter is printed in double sets, such as AB, CD, or XY. Under each set of those letters are designated numbers, in no particular sequence. When we send coordinates, we'll 'shackle' the numerical information before sending out our position. Each sheet is good for twenty-four hours, and every support unit in I Corps has identical ones to ensure accuracy. After the active time period passes, we'll destroy each sheet. Put 'em in your pocket and don't let 'em get wet."

Jackson grinned. "Nice to see you too, sir."

Rivers was all business. "Look, Paul. This is serious. While I respect your ability in the woods, the fact is I've done this a hell of a lot more. Being on a LRRP is a lot different than being with the grunts. So I'm going to be the teacher out there. I want you to add anything you feel is important, but if there's a question, I'll make the decision."

"Roger that, Skipper."

The captain turned in the seat so he could see Jackson clearly. "Sorry, but you're going to have to hump the radio. Break out your notebook and copy down these freqs. We'll use them and a set of call signs I've got for air and artillery support. Our team code is 'Deuce.' I'm 'Deuce One,' and you, obviously, are 'Deuce Two.' We'll use these names when we transmit so the receiver will know which of us is talking. Got it?"

"Yes, sir."

"Any questions so far?" The jeep pulled up next to a small helicopter parked between two very large steel-reinforced walls before Jackson could respond. Rivers jerked his thumb upward, and Jackson got out and threw their gear into the waiting chopper. He spoke to the pilot, then told Jackson, "This bird'll take us to the Rock Pile. It's the closest firebase to our insertion point."

After the two Marines climbed on board and strapped themselves in, the engines began to whine and the overhead rotor began to turn. As the blades gained speed, two more Marines appeared and took seats behind M60 machine guns affixed to a stand just inside each door.

The crew chief spoke to Rivers. "It's fifteen minutes flying time, sir. Just sit back and relax."

Just then, Colonel MacDonald filled the door next to Rivers and yelled, "Good luck."

"What brought him down here, sir?" Jackson asked after the colonel had stepped back. "Is this type of send-off common?"

"Not at all. His presence should tell you how important the mission is."

The Huey increased power and became light on its skids. As it did, the pilot moved it forward by lifting the collective, which changed the pitch of the rotor blades; the bird began to fly. Steadily, the Huey moved out of the confinement and toward the active runway. Once there, it gained additional forward speed and altitude until Team Deuce left Phu Bai behind in the early dawn.

Jackson stared out the open door and shouted at Rivers, "It's beautiful up here. I can see the Ben Hai River. Look how blue the Pacific is, and the jungle makes the mountains look almost purple in the mist."

Rivers nodded and pointed down. "That's Highway 1. It runs from North Vietnam to Da Nang along the coast. As we come up on the Cua Viet River, we'll veer west and follow Route 9. That'll get us to the Rock Pile."

As the Huey settled onto the firebase, Rivers said to Jackson, "We'll be staying here until after nightfall. Then we'll go north and west to the insertion point. It's only a few klicks from here. We're supposed to enter our LZ at the same time artillery fires the night's harassment, so we have plenty of time to go over our gear and get in some hot meals before jumping off. There will be no hot food after we leave, so let's eat as much as we can before we're forced to live on LRRP rations."

"Sounds good to me, Skipper."

The captain shook his head and laughed. "I'd like to cover a few last-minute things while we eat," Rivers added.

"Yes, sir."

Rivers flared. "And that's number one. No more use of rank between us until after this is over. Clear?"

"Roger. I'm not going to set you up as a target."

"Good. We'll communicate mostly with hand signals, but if we have to talk, we'll do it by whispering directly into the other's ear. Are you familiar with Rogers' Rangers?"

"British outfit. French and Indian War; first of the Pathfinders if I remember my American history."

Rivers was impressed. "That's right. Major Rogers' first rule was one we will strictly adhere to: 'Don't forget nothin'.' So bear with me if I repeat myself as I go over this stuff."

Jackson scratched his ass. "Fine, but can we do it over at those tables while we finish a hot meal? By the looks of it they're servin' corned beef and powdered eggs."

"You really eat that crap? The LRRPs call it 'red death.' Tastes like salted shit."

Jackson laughed. "Well, I don't imagine this'll be any different, but it's hot. Besides, the taste comes from the meat, not real salt. It'll help us sweat and keep our bodies cool."

"Yeah, I've heard that, but no one needs anything to make them sweat here; the heat's enough." While they ate, Rivers handed two bags of clear fluid and several vials of pills to Jackson. "I scored these off a couple of corpsmen last night."

"The fluid is serum albumin, a blood expander. If either of us gets hit it'll slow the effects of blood loss. The pills are salt, Benadryl, and chloroquine primaquine phosphate. We'll need these to ward off the effects of heat, insects, and malaria. If either of us gets hit, the other will need to keep him alive long enough to be extracted. Because we'll be alone, it's far more important that we be capable of providing emergency first aid than it ever was in the grunts. On top of that, we'll need to examine each other for rashes and leeches. We look after each other as a primary responsibility. Clear?"

"Crystal."

"If you have underwear on, take it off and throw it away. In this heat, it will rub you raw and give you jock rot. You'll have to free-ball it from here on out." Rivers handed him two packages of prophylactics. "When we're in the bush, use these to secure your trouser legs to your boots, and then tape over the cuff."

Jackson lifted his leg to expose a trouser well taped to the top of his boot. "Done."

"Good. Keep the rubbers just in case. If you don't have two pairs of socks on, take off your boots and put an extra pair on now. We won't be takin' our boots off unless we're secured for the evening, and then only long enough to put on dry socks. Wearing two pairs will cushion your feet from blisters." He ticked off other items. "We won't shave in the bush, so if you got any equipment with you, throw it away. Cammie paint sticks to a beard better than it does to a clean-shaven face. Finally, put these in your unit 1 bag."

Jackson didn't want to hump the extra weight. "What are they?"

"RAPS. We'll use them to mark the locations of bridges and other fortifications so the fly-guys can carpet-bomb the area after we leave. Our purpose is to see what's happening and report back. We're not supposed to engage the enemy at any time, but I just can't go in there, see all of their shit, and not fuck with Charlie's lifestyle. So, we'll plant these and arrange for the Air Force to provide a wake-up call."

As they waited for dark, the two men practiced immediate-action drills. The captain carefully repeated their practiced communications, stressed how they would be handled in the bush, what signals would be used, and what each one meant.

"Look, I know it's boring as hell, but let's go back over the order of march. Each of us will alternate walking point and tail. The geographical characteristics of our AO are rugged, jungle-covered mountains, and Division said elements of the 101st Airborne and the 26th Marines will be operating around us. If we come across anybody, we treat them like they're gooks and avoid."

Jackson's eyes registered his strong concurrence. "You bet your ass. Too many people fire first and ask questions later. Most figure there's no one outside the wire except gooks and if they're wrong, well, God can sort 'em out after the killing's over."

"I know you've been out there before, Paul, but we have to be perfect. Nothing will be left to chance. Get your gear on, jump up and down several times, and shake your body while doing it." Jackson looked at Rivers as if he'd lost his mind, but he complied. After he finished, Rivers did the same thing.

Rivers watched Jackson hold back laughter as he jumped around. "That was a noise check. Anything making noise has to be secured. I brought some black electrician's tape we can use. Finally, everything shiny I want either discarded, taped over, or covered with cammie paint."

"What's your blood type?" Rivers asked while Jackson worked. "Mine's O negative."

"Me, too."

"Good, that makes it simple. We can give each other an emergency transfusion if necessary, a blessing I hope to God we won't need."

About 2100, Rivers said, "Saddle up," and both men walked over to a Huey where several FNGs were off-loading. Rivers nodded to Jackson. "This works great. To the untrained eye we look just like those cherries. Our equipment isn't faded or worn, and there's no mud covering our uniforms. The new stands out like a neon sign. It'll keep others from asking questions we can't answer."

They climbed on board and the Huey lifted off into a humid and very dark night. It climbed steadily until the air became cold and bit at the heavily painted faces of the two men.

Rivers signaled, "Get over here." When Jackson was seated next to him he said, "Give me a hand with this cammie paint. Make sure all exposed skin is covered and my features are well broken up. Use the dark green paint over the bone structure and the lighter green to fill in and break up any pattern you think is too revealing. Then I'll check you." Rivers finished with one last warning. "When we get there, we'll exit from the right side. It's going to be darker than midnight in a coal bin, and I don't want to walk into the tail rotor. Once we're clear, we'll move into the trees."

Jackson looked out the open door. "How far above the ground will the bird hover?"

"Couple of feet, but in the dark it'll look like twenty. It will hover for only a few seconds. That's when we jump. The second we're clear, the bird will continue on and make several touch-and-goes before heading for the barn. Hopefully, the extra landings will confuse the gooks long enough for us to get the hell outta Dodge."

Jackson prayed silently as he felt the helicopter start its descent and the outside air once again grew heavy with the humidity and heat of the jungle. "Hail Mary, full of grace . . ."

TEN

Laos, Vietnam, and DMZ Borders

2300, January 7, 1968

THE PILOT SAW the LZ and nosed the bird over. The downward spiral was rapid, and within seconds the helicopter was two feet off the ground. It drifted slowly across the face of the earth, its nose level with the horizon.

As soon as the bird hovered Rivers shouted, "Go." Both men hit the ground hard. After a brief moment of orientation, Rivers moved toward the tree line to the south. Jackson followed about three feet behind. As soon as they entered the jungle they lay face down to listen. Jackson followed the instructions Rivers had given him earlier in the day and kept his feet touching the captain's and his body facing in the opposite direction from Rivers'. The captain was facing north to observe the edge of the tree line and meadow, so Jackson faced south into the jungle.

After ten minutes passed without a sound, Jackson felt Rivers come to a kneeling position, so he assumed one as well. Rivers' hand applied pressure to the sergeant's shoulder, and in a barely audible whisper he said, "Face me." As soon as their eyes met, Rivers made the hand signals for "follow me" and moved out toward their first night's objective, a cave about two klicks to the north and east.

Earlier, while they were forcing "red death" into their mouths during lunch, Rivers had carefully gone over the mission's SMEAC—the situation, mission, execution, admin/logistics, and command/signal. "The harbor site will serve as our base of operations. We'll store the heavy packs there and conduct patrols carrying only minimum gear. The fewer things we carry, the less chance of noise. There's also the benefit of not having to hump all that shit. That's going to be especially important to you, 'cause we're taking the radio everywhere we go."

As they neared the cave, Rivers called a halt and placed his mouth next to Jackson's ear. "We can't move straight in. Need to make sure no one's following, so we'll buttonhook across the mouth of the cave. When we're about a hundred meters past the opening, we'll swing back in a large arc and move inside. "If we do it right, it'll force anyone following our trail to cross directly in front of us. We'll hear them before they realize where we are."

★

The captain was all business once they were inside the cave. "Set up your half of the defensive devices. We'll use the personal seismic intrusion devices. PSIDs are sensitive as hell, but they'll give us a warning buzz if there are any vibrations in the ground."

Jackson took his PSIDs from inside a pouch on the side of his haversack. "Which setting do you want me to use?"

"Use them all. Start with the lowest and move up the scale as you set them in. Position each transmitter so a dissimilar signal will be sent. That way we'll not only know if Charlie's about, but also what direction he's going. Set the first group at right angles to the mouth of the cave, and the second starting at the opening, moving in a straight line away from us. Insert them carefully and cover them with leaves. That way, they'll look like blades of grass."

After Jackson returned, Rivers planted his half of the defensive perimeter, four claymores.

When he returned he told Jackson where he put each one. "I laid them out so each blast will overlap the next. That will give us a kill zone nearly 150 meters wide and 50 to 60 meters deep. Hook the wires to a single hell-box detonator and sit it next to your PSID receivers. Keep the detonator rod clear in case we need to use them in a hurry."

When the area was secure, Jackson took his place at the edge of the cave looking out. His would be the first watch. The schedule had been set back at the Rock Pile, and the decision of who took first watch told Jackson a lot about the skipper. Rivers flipped a coin and won, but at least it wasn't an order.

At the beginning of the first watch, Rivers laid out the radio call pattern. "Get our position back to Phu Bai first. Use Colonel MacDonald's reporting procedure. Tell them we're at our first objective, then every fifteen minutes Phu Bai will call and identify themselves. Your response will be a single click of the handset button. The interruption of the line static means all is well." Next Rivers laid out his plan for the following day. "We will patrol in a star pattern starting at the mouth of the cave and continuing south, following a different compass heading each night. We'll cross the Quang Tri River and recon a twelve-kilometer grid, including the one the colonel's worried about. Don't forget that the S2 pogue told us to expect large concentrations of VC along with NVA."

Jackson snorted. "Yeah, I remember. He said the 456th VC Regiment is headquartered in the patrol area. Made me feel good."

Jackson's watch passed quickly as he alternated between listening to the radio, visually observing the area in front of the cave, and concentrating on the PSIDs. If any of the receivers indicated movement, Rivers was to be awakened immediately. "If they're coming toward the cave," he'd said, "blow the claymores and we'll escape through the confusion."

The first night passed uneventfully. Each man woke the other at two-hour intervals until the morning brought daylight into the cave. With it came clouds of insects.

Jackson wiped a host of mosquitoes off his face and peered at Rivers over his can of C ration peaches. "What're you eatin'?"

Rivers stretched. "Probably choke down some pork and beans, but not until after I get a new layer of paint on my face."

To cover his galloping nerves, Jackson ate and watched Rivers position a mirror on his knee and grab a bottle of insect repellant. Sweat trickled down Jackson's face, stinging his eyes. "I like to squirt the bug juice into my hand, then dip the cammie paint into the liquid to break it down. I think it makes the grease go on easier, and it leaves a smooth, even finish."

Flies buzzed around Rivers' face. He pulled a cammie stick free from its pouch and applied it as he spoke. "You do what you think best. When we're ready to go we'll retrieve the claymores and PSIDs. There's a crevice in the wall where we can store our gear. It should be invisible from prying eyes, but for added insurance we'll leave a frag beneath each pack with its pin pulled. If someone tries to remove them, the grenades will put an end to his curiosity."

When his face was newly painted, Rivers motioned to Jackson to saddle up. Before leaving they swept the dirt floor free of footprints as they carefully backed out of the cave.

Rivers held up his fist. "Don't silhouette yourself, and stay close to the cave wall. When we reach concealment outside, we'll resweep the ground and head off in our first direction."

"Where are we headed, exactly?"

"South. Past some old villages the map has marked as destroyed. We'll give them plenty of space anyway. We won't get closer than twenty meters."

When they got near the first village, they found a position where they could observe effectively and remain undetected. Rivers wished he'd thought to piss before settling down. He thought about pissing his pants, thinking that in this heat Jackson wouldn't know it from sweat.

Jackson looked at the village. "It looks exactly like what the map shows. I don't see any movement—people *or* animals—or hear any sound. The buildings look like they were burned to the ground. I don't see anything except charred supports."

Rivers knelt and rubbed the knots out of his calf. "Sometimes, what you don't see is the most dangerous. I vote for staying as far away as possible. Seeing those villages close up scares the shit outta me. If Charlie weren't here, the rice paddies would be filled with farmers. Where are they?"

About midday, with Jackson walking point, the team came across a trail showing evidence of recent heavy traffic. Jackson wiped sweat out of his eyes and signaled Rivers forward. He pointed at sandal prints along both edges of the trail. "Looks like Ho Chi Minh thousand-milers."

"What?"

Jackson chuckled. "Sorry, sometimes I forget you're a zero. The prints indicate VC. They make their sandals out of old tires. Grunts refer to them as 'thousand-milers.' The footprints look as if a square tire banged its way down the path."

"I saw those awhile ago," Rivers said, "but there's more. Whoever made those tracks was carrying something damned heavy, maybe ammo. See how the toes dig deep into the sand? But what worries me is there are no leaves or grass inside any of them."

"That's it, Skipper. They were made recently."

Rivers nodded agreement. "The gooks are traveling east to west, further into the jungle. We'll cross the trail carefully, then remove our boot prints."

"You think we should follow the trail and see what we can identify?"

Rivers wiped a swarm of mosquitoes off his arm and shook his head. "No. In fact, let's make never walking on a trail we didn't make a cardinal rule. If we didn't make it and don't know who or how many did, then we avoid it. The only thing at the end of an unknown trail is disaster."

Jackson understood completely. "Roger that. There's an outcropping of rock up ahead. We can cross the trail and belly up to the point. From there we should have a clear view of the trail for about a hundred meters in both directions."

Rivers nodded. "Good. Move out."

When Jackson reached the point, he eased the overhanging leaves and vines aside to provide a clear view of the path. As Rivers crawled up, Jackson signaled for caution. Using two fingers, he pointed to his eyes and then toward a position directly across from theirs. The message was clear: "Look there."

Rivers knelt close to Jackson, and the sergeant whispered, "What's it look like to you?"

Rivers peered through the grass and spoke into Jackson's ear. "A large cave. Bigger than the one we used last night."

Jackson's eyes swept the area again. "I think it's a bunker. Looks active, too."

Rivers quickly freed his binoculars and made a quick sweep up the road. "Looks like we've got company—about thirty gooks, and none are wearing pajamas." He handed the glasses to Jackson.

Jackson's heart rate jumped when his eyes focused on the oncoming soldiers. "Jesus. They're not VC. They're wearin' brown uniforms and helmets, and they're carrying AK-47s, muzzle down."

"NVA." Rivers carefully eased away from the edge, cautiously replacing the leaves and vines in their original positions. "We can't stay here."

"Why not? They can't see us up here."

Rivers chuckled softly. "That's right, but we can't see them either. Our job's to observe, so we're going to move to where we can see what's going on. Let's go." As they crept along the ridgeline, Rivers periodically slid back just enough leaves to allow his binoculars to poke through. He held his breath as he observed the hidden bunker and the NVA below their position.

Jackson, facing in the opposite direction, controlled his nerves by remembering the instructions Rivers had given him before they left the harbor. "When we stop, especially when there are gooks about, watch for movement from behind." He wiped sweat from his eyes and red ants from his hands. The ants were vicious, and he bit back his desire to curse. "We can't see them either," Rivers had said. *He's got balls all right. Great big ones.*

Signaling Jackson forward, Rivers whispered, "What I see ain't good."

Jackson tightened his grip on his Stoner and moved the selector knob to automatic.

Rivers saw the rifle tighten against Jackson's shoulder. "If you have to fire. Put all your rounds down the path and then look out, 'cause I'm going to be moving past you like a bat outta hell. There's about a hundred NVA down there, and more VC coming down the road."

Jackson watched the trees behind him.

After a few minutes, both men began to relax as they studied their areas of responsibility.

Rivers reached for his notebook and signaled Jackson to do likewise. "If we have to didi, it's each man for himself. If only one makes it back, he has to know everything we've seen."

Jackson nodded, then wiped a swarm of mosquitoes off his face, smearing his own blood across his cheek.

Rivers whispered, "The bunker's entrance matches the earth around it, and that means recent construction. The leaves and branches littering the ground indicate something knocked down the camouflage."

Jackson nodded. "Otherwise we never would've seen it."

Rivers could feel sweat pooling on his chest. "I watched as they removed the camouflage. What we thought was a single bunker is a complex with multiple gun positions."

Jackson nodded.

When the Vietnamese had moved inside the bunker, the Marines moved close together again. Rivers spoke first. "We wait and take a closer look after they leave."

"What makes you think they'll leave?"

"Why not? They're in their element. They don't know we're here and have only come to repair damage. When they're done, they'll leave. For now, let's have lunch."

Rivers ate first. When he finished eating, Rivers assumed Jackson's position while the sergeant ate.

Jackson grimaced as he shoveled food into his mouth. "This crap is awful. I thought LRRP rations were supposed to be edible when you mixed them with water, but these suck worse than C-rat lima beans and ham."

Rivers chuckled. "You need to heat it first. Add water, mix the contents by squeezing the bag gently, and then pour it into your canteen cup. Then shave several slivers of C4 off a block and set them on fire. That'll give enough heat for whatever you got, but it'll only last a few seconds."

There was no smell, and no smoke. The concoction inside the cup bubbled its warmth, and Jackson ate quietly.

Rivers saw Jackson stowing his cup. "When you're done, get back here and observe to the rear. I want to see what's cookin' in the bunker."

Rivers carefully pushed his binoculars through the vines and swept them back and forth across the bunker complex. "Damn! There's a bunch of logs lying on the roadbed. The VC are carrying them into the complex one at a time."

While the VC worked, their constant babble was clearly audible, but the NVA soldiers said little. They simply squatted in little groups with their weapons held across their legs. Not vigilant, but not sleeping either.

Rivers' voice became edgy. "There must be a shitload of gooks close by, 'cause the ones below act like they're not worried about a damned thing. That gives us an advantage. If they're this sure of themselves, they won't be watching carefully, and that's all we need to see what we need to." Rivers retrieved his binoculars and told Jackson to break out his notebook. "Take this down."

Jackson nodded.

From his pocket Rivers produced a map marked off with a series of lines that formed small squares. Small numbers around the edges of the paper were the map's coordinates. "I make our location at Bravo two-seven, Papa one-three. Mark this location as bunker complex—twelve openings. From here on, the plan is simple. We sit and wait until the gooks leave. When we're sure we're alone, we'll enter the bunker. I need to see what's inside."

Jackson rubbed his forehead in a vain attempt to rid himself of the prickly heat rash he was developing. "Sounds too risky. What if only one of us goes inside and the other sits alongside the road where he can observe in both directions?"

"Sounds good. I'll go inside. If you spot any gooks, avoid contact at all costs. If the shit hits the fan, get the hell outta Dodge. You will not, repeat, *will not*, wait for me. At the first sound of gunfire, we'll return to the harbor and wait for only one night. If the other doesn't return, the one who does will destroy the gear and call for extraction."

Jackson nodded.

★

The afternoon sun turned their position into a sauna. Finally they heard the noise made by the commotion of men moving in large numbers.

Rivers returned to his prone position, stuck the binoculars under the vines, and was rewarded with a view of enemy soldiers moving down the road toward the west. Using hand signals he told Jackson, "It's time to have a look. You lead off."

They crept silently, each aware of the need for stealth. Heel down first, then rotate weight to the ball of the foot. When the foot was flat, they hesitated and listened. It took them twenty minutes to descend the hill.

When they reached the road, Rivers looked in the direction in which the NVA and VC had gone. "Find a good spot. I'll leave my gear with you. If there's trouble, get the fuck outta here. I'll be back ASAP."

Jackson moved to a point where he could see two hundred meters in both directions and still keep an eye on the bunker.

Rivers watched until Jackson was in position, then carefully slid his hands between the leaves and spread the vines shielding him from view. From the road he couldn't see the opening to the bunker. *Shit,* he thought. *Things look a lot different close up.* Then he chastised himself. *Hey dumbass, look at the footprints on the road. See where they move into the jungle? Follow them.* He darted across the road and under the jungle vines. As soon as his eyes grew accustomed to the dark he was thunderstruck by what he saw. *Holy shit! There's an entire base camp under here!* Clean, well-packed footpaths connected the bunker positions and led to a larger path that continued to the bottom of the valley.

Sweat dripped down Rivers' chest and ran across his stomach as he smelled the air for cooking fires and latrines. He was scared, but he forced himself to be calm. *No one's down here. If they were, there'd be smoke.* He was careful to stay in the center of the path. It was imperative that he leave no boot prints, especially at the bottom of the complex. When he'd gone about ten feet, the path dropped off sharply and disappeared around a turn.

Careful now. Move to the edge of the path. Press your body against the side of the hill and peer around the corner. My God! There must be thirty buildings on the valley floor. But no movement or campfires. Looks deserted. Okay, move carefully and stay in the center of the path.

Rivers wanted to look inside every one of the buildings, but that would have taken too much time. With every step his position became more untenable. What if the NVA returned? He desperately tried to make sense of what he saw. *Let's look in here. Jesus H. Christ. Look at this, will you? There's got to be a thousand mines and mortar rounds in here.* He copied down some of the lettering on the ammo boxes after realizing he couldn't take any samples; the weight would be too much to hump out of the bush.

Rivers left the building and looked at a group of smaller huts to his left. He pushed the first one's door open and his mind hit overdrive. There were hundreds of automatic weapons, along with more mines and too many mortar rounds to count. It looked as if Charlie was stocking up for heavy action. He counted seventy boxes holding ten mortar rounds each. In the corner were more than fifty boxes of AK-47s, still in preservative wrapping.

Rivers wanted to see more but didn't have the time. The NVA could return at any moment and Jackson would be anxious, so he planted two RAPS under what he thought was the command building. He knew if the fly-guys hit it, collateral damage would get the rest.

It was late afternoon when Rivers finally stuck his head out from under the camouflaged netting. He wanted to get as far away as possible, and damned quick. Charlie would be coming back soon to set up the evening ambush.

Jackson signaled urgently from the other side of the road. "*Hurry up!*" He pointed down the road where singsong voices were barely audible.

Rivers crossed to Jackson's position and reached for his pack. "Let's didi. I've seen enough."

ELEVEN

Harbor Site, Northeastern Quang Tri Province

1845, January 9, 1968

RIVERS WANTED to debrief as soon as they reached the harbor. "I'll tell you everything I saw, and you make sure nothing is left out."

Jackson wrote the captain's detailed information in his notebook and added some facts regarding what he had observed. Then he asked pertinent, no-nonsense questions. "How deep was the valley?"

Rivers nodded his approval. "Good. That will tell the Air Force what type of bombs they should drop."

"What type of canopy was overhead?"

Rivers shook his head. "Jesus, did I forget that, too? It was triple. The fly-guys will need deep-penetration bombs to hit the target; otherwise they'll explode against the trees. I figure the bottom canopy was seventy feet below the point where I entered the complex."

"How many campfires did you count?"

Rivers chided himself. "Shit. I got too damned excited. No fires, but I counted more than fifty sites, so the camp should hold about five thousand."

"Did you see any tunnels under any of the buildings or at the base of any bunkers?" Jackson kept writing and didn't look up for the answer.

"There was a tunnel entrance in each bunker leading back to a common room cut deep into the hill. That would make it easy to move from one position to another and pull their heads in during an airdrop or artillery barrage. They can literally withstand just about any assault and don't have to worry about the effects of the heavy stuff."

Jackson continued writing, stopping every minute or so to ask questions. After an hour, both men thoroughly understood what Team Deuce had seen.

Early evening brought a change in the weather. The hot, humid, still air gave way to a wet wind that howled through the cave. Outside, steel-gray clouds pushed the blue sky into night earlier than anticipated. Soon streaks of lightning began to illuminate the sky, followed by the inevitable thunderclaps—a serious problem for Team Deuce.

Rivers was worried. "We have to stay on our toes. PSIDs have one serious flaw:

they're stupid. They can't detect the difference between the vibration of a walking man and the rumble of thunder. So we don't let confusion reign supreme, clear? We will assume each warning beep is first a gook, second an act of nature. Each watch will be stressful, so keep your eyes focused and don't let the lightning ruin your night vision. Keep your eyes down. You'll still be able to see the light. If we get a PSID alert afterward, we'll consider it thunder. Scan the area immediately in front of the cave first, and if nothing's moving, turn off the alarm."

By midnight the temperature in the cave had dropped from a steamy 95° to a bone-chilling 60°. The cold was made worse by a strong wind. The cave helped break the storm's intensity, but the men still shook inside the cold, damp environment.

Jackson wasn't in good shape when the watch changed. His legs were severely cramped because standing up or stretching in the close confines of the cave's entrance was out of the question. "This weather isn't going to make the rest of the mission any easier."

Rivers nodded. "That's right, but we continue as planned. I'll wake you at 0400 and we'll move out . . . ninety degrees away from the bunker. The rain is going to drive all manner of shit inside this cave," he added, "so be on the lookout for snakes. They'll try to get close for warmth."

Jackson swore. "Shit. You're just full of good news, ain't cha?"

The rain and wind intensified throughout the day but didn't stop the patrol. Jackson was glad to be able to walk out the cramps. "The rain helps me relax," he told Rivers. "Only the stupidest people venture out in weather like this."

The noon radio check brought more bad news. "Phu Bai says the storm's expected to intensify with ninety-knot winds," Rivers told Jackson. "They want us to protect ourselves from what they're calling a typhoon. But you understand, that came from people who are warm, dry, and enjoying the security of the rear area." Both men laughed as they copied the message into their notebooks.

The day's search passed uneventfully. After they returned to the harbor and completed their debrief Rivers said, "Tomorrow, we're going back to the bunker and explore west from there."

Being in a cave thirty-five miles from any manner of safety scares the shit out of me, Jackson thought as he assumed the watch. The leg cramps returned, and he bit his lip to keep from crying out. He watched enviously as Rivers put his head down and fell asleep immediately. He didn't think he could sleep in a storm like this. The wind was incredibly strong, and both men were so soaked that their skin started to wrinkle.

Shit. What have we gotten ourselves into? Why doesn't Rivers have cramps? This two-man LRRP is bullshit. MacDonald must be off his nut. Is he taking the safe way out, ordering two men to their deaths rather than ten? But Rivers is sold on the idea. Me, I'm just too scared to care.

Throughout the night they listened to the PSIDs emit their continual *beep, beep, beep* warning. By morning, both wondered which would stop functioning first, the PSIDs or themselves. Rivers shouted above the wind. "There's no way we can deal effectively with weather like this, or the effects it'll have on equipment. Let's hope the sensors don't come loose and blow away."

By morning the winds were down but the rain continued unabated.

Rivers radioed Phu Bai. "This is Deuce One, over."

"Roger, Deuce One. This is Alpha Green Six, over."

"Six, this is Deuce One. Will remain in harbor until weather eases. Soaked to the bone, hands and feet soft and swollen."

"Roger. Team Deuce staying dry. Alpha Green out."

"Okay," Rivers said, "Standard watches, but when you're off move to the rear like we did last night. It's not much, but it'll help."

Neither man was able to dry out completely, and Rivers too started to cramp. However, the lighter winds were a welcome relief, and life inside the cave soon took on more than the rituals of survival. With both men awake and Jackson on watch, Rivers started a fire. He gathered sticks and twigs, then ignited them with a pile of C4. "I'll make coffee," he said. "It'll take the edge off, even if tastes like shit." The shavings burned hot, and the fire heated the cave.

"You ever build a fire using C4, Paul?"

"No, never had reason."

"You set a C ration can full of water next to the flames. When it boils, stir in the coffee, a packet of powdered cream, and an ounce of brandy." He passed one of the cans to Jackson and sat on the ground, just far enough inside to stay out of the rain and stretch his legs. "What do you think? Are we having fun?"

Despite being cold, wet, and thoroughly miserable, Jackson laughed. "I guess so. Shit, I can't remember a better time."

Gales of stifled laughter erupted. For a moment, both forgot the miserable night and the importance of their mission. When the moment was over, they resumed their positions and worried about what they might uncover next. Neither man shared his concern with the other.

Rivers knew staying busy would keep their minds off the miserable conditions. "Let's clean our weapons and repack our unit 1 bags. I figure about 1700 it'll be dark enough for us to return to where we uncovered the bunker. The harassment fire will cover our noise."

As they left the cave, American artillery rumbled to the south. Incoming shells sounded like distant trains until they exploded. Jackson grumbled, "Christ, even the explosions are muffled against the rain."

They exchanged the point position several times but saw no movement along the trail.

Rivers said, "I guess the rain and cold has everyone huddled up next to a warm stove."

Jackson wiped water from his eyes and let it run down his shirt. "Yeah, everyone except us."

By 2030 they were concealed by a bush, twenty meters off the trail and five from the rain-gorged waters of the Quang Tri River. Yesterday it had been a placid stream about thirty meters wide; now it was a raging torrent. Jackson asked, "How wide do you think it is?"

Rivers shook his head. "Too wide . . . and too damned fast for us to cross. We'd drown sure as hell. Let's move back to where the trail leads to the bunker, then turn west."

Two kilometers later the path opened into a large road. As they started to step out onto the hard-packed surface, Jackson's heart stopped. His hand immediately closed into a fist and his lips formed the word, "Gooks."

Ten feet away, a man stood silhouetted in the dim light. As the shape disappeared into the bush, another immediately replaced it. Very carefully, Jackson stepped back into the covering jungle. He used hand signals to report. "Two gooks, both carrying AKs and wearing NVA helmets."

Rivers signaled back. "We'll wait and listen."

After half an hour of hearing nothing, they stuck their heads through the vines covering their position and saw men bunched up on the road as if they were waiting for something. Jackson pulled his head in and signed, "Ten NVA."

Rivers nodded. "Right. Did you see the .50 caliber?"

Minutes that seemed like hours passed as both men periodically consulted their watches. When a loud squeaking sound came from the other side of the NVA position, Rivers signaled, "I'll look. You stay put." He dropped to the rain-soaked ground and stuck his head out just enough to see the source of the noise. Pulling his head back in quickly, he whispered. "Wooden cart. Square sides with a pointed front and a bottom that's angled like a boat. It's full of weapons."

Jackson stuck his head out for just a second and then looked at Rivers. "They're standing in a semicircle around the cart, not even trying to be quiet."

Both Marines remained absolutely still. Seconds later, they were startled by the sound of a large truck grinding its way up the road. Jackson gripped the captain's arm and mouthed, "What now?"

Rivers whispered, "Let's move deeper into the jungle." Both men slid silently back into the concealment. Once he felt safer, Rivers said softly, "Let's watch for a few more minutes." Through the vines Rivers could see the truck parked in the center of the road. The red star of the North Vietnamese Army was painted on the truck's door, and it was loaded with wooden crates. Rivers' breath roared in his ears. *There's got to be twenty mortars on the truck; tubes on one side and baseplates on the other.* He watched as the mortars and crates were unloaded in the deepening darkness until one of the soldiers brought out a lantern and placed it in the roadbed.

A soldier stumbled and spilled his crate. Box after box of containers that looked like U.S. issue ammo cans fell open. Rivers was stunned. *Christ! If those crates are full of ammunition, there must be a million rounds down there.*

Jackson didn't try to conceal his fear as he shook the captain's arm. "We got to didi, now. There's fifty, sixty NVA sweeping the sides of the road and coming straight toward us." He moved back, and Rivers followed. More vehicle sounds came from up the road, and men started running and shouting.

Rivers and Jackson froze. Then, overhead, they heard the sound of incoming 155s. It was 2100, and the nightly harassment was inbound.

Rivers shouted over the explosions. "Hold up! I'm not passing up a chance like this. Let's inflict some damage of our own." Turning around, they went back toward the truck. "Wait until the sound of impact indicates the next round should fall on this location, then toss your grenades into the truck and run like a son of a bitch."

After he threw his grenades, Rivers turned and ran as fast as he could, with Jackson right on his ass. Yelling over his shoulder, he said, "Get as far away as possible before the grenades go off."

They made it about twenty meters before the concussion threw them to the ground. The grenades ignited a secondary explosion in the truck that sounded like a direct hit from a 105-mm shell. The two Marines regained their feet and raced into the jungle. Neither man looked back or slowed down. They ran for another ten minutes before Rivers slowed to a normal pace. "Catch your breath. We'll rest later, but first let's get the fuck outta Dodge."

Jackson led them due east until they cut a trail heading south. He signaled Rivers. "No sign of recent use."

The two men crouched and listened for anyone who might be following. "We'll wait here for a few minutes."

Jackson signed, "I don't hear anything." He watched as Rivers stepped out on the trail and surveyed it in both directions.

"Move south down the darkest edge of the trail," Rivers ordered. "I'll be about fifteen feet behind you. Stay in the friggin' shadows."

The five-kilometer hike back to the harbor took more than two hours. As they entered the cave, their adrenaline rush crashed and they collapsed on the floor.

When their breathing returned to normal, Rivers radioed Phu Bai. "Alpha Green, Alpha Green, this is Deuce One, over."

"Deuce One, this is Alpha Green Actual, over."

"Actual, Deuce One requesting early pickup. Point Zebra two-nine at 0430. Over."

"Roger. Alpha Green out."

Rivers was visibly shaken. "We're done for here, and we're gettin' out while the gettin's good. Our bird will be at the LZ in an hour. Saddle up."

They policed the area, dug up their claymores and PSIDs, brushed the ground in front of the cave, and scattered leaves and twigs in front of the opening.

Jackson was glad they were going and said so. "I don't like the neighborhood."

Rivers nodded agreement. "Let's didi. This place gives me the creeps."

TWELVE

Headquarters 26th Marines, Phu Bai

0600, January 12, 1968

JACKSON GRUMBLED FROM under his blanket. "It's our first morning back. You'd think I'd get one day to rest. Instead it's 'report to S2 by 0800.' I'm so blessed." Reluctantly he dragged his ass out of the rack, got dressed, and ambled down to the mess hall for his first hot food since going into the bush.

A messman looked in awe at Jackson's tray. "Wow, Sarge, you gonna eat all that?"

"Yup. You know the rule, 'Take all you want . . .'"

The messman laughed. "But eat all you take."

S2 was full of people Jackson didn't know. Officers were standing about, and several enlisted typists sat at desks. Captain Rivers was engaged in an aggressive discussion with a gunnery sergeant Jackson didn't know. "Pittsburgh's going to kick the shit out of the Patriots, Gunny. Those shitbirds shouldn't be allowed on the same field."

The gunny wasn't having it. "If you weren't an officer, I'd tell you straight to your face you was full of shit, sir."

Rivers laughed. "Excuse me, Gunny. Let's continue this later." He turned to Jackson and shook his hand. "Have you ever been through a debriefing session, Paul?"

"No, sir. This is my first."

"Keep one thing in mind; most of the people you will be talking to are REMFs— staff officers who have no idea what it's like outside the wire."

"So how do I handle that, sir?"

"Simple. Just tell 'em what happened and what you saw. They'll use what we say to build their intelligence assessment. No need to sweat anything here. There'll be no chickenshit."

Jackson wasn't at all sure he wanted to go through debriefing, but he gave the only answer possible. "Aye, aye, sir."

A door opened and a lieutenant motioned them inside. Jackson remembered him from Colonel MacDonald's office. That now seemed like a very long time ago.

Inside there was a large table with several officers sitting on one side. The lieutenant pointed at the chairs facing the table and spoke to Rivers. "Will you please sit over there, sir?" Once they were seated he continued, "Let me introduce the panel for the record, sir. This is our senior member, Colonel MacDonald, whom you both know. Next we have Major Lowing from the S2 section, and Captain Okura from Division G2."

Jackson leaned over and whispered to Rivers. "Jesus, Skipper, the captain looks too young to shave." *In fact*, thought Jackson, *he looks like a big-time REMF with pale skin and a shit-eatin' smile.* His assumption was verified when the captain asked him where he'd gone to college.

Jackson thought it was a stupid question and answered briefly. "No college, sir." *Hell, anyone with more'n a day in the bush would know you don't ask an eighteen-year-old sergeant a question like that.*

At times the officers asked the team questions simultaneously, stumbling over themselves to gain the information they needed, but most of the time it was the colonel who directed the effort. The gunnies sat at desks in the rear of the room, huddling over transcription machines and taking down every word spoken.

Colonel MacDonald saw Jackson eyeballing the gunnies. "Triple redundancy ensures not a single word will be missed from this conversation, Jackson."

The interrogation lasted for three days, with the second and third being mostly repeats of the first. The colonel asked the majority of the questions, and the junior officers picked at specific points in the answers provided. They tacked maps to the wall and asked Rivers and Jackson to verify the location of a wide variety of enemy positions.

Jackson wondered where they got their information about those positions. He figured if they believed what was on their charts, they didn't know squat. Every question they asked about the VC and NVA reinforced Jackson's opinion of just how wrong their information was. They were grasping for details to fill in what smelled like an overwhelming level of ignorance. But what really surprised the sergeant were the attitudes of the younger officers, who seemed to think the VC were a bunch of fuckups who'd only done as well as they had because they were largely facing the ARVN, who everyone knew were even bigger losers.

"That's not right, sir," Jackson said when a lieutenant commented on the NVA. Unable to stop himself, he continued, "I don't know where you get your information, sir, but Charlie is hardly 'untrained and ill-equipped.' They're dedicated, hard-nosed professionals who, to the man, are tough as hell. And they're superbly disciplined. There's a respect between their officers and enlisted men that's much better than anything I've seen in the American military. Officers are expected to do every job they ask their men to perform. They may think nothing of belting an enlisted man in the mouth, but they're honest and work hard to keep their men healthy and engaged. The discipline makes their life simpler. If someone senior tells you to do something, you do it . . . period. If you don't, you're either beaten or shot."

Jackson stopped short as the division commander entered the room. "Carry on," was all the general said before sitting on the interrogators' side of the table.

"Yes, sir. So what you're hearing about how unprofessional the NVA is," Jackson continued, "is giving you the wrong idea of its capabilities." He pointed to the wall.

"Look at this map. Captain Rivers and I saw emplacements here, here, and here. They were better than anything we have on any of our bases, anywhere in the 'Nam. The construction was always first rate, and the effect they would have on any assaulting force is unimaginable."

From time to time the general chuckled, as if he thought Jackson didn't know what he was talking about. Each time it happened, the sergeant stopped talking until ordered to continue.

Screw you, Jackson thought. *When was the last time you spent three nights in the middle of Charlie's backyard? Fucking never, that's when.*

With another, "Carry on," the general rose and left the room.

Jackson turned to Rivers and asked, "Why did he laugh when I was talking, sir?" For some reason, the officers present, especially Colonel MacDonald, thought the question was funny. All of them, including Captain Rivers, laughed, but none gave him an answer.

"Christ Jesus," Jackson bitched under his breath as he walked to S2 the next morning. "Every day it's the same damned thing. Get to S2 by 0800 and finish after 1700. Then they say, 'come back tomorrow.' Well, being at Phu Bai beats the hell outta Duc Lo or, heaven forbid, going back into the bush with Rivers. I could get used to livin' like a REMF, but I'm talked out. If there's anything they haven't asked, I can't think of what it might be." On this day, though, when he entered the room, the only person he found was Captain Rivers.

"Come in and close the door behind you, Paul, then help yourself to coffee. We need to talk."

"Yes, sir. I know I got a little carried away, but those zeroes . . ."

Rivers smiled. "Relax. You did fine."

"Shit, sir, I thought you wanted to ream me out about some of my answers. I know officers don't like it when an enlisted man thinks they're full of shit, and they especially don't like newly minted sergeants telling 'em so. I guess its time for my first real ass-chewin' from you, huh?"

"Forget it. According to Colonel MacDonald, the information we just gave S2 is the best intel they've received in months. What you said was right on the money, and it's not what I wanted to talk about."

"It's not?"

Rivers laughed. "No. I've been wondering if you've given any thought to what we'll be doing next?"

"Is the debrief over?"

"For now it is."

"Well, then no, sir, I haven't. I'm still too green to have an opinion as to what you or the colonel might need next."

"Don't bullshit me, Paul."

"Well, sir, I'd like to complete my tour as a sniper."

Rivers frowned. "That, I'm afraid, is out of the question. After the performance you just turned in, I'll be lucky to hold onto you for the rest of your tour."

Jackson panicked. "But why, sir? I didn't do anything wrong. I told the truth and reported only what we saw."

Rivers didn't reply directly to the question. "Listen, Paul. This war's about to expand. Charlie's going to blow things wide open in the very near future. That means we'll need a lot of intelligence of the type we just delivered, which is a hell of a lot better than what the LRRPs are reporting. To obtain it, you and I are going to be kept very busy."

"I don't know," Jackson said, more thinking aloud than making a direct reply.

Rivers' face was set with determination. "Well, I do. You're needed here. Therefore, your request to return to Special Weapons is denied. You and I are going to be the cadre of a new form of intelligence unit, one comprised of very small teams that operate strictly on an independent basis. We won't be allowed to pick our missions— those will be based on the needs of the division—but how we conduct the operation will strictly be up to us. I need you to help me train others to do what we've already done."

Jackson sat up straight in his chair and stared at Rivers. "Wait a minute. I told you before we started this that I didn't see myself getting killed because some cherry didn't know what he was supposed to do."

Rivers took a step back but responded quickly. "We won't be using cherries. They'll be handpicked veterans who've spent a minimum of six months in the bush. People with exceptional abilities, like yours."

"I don't know, sir. I'd like to work as a sniper. I mean, I like working with you—it's a damned sight better than being a grunt—but I don't like the idea of training others."

"Tell you what. I want you here, but I'm not going to beg. Take some time and think about it. I can only promise you more of what we just came through. Find me tomorrow."

THIRTEEN

Phu Bai

1300, January 16, 1968

JACKSON THUMPED HIS beer bottle down on the bar in the NCO club and openly expressed his feelings. "This place really sucks."

The overweight bartender replied, "If you don't like it, take your ass the fuck outta here."

Jackson figured fat REMFs to be the worst kind of feather merchants. "Don't get your panties in a knot. This shithole's a hell of a lot better than the bush. I'm only here 'cause it's cool inside and hot as hell outside. That and the beer is cheap." He picked up the bottle just as American artillery opened up. The barstool vibrated with the sounds of outbound 175-mm rounds, glasses rattled, and a brown-and-blue Schlitz beer sign fell off the wall behind the bar. Jackson watched two newbies at the end of the bar cringe as the noise grew louder.

The bartender chuckled as he slid a second ice-cold beer down the bar. "Don't get in the habit of flinching, cherry," he said to one of the newbies. "That's outgoing. If you can't control yourself when you hear that, you'll shit yourself when you hear incoming."

Jackson frowned. "Shut up, asshole. When's the last time you spent a night with your ass in the grass? God, I hate REMFs, and you, you fat, pasty-skinned bastard, are a classic example if I ever saw one. Even a cherry on his second day in the bush doesn't have pale skin or long hair. Every real Marine has a deep tan from humpin' in the hot sun and knows enough to keep his hair short."

The bartender hunched his shoulders. "Who the fuck you talkin' to, grunt?"

Jackson was full of menace. "You, you candy-ass feather merchant. Leave the kid alone. It ain't his fault he just got here."

The bartender took up a post at the far end of the bar.

Jackson motioned to the FNG corporals. "You two. Join me over there." Both men, obviously new replacements, picked up their beers and walked to a table near the door.

Jackson had first seen the FNGs outside. They couldn't have been more obvious with their stateside utility uniforms, complete with creases, and he felt sorry for the poor bastards. Thirteen months is one hell of a long time. The thought of having to do a full tour again made him cringe. Jackson knew he'd screwed up as he watched the corporals walk toward the table. "You two better wise the fuck up. I should have kept my mouth shut and let you take care of yourselves."

"Why *did* you help, Sergeant?" the taller of the two asked.

Jackson shook his head. "Because I don't like being called a cherry either, especially by some fat REMF who's never been outside the club, and 'cause I know you're going to be in the shit soon."

"Can I sit here?" the cherry asked, touching a chair.

Jackson scowled. "I asked you over here, didn't I? Don't make me regret it by acting like a candy-ass."

The other cherry nodded in the direction of the REMF bartender. "Thanks, Sarge."

Jackson nodded. "Don't mean nothin'."

Not wanting to be left out, Cherry 1 asked. "How long have you been in-country?"

"Nearly five months."

"And people still call you a cherry?"

"Corporal," Jackson said with more patience than he felt. "You're going to be a cherry as long as there's one guy in this miserable shithole one day shorter than you are. Get used to it."

"Who're you with, Sergeant?"

"No one right now. I just left Alpha 2-26."

"That explains why you're in the club so early."

"I guess so. My being here bother you?"

"Not at all, Sarge. We just haven't seen anyone quite like you since we arrived."

"Well, you couldn't have been lookin' too friggin' hard. There's a couple thousand of us around. More if you count the air wing pukes."

"Not with jungle utes on, red mud caked into the webbing of his boots, and sportin' a soft rain cover, there ain't."

Jackson grinned. "Well, I'll be goddamned, an observant cherry. Don't see too many like you 'round here. They usually end up with the LRRPs. If I was you, I'd keep that a secret until after I was assigned."

"Too late. We were assigned this morning. First Battalion, 26th Marines, at a place called Khe Sanh. Know it?"

Jackson nodded. "Yeah, I know it. Been there a couple of times and was always glad when I left. Fuckin' place gives me the shakes."

"That's encouraging," Cherry 2 said. "Why'd it bother you?"

"The jungle around the base is just lousy with gooks. The place sits at the bottom of several large hills high enough to see Laos to the west and the Z to the north. All around it the jungle grows three canopies high and is home to every gook on his way south. Lots of NVA, and plenty of VC too, especially this time of the year. But what really bothers me is the friggin' hills. Every time I'm there, I feel like a Frog at Dien Bien Phu."

Cherry 1 stared in awe. "A what?"

"A Frog," Jackson snapped. "You know, a Frenchman. They got their ass kicked back in the late forties by the same gooks we're fightin' now."

Cherry 2 was hanging on Jackson's every word. "What do you mean by 'this time of year'?"

"It's almost Lunar New Year, or Tet, as Charles calls it. A big gook holiday—the biggest. Every year, Charlie gets filled up with religion, drinks himself blind, then prays to his long-lost ancestors. Makes him brave as hell. That kind of fervor scares the shit outta me."

Cherry 1 frowned in disbelief. "How do you know all of this stuff? This has to be your first New Year. You said you've only been here five months."

Jackson grabbed his beer and started to get up. "That's right, asshole. Me, I'm lucky. My thirteen months only includes one of the fuckers. You two just got here, right?"

Heads nodded.

"Well, your thirteen months will take you through two of 'em. The last one'll be especially bad because you'll be short. Things get crazy when you're short."

Cherry 2 pushed his buddy. "Sit down, Sergeant. My dumbass friend didn't mean any disrespect. It's really that bad at Khe Sanh?"

Jackson returned to his seat. "Yeah, it can be."

Feeling like a fool, Cherry 1 changed the subject. "What've you been doing if you're not assigned to a regular outfit?"

"I'm part of a special recon team. My CO and I've been doing some work for the skipper of the Twenty-Sixth. Before that I was a rifleman walking patrols out of Duc Lo."

"Where's that?"

"About halfway between where you're headed and the Laos-DMZ juncture. It's a small firebase used to mount ambush and harassment patrols. Cute piece of real estate about half a klick from the Z."

The smarter of the two cherries asked the obvious question. "Can you tell us a little about what to expect?"

Jackson nodded. "It's war. For-real combat. I don't care what all those pricks back in the world told you, or what you might've heard on NBC. This is a gut-bustin' shootin' war where real men, your friends, get killed." He drained his Budweiser. "Hey, you've just helped me make up my mind."

"We did what?"

"I came in here to decide if I wanted to stay with my present assignment. Now I know what I need to do. Seeing you two made me realize just how safe I am with Captain Rivers. Nothin' in the 'Nam, and I mean nothin', is more dangerous than leading cherries like you outside the wire." Jackson rose to his feet. "Thanks, gentlemen." He threw a twenty-dollar MPC note on the table, told them to drink up, and left to find Rivers.

FOURTEEN

Headquarters 26th Marines, Phu Bai

1330, January 18, 1968

JACKSON WAS IN THE MOOD to bitch. "If this job is anything, it's boring."

Rivers had no pity. "You complain too much. Besides, you volunteered."

"True enough. Actually, things are good except for your brutal physical training routine. Why do we come to the beach every day and run in the water? Back and forth until we're too tired to walk."

Rivers laughed. "Tired? You haven't seen shit, Paul. From now on, after we're done at the beach we're going to Supply and unload trucks. We'll lift the heaviest boxes I can find. That will take the place of a normal weight-training program. I thought of it because I couldn't find any weights on the base or buy any in the ville. We're also going to run and perform calisthenics to develop our wind, endurance, and strength. And we'll eat double portions of vegetables, meat, and eggs; all high-protein stuff. The combination of high-potency food and strenuous exercise will have us looking and feeling better than we ever have. There's no hard booze allowed, but you can drink three beers a day for the carbs."

Jackson laughed. "It won't take much encouragement for me to comply with that order."

Rivers suddenly got very serious. "Major Potts wants us to spend several hours a day at S2 so we can learn as much about intel as possible: what we need to look for, what we should ignore, and how to identify specific gook units. And that's just the beginning. We're going to refine our skills with time-delay incendiary devices, unmanned ambushes, hand-to-hand techniques, and making high-impact rounds out of our Stoner shells. Long-range killing techniques using the M40 sniper rifle will be a fundamental skill. In fact, I asked the colonel to have the weapon included as part of our table of organization and equipment. I got no argument. So the big rifle's yours, Paul."

Rivers handed Jackson a rifle mounted with a large scope. "This is a very special weapon, so take good care of it. It's a lot heavier than your Stoner, which you'll also hump. I had some friends in Lang Vei fit it with a high-magnification night scope. It can see through the darkest night, and that makes it the perfect weapon for someone with your talent."

Jackson was happier than a pig in shit. "It's incredible."

"Yes, it is. It fires the standard NATO 7.62-by-51 round, but with an unjacketed hollow-point."

"I'll be able to take something down at one hell of a distance."

Rivers chuckled as he watched Jackson act like a little boy with a new toy. "Strip the weapon until you can do it blindfolded. There's no telling when you might have to do it in the dark. Keep the metal components covered with a light coat of sewing machine oil. Next—"

Jackson interrupted. "Next, I'll rip a camouflaged cloth into pieces and tape them around the stock and hand guards to keep them from rattling and help break up the weapon's signature."

When Jackson completed the task, the only thing regulation on the rifle was the barrel. There was no practical way to conceal the black metal sticking out from the camouflaged hand guard. He later had an armorer thread the flash suppressor so a silencing device could be screwed on, allowing him to muffle both flash and noise.

★

By the end of the second week of training, it was a vastly different Team Deuce that was called into the colonel's office for briefing.

MacDonald started. "The information you brought us last time has proven invaluable, but we still haven't learned what Charlie's up to."

Major Potts added, "For example, we know there's heavy concentrations of NVA moving down the Ho Chi Minh Trail, but we don't know if they're staying in Laos or if they're coming across the border in groups too small to detect."

Rivers raised his eyebrows. "What have the LRRP teams turned up?"

Colonel MacDonald answered. "Not much. Just a bunch of tracks and surface evidence indicating a large-scale movement south; but we don't know how many, what kind, or how well they're equipped. Every time we've sent out a LRRP since you returned, the results have always been the same. They see little, hear nothing, or wind up being ambushed before we can get them back. We've lost twenty men since last Sunday. One team alone lost five."

Major Potts focused the conversation. "We need to identify specific units, equipment, and morale."

Moving to a large map, Colonel MacDonald pointed to a spot close to the Laos-DMZ border. "We'll insert you here and expect you back in no more than five days. We'll use the standard harassment fire devised by our good sergeant." A head nod passed along the credit to Jackson. It was now SOP for inserting LRRP teams throughout I Corps. "If you get the information sooner, we want you out. Do not, I repeat, do not spend any longer than absolutely necessary. We'll have a weather bird standing by twenty-four hours a day for extraction. You call the moment it gets too hairy or as soon as you have what we need."

"By the way," Major Potts said, "the information you brought back from your first mission identified the 456th VC Regiment and the 1278th and 401st NVA Regiments. Additionally, we had an Arc Light eliminate the bunker complex you uncovered. Smart thinking to plant a RAPS. We dropped a shitload of bunker-busters and incendiaries on the exact position. A recon bird following BUFF reported secondary explosions going off for more than five minutes."

MacDonald smiled. "Destroying the complex was a real win. Questions?"

There were none, and the briefing stayed quick and concise.

Team Deuce finished breakfast by 0600 the next morning. Captain Rivers wanted to make sure they ate enough high-protein and carbohydrate-rich foods to last for several days. LRRP rations, even though they were heavily laced with vitamin supplements, weren't enough to provide the energy the two men would need in the bush. "We need to be at the flight line by 0800 so the colonel can brief us before takeoff. It's not a necessity; more like he wants to see us again to wish us good luck."

Jackson jumped into the jeep. "I really admire the colonel. He's a hell of a Marine."

"None better, Paul. He'll be getting his general officer's flag pretty soon. When that happens the Corps will lose the best regimental commander it has."

When they arrived at the flight line Jackson saw an Army CH-47 waiting for them. "Will you look at that? I guess the time we spent working with the 101st at Camp Eagle didn't pay off. I thought we'd be ridin' a Huey, not this big bastard."

Rivers chuckled. "Relax. The Chinook's larger than the Huey, but its twin rotors provide more lifting capacity, and we're not the only cargo being carried."

"If you'll excuse me, Skipper, I personally don't give a shit if it can lift the *Queen Mary*. I don't like the idea of being inserted by an overgrown target. These things need too much area to sit down and make too damned much noise doing it."

Rivers laughed. "The fact that they're slower and draw more ground fire doesn't have anything to do with your reluctance, does it?"

The Chinook's crew chief told Jackson, "Don't sweat it, gyrene. We're only ferrying you two as far as Khe Sanh. A Huey will take you on to your LZ. Where you guys are goin' you don't need the additional excitement flying in one of these converted coffins can bring."

Jackson shook his head. "I remember the first time I flew in one of these eggbeaters. I was so green I thought the light beams appearing inside the bird were pretty. Didn't take me too long to figure out it was gook bullets makin' 'em. The prospect of repeating that scenario isn't something I want to contemplate."

The crew chief laughed. "We'll be at Khe Sahn by 1030. You'll be on the ground until after dark, then you'll get your Huey."

Just as he did before their first mission, Colonel MacDonald, accompanied by the sergeant major and, this time, Major Potts, came to the flight line. "Good luck and good hunting," he yelled through the gunner's door.

The pilots were strapped in, but MacDonald leaned in and spoke to one of them. As soon as the colonel's group left, the chopper lifted off.

"Get comfortable," the crew chief yelled. "We don't have any of the luxuries you grunts are used to, but take a seat on those canvas benches. We'll hang out behind these M60s and keep you safe." He laughed and waved his arm to include a second door gunner.

The gunner yelled over the rotor wash. "We took out the windows. Seems all of you gyrenes bitched when ya got cut by the glass the gooks shot out. Now, as we gain speed, the wind will make it so you can't hear shit."

The flight to Khe Sanh lasted only a few minutes, and the helicopter never rose above a thousand feet. Much to Jackson's chagrin, they flew a course that took them directly over some of the country's heaviest jungle, which upped the possibility of ground fire.

Jackson yelled to Rivers. "I hope those clouds over the ocean don't turn ugly. This has been the first serious break in the rain since the monsoon started."

Rivers had to yell. "We'll get in a couple more hot meals and do the checklist when we get to Khe Sanh."

★

Every second on the ground was consumed in some sort of activity, and both Marines were soaked with sweat when the Huey finally lifted off and headed northeast.

Jackson looked at the sky and swore. Heavy clouds showed in the east. The vapor rising off the placid Pacific tides was drifting slowly westward to pile thunderheads along the coast. "Shit. Wouldn't you know it? The weather's changin' again. Those friggin' clouds mean there won't be any relief from the rain again this trip."

The Huey's crew chief gave the signal to get ready. He raised his hand with his thumb extended upward. The bird lost altitude quickly and made two false inserts before entering the primary LZ.

Rivers told Jackson, "The fake landings are made because some REMF thinks it'll confuse the gooks. The idea is to keep Charlie from sending out a patrol to investigate the helicopter. But what the REMF doesn't know is Charles *always* sends out a patrol. The only benefit we get is it takes him longer to investigate three areas than it does one. We'll use the time to exit the LZ as rapidly as possible."

As they entered the landing zone, the behavior of the two door gunners changed dramatically. They kept fingers on the triggers of their M60s, and their eyes carefully swept the ground for anything unnatural.

During the day's briefing, Rivers had made the insertion plan clear to Jackson: "Our plan calls for us to exit the bird while the skids are still off the ground. As soon as we're off, it will depart immediately. After it's gone, we'll listen, orient ourselves to the landscape, then bug out. Make goddamned sure you stay close, 'cause I'm makin' it to the jungle as fast as I can." And so he did.

Major Potts' words ran through Jackson's head as he chased after Rivers. "You're going to be operating at a significant disadvantage. Not only will you be deep in Charlie's backyard, but you'll be inserted at an LZ that's completely surrounded by hills. The gooks will be able to see it from any one of them." He heard MacDonald's voice next. "Once on the ground, it'll take you time to get clear. Charles will have troops in the area by then, so I've ordered the chopper to circle until you send two clicks on the radio. They'll stay above five thousand feet and use thermal imaging to spot any movement in the jungle. If they see anything coming your way, they'll give you a shout."

"That's no good unless they can give us an estimate of the number of troops," Rivers had said, "and their direction of travel and speed."

MacDonald had nodded. "I'll see to it."

FIFTEEN

Near the Laotian Border

2230, January 22, 1968

JACKSON COULDN'T BELIEVE IT. *We haven't moved a thousand meters from the LZ and he stops to "listen" to the friggin' jungle.*

Kneeling next to a large tree, Rivers whispered directly into Jackson's ear, "We'll stay here a few minutes. Get the chopper outta here and send MacDonald the 'all clear' message."

After the radio transmission was acknowledged, Rivers signaled, "Move out to where those two hills come together."

By midnight they had reached their intended AO and found a suitable harbor site. Rivers kept his voice just above a whisper. "This spot provides us enough elevation to observe and good concealment from above."

Jackson slid forward. "Looks good. The ground is hard and dry; no need to worry about leeches. Nearly six feet deep with jungle covering the entrance . . . damn near perfect."

After setting up PSIDs and claymores, they scanned the hill for any sign of Charlie. Rivers lifted his nose. "Do you smell it?"

Jackson nodded. "Yeah, and it tells me we ain't alone. Smells like someone's burning chicken feathers in a rubber boot over a buffalo-shit fire. It stinks, but it's not very strong so they aren't close."

Rivers stifled a laugh. "Campfires, for sure; but I don't see any glow in the sky, so we stay as deep in the harbor as possible. Okay, let's flip for first watch."

The morning was overcast with the scent of rain as the two Marines prepared for the day's mission. Rivers looked out and spoke with trepidation. "We're deep in Charlie's backyard, you know; only a stone's throw from Laos. It's on the opposite side of the hill above us."

The overcast thickened, and by the time they departed the harbor the cloud cover reduced their visibility to just over a hundred meters. Jackson reminded Rivers as they started downhill. "Don't trample the elephant grass. If we do, we'll give Charlie a direct line to our gear and time enough to prepare a truly unwelcome surprise when we return."

Rivers understood. "You bet. If we're careful, this position will be completely safe. If not, the inquisitive will get a close-up look at the surprises we've left."

About an hour out, Jackson signaled, "Freeze." Two Vietnamese were walking along the trail the team wanted to observe.

Rivers pointed to his eyes and then to the enemy. That told Jackson, "We'll watch from here. See if you can spot where they're going."

Jackson broke out his notebook and wrote down what he saw. "First gook: Tan jacket; dark trousers; suspenders with grenades. Two bandoliers of ammo around neck; carrying AK-47. No headgear; wearing thousand-milers."

Rivers added in a whisper, "No canteens. He isn't far from base. No one, not even Charlie, goes into the jungle without plenty of water.

Jackson nodded and continued to write. "Second gook: Pistol only; brown leather holster with Sam Brown–style belt. Red color tabs on blouse makes him an officer."

Rivers wanted more. "See if you can identify his rank through your scope."

Jackson sighted the big scope. "NVA colonel. Shoulder boards have three large gold stars and the number 488."

Rivers nodded. "That makes him the commanding officer of the 488th NVA Regiment. We stay here. They can't see us from below, and we can see the entire trail."

The two men stayed behind the underbrush and observed for more than an hour. There was a lot to see.

★

After they returned to the harbor and could speak freely the two men compared notes. Rivers asked, "How many did you count?"

"Over two hundred VC and more than two thousand NVA. Every one carried an automatic rifle and at least two mortar shells and grenades."

Rivers nodded agreement. "That's my count too. The first VC we saw must've been a scout. I saw him more than twenty times, moving against the flow, then returning with another group of NVA. He's probably the local VC guide directing the NVA movement south."

Jackson nodded. "There has to be a staging area close by. That accounts for the smell last night and for the movement we're seeing now. Major Potts thought it was inside Laos, but this looks like a direct feed to the Ho Chi Minh Trail."

Rivers' tension spilled out. "I almost shit when those B-52s came in and dropped their loads on the trail. BUFF really *is* a big, ugly, fat fucker, but he sure as hell got some. I've never seen concussion circles grow outward from the point of impact before.

Jackson chuckled. "The noise was deafening. I shudder to think what it was like where the bombs went off."

Rivers remained tense. "Just as soon as BUFF left, though, the movement south started right back up."

"Yeah, and it didn't stop. Two NVA regiments and a VC force I couldn't identify passed directly below us within an hour. Whatever Charles is up to, it's huge."

Rivers finally let down his guard. "I was scared shitless, Paul. I was damned glad it rained hard as we were leaving. On a clear day they might have seen us, and that would have been it."

"You okay, Skipper?"

"Yeah."

"I felt the same way. As long as the com line with the Rock Pile remains good I'm okay with continuing, but I gotta tell you, I was damned glad when you wanted to go."

Rivers laughed and broke the melancholy. "Shit, Jackson, we bitch too much. This trip's a cakewalk. Remember, the colonel said no night patrols."

"Yeah? Why'd night patrols concern him?"

"Because he thought there'd be too damned many gooks out then and doesn't want us exposed. Hell, man, we can get a good night's sleep."

By midnight the rain was falling harder and was accompanied by thunder and lightning. The temperature dropped sharply. Each man, when not on watch, huddled in his poncho to ward off the cold.

About 0230 Jackson woke Rivers by placing his hand firmly on his shoulder. His finger against his lips warned, "Be quiet." Another series of hand signals said, "Gooks inside the PSIDs, moving left to right across the front." Jackson thought he saw fear in Rivers' eyes, but it was gone as quickly as it came. He whispered, "There's a steady stream of them heading past in single file. Their direction of march takes them from behind us at about a thirty-degree angle, then down the slope into the jungle. They're quiet, orderly, and well disciplined. I haven't seen a single one look up the hill, so we're okay for now."

He took a look quick outside and then continued, "Too many to blow the claymores. We're up to our ass in NVA. We'd just piss 'em off. But I put them all right in front of the opening. If Luke gets curious, he'll get a face full of something he won't soon forget."

Rivers shivered and wondered if it was because he was wet or because he was scared stiff. "They must be close to a shitload of their buddies. So close they're not concerned with looking for anything hostile, regardless of its size. This isn't good, Paul. We have to move our house."

When dawn broke through the jungle canopy, Jackson crawled out to investigate the tracks. The continuous rain had wiped away anything useful. Only the trampled elephant grass remained.

Rivers talked while they ate breakfast. "Look, we know Charlie moves at night; that's the reason MacDonald restricted us to daylight. But we're far too exposed here. What we saw last night was just too damned close. I say we move as soon as possible."

When communication was established with Phu Bai, however, the team was instructed to continue their observation of the trail. "You're not to risk discovery, but Colonel MacDonald wants to know where the gooks are heading."

Rivers keyed the mike. "Bullshit. If he wants to know that, have him come look for himself. If we go down the hill again we'll be seen."

A metallic reply came instantly. "Are you refusing, Deuce One?"

Rivers shot back, "You bet your ass."

The radio voice became angry. "Get this, hotshot. MacDonald needs that information. So you get your ass down the friggin' hill. You got it?"

Rivers snapped the radio off, but not before a parting shot. "Go fuck yourself." He turned to Jackson. "Look, Paul," I don't care what they say, we can't go down the slope. This hill is just too hot. Let's head toward the border. Charlie won't patrol as aggressively inside Laos, so I say we hide there."

"Are you serious?"

"It's our only option," Rivers explained patiently. "Going around the hill is out of the question, so we climb. We're in the middle of the heaviest concentration of NVA I've ever seen. What we observed yesterday, and the movement last night, tells me Uncle Ho is close and in huge numbers. When we saddle up, we're going straight up the slope."

Jackson's expression made it clear he thought the idea was insane. His voice trembled and gave away the fear both men felt. "S2's maps show the top of this hill as open meadow. We'll have to cover at least a hundred meters of open terrain."

"More like one fifty," Rivers said. "And we'll have to do it humpin' all this shit. I don't like it either, but there's no choice. If we stay here another night, Charlie will find us. We're too close in. We have to back out, find a safe place to hole up, and then recon back in to find out what's here."

"What do you say we give ourselves a chance?"

"What'cha got in mind?"

Jackson wiped sweat out of his eyes. "Just before we move into the open, let's call in an air strike on this side of the hill. Get whatever unit we can to bomb the whole area back to the Stone Age. That'll keep Luke's head down."

Rivers nodded his agreement. "Sounds like a plan. Let's go."

Staying deep in the shadows, Team Deuce moved slowly from one tree to the next, each man living within his own fear. They continually listened to the sounds of the jungle. Once, the monkeys and birds stopped their constant racket and both men's hearts stopped beating. They stood silent, straining to hear any sound of movement. When none came and the sounds of the jungle returned, they resumed their upward trek. They gained the summit by noon. The edge of a broad meadow sat squarely before them.

Sliding close to Jackson, Rivers whispered, "It must be three hundred meters wide at the narrowest point." He parted the vegetation at the edge of the jungle and looked out into the meadow. "Oh, shit! There's gonna be snakes in those weeds."

Jackson's face paled. "Snakes! I hate fuckin' snakes. Can't we go around?"

Rivers chuckled as he saw his own fear reflected in Jackson's face. "No. We'll stay here for a few minutes and try to get some support. See if you can get some naval gun in here. If we can, the results will scare the shit out of everybody within twenty klicks, including the friggin' snakes."

Jackson scanned his shackle sheet for the correct call sign and pressed the transmission key on the PRC 77. He kept a wary eye on the grass for snakes as he plotted the exact location of their harbor site to use as a base coordinate for the inbound fire. "Romeo Two Six, this is Deuce Two. Romeo Two Six, this is Deuce Two."

"Roger, Deuce Two. This is Romeo Two Six."

"Roger, Romeo Two Six. I have a fire mission for anything with a long arm."

"Roger, Deuce Two. We have a very long arm. What's your target, over?"

"Heavy troop concentration at Alpha Zebra Tango by Fox Romeo Alpha.

"Roger. I repeat, Alpha Zebra Tango by Fox Romeo Alpha," the squid gunner said. "You're on the edge of our arm, Deuce Two, but we'll reach you. Shot away, adjust as necessary."

Jackson smiled as he saw Rivers scrape fire ants off the top of his boots. "They're firing the first shot directly at last night's harbor site; then we'll correct."

About sixty seconds went by without a sound, and Rivers asked, "Who'd you call? The round should've been here long ago."

Jackson smiled and said, "Here it comes." Just then a dull, angry rumble came screeching through the afternoon sky. "This one'll sound like a locomotive as it closes; very loud and very deadly. Look there."

Just before the sound reached them they saw the earth down the hill lift up in a massive convulsion. Even a thousand meters away their position trembled with the impact.

Jackson whispered into the headset, "Roger, Romeo Two Six, drop two hundred, left and right two hundred, and fire for effect."

Rivers nodded agreement. "That's it, Paul. Those distances will put the shells right on top of the gooks."

As soon as they heard the sound of the next set of rounds, both members of Team Deuce were up and running across the meadow, snakes be damned. They hadn't gone more than fifty meters when all hell broke loose. The ground they were running across heaved and bucked as round after round struck the impact zone. They ran over roller-coaster terrain toward the safety of the concealing jungle.

Rivers wheezed as he lay on the jungle floor. "What the hell *was* that?" The heavy concussions shook the ground for several more minutes before they stopped.

Jackson laughed. "That, my man, was the U.S. fuckin' Navy. Major Potts said the *New Jersey* was operating off the coast. It has 16-inch guns and hurls a 2,000-pound projectile over 30 miles to a target no bigger than a flea's ass. I was skeptical, but now I'm a by-God believer."

"My God," was all Rivers could say.

Without looking back, the dirty, tired, and hungry team moved out to find safety inside Laos.

The cave they selected as a harbor sat within a stone outcropping and was some fifty feet above a trail that ran beside a small river. Rivers and Jackson quickly laid out their PSIDs and claymores paralleling the path leading to the cave. Once they were sure their new harbor was safe, they crawled in, ate, and began their two-hour routine of sleep and watch. They enjoyed an uneventful night, but that peace ended at dawn.

As he shook Jackson awake, a wide-eyed Rivers whispered, "Get your scope and look at what's outside."

Crawling to the opening, Jackson poked his scope carefully around the edge and focused on the river directly below. The sight that filled the aperture caused him to snap back from the cave's mouth. "Shit," he gasped. "There's hundreds of Ho Chi Minh's best camped a hundred meters upriver from here."

Rivers nodded. "Yeah, thought so. I heard them just before dawn. I think they stopped to cook morning rice."

"Right. There's small campfires as far as I can see beyond the river bend, and for three hundred meters behind us. I figure it's at least a reinforced regiment." Jackson saw fear flit through Rivers' eyes once again.

"Let's stay back as far as we can," Rivers said. "We'll talk to MacDonald, tell the relay we're going off the air, and then turn the noisy son of a bitch off." Shutting down the radio would instantly tell Phu Bai how desperate the situation was. He moved to the back of the cave, spouting orders as he went. "Get against the wall. Press yourself into the rock face and stay as motionless as possible."

The short period the NVA camped by the river seemed like a lifetime. After their noise faded into the distance, the two Marines waited an additional ten minutes. Then Rivers signaled Jackson to get back to the opening with his scope.

"They're gone, Skipper."

"Thank God. Can I breathe now?"

Jackson's nerves were about to snap. "That's too friggin' close. Christ, the woods must be lousy with the bastards."

"Well, that's what we came here to find out. I figure we can recon on a path parallel to the one the gooks took. So saddle up. I don't want them getting too far ahead."

Jackson looked at Rivers like he was off his nut.

After a half hour on the trail Rivers whispered, "This is what, the seventh or eighth road we've seen that's big enough to move heavy trucks?"

"Eighth. Christ, there's activity everywhere. Looks like most of the troops are on foot. There's thousands of thousand-miler footprints covering the roads."

Rivers nodded. "Well, we can't follow them down the road, so we'll walk just inside the jungle edge. Make sure we don't leave any boot prints where they can be seen. I figure we can follow until Charlie disappears into the jungle just north of where we called in the naval gun. When we can't see them any longer, we'll didi back to the harbor."

★

When they finally turned back, Jackson shook his head. "Shit. I've counted more than eight thousand NVA, fifty-five officers in the rank of major or above, forty trucks, and an unlimited number of thousand-miler prints."

"Yeah, there's a shitload of 'em alright. I'm convinced we're witnessing at least four different NVA divisions moving south," Rivers said. "I've counted more than fifty units, heavy weapons, and a movement of personnel on a scale, up to this point, no one would have believed possible. We need to get this info back first thing tonight."

Jackson looked doubtful. "Are you concerned about our position, or is it just the urgency of the information?"

"Look, Paul. If we don't make it back, and that's a real possibility, the colonel still needs the intel. There is no other choice."

During the communication the colonel asked the team to recon an old French army base about two kilometers south of their position before returning. "Division wants to know if the gooks have improved the camp, and if so, how much. Once you've reconned the site, I want you out. Understand?"

"Aye, aye, sir."

"Shit, Paul," Rivers said when he had ended the transmission. "I don't like the idea of looking at old French real estate. I think it's too risky."

Jackson's fear and anxiety showed in his answer. "Me either. Christ, it's just you, me, and a shitload of Uncle Ho's buddies. I'm not willing to risk my ass for a bunch of REMFs who ain't ever going to know more'n what we tell 'em."

"I agree, but you heard the man. Division needs to know. We'll give it a look-see, but nothing more."

Jackson persisted. "Looking at any fortification, even one that's been abandoned for twenty years, means we'll have to cross open terrain. The prospect of exposing ourselves for even a moment ain't makin' me happy."

The team moved out before daybreak carrying all of their gear. They walked down the hill with absolutely no intention of returning. After they had moved a hundred meters, Rivers held up his hand and signaled, "Freeze." He whispered, "That big junction is just ahead. We can't avoid it, but when we cross, we move fast." Poking just enough of his face out of the jungle to see in both directions, Rivers made sure there was no movement on the road before he started to cross. Had he paused for a half a second, Jackson would have run over him.

When they were safely on the other side of the road Rivers said, "Let's leave a parting gift for our little friends. Get out the claymores. We'll plant them in a series of maneuvers that'll kill anyone moving down the road. Position the balls to travel about waist high and down the length of the road. I'll secure their firing mechanisms to a trip wire and hide it along the edge."

Jackson rubbed feeling back into his shoulders. "I like it. All we need is for one gook to take a piss. As soon as he steps into the jungle it'll be good night Irene for everybody standing on the road within a hundred meters."

Rivers was bone-tired and not in the mood for Jackson's humor. "Yeah, well, let's just do it and get the hell outta Dodge. Our chance of observing solid activity and living to report it is still good. As long as we remain in the jungle there's more than sufficient cover to hide us from prying eyes, so I feel relatively safe."

Jackson couldn't believe it. "Well, I'm damned glad one of us does."

They reached the Frog fort at 1100. Rivers observed the open ground surrounding it for a long time. "There's no way we're going in there. We'll recon from over there." He pointed to an adjoining hill. A half-hour's climb took them to a small overhang well above the old fort. Seen from this angle, it was clearly deserted. The ground around the half-filled trenches showed no use for many years. Fighting holes cut into the mountainside twenty years ago were still visible but half-filled with debris.

Jackson put away his scope, wondering how in the hell the French had been defeated here. "Looks like everything is overgrown, but the fight here must have been savage."

Rivers nodded. "Damned glad I wasn't trying to take this place. There's rusty old barbed wire everywhere. If Charlie's using the fort at all, he's doing so underground, and that's something we are not going to investigate. Let's get out of here."

★

Jackson led Rivers to a small meadow on the far side of the hill's crest, never leaving concealment. Once there, they tuned the PRC 77 to the extraction helicopter's frequency and waited nervously for the bird to arrive.

"Team Deuce, this is Peepers One Seven, over."

Jackson took the handset and confirmed the team's position with the unseen chopper.

The driver's microphone squawked, "Mark position with yellow smoke so I can identify location on my first pass."

Jackson's hand shook as he strangled the mike. "This guy's a goddamned cherry," he said to Rivers. "Peepers One Seven, this is Deuce Two, no smoke; repeat, no smoke."

"Negative Deuce Two, we require smoke. Will not wait on ground." The pilot spoke firmly, but his voice betrayed his fear.

Jackson hissed into the mike, "Listen to me, you chickenshit son of a bitch. We ain't popping smoke, and that's final. Now you get that fuckin' bird on the ground and we'll find you."

Rivers took the handset and talked politely to the young pilot. "Peepers One Seven, this is Deuce Actual. Area is within heavy NVA concentration. Smoke is not an option. Bring your bird to a heading of one eight zero degrees and we will sound our location as you pass. Over."

"Negative, Actual. I require smoke or will not land. Over."

Rivers didn't raise his voice. He didn't have to. The violence contained in his words said it all. "Listen to me, you REMF motherfucker. If you don't land, we'll walk the fuck outta here, and when we get back to Phu Bai there won't be a place in 'Nam you'll be able to hide from my sergeant. Now quit fuckin' around and get our bird on the ground."

"Negative, Actual. Say again. Negative. No smoke, no landing."

"We're not popping smoke, asshole. So it looks like we got us a Mexican standoff. If you don't want to land, then get the fuck outta here so Charlie doesn't get curious and investigate why you're flying around in his backyard. Second, and this is an order, mister, when you get back to your base, you go find your CO and tell him Colonel MacDonald of the 26th Marines wants to see him in his office immediately. Next you tell him he should pick out a court-martial site for you and your copilot, because if you leave us out here, I'll have your ass up on so many charges it'll make your fuckin' head spin." This time Rivers made no effort to contain himself. By the time the transmission ended he was screaming into the handset.

Two minutes later, the chopper landed and Team Deuce boarded. They kept their weapons on full automatic and pointed at the back of the cockpit as they enjoyed the coolness of the late afternoon air.

SIXTEEN

Headquarters, 26th Marine Regiment, Phu Bai

0900, January 25, 1968

FOUR DAYS AFTER their return to Phu Bai, Rivers received new orders from the colonel for Jackson and himself. "You're gonna love this, Jackson. Colonel MacDonald believes our information is too important to be transmitted via written order. He's afraid his current crop of S2 staffers might not grasp its urgency. He also believes, like most grunts, that 'military intelligence' is an oxymoron. To get the full impact across, he wants his commanders to hear it from the horses' mouth—us. The COs are all experienced commanders, but the young S2s don't know a platoon from a division."

Jackson turned to stare at Rivers. "You're telling me MacDonald believes the same things about Intel pogues that line grunts do?"

"In this instance, anyway. But, in his position, he can't openly express it. He thinks that what we discovered is just too important to trust it to anyone who didn't see it firsthand. We're going to have to do the briefings ourselves."

Jackson shook his head in disbelief. "Let me get this straight. An experienced officer, probably the best MacDonald has at the company level, has brought back crucial information, and the only people who can pass it along are the ones who saw it firsthand?"

Rivers flashed his exasperation. "That's about it. So I get to visit the vacation spots of Gio Lin, Cam Lo, Quang Tri, Camp Carroll, and Con Thien, while you will holiday at Khe Sanh, the Rock Pile, Cau Lu, and Duc Lo. The colonel will call the base commanders and stress the urgency of what we're going to share."

It was late afternoon by the time Jackson reached Duc Lo, having stopped along the way at Con Thien and Khe Sanh to conduct briefings. The chopper banked tightly and circled the firebase, then dropped quickly into a tight spiral. Each turn of the coil brought the bird closer to the firebase. Jackson spoke as he looked out a porthole window at the LZ. "Jesus Christ, there's a lot of body bags down there."

The door gunner couldn't resist. "Well, cherry, this place ain't no fuckin' re-sort. See dem boys standin' next to da bags? Those be da boys who gonna load da bodies on this heah bird, so's we can get 'em to Da Nang to start their horizontal trip to their mommies. We ain't gonna spend more'n a second heah longer'n we need to," the gunner continued. "So you be gettin' yo' cherry ass outta my bird the second we touch down. We're too damned close to the Z for me."

Jackson picked up his Stoner and hung it muzzle down from his shoulder. "No argument on that point."

"You can do me a big fav'ah if you grab a couple of them C-rat cases and carry 'em off when you go," the gunner said.

As soon as the Huey's skids bounced, Jackson grabbed three cases of C-rations and moved toward the right door of the chopper. Just as he was about to exit, a work detail filled the door. Several two-man teams entered, each carrying a single black bag that they placed reverently on the floor.

"Make a hole," a big Marine yelled as he fought to carry the boot half of another bag on board. The man carrying the shoulder and head half looked for a place to lay the bag and fixed on a spot behind Jackson. "Get the fuck outta the way, cherry."

Jackson took a long, hard look at the bag and thanked God he'd gotten off this hill when he did.

"Hey," came a shout. "Here's the last one's hat." A steel helmet with a large hole through both sides came spinning through the machine-gunner's door and landed with a bang on the metal floor.

"One thing about Marine grunts," Jackson told the gunner, "they sure as hell understand what tender lovin' care is."

Jackson heard two loud *krumpf*s as he moved away from the spinning rotors.

"Move it, Marine," yelled a voice.

Jackson looked around to see who had spoken.

"Keep standin' there with your ass hangin' out and that gook mortar crew will put their next round in your back pocket." The voice came from behind a nearby bunker. The officer it belonged to didn't come out from his hiding spot when he asked, "You Jackson?"

"Yes, *sir!*" Jackson responded with as much emphasis as he could muster. He looked the lieutenant up and down. *Another cherry zero. Those mortars landed on the far end of the line, nowhere near us, and this college boy is hiding behind the bunker. Chickenshit asshole.*

The skittish lieutenant yelled again. "Come with me. The skipper's waiting. Regiment called, so I guess you're something important, but you don't look like much. Are those clean ripstops you're wearing? What kind of a weapon is that? Looks like some kind of a toy."

Jackson cradled his Stoner and repeated John Macon's words. "I can assure you, LT, this ain't no toy." Jackson didn't think the zero saw the sniper rifle hanging down his back, because if he had, he would've made more stupid comments.

The cherry lieutenant mumbled, "Fucking REMF gopher taking me away from my platoon at a time like this."

Jackson smiled. *Screw you. I didn't ask to be here. I'm back on this shit-eatin' hill 'cause the colonel thinks it's important. Fuck all you assholes. I know what's out in those woods, and I'd like nothing better than to be back in Phu Bai cuddled up next to a cold beer.*

The lieutenant started up the hill with Jackson in trail. They passed through several entrenchments before reaching a large bunker set deep inside the ground about fifty meters from the top. In his four months as a grunt here, Jackson had never set foot inside the command bunker. Now he was back as a representative of the regimental commander. Inside, several Coleman lanterns cast a dim yellow glow over the scattered maps and field desks. The battalion commander stood in the far corner looking over a map taped to a broken piece of Plexiglas.

The college boy stopped Jackson. "Wait here."

Jackson figured the lieutenant wanted to go suck up to the major. Then he saw the zero point at him. *Jesus. Whatever he said must have struck a nerve. Look at the skipper stomp his way over here.*

When he drew close, the expression on the officer's face changed and he actually smiled. Sticking out his hand, he said in a voice loud enough for the tight-ass lieutenant to hear. "Well, I'll be goddamned. They said a sergeant was coming up here. They didn't screw up and make you one, did they, Jackson? MacDonald must be getting soft."

Jackson grinned. "Yes, sir, I guess that's it." He'd met the battalion commander just after the line incident that got him promoted into Team Deuce.

"Was it you sneaking around out there with Rivers?"

"Yes, sir." Jackson decided to watch his mouth and show more than normal respect. The skipper was Maj. F. J. Kruzak, eldest son of Lt. Gen. Bobby J. Kruzak, Commanding General, Fleet Marine Force Pacific. Not that his lineage meant shit out here, except maybe to college-boy wizards like the asshole lieutenant. What Jackson knew about Kruzak was the only thing that counted in the bush: he was a damned fine officer, one who held the respect of every grunt he served with. He was not the sort who risked his men to advance his career. A Marine's Marine, just like Rivers.

"It's Paul, if I remember correctly."

Jackson remembered his military responsibilities when reporting to a commanding officer and pulled himself to attention. "Sergeant Jackson reporting as ordered, sir."

The boot lieutenant and the rest of the gathered officers clearly heard the exchange. Each knew the major wasn't lavish with praise, and the warmth of his greeting to Jackson gave the kid sergeant instant credibility.

Major Kruzak grabbed the Stoner and examined it closely. "What the hell is this, Paul?"

"It's a Stoner 5.56, Skipper," Jackson said, adding the title of respect to his reply. "I picked it up when Captain Rivers transferred me to his unit. It's a hell of a weapon, sir." For the sake of the asshole lieutenant he added, "And it sure as hell isn't the toy it looks like."

Kruzak's eyebrows rose. "What?"

"I said, sir, it isn't a toy. It's one mean son of a bitch. Great hitting power and very lightweight. Its smaller ammo makes it a lot easier to hump, too."

"And what the hell is this?" Major Kruzak grabbed the fancied-up M40 sniper rifle and spun Jackson around to get a better look.

"Just a minute, Skipper, and I'll take it off." He lifted the weapon over his head and handed it to the major. "It's the new vintage M40 sniper rifle, Skipper."

The major spun the big weapon in his hands to examine the action and the scope. "Well, I'll be goddamned. This is one hell of a weapon, Paul. Where do I get mine?"

"Well, sir, the major's welcome to take my place with Captain Rivers. I'd be happy to spend my tour inside this bunker."

Kruzak laughed. "Not on your life, Marine. I wouldn't be caught dead runnin' around the hills with that crazy son of a bitch. It's a wonder he hasn't got your ass shot full of holes by now." He grabbed Jackson by the shoulders and shoved him in the playful manner common among Marines who held each other in high regard. When the major handed the M40 back to Jackson, he did so with something akin to reverence.

"I wanted my officers to hear your briefing," Kruzak said as he returned to the business at hand. He turned to face the small gathering behind him and introduced each officer. Jackson recognized Captain Johansen, his former CO and skipper of Alpha Company. There were two more company commanders and several platoon leaders, including the asshole lieutenant who now looked at Jackson very differently. In addition to the line commanders the battalion staff was also present.

A voice from behind Jackson asked, "How about some coffee, Sergeant?"

Jackson turned and saw the battalion first sergeant, and greeted him warmly. "Sounds good, First Sergeant. Just as long as you didn't make it in your helmet."

The comment brought laughs from the major and Captain Johansen but a scowl from the first shirt. "Some things never change, Skipper," he said to Major Kruzak. "Like wise ass boots who forget their place." The first sergeant's welcome home was over.

Kruzak moved to the far rear corner of the bunker and stood next to the large map. "Okay, we've got the bullshit out of the way. Let's get on with the briefing. If you please, Sergeant?"

"Yes, sir."

The officers sat on or leaned against sandbags. Each made sure he had an unobstructed view of the map and the visiting "cherry."

Major Kruzak kicked off the briefing. "Can you begin by indicating the area you patrolled?"

"Yes, sir." Jackson took the red grease pencil the major pushed in his direction. "Let me orient myself as to how our AO would appear on your maps." The map was mounted behind a large piece of Plexiglas so it could be drawn on with the grease pencil without damaging the paper. Speaking in a loud voice, he started with, "This is the Duc Lo AO. The firebase is located in the center and these are the fire coordinate lines the base supports." He carefully drew red lines around Team Deuce's AO before continuing. "As you were informed, sir, Captain Rivers and I form a special reconnaissance team on Colonel MacDonald's staff. This is the area we operated in. We were inserted at this point and made our first harbor site along the edge of these ridges."

The insertion point piqued the interest of men listening because it was well within their AO and at a spot where they'd been taking extremely high casualties of late.

Jackson marked another spot. "This position gave us a clear view of a major gook trail that moves from left to right across the AO. We observed extremely heavy activity on it at all hours, both day and night."

One of the company commanders asked, "What kind of activity, Sergeant?"

"All kinds, sir. Heavy troop movement—divisional strength, at least. All NVA, with VC guides, heavy trucks, and support equipment."

"Tanks?"

"No, sir. Nor did we find any evidence of any."

"How can you be sure?"

"Because the roadbed was hard-packed dirt. If a tank passed, the surface would've been chewed up. It wasn't."

Major Kruzak interrupted. "Let the sergeant finish. There'll be a Q&A session afterward."

Jackson nodded. "Thank you, sir. As I was saying, we observed heavy foot traffic. In fact, we counted several thousand men in the single day we observed from this point. Heavy trucks, as large as six-bys, frequently interrupted the troop movement. They came in small convoys of four to six vehicles, each commanded by an NVA officer in a smaller vehicle. Each truck carried large boxes of ammunition, mortars, and 122-mm rockets. This we're sure of because we examined similar crates inside a bunker complex on a previous mission. These were the same size and shape, with identical markings. Additionally, we counted over three hundred mortar tubes and two hundred portable rocket launchers."

"We identified elements of the NVA's 1248th, 567th, 4066th, and 488th Divisions heading south from Laos. They traveled in groups of twenty-five to one hundred, with at least one officer and several noncoms in each. Each man carried either an SKS or an AK-47 and a pack showing a minimum of two mortar shells. Every soldier wore a standard NVA uniform and displayed a high degree of confidence. Their morale appeared extremely good. They acted like well-disciplined and veteran soldiers. There were no Chu Hoi candidates anywhere."

Ignoring his own instructions, Major Kruzak interrupted with a question. "How did you know there was high morale and good discipline, Paul?"

"Disciplined troops move differently. The soldiers we watched stayed to the jungle side of the road and kept in the shadows. They continually watched the sky for aircraft and moved in well-dressed formations. The noncoms spent their time providing encouragement. We saw no evidence of disease, malnutrition, or fear. But the biggest reason I say they were disciplined and in a state of good morale is they didn't make any noise—*none at all*. Their equipment didn't rattle and they didn't talk. They watched, listened, and moved silently."

The major nodded, and Jackson continued.

"During the second night, our harbor was nearly discovered by NVA, so we abandoned the location and moved to a new harbor . . . *here*."

"Jesus Christ, man, that's inside Laos."

"Yes, sir."

Another officer asked, "Did you know where you were?"

"Yes, sir. Every minute."

Jackson spoke directly to Kruzak in support of the decision to move into Laos. "Captain Rivers and I were alone and cut off by a vastly superior enemy. We were aware we violated a major command order, but the captain exercised what he felt to be in our best interests at the time."

The belligerent officer persisted. "Violating a 3rd MAF directive is in your best interest?"

Jackson shot his answer across the room. "Begging your pardon, sir. You weren't there." There was no mistaking the rebuke in Jackson's statement.

The young officer started to remind him of his place, but Major Kruzak cut him off. "Does Colonel MacDonald know about this?"

Jackson nodded. "Yes, sir. The captain told him and Division."

Everyone present knew that a commander in the field has every right to exercise his judgment in the best interest of the mission and the safety of his men. Captain Rivers had done nothing more; however, the political ramifications would be severe if the team's movement into Laos became public knowledge.

Major Kruzak looked at his officers. "Let's suffice it to say, gentlemen, that *we* were not there, and Captain Rivers, an officer with an exceptional combat record, simply exercised command judgment. You will not speak of this outside these walls. Am I clear?"

The agreement was unanimous, but the lieutenant who had suffered Jackson's rebuke continued his hostile glare.

Jackson didn't think it made any difference *where* they were. Their job was to recon the AO. The only reason they went into Laos was to save their butts. He felt the war was some kind of screwed up when people could ruin someone as good as Rivers over something as stupid as an imaginary line on a map.

The briefing went on for another hour, during which Jackson related everything Team Deuce saw. He left nothing out and did not color any of the details. His delivery was straightforward—a simple matter of relating facts.

Captain Johansen asked, "Are you sure of the numbers of NVA you counted, Sergeant? I'm not questioning the assessment; I just want verification. Those numbers are far greater than what my LRRPs are telling me."

"Well, sir, I'm sure your LRRPs are telling you exactly what they've seen, and that is precisely the reason the captain and I were put together and sent out to observe."

"I don't understand."

"You send out a ten-man patrol, correct, sir?"

"Yes."

"Well, sir, Colonel MacDonald believes ten is too many. They make too much noise and Charlie simply hides. If a team does get lucky and sees something important, he kills them."

The nods all around the room verified the truth in that, but the officers still wanted to eliminate any possibility that Jackson was exaggerating. Jackson responded confidently to repeated questions about the size of the NVA forces and repeated the original estimates he and Rivers worked out in their debrief with Colonel MacDonald.

When the questions started to peter out, Major Kruzak faced his officers. "That's it, gentlemen. I suggest we treat this information very seriously. I've known Colonel MacDonald for a long time, and he wouldn't have sent Jackson out here if he didn't think the information was critical. I expect you to evaluate necessity before sending out patrols. With the woods this full of gooks, let's keep our heads pulled in for a few days. We are now on 50 percent alert. Dismissed."

With the major's pep talk ringing in their heads, the officers moved toward the bunker's opening. They grouped themselves at the entrance so they could move through the blackout curtain without letting too much light outside. The sun had set during the briefing, and it was now completely dark on the other side of the heavy black canvas.

"Incoming!"

The bunker's interior exploded in a violent white light.

SEVENTEEN

Duc Lo Firebase

1730, January 27, 1968

THE NVA GOT LUCKY. Their first rocket was a direct hit on the entrance to the command bunker. With a single shot they effectively destroyed the Duc Lo command structure.

The explosion knocked Jackson off his feet, but his position in the very rear of the bunker saved his life. As soon as the air rushed back into his lungs, he pulled himself up to a crouch and surveyed the immediate area. The bunker was gone. The wall of sandbags that had formed the door had been replaced by a ten-foot hole. A lieutenant screamed in agony as he pulled himself out from under an overturned desk, clutching his groin. "Corpsman. Help! Oh, Christ. Help me, I'm hit." Jackson winced when he looked closer and saw the man holding his intestines in his hands, feverishly trying to stuff them back inside his abdomen.

Bursts of M60 machine-gun fire intermixed with the constant *krumpf* of exploding mortars and the higher whine of 122-mm rockets. Hundreds of them screamed overhead before striking the lower slopes of the camp. Jackson heard the high-pitched bang of American M14s interlaced with the heavier cracks of AK-47s. The horrendous noise that is the hallmark of modern combat filled the air within a single heartbeat. It was as if a switch was flipped and the whole world turned to instant shit.

He screamed so his voice would carry over the noise of the attack. "Is anybody in here?"

A weak voice responded, "Over here. The rocket hit the bunker doorway."

"No shit, Sherlock. Are you hurt?" When no answer came, he pushed past a couple of overturned desks to the spot where most of the wall had blown away—four feet of sandbags and railroad ties gone in a split second. He pushed aside a six-foot piece of crushed Marshall matting, and it fell at his feet. He saw part of a body lying on top of a field desk. The man had been ripped in half just below the ribcage, and the legs and lower torso twitched their way into silence. The upper half was just gone.

Major Kruzak crawled from under a desk and stood up. "Over here. I'm hit."

Jackson examined the wound. Blood was flowing out of a hole in the major's leg. Jackson applied a tourniquet and breathed a sigh of relief when he saw the blood wasn't pulsing in time with the major's heartbeat. He grabbed Kruzak's first-aid kit, ripped open the sterile bandage, and pressed it tightly against the wound. "You got a hole in your leg about the size of a truck, Skipper, but no artery was hit. It's bad, but I think you'll make it. Lie down, sir, and hold this." Jackson tightened the tourniquet. "Blood flow is slowing down, Skipper." He took a second bandage from his unit 1 bag and placed it against the damaged leg. Kruzak screamed as he pressed the dressing into the wound. When he was convinced the major wouldn't bleed to death, Jackson left him and searched the remains of the bunker for anyone else requiring help.

When he returned, Kruzak asked, "Who's left?"

"No one, sir. Just you and me."

Turning over a field desk, Jackson saw the body of Captain Johansen. Shrapnel had cut off the top of his head, and his brain lay exposed to rapidly swarming flies. Jackson almost gagged as the sweet smell of fresh blood reached his nose. "Stay here, I'm going to have a look-see outside."

He stood up and took a long look below their position and around the perimeter. Mortars and rockets exploded across the entire compound, and the Marines were pouring a hell storm of return fire into the enemy. "Looks like our guys are givin' 'em hell, Skipper," he yelled back to the major. "I can see red tracers from the perimeter hitting out hard." What he didn't say was that there was a hell of a lot more NVA green tracers than American reds.

Looking farther out toward the perimeter Jackson gasped. The wall of concertina wire was covered with thousands of NVA. Someone had fired the foo gas, and the NVA were using the acrid black smoke and dead bodies as cover against the devastating fire being poured into their ranks.

An object whistled past Jackson's ear and slammed into the bunker behind him. A second later something bounced off the four-foot wall he was standing behind and a ripping explosion blew him backward into the bunker. He screamed and felt sticky warmth creeping down the sides of his face from his ears.

Major Kruzak yelled, "We've gotta get the hell out of this bunker or we're not gonna make it. Follow me." The major started around the wall of sandbags, but his injured leg wouldn't support his weight and he collapsed.

Shaking his head to clear the dizziness caused by the second explosion, Jackson struggled to his feet and grabbed the major underneath his arms.

Kruzak shook his head. "Don't worry about me. There's a cave up and to the left. The opening's very small and shielded by a solid rock wall. I can make it that far. Get an M60 up there ASAP. There's more ammo than we need inside, but no guns. I'll meet you there."

Jackson crawled into a solid wall of noise and a scene of near complete devastation. "Where the hell am I going to find an M60?" he yelled, trying to keep his mind off the destruction around him. NVA mortars and rockets were still lacing the camp. There were more than a hundred craters between Jackson's position and the perimeter. The bunkers were gone, and bodies lay everywhere. He saw not a living soul. Jackson's mind raced as he searched for an M60. *There's one. Looks okay. Where's the fuckin' ammo? That's right, Kruzak said we wouldn't need any.* Moving into one of the secondary gun positions, he pushed a body off the M60 and hoisted the gun. He pushed aside two more bodies and moved back up the hill toward the cave.

As he approached the entrance, he yelled, "Friendlies coming through," and dove onto the stone floor. He hit hard. The M60 landed against his back and punched the air from his lungs. After he got his shit together, he stood and examined the cave's interior. "Shit. This is the friggin' ammo bunker." The cave was about thirty feet long with a ceiling fifteen feet above the floor. Thousands of grenades and a few mortars were stacked inside, along with more ammo than Jackson could count.

An order came from the cave's entrance. "Get over here and set up the gun."

Even though the speech was thready, Jackson recognized Kruzak's voice. The major's wound was bleeding again, so he retightened the tourniquet. "You got to stay off your leg, sir."

"Yeah? Let me worry about it. Right now I have to get back to my men and organize a counterattack."

"You're not going anywhere."

"Fuck you, Sergeant. Who the fuck are you to tell me what I'm going to do?"

Jackson pushed Kruzak onto a box of mortar shells. "Look, Major. We'll worry about who the fuck's in charge tomorrow. Right now these are the facts. Your command is gone. Charlie took most of it out with mortar and rocket fire. The few survivors are making a last-ditch effort to keep the gooks from overrunning the base. It's over a hundred meters from here to the line. If you could run, you might make it, but in your condition a gook sniper would blow your head off before you got ten meters. Even if you did get to your men, they'd shoot you before they realized who you are. There's nothing out there except Charlie. So stay put and shove your rank up your ass. I put the M60 next to the wall. Get behind it while I go get us a radio."

The dumbfounded major nodded and crawled behind the M60.

Jackson positioned him where he could shoot straight down the hill. "Don't fire unless Charlie comes in this direction. I'll be right back." He slipped out of the cave and disappeared toward the command bunker.

When he reappeared, he called out before entering. "Major. Major Kruzak." When no answer came, he set the radio next to the mouth of the cave and pulled out the .357 he carried in his shoulder holster. Holding only the pistol he rolled into the cave. There was no one inside except Kruzak, unconscious behind the machine gun. His leg was bleeding again, and he looked pale from loss of blood.

Jackson slapped the major's face hard. "Wake up, Skipper."

The major opened glazed-over eyes but didn't protest the slap. In a very low voice, he mumbled something Jackson couldn't hear. The voice was too weak to overcome the noise from outside. The lack of response, weak voice, and thousand-yard stare in Kruzak's eyes were sure indicators of shock.

Scared of losing the major, Jackson yelled, "Listen, goddamn it. You're going to die if you don't wake up. Gotta stop the bleeding. Where the fuck's the blood expander?" He reached for his unit 1 bag and found what he needed. "This is going to hurt you more'n me," Jackson laughed as he jabbed a needle into Kruzak's arm. He hooked the bag of serum albumin above the major's head. "If Captain Rivers is right, this shit will keep you from dying on me."

Jackson moved the major away from the M60 and took his place, then yanked the PRC 77 over to his side and keyed the mike. "Shit, what are the fucking day codes?"

Jackson's scream bounced off the rock walls. He rifled through the major's jacket and found the shackle sheets in the left breast pocket. After locating the call sign for the day, he keyed the mike again. "Alpha One, Alpha One, this is Romeo Two Niner, over."

Jackson waited ten seconds then repeated his transmission. "Alpha One, Alpha One, this is Romeo Two Niner, over."

"Romeo Two Niner, this is Alpha One."

"Alpha One, I have a sitrep. Have received extremely heavy mortar and rocket attack, followed by regimental-sized ground assault. All command personnel are dead, or . . ." looking at the major he evaluated the remainder of the sentence, "unable to function. We have large enemy force inside compound. All forward positions have been overrun. Advise, over." Jackson released the transmission key so he could hear the incoming response.

"Romeo Two Niner, this is Alpha One Actual. All command personnel are dead. Is that your transmission, over?" The voice was Colonel MacDonald's in Phu Bai.

"That's right, Actual," Jackson said into the handset. "Everyone except Major Kruzak. He's badly wounded and out of action. We're in the ammo cave behind the command bunker."

"Who is 'we,' Romeo Two Niner?"

"Major Kruzak and me, Deuce Two," he spilled into the radio. "All other officers are dead. We're in a well-shielded position with light weapons. We need artillery support and an air strike, and we need it now."

"Give me the coordinates, son. Just relax and give me the exact location of the enemy."

"The gooks are everywhere around the base of the camp up to the secondary defense perimeter. They were inside the wire the last time I looked. I don't hear any firing from our side. I don't have a map and can't give you any better location than the perimeter. Put it on the camp. Charlie has it, we don't." Abandoning all proper technique, he simply let go of the transmission key and waited for the response.

Colonel MacDonald's voice was overridden by the fire coordination center at Khe Sanh. "Romeo Two Niner, we can't use those coordinates. What about the Marines still out there?"

Jackson's voice came out cold and strong. "Listen. There ain't nothing out there except gooks. If there's anybody who isn't dead yet, Charlie's killing them as we speak. Get the lead out and put your arty where I told you." He focused all of his command presence into his voice, and the words came across with calm, measured finality. He knew what he was doing.

"Roger, Romeo Two Niner. Shot out."

Jackson screamed into the mike. "*Fire for effect, goddamn it. We can't spot a round. Just fire your maximum effort!*" He raised the radio volume to maximum so he could hear the radio when the incoming started to explode around his position. Then he dropped the handset, placed the albumin bag against the major's chest, grabbed him under the arms, and dragged him away from the cave entrance.

Returning to the mouth of the cave, Jackson picked up his sniper rifle and sighted toward the wire. As he panned the scope back and forth across the perimeter, he saw nothing but carnage. Dead Marines lay everywhere as Charlie carefully moved through the bunker complex searching for wounded. To stay in control of his emotions the young sergeant talked to himself as he waited. "Okay," he screamed as he watched a survivor dispatched by a bullet through the head. "You bastards don't even care if it's a wounded comrade or a Marine; you're killin' everybody."

Looking down the hill, Jackson saw a group of ten Marines with their hands above their heads standing in a circle. Several NVA ran up and opened fire. Charlie wasn't taking prisoners.

Elsewhere, NVA moved among the bodies removing boots, shirts, and weapons. It was a thorough search that left the dead Marines without dignity. Jackson's stomach roiled. When an NVA officer came into view, Jackson laid the crosshairs of the big scope just under his forehead. "You just wait, you son of a bitch." Within a few seconds he heard the sound of incoming artillery rounds. Before the first one hit, Jackson closed the slack off his weapon and a NATO round tore through the NVA officer's forehead.

Jackson looked for another officer. "Where are you assholes? There you are. Take that, you rice-burnin' son of a bitch." After the second shot, the NVA started looking up the hill. He dropped two more officers before the first American salvo struck the compound.

Laying the M40 aside, Jackson grabbed the M60 and ran a belt of ammunition across the positions below him. "Get some," he yelled as the gooks started clutching their bodies. When one of the incoming shells hit near his line of sight, he fired through the dust until he saw body parts fly into the air.

Picking up the radio handset, Jackson screamed into the microphone. "Keep it coming. Drop fifty and move left and right around the base of the hill. I need you to take out as many gooks inside the wire as possible." While he was waiting, he grabbed several claymores and laid them in a semicircle around the cave opening. He pulled their wires back, laced them together, and thrust them inside a single hell-box. He yelled to the major, "This will be our last stand. If they get this far, I'll fire all of them at once. We'll take a lot of gooks with us when we go, Skipper."

The radio squawked, "Romeo Two Niner, this is Navy Delta Flight, over."

"Roger, Delta Flight. Where are you?" The sound of exploding shells was deafening, and Jackson screamed into the handset to be heard.

"Staying out of range of the artillery, approximately six zero seconds west of your position. We're six F4s with napalm and frag. Where would you like it? Over."

"Put it on the eastern slopes of the camp. The gooks appear to be massing for a second assault from there."

"Roger, Romeo Two Niner. It'll only take a second."

Jackson laughed at the cocky response, which calmed nerves that were at the breaking point. Sixty seconds after the artillery stopped he heard the first jet pass overhead. He knew if they were dropping napalm he'd better get as far back in the cave as possible. He rolled Kruzak onto his stomach and lay down on top of him. Rivers' lessons raced through his memory, "If you lay it in close, get your face in the dirt so the napalm doesn't suck the air out of your lungs when it consumes the oxygen it needs."

A high-pitched whoosh and several very large explosions followed the sound of the jets passing overhead. Jackson felt the pressure drop as the blast sucked out the air inside the cave. With another whoosh it flowed back inside. Nature abhors a vacuum.

"Good, you're still alive," Jackson said to reassure himself. "Don't run away, Skipper. I'm gonna get some." He returned to his position by the cave's mouth and loaded his M40. He panned the scope across the area in front of the cave. "Fuck! There's nothing down there." The eastern side of the camp resembled the surface of the moon. Burnt-out craters were all that remained of the compound. No longer did he hear the *pop, pop, pop* of small-arms fire; nor was there any dust in the air. Burning flesh smoldered like small candles. *Shit, there's nothin' left.* The sickening smell of burning flesh cast an unholy pall over the camp and worked its way into every pore of Jackson's body.

A panicked Vietnamese voice called for help, "Giúp tôi."

"Kong biệt. Biệt Thự Kong." The order to advance came from the base of the hill. The officer giving the order was still some distance away, but as Jackson moved his scope toward the tree line to the east, he saw a shadow standing next to a big rubber tree stump. "Okay, shitbird," Jackson screamed, "you just stand right there." *Careful, he's a long ways away. Squeeze out the slack. Ease back until the big bastard surprises you.* He released the air from his lungs until the weapon discharged in an incredibly loud bang. The noise echoed off the walls of the cave and roared through Jackson's ears, which started to bleed again.

AK-47s fired in response but fell well short of their mark. Jackson's position was more than five hundred meters from the closest living NVA soldier.

Jackson yelled down the hill. "I'm too far away, assholes. I'm way up here and you fuckers ain't." He heard the sounds of the departing Navy jets overhead as they turned and headed back to their ship. In a panic, Jackson yelled down at the enemy. "Just stay in the trees, goddamn it. What I don't need is a fresh ground attack."

The *klink* of a mortar round leaving its tube echoed through the night. Jackson heard the soft *klink* of another round leaving the tube just seconds before the first round impacted thirty yards to his front. The next round hit the ground twenty yards to the left of the first and was followed by six more walking the face of the inner perimeter.

They don't know where I am! They think I'm at the edge of their range. That gives me a hell of an advantage. Convinced the area where he saw the last shadow contained the enemy command unit, Jackson kept his scope trained there. A few seconds after the last mortar round exploded he was rewarded with a new shadow. As he watched through the scope, he saw his second round strike the silhouette and throw it over a fallen tree trunk. It was immediately replaced by another, and then another . . . and another.

Carefully sliding down inside the cave's entrance, Jackson picked up the radio's handset. "This is Romeo Two Niner. Who do I have on here?"

"Romeo Two Niner, this is Able Fox Actual."

"Roger, Actual. I have a fire mission. Drop five hundred from last coordinate and move your shells left and right at the foot of the slope."

"Can we send a spotter round in first to confirm the coordinates, Romeo Two Niner?"

"Negative. A spotter round will give them a chance to depart impact area, over." Jackson's voice was firm, flat, and unemotional. "Suspect command force at last location. Fire for effect." He dropped the mike, returned to the cave mouth, and picked up the sniper rifle, then trained the scope on the area where he hoped the big shells would fall. Within seconds he was rewarded with the sound of more shells whistling their way into the edge of the jungle. He dropped the scope to avoid being blinded by the flash as he heard the impact of the second wave of American rounds rip into the ground beneath the hill.

The radio squawked. "Romeo Two Niner, Romeo Two Niner, this is Able Fox Actual. Are you still there?"

"Yeah, we're still here, but they ain't. Nice shootin', sir," Jackson said softly. Feeling immensely tired, he barely heard the voice tell him to stay under cover until the relief force was on the ground.

EIGHTEEN

Duc Lo Firebase

0300, January 28, 1968

THE RELIEF FORCE arrived several hours later. Helicopters from Camp Eagle, Quang Tri, Marble Mountain, and Phu Bai brought two companies of the 1st Battalion, 9th Marine Regiment out of Camp Carroll. They moved into the camp unopposed. Charlie was gone, back inside the protection of the surrounding jungle.

The newcomers searched frantically for survivors. They found none. A Navy corpsman, horrified by the state of the camp, talked aimlessly to himself as he went from body to body. "The camp's FUBAR. The bunkers are gone. Nothing but overlapping craters filled with dead. The fight must have been brutal."

An officer yelled at Marines attempting to straighten some of the clutter. "Don't touch a thing. Just push everything out of the way and establish your new perimeter. We need to be ready if they come back."

When Jackson saw Americans moving into the bunkers and taking up position, he tried to move the unconscious Major Kruzak toward the mouth of the cave, but he was too weak. Instead, he yelled for help. "Corpsman. Corpsman, up here." Jackson's voice echoed across the eerie silence of the inner perimeter and focused the relief force's attention on the cave.

A voice choked with emotion called in the dark. "I can't find anyone alive up here."

A big sergeant with a Georgia accent yelled back, "Keep looking, goddamn it. I heard somebody."

"Hey, Sarge, we searched over there. Are you sure you heard something?"

"You goddamn right I did. And it was an American voice coming from the top of the hill. Skipper says only one fire team is to investigate. He wants everyone else in their holes. He's not taking any chances. Doesn't want any of us ending up like these poor bastards."

A PFC on his first trip to the bush asked, "What if it was Charlie pretending to be one of us?"

"Well, if it's a gook, he's about to get a reception he'll never forget."

The fire team circled around to approach the cave from behind. The team leader, a twenty-one-year-old from Topeka, Kansas, named Wickerman, held a grenade in his hand and prepared to pitch it inside the cave. "Identify yourself, goddamn it, or we're going to frag the shit outta your hole."

"Jackson, Paul A., sergeant, U.S. fucking Marine Corps, with Major F. J. Kruzak, commanding officer, 1st Battalion, 26th Marines. Now get your ass down here with a pecker-checker before the fucking major bleeds to death."

The sergeant called to his fire teams, "He's gotta be American. Ain't no gook alive can swear like that." He told his automatic rifleman to cover the mouth of the cave and slowly edged his way along the inside wall until his eyes became accustomed to the darkness. When he saw Jackson trying to lift Major Kruzak, he called for help. "Get Doc Peterson down here ASAP." Then he moved to a position next to Jackson and put down his weapon. "You okay?"

"Never better."

"Here, let me do that." The squad leader took the major, laid him on the floor, and pushed Jackson to a sitting position next to a crate labeled "Hand Grenade—Fragmentation."

Wickerman examined Jackson, amazed the sergeant was still breathing, and yelled through the opening of the cave. "Corpsman! Get a fucking corpsman down here *now*."

A voice responded, "On the way."

When rough hands grabbed Jackson's shirt and slapped his face, he started to focus. "The major! See to the major." His voice was like sandpaper.

The large corpsman continued his examination. "All ready being done, bro." The big hands unbuttoned the front of Jackson's shirt to search for the source of the blood covering the sergeant's uniform. "Where you hit, bro?"

Jackson voice came in short rasps. "Ain't hit."

"Like hell you ain't. Nobody bleed like that ain't hit sumplace." The corpsman's hands carefully patted Jackson down until he came to the ribcage. When he placed his hands against Jackson's left side, the sergeant winced. "Got you some broke ribs. Big cut on yo' head too, but nuthin' else I can see. Yo' hands be pretty badly burned, and it looks like you got a ruptured eardrum. Nuthin' gonna get you a ride home, though. I still cain't figure how you got all that blood on your bad self, bro."

The corpsman's slow, southern drawl made him sound like a L'il Abner character. It brought a vision of Dogpatch, USA, and Jackson tried to laugh. It hurt like hell. Jackson looked toward the rear of the cave. "I'm all right. How about the major?"

"Don't know. He be real bad. Got a dust-off comin' fo' him now."

Jackson saw several men bent over the major. He was on a canvas stretcher, and a red tube ran between his arm and another Marine. They were giving Kruzak a transfusion.

Seeing Jackson's expression, the corpsman said, "He lost lotsa blood, but he be watched by a fo' real doctor."

"Yeah, I can see the caduceus and bars." Jackson crawled over and patted the major's shoulder.

The doctor's eyes filled with tears when he saw Jackson's deep concern. "He'll be fine, Sergeant. He's tough."

Two corpsmen picked up the stretcher and moved toward a newly arrived chopper. As soon as Kruzak was loaded, it lifted off and began a speed run to the waiting USS *Sanctuary*.

After Kruzak left, the cave started to fill up with the curious. A tall, very erect man with a weatherbeaten face and a silver eagle pinned to the facing of his cover pushed his way through the crowd and knelt next to Jackson. "You must be Romeo Two Niner?"

Jackson looked at the colonel and nodded.

The big corpsman, satisfied that Jackson's only problems were the cut on his forehead and two broken ribs, set about repairing the damage. Jackson winced as the rough hands pinched the two sides of his forehead together and applied several small bandages. An Ace bandage wrapped the broken ribs.

The colonel watched the corpsman work. "I'm McManus, 9th Marines. Glad to meet you, Sergeant."

"Yeah, me too, sir. It's a real pleasure."

McManus ignored Jackson's sarcasm and turned to the big corpsman. "Is he going to be all right, Doc?"

"Yes, suh. He'll be just fine in a few days. Nuthin' wrong with him some clean sheets and a bath won' cure."

"Can he stay here or do we have to medevac him tonight?"

The corpsman looked down at Jackson and then up at the colonel. "No need for medevac, suh. Just those ribs that needs attention.

Jackson was dumbfounded. *My luck has run out. This chickenshit son of a bitch is going to keep me here. He's pissed because I didn't follow the book when I called in the fire missions. I am fucked.*

The colonel turned to Jackson. "I'd like to keep you for a few hours so I can understand what happened, but I won't force the issue. If you want to get on a medevac, you got it, but before you decide, will you take a short walk with me?"

The colonel sounded sincerely concerned, but Jackson didn't care. *I'm gettin' on the next dust-off that sets its ass in the grass, and there's nothing this chickenshit zero can tell me that'll change my mind.* Jackson started to stand up, but he was too weak. He stumbled and the big corpsman caught him before he fell. He shook his head to clear the cobwebs, and pain scorched through his body. The tightly bound ribs made his chest ache, and his head still pounded from the blast of the concussion. He needed help to stand. "Can someone hand me my rifles?"

"Sure, Sarge," the big corpsman said. "Which are yours?"

"The black one," Jackson said, "and the big one with the scope."

Two Marines picked up the weapons, but when they handed them to Jackson, he couldn't raise his arms high enough to put them over his shoulder. The tape on his ribs kept him from rolling his arm under the sling as he normally would have, and he almost dropped the Stoner.

The colonel's voice was tight with emotion. "Give him a hand."

The two Marines silently grabbed Jackson's weapons and hung them over his shoulder and down his back. The colonel helped him walk the few steps out of the cave. Together, the two moved through the devastated camp toward the ruins of the command bunker, passing groups of men who were picking up the dead and gently placing them in a single line at the rear of the secondary perimeter. Others placed the bodies inside zippered black plastic bags. Everyone who touched a body did so with reverence. The dead NVA didn't receive the same treatment. Marines carried them to a large crater and tossed them inside.

As the two men stood next to the command bunker, a young captain approached and addressed the colonel. His face was ashen and he was out of breath. "Skipper, we found a group of ten . . . dead . . . at the foot of the hill, sir."

"Yes?"

"There are no weapons near them, and they're lying in a circle. The location isn't like the other sites, Skipper. It looks like they were executed." The captain's voice cracked.

"They shot them when they tried to surrender, sir," Jackson said. "After they put their hands in the air. I saw it. Charlie never intended to take prisoners."

The colonel's face paled. "It's too bad some of those hippie bastards back home weren't here to see this."

The captain threw up.

The colonel turned Jackson toward the line to give the captain some space. "Sergeant."

"Yes, sir."

Colonel McManus stared into the ground. "I suppose you think I'm an asshole for not putting you on a bird back to Phu Bai."

Jackson's silence spoke volumes.

"I asked you to stay because my men need to know someone made it off this hill alive. I need you to walk through the perimeter with me and give them a reason to be here. Will you do that?" The colonel was biting back tears, overwhelmed by the captain's description of the executed men. *To lose men in battle is one thing, but to have them shot down like vermin is something else all together. Twenty years in the Corps hasn't trained me for dealing with the brutality I've found in 'Nam.*

Jackson's response was barely audible. "Yes, sir." Tears ran down his face, and the colonel tightened his grip on the younger man's shoulders. Both men understood what had happened here, but it would be take years before either one would be able to live with the memories. They slowly walked through the camp. Here and there the colonel spoke to his Marines. As the two walked, Jackson related what he saw during the attack. He left nothing out; nor did he embellish. He identified NVA regiments he remembered from their uniform markings and told McManus of the command group he spotted in the tree line. The colonel sent some men to investigate.

When they reached the command bunker, McManus said, "Get some sleep, Sergeant. I'll get you on the morning bird."

Excerpt from after-action report filed by Colonel McManus, CO, 9th Marine Regiment, January 20, 1968:

The attack on Duc Lo was a well-planned operation led by General V. N. Ng, commanding the 11th NVA Division. It involved five reinforced regiments and lasted for forty-three minutes. Casualties were horrendous on both sides. We lost 361 enlisted, 21 officers, and 6 corpsmen.

Of Alpha Company's assigned strength, only its commanding officer remains alive. North Vietnamese losses are estimated at 1,500 dead, of which 1,380 bodies have been recovered, including 42 officers. Of those 42, 11 died at the edge of the tree line, outside the perimeter. Each officer died from a single projectile through the head; no other wounds were uncovered.

Sgt. Paul A. Jackson, Headquarters Company, 26th Marines, was the only other survivor. His actions, all undertaken at grave risk to his life, reflect great credit upon the United States Marine Corps and the Naval Service. He is recommended for the highest commendation this country offers.

NINETEEN

85th Medevac Hospital, Da Nang

1745, January 31, 1968

JACKSON WOKE UP between clean sheets. He felt hung over, but his head had never hurt this bad from drinking. When he tried to focus, the room spun. He quickly shut his eyes to regain his center. He remembered arriving by medevac, but not what happened after he was treated in Emergency. His hands hurt. That would be from the burns he got changing barrels on the M60. He guessed that was what the layers of gauze covered. He wondered how bad the cut on his forehead was. It didn't feel serious when he walked in, but the corpsman seemed concerned.

"Infection," the corpsman said, "spreads fast in this miserable heat and humidity."

Jackson knew the gash wasn't infected. Rivers had taught him what that felt like, and he didn't have any of the symptoms. Besides, the big corpsman at Duc Lo shot him up with enough antibiotics to cure the clap. The pecker-checkers here said they were concerned because his wounds were open to the air for several hours.

Jackson let his mind wander, the throbbing in his hands his only connection with time. It provided a pulse, but that could have occurred every second or once a day; he didn't care. He wanted to emerge from his stupor but didn't feel like he could break through. He knew he was in a hospital, so it really didn't matter how quickly he got his shit together. Tomorrow, or even next week would be fine.

Far from the sergeant's bed, in the ancient city of Hue, the full might of the 26th Marines gathered on the southern shore of the Perfume River preparing to reenter the city using the only bridge left standing.

His throbbing hands paced him through the day. He slept, woke, and alternated safely between the two. He didn't hurt very much, just couldn't find the strength to fully wake up. The throbbing in his hands and the drumbeat of his heart pulled him from his stupor. When he tried to sit up, pain shot behind his eyes. And something else. *A leech? They have leeches in the friggin' hospital? It's sucking the blood from my arm.*

He knew he had to move slowly or his head would split open. He rotated just enough to see what was hanging on his arm. *There's a friggin' needle in my vein. Someone's taking my blood.* Through a vise of pain his eyes followed the tube attached to his arm; it traveled over the edge of the bed, then down toward the floor. And then back up to a person. The man was sitting in a chair reading *Playboy* magazine.

He looked up. "You with us, Sarge?"

Jackson managed to raise his head. His voice came out raspy and broken. "Blood. You're taking my blood. What for?"

"Your doctor said it'd be okay to take a pint. I'm almost through." The corpsman rose and checked the needle in Jackson's arm. "It doesn't hurt, does it? I stuck you real careful. Didn't want to wake you up. You're kind of a celebrity here."

"A what?"

"Visitor after visitor, man—couple of captains, a colonel, and a general's aide. We were told to call them all when you woke up. I guess I'll have to do that now."

Jackson rested his head back on the pillow. Sitting up made him nauseous. He asked the corpsman why.

"When you came in, they shot you up with enough Demerol to fell an ox. It'll wear off in a bit."

"Why do you need blood?"

"For all the casualties. You're O negative, the universal donor, so we helped ourselves."

"What casualties?"

"NVA have been hitting bases all over the country. Our embassy in Saigon was attacked. Blew a big hole in the wall and killed some Marines. Things have been hot everywhere. There was a ground attack on the airbase, another at Freedom Hill, and they even tried to get in here. Charlie violated the cease-fire and has spent the night killing anybody and everybody. We've had more than three hundred casualties since noon. The brass are shittin' in their hats. Don't know what to make of it, but it's a big push."

Jackson shifted his weight to ease the ache in his head. *This can't be real . . . none of it. Not the casualties, not even this hospital.* The movement made his stomach lurch, and he fought back the urge to vomit. When he focused on the corpsman the room stopped spinning. He concentrated on calming his voice and spoke carefully. "What time is it, Doc?"

"About 1800."

"You mean I've been in here for over eight hours?"

"More like a full day plus eight hours, Sarge."

"What? What day is it?"

"Friday. You came in yesterday morning." The corpsman moved closer, his face showing concern. "You arrived on the dust-off. Your ribs were treated in the ER, and they kept you here because you had a slight concussion. Since then, we've been pumping antibiotics into you and tendin' your head wound. You feeling okay, Sarge? I can call a doctor and have him take a look."

"No. I'm all right. Where are the casualties coming from?"

The corpsman shook his head. "Up north. Place called Khe Sanh. They say it's surrounded by thousands of gooks. Can you believe it?"

"Yeah," Jackson said quietly, "I can believe it." *Christ! Khe Sanh is where those two boots I talked to in the NCO club went.*

The corpsman finally removed the needle from Jackson's arm and held up the bag containing his blood. "Keep your elbow bent for a few minutes. Get some rest. Those drugs will be wearin' off soon and your hands will start to ache. If you need anything, press this button."

Jackson watched through foggy eyes as the pecker-checker carried the bottle through the door. After it closed with a soft clang, Jackson became aware of others in the room. He was in a ward filled with occupied beds. Each occupant appeared to be in a different stage of recovery. Some sat on the edge of their beds; others were unconscious and sheathed in white gauze. In the bed across from his, sheets formed a sort of tent. A single foot extended from beneath it.

He lay back and slept until he felt someone pushing against his leg. The small movement wasn't uncomfortable, but it made his head ache, and that pissed him off. He opened his eyes to tell whoever it was to fuck off and saw Captain Rivers standing next to the bed. "Skipper, what're you doin' here?"

"Trying to wake you up, asshole. If you ride the gravy train any longer you'll miss all the fun."

"What *fun?*"

"Luke the Gook has been turning life into nothin' but."

"I don't understand. How is Charlie *fun?*"

Rivers pondered for a moment. "Well, maybe fun's not the right word. He's finally come out of the bush, and we're having our first opportunity to kick some real ass."

"Yeah, well, he did some serious ass kickin' at Duc Lo."

"So I've heard. Lotsa people upset about that. Gooks shooting unarmed men trying to surrender has pissed off the entire division, and everybody wants some payback. I guess they believe our numbers now, by God."

Jackson didn't react. "Yeah, I guess so." He felt uneasy hearing about how men dying in large numbers were verifying the estimates they brought back from their last mission.

"We have to talk," Rivers said.

The sarcasm dripped off Jackson tongue. "About what, our next adventure?" He didn't feel like reliving Duc Lo, and he damned sure didn't want to talk about what was going to happen tomorrow.

"Get a hold of yourself, Paul. You aren't hurt so bad I won't kick your ass." There was steel in Rivers' voice but laughter in his eyes.

"Sorry. I'm just not into talking right now. I'd rather lie here and not hear a word about what Charlie's doing. I've seen enough."

The captain nodded. "Probably. I'm sure as hell glad I wasn't up there with you. But that's not what I meant."

"Well, shit. That's all we talk about, isn't it? Where we've been, what we've seen, and where we're goin' next."

"Yeah, you're right. Our conversations have been pretty limited. But that stops now. We have plans to make."

"Yeah, what kind?"

"Well, it seems there are plenty of folks around here who are interested in the information we developed. Suddenly there's a lot of interest in creating specialists in small unit recon tactics. But let that rest a minute. First, we need to talk about what happened at Duc Lo."

Jackson told the story briefly, honestly, and modestly.

Rivers shook his head. "You are one lucky son of a bitch. No one was supposed to walk away from that."

"The cave was the reason we made it. The gooks had to come straight up the hill, and it gave us an advantage."

"It gave you a hell of an advantage."

"And Kruzak was there too."

"Yeah. Hurt so bad it's fifty-fifty whether or not they'll cut off his leg. I've talked to him. He told me he was unconscious most of the time, and even when he wasn't you took charge. Don't be modest; it doesn't fit."

Jackson shifted on the bed. "You know, Skipper, listenin' to you tell me how my body should be ripening in the hot sun instead of being in the hospital is just about too much. Maybe I *do* feel guilty about making it through the attack. Should I? I don't know. Before they flew me out of Duc Lo I talked to a bird colonel named McManus, and he told me about how men deal with watching others die and the fear of their own death. He said, 'Some see themselves as cowards, not brave enough to face the death others found. Others just feel isolated and alone for long periods of time afterward.' But you've made me realize just how I do feel. I feel just plain lucky."

Rivers broke into a wide grin and belted Jackson on the arm hard enough to make him wince. "Better to be lucky than smart, I always say." Then he laughed.

Jackson settled back onto his pillow. "I don't see anything that goddamn funny."

Rivers laughed harder. "I was just thinking you must've shocked the shit out of those gooks when you let go with the M40. Must've driven 'em crazy when they couldn't get to you."

Jackson tried to remain morose but ended up breaking into a wide grin. "Yeah. They were pissed when they couldn't find me. They kept tearing up the perimeter, thinking I was down there and not another five hundred meters up the hill. While they were trying to gauge my range, I dropped a few of their officers."

"Eleven, if the body count is correct," Rivers interjected.

"Whatever. I didn't count. I just remember how stupid they were, stepping in to assume their leader's position again and again. And then there were some who charged up the hill. The one who got the closest was no more than twenty feet away when my bullets ripped into him. The rounds aren't that big, but I fired a shitload when I switched to rock and roll."

Rivers interrupted again. "Well, others counted for you. There were eleven gook officers. We know those were yours because each had a single heavy-caliber shot through the head. Then there were seventy-three others coming up the hill directly toward the cave entrance."

Jackson desperately wanted to change the subject. *Shit, why doesn't he just shut up? I'm in no mood to have anyone rehash the situation secondhand.* "You said there were things we should talk about."

Before the conversation could resume, a corpsman came in carrying coffee. "You're discharged, Sergeant. We need the bed. There's a shitload of medevacs comin' in. I brought you a clean set of ripstops and your boots."

"Well, all right," Rivers said. "Get dressed."

"Change the bandage on your head every day for a week," the pecker-checker said. "Then report to a medical unit so they can check for infection and tend to your ribs."

Rivers turned to the corpsman. "Doc, call Colonel MacDonald at 26th Regiment and tell him I've got Jackson."

"Yes, sir. What about the general's aide? He's been callin' every fifteen minutes."

"Him too."

The two Marines left the bed, and the coffee, to grow cold.

Outside, the sun made Jackson wince. "Let's find someplace dark to talk."

Rivers laughed. "Gotcha. Let's go to Tien Shau. We can sit inside the Elephant, have a few beers, and continue our conversation. It's dark in there."

"You forget, *sir*, enlisted men and dogs aren't allowed." Jackson held up his chevronless collar point to drive home the fact that NCOs weren't welcome in the Stone Elephant.

Rivers waved his hand. "Don't sweat the small shit. REMFs are the only ones who care, and if anyone has balls enough to say anything, I'll deal with it."

Jackson nodded, and the two departed for the Air Force side of the base.

Their eyes quickly adjusted to the dark. "Looks like we got the place to ourselves anyway," said Rivers.

"Must be the early hour," Jackson noted.

"Nah, this place is full all the time. Must be our boys are out hunting Cong."

They ordered beer, and cold bottles of Budweiser appeared within minutes.

Jackson figured Rivers wanted to talk more about Duc Lo, and he wasn't disappointed.

"I'm sorry, Paul, but it's customary to go over these kinds of circumstances several times so all the facts can be pieced together."

"Like what?" Jackson asked.

Rivers proceeded cautiously. "Well, for starters, how did a single sergeant survive? People, especially REMFs, talk, and all kinds of scuttlebutt will be going around. Therefore, the hammering I'm going to give you is appropriate, even if just to keep down the rumors."

The inquisition went on for hours. When Rivers finally stopped, Jackson took a long pull on the neck of his fifth beer. When he set it down, Rivers brought up a new subject.

"We need to talk about what you'll be doing next."

"Christ! The REMFs don't waste time. Not that I was expecting anything different, but a couple of days off wouldn't be a hell of a lot to hope for."

"Save it, Paul. We need to talk seriously. So don't start with the crap, okay?"

The harshness in Rivers' voice knocked the cockiness out of Jackson's response. "Okay, fine. It's not your fault REMFs don't have a conscience."

Ignoring the comment, Rivers continued. "Have you ever given any thought to becoming an officer?"

The totally unexpected question gave Jackson pause. "Not really, no. I'm too young, and I don't have a college education."

"Those things can be waived by proper authority . . . if you're interested."

Jackson thought for a moment. He knew that a great many Marine officers were former enlisted men. These "mustangs" had commanded units as large as battalions. The most famous of them, Chesty Puller, commanded the 1st Marine Division in Korea and rose to the rank of lieutenant general. "Honestly," he said at last, "I've always thought I could be a warrant officer or a limited-duty officer in time, but what you're talkin' about seems more immediate."

Rivers waved at a waiter for another round. "That's right. I'm talking about right now. This is a unique situation, Paul. We're in one of the ugliest wars this country has ever fought, one a lot of us believe we're losing. The attacks in the last few days have driven that home in the minds of many senior officers. They agree we're going to have to do things differently if we're to come out of this situation with our heads up. Many believe we can start by aggressively adopting guerrilla tactics. The first thing they propose is to change how we gather intel and how we go about eliminating key targets. They're going to need highly skilled individuals to lead recon. People like you, in other words. Interested?"

"I don't know. I hadn't planned on making this a career."

"That's not necessary," Rivers responded. "Officers can resign their commission after four years of service. That adds less than a year to the time you've got left anyway."

Being an officer, Jackson thought, *is without a doubt one hell of a lot better than being an enlisted man.* Aloud he said, "When we met, I told you there were several things I didn't want to end up doing, such as ordering others to their deaths. I remember how it affected platoon leaders at Duc Lo, and I don't know if I can handle that. I also know the Corps assigns officers where they're needed. If I accept a commission, there's no doubt what my MOS will be."

"Yup," Rivers agreed; "0302, Infantry."

"A grunt platoon leader? That's one position I absolutely don't want. I don't want to wind up in a place like Duc Lo waiting for my ticket to be punched."

"That won't happen," Rivers responded with confidence. "Do you remember what I said about forming a special recon group within the Corps? How this group would be developed using only handpicked, experienced, and elite individuals?"

"Yes, sir."

"Well, we're going to do it."

"Who exactly is 'we,' sir?"

"You and me, Paul, provided you accept what General Lew is offering. You've distinguished yourself more than I think you understand, and the Corps needs you right now. Not necessarily because of what you did, but because you survived. This lousy war has caused the Corps to rethink a lot of its values, and what you did at Duc Lo is something special. I've spent a lot of time telling the right people that you and I are the ones who can create this recon team. They were slow to agree, but after Duc Lo they've seen the light. They're willing to let us set it up, but we have to get you commissioned first."

"Okay, suppose I accept. How does it work?"

"The process is simple," Rivers said. "You submit an application. Then you'll appear before a review board at III MAF. The purpose is to evaluate you under pressure. After the board provides formal approval you'll be sent to Quantico to attend OCS. You'll be trained, commissioned, and shipped back here. When you return, we'll build our unit."

Jackson was unconvinced. "And what about you? What happens to you while I'm enjoying the Virginia countryside? What if you get killed? When I get back, I'm saddled with some REMF or assigned as the leader of 3rd platoon, Alpha Company."

"That isn't going to happen. I've been told to stand down and confine my talents to locating the right men to form our group, which should take about the same amount of time you'll be gone. Besides, I was keeping myself out of the shit a long time before you happened along. I can still take care of myself."

"I'll have to attend OCS with a bunch of college boys?"

"Going to college does not make one inferior, Jackson. I know some damned nice people who've graduated without deformity." Rivers held up his right hand and proudly displayed the Annapolis ring on his finger.

The ring meant nothing to Jackson. "I mean, I'm not sure I can cut it in that kind of company. All I have is a high school diploma."

"And combat experience," Rivers added quickly. "Something that will give you one hell of an advantage at Quantico."

"You really think I'd make a good officer?"

Rivers didn't hesitate. "I do. But the only way we'll know for sure is if you set your mind to it. I think you can be a hell of a lot more than just another sergeant."

"Okay. If you think I can."

"Listen, Paul, what I think doesn't mean anything. It's what you think and are willing to go through. You've known your share of second lieutenants. Don't you think you could do the job as well as or even better than they did?"

"Yes, sir, but I never thought I'd get the chance."

"Well you've got it. Now it's time to put up or shut up."

"What've I got to lose?"

"Christ, don't be so enthusiastic. Being an officer is a privilege, Jackson. Some damned good men have worn bars."

"Okay. Okay, I'll volunteer," Jackson laughed, holding his hands up in surrender.

TWENTY

Da Nang

2305, January 31, 1968

JACKSON WAS SURPRISED when Rivers produced the OCS application right there in the Stone Elephant, but he signed it. "You son of a bitch. You knew what I'd say. You prepared it before you came to get me."

"You bet your ass," Rivers said. "While it makes its way through the messed-up bureaucracy that runs the Corps, we're going to be attached to S2. MacDonald wants us to write up the requirements for Force Recon. Put the whole OCS business out of your mind 'cause it'll take a long time. Besides, we have more important issues to deal with."

Jackson confided, "I doubt I'll ever be commissioned, sir. I'm not sure combat experience will overcome my age and lack of education. What's worse, I think Duc Lo has a lot more to do with this harebrained idea than it should."

Jackson's negativity didn't sit well with Rivers. "Look, goddamn it, you're wrong if you think the review board will reject your application. They'll understand that the leadership abilities you showed at Duc Lo are sufficient reason to warrant waiving the age and education requirements. Right now, though, we need to think about what's going to be needed for the new unit. What kind of equipment? What type of men? How many of each rank and MOS? What will the command structure look like and how the unit will be organized?"

"Okay, okay," Jackson said, pushing aside his doubts. "The units have to be very small and highly independent. But will HQMC buy what we have to sell?"

"I doubt it. Headquarters Marine Corps is a stodgy organization filled with incredibly out-of-touch people who think we're still fighting the Japanese. A lot of people think the present-day Crotch is the result of nearly two hundred years of tradition unhampered by a single moment's progress."

Jackson laughed and nodded.

"Look," Rivers said, "I'll keep your sorry ass around even if the officer board turns you down, but in what capacity I don't know. I certainly can't bring in a bunch of highly skilled staff NCOs and move them out of the command structure in favor of a junior sergeant."

Jackson shook his head. "Highly skilled? Here's how things will really happen. When the order comes down for volunteers, the ones we'll get are the ones each organization feels it can most easily do without. They won't be cherries, but they'll damned sure be fuckups and malcontents. We won't be able to find a good man in the bunch."

"You're right," Rivers agreed; "and that's why I'm not going to ask the commands. I'm going directly to the men. If we take what command sends us, we'll be screwed from the beginning."

"That might work. But even if we're given the priority you think we'll get, there aren't more than a handful of men in 'Nam we'll really want, and none who've run small units."

As the next few days passed, a thousand things occupied Jackson's mind. The time since the Year of the Monkey was heralded in with massive gunfire instead of celebratory fireworks had been among the busiest, and bloodiest, the Corps had seen in Vietnam. In the Tet Offensive, as it was now being called, Charlie came out of the woodwork in full strength and hit hard at nearly every strategic point in the country. Well-coordinated attacks were launched against U.S. and ARVN bases and Vietnam's civilian leadership. The assaults created a mountain of casualties. Some estimates put U.S. and ARVN dead at 4,500, and wounded at near 16,000. The *Stars and Stripes,* if you could believe anything that rag published, set NVA and VC losses at over 50,000. U.S. news correspondents reported that the situation was out of control. Even Congress was talking about the war being unwinnable, and opinion against it appeared strong.

The siege at Khe Sanh was finally broken, but only after six thousand Marines relieved the defenders. There was tremendous loss of life on both sides of the wire. The city of Hue was destroyed by the artillery and air strikes needed to drive the NVA out of the ancient capital. It took four Marine regiments—the 1st, 5th, 9th, and 26th—leading a very reluctant ARVN to regain control of I Corps. The 1st and the 5th Regiments recaptured Hue, and the 9th and 26th survived Khe Sanh. Together they beat Ho Chi Minh's forces in large-scale, face-to-face combat for the first time.

The possibility that he'd be approved to attend OCS seemed to be fading when the summons to attend the screening board in Da Nang finally arrived.

Rivers told him, "Put on your best uniform, scrape the mud off your boots, and try to look like a REMF for a couple of hours."

When Jackson arrived at headquarters he was told to present himself immediately to a line of officers seated behind a wooden table. A lieutenant colonel was the senior officer. He was joined by two captains and two majors, with a first lieutenant acting as secretary. Jackson realized one thing quickly: they all had the pale skin that signaled REMF. The lieutenant said, "Sit down, Sergeant."

Jackson did as he was ordered and sat in the chair in front of the table. Rivers had coached him earlier to "sit at attention. Keep your back straight and your ass on the first three inches of the chair. Keep your forearms in line with your thighs and your hands over your knees." He'd practiced until he thought it was the only way to sit.

The officers looked at him with open curiosity and what appeared to Jackson more than mild disapproval. The light colonel looked up and down the table before beginning. "What we have before us is a young but well-turned-out sergeant of the regular Marine Corps. He has been recommended by his commanding officer, Captain Bartholomew Rivers, a regular officer and an Annapolis graduate. Colonel R. F. MacDonald, commanding officer of the 26th Marines, has countersigned the recommendation, and it has been endorsed "recommended with enthusiasm" by the commanding general of the 3rd Marine Division. These recommendations are largely based on the sergeant's remarkable combat record. 'Brilliant and extraordinary' is how General Lew referred to it."

Before speaking to Jackson the colonel looked him up and down closely. "In your own words, Sergeant, please tell me why you feel you're qualified to be an officer of Marines."

"I'm not at all positive I am, sir."

The colonel was shocked. "That, Sergeant, is an entirely unexpected response. You signed an application applying for Officer Candidates School. Your commanding officer, his commanding officer, and their commanding general all believe you *should* be an officer. Can you give us any reason why you think their recommendations aren't in order?"

Jackson's face paled. *Shit. I'm facing a group of officers who resent some wannabe enlisted man trying to enter their exclusive club. I don't see any objectivity. Rivers was wrong when he said I'd be given a fair shake.* "No, sir," Jackson said. "I'm not trying to be difficult, sir. I have serious concerns about my ability to be an effective officer."

"Could you tell this board what those are, Sergeant? We're expected to provide a fair and thorough review of your qualifications after this meeting. What you add will help us do so."

A major seated to the left of the colonel spoke. "Tell us why you have reservations, Sergeant."

Jackson focused on the new officer. "I don't have a college education, sir, and I don't meet the minimum age requirement."

The major smiled. "That's all? You think a lack of education and youth will hamper your performance? Is that what I'm hearing?"

"That's it, sir."

The major shook his head. "Now tell us the real reasons you don't think you're qualified, Sergeant."

This is friggin' surreal. How do they expect me to respond to a question like that? He felt perspiration on his forehead, and his nervousness began to piss him off.

When Jackson didn't respond, the major said, "You know lieutenants. Pick out anything you've seen them do you that you can't."

"Sir, the officers I know have a special way of communicating. Each one possesses a command of the language I don't feel my educational background has prepared me with."

One of the captains asked, "You have combat experience, do you not, Sergeant?"

"About six months, sir."

"Of that time, Sergeant, how much was actually been spent in the bush?"

"All but the last three weeks, sir."

The colonel interrupted. "What happened to bring you out of the line, Sergeant?"

"Sir, I was medevaced and assigned to other duties."

"In fact, you were one of the two survivors at Duc Lo, and you were medevaced because you were wounded standing off a vastly superior enemy force. Isn't that true, Sergeant? A standoff, I might add, that resulted in you saving the life of the commanding officer of the 1st Battalion, 26th Marines."

"That's correct, sir." Jackson was embarrassed. He didn't want the board to think he was trying to benefit from what happened at Duc Lo.

Looking up and down the board, the lieutenant colonel addressed its members. "Sergeant Jackson is a member of a special two-man reconnaissance team formed by Colonel MacDonald to uncover information our LRRP teams have been missing. That team was primarily responsible for gathering all of the good data we received prior to Tet. Without his information, things would've been one hell of a lot more dicey around here, I assure you.

"He was conducting a briefing to dispersed unit commanders, again at the request of Colonel MacDonald, when he was caught at Duc Lo and survived the destruction of its command bunker. Afterward, he provided emergency medical attention to the commanding officer and forcibly held off an organized assault by a regiment-sized attack force. He called in artillery and air strikes on his own position, not once but several times. He performed exceptionally well under extremely adverse circumstances and was able to communicate clearly with rear support areas throughout the engagement. Is that about it, Sergeant?"

"I'm sure the colonel knows more about Duc Lo than I do, sir."

"Perhaps." The colonel seemed to understand Jackson's reluctance to talk. "Is there any other reason you don't feel you should be an officer?"

"I wouldn't know how to act like one, sir."

"The important things I believe you understand very well, Jackson," the colonel said. "The other things they'll teach you in Quantico. But I'd like an answer to one last question."

"Yes, sir."

"Do you want to be an officer?"

Jackson took his time considering his answer, ignoring the disapproving looks that appeared on the officers' faces.

"Yes, sir. Very much."

With that, the board was over and Jackson was dismissed. Each member recommended, with enthusiasm, Jackson's approval.

Two days later, Jackson reported to Colonel MacDonald's office. "Sir, Sergeant Jackson reporting to the commanding officer as ordered, sir."

"Stand at ease, Sergeant," MacDonald said. "You've been called here to receive the recommendation of the Officer Review Board."

"Yes, sir."

"It has been brought to our attention," the colonel said, sweeping his arm in an arc that included Captain Rivers, "that you conducted yourself in a hesitant and unsure manner."

"Sir?" Jackson congratulated himself on reading it correctly. The chickenshit REMFs turned him down. What the hell. He didn't expect to make it anyway.

"But, your deplorable conduct notwithstanding, the board voted unanimously to approve our recommendation." The colonel extended his hand. "I might add that this has been the one bright spot around here for the past week."

Rivers shook Jackson's hand warmly. "Congratulations, Paul."

Colonel MacDonald grinned. "Now, you'll stand at attention, Sergeant."

Just as he did, the door in the rear of the office opened and in stepped a three-star general, a major general, and several staff officers. The generals moved to the front of the room and were introduced as Gen. Walter Lew, commander of the 3rd Marine Amphibious Force, and Maj. Gen. Raymond Davis, assistant commander of the 3rd Marine Division.

General Lew stepped in front of the little group and spoke. "All of us had a small hand in your recommendation, and none of us wants to see you go to Quantico under normal circumstances."

Jackson was far more than slightly dumbfounded. "Sir?"

"I believe you are at attention, Sergeant," the general said with a straight face. "That means you don't speak unless directly spoken to, and then only if given permission."

Jackson pulled his eyes back above the colonel's desk and locked his arms at his sides.

The general tried hard to keep a straight face. "As I was saying, none of us wants you to go to Quantico in the standard manner. Therefore, we've arranged for you to go in a manner befitting your performance at our board of review. Which, I'm told, wasn't what we expected. Can you help me with this, Chuck?"

The junior general took over. "What General Lew is alluding to, Sergeant, is we don't want some chickenshit REMF giving you a lot of shit as you go through the course. Is that clear?"

"Sir, I don't understand the general, sir."

General Davis smiled. "Why? It should be crystal clear to the most simple of men. You did say this was a brighter-than-average Marine, did you not, Rivers?"

"Yes, sir. Very much so."

The smile grew wider on Davis' face. "Well, then, perhaps it's me." He turned to MacDonald. "Could you enlighten him, colonel?"

"I can try, sir, but, with your permission, I think the gentleman who started this little fiasco should speak for all of us."

There were nods of agreement and broad smiles all around. Except for Jackson, who remained utterly confused.

"Sergeant," Captain Rivers began. "At Quantico you're going to be met by drill instructors who will believe you're an asshole trying to get ahead. People who are thoroughly prepared to make your life miserable. Do you realize that?"

"Yes, sir. I've anticipated it to be much like boot camp, sir."

"Oh, it'll be much worse than that, Sergeant."

The comment brought chuckles from all the officers.

"In fact," the captain smothered his laughter and continued, "we believe your treatment will be brutal if you report as an NCO trying to receive a commission."

"Therefore," interrupted General Lew, "we've decided the only way you can avoid the hazing is to report already commissioned. We are here to do just that. Raise your right hand and repeat after me."

Jackson did as he was ordered, and General Lew administered the commissioned officer's oath of allegiance. "You can drop your hand now, Lieutenant." Lew took a set of second lieutenant's bars out of his pocket. "Chuck, can you and Mac help me with this?"

"With respect, sir," said MacDonald. "Captain Rivers has something he'd like to add before we continue."

"By all means, get on with it, Bart."

"Thank you, sir." Turning to face Jackson, Rivers said, "Paul, these were my bars. I hope you'll wear them and that they'll bring you the same success they've brought me." The emotion in Rivers' voice had all of the officers clearing their throats and looking away. Rivers handed the bars to Lew and stepped back.

"I hope you realize the quality of man who wore these bars before you, Lieutenant," Lew said. "You have a special obligation to conduct yourself in a manner that will reflect well upon him." The general's voice was soft because his throat was choked with emotion.

"Yes, sir," Jackson said, equally moved. "I'm deeply honored, sir."

The two generals stepped in front of Jackson, removed his sergeant's chevrons, and replaced them with the well-worn second lieutenant's bars. "Congratulations, Lieutenant," each general said as he shook Jackson's hand.

Colonel MacDonald bellowed at the closed door of his office, "Sergeant Major!"

"Yes, sir." The door opened to admit a cart piled high with coffee and donuts.

The celebration lasted fifteen minutes, then both generals offered their congratulations again and departed. After they were gone, MacDonald told Jackson to go to S1 and pick up his orders. He was booked on the morning freedom bird.

Captain Rivers walked the bewildered new lieutenant over to the company office and then to Supply to procure a decent set of utilities to wear to Okinawa, the first stop on his trip back to the world. "Look, Paul, "he said. "Buy only a basic supply of officer's uniforms in Okinawa. It's summer, so you'll need a good set of trops to wear when reporting into Schools Battalion. But don't buy more than two. The healthy food and physical training you're going to receive at OCS will alter your physique and put some weight back on you. So instead of buying uniforms that'll soon be too small, wait and purchase them at Quantico—or better yet, at one of those high-dollar uniform shops in New York City. Quality matters."

After Jackson paid for a new utility uniform, they went to the 24th Corps officers' club to celebrate.

The next morning, a very hung-over Rivers put Jackson on board a freedom bird to Kadena Air Force Base in Okinawa, where he was assigned a seat on American Airlines flight 002 to Norton Air Base near Los Angeles.

★

Jackson suddenly found himself back in a world he hadn't seen for far too long. The plane was staffed by a bevy of very pretty round-eyed women who were more than willing to spend their time talking to the returning servicemen. They moved up and down the aisle bringing a touch of home to each man and were rewarded with compliments and polite conversation.

"I can't remember the last time I saw American servicemen with nothing to say around beautiful women," Jackson told the first stewardess he spoke to. "But seeing you does make it difficult to speak. Christ, you smell good."

"Thanks, Lieutenant. It's Chanel No. 5."

"What it *is* is intoxicating."

"I'll bet you say that to all the girls, Lieutenant. I think it's just the reality of going home."

"You're probably right," Jackson said, "and that's what's going to keep me from making a fool of myself."

For most of the flight he sat next to a Marine pilot, a major from Alabama who was reporting for duty at Beaufort, South Carolina. "I was the S4 at MAG-36," the major told him. "Phu Bai was a real shithole, but I've got orders to Beaufort. It's close to my home state, and that makes my wife happy."

"What did you fly, sir?" Jackson asked.

"OV-10s."

They reminisced a little about Phu Bai and the surrounding countryside. The major inspected Jackson's ribbons. "Bronze Star, huh? What did you do in-country?"

"Reconnaissance, sir." After that, conversation lagged and each man retired into his own thoughts. There were no tough questions asked and no bullshit answers given.

The plane landed in San Bernardino at about 1400. "Damn it," the major complained. "We have to process through Customs here. I've got a flight leaving in four hours, and it's a long ride to LAX."

Inside the customs area fat, sloppy civilians went through the men's luggage looking for contraband and drugs. By the time they completed the procedure it was nearly dinnertime.

"Want to share the cost of a cab, Lieutenant?"

As the taxi rolled through Norton's main gate it passed a large gathering of long-haired, scantily clad demonstrators holding signs denouncing the war in Vietnam. Jackson saw one that read "Hell No, I Won't Go." While he found that disturbing, it was another that really caught his attention. In red letters painted to look like dripping blood, it said "Welcome Home, Baby Killers." *Yeah, welcome home.*

TWENTY-ONE

Los Angeles International Airport

1800, February 27, 1968

JACKSON STOOD NEXT to Major Mills outside a concourse bar. "We've walked past this place a dozen times, sir. Your flight doesn't leave for another hour and I'm thirsty. Why don't we go in?"

Mills shook his head. "I don't drink, so I think I'll go on to my gate. Nice meeting you, Jackson. Good luck."

"You too, sir. I think I'll have that drink; in fact, I'll have several. It'll take that many to wash the taste of homecoming out of my mouth." Bad enough that a fat, dirty civilian had ransacked his bag at Norton, but the demonstrators outside the gate had really pissed him off. Jackson was livid. "Did you see the sign that said 'baby killers'? I might understand if the bastards were Vietnamese, but to be called a 'murdering fucking pig' by another American is too much."

Major Mills shook Jackson's hand. "We know better, Lieutenant. What idiots think doesn't amount to squat. You take care of yourself in Quantico."

Jackson said goodbye, walked into the bar, and ordered a beer.

The bartender smiled. "What kind?"

Jackson thought he was being made fun of. "You mean you have more than one kind?"

That sent the bartender into a fit of laughter. He pulled out a Heineken, poured the first few swallows into a frosted glass, and pointed to a Marine Corps plaque over the bar. "The first one's on the house, Lieutenant. I was in World War II, and it's my policy to give the first beer free when a brother Marine comes home."

Jackson thanked him, and the two men reminisced for a few minutes, neither asking the tough questions but both wanting to share.

Looking past Jackson, the bartender said, "You're being watched. Be careful, this place is lousy with queers."

Jackson glanced over his shoulder. "Who is he?"

"Beats the shit outta me. Looks like a poster boy for Harvard: smartly tailored suit, white shirt, and Ivy League tie. But he's definitely watching you. Probably just a rich kid on his way back to school after a big weekend of action."

That made Jackson laugh. "Yeah. We call L.A. 'The Land of the Whispering Bushes.'"

"Ain't it the truth? Gotta fetch another round for those squids at the end of the bar. I hate them cluttering up the place, but money is money."

Now that he was paying attention, Jackson found the young man's steady gaze unnerving. Even worse, the guy was smiling at him the whole time—as if he was trying to develop the courage to hit on him. Jackson stared at his beer. "Christ, I know LA is full of them, but having one this close makes me nervous."

The bartender laughed. "Just ignore him and enjoy the show."

"What show?"

"Are you blind? The women! Look at them parading themselves around in skirts so short they leave nothing to the imagination."

"Yeah, I saw a few of 'em out at Norton," Jackson said. "Makes their legs look great but doesn't do a hell of a lot for their attitude toward the military."

"Attitude? What are you talkin' about? Christ, man, ever since the miniskirt's become popular I've been reaping the rewards."

Jackson watched the concourse outside and tried to remember when he'd seen so many women wearing so little. "I see what you mean."

"Jesus, those bare midriffs and long legs are screamin' to be touched, and the selection is endless."

★

The airplane was a Boeing 707 with seats in sets of three on either side of a single aisle. Jackson wasn't at all pleased with his seat assignment. *Shit. I knew something would go wrong. I can't believe I have to sit with a woman takin' her three screamin' kids all the way to Washington. And here I am in the middle seat between one of the brats and Mommie. Looks like it's gonna be a very long flight.*

Just when he was about to lose it altogether, a very pretty blonde stewardess with a killer body walked up. "I have a different seat for you, Lieutenant." Her nametag indicated that her name was Karen.

Jackson looked around the tourist cabin for a likely spot. "I don't see an empty one, miss—uh, Karen."

"It's in first class, and it's yours if you want it."

"You bet! Thanks." *Hot damn!* he thought.

The stew reached up to get his bag from the overhead, giving Jackson a nice view of the best legs he'd ever seen. He followed her to a seat just in front of the first-class curtain. Her smile warmed Jackson down to his toes. "I have to work the back," she said, "but I'll bring my address up in case you'd like to see some of D.C."

After she left, Jackson stowed his bag and bent to sit down. The well-dressed man who had been watching him in the bar smiled up at him. "Sit down," he said, patting Jackson's seat with one hand while he lifted a glass of champagne to his lips with the other. The man's choice of drink all but confirmed Jackson's suspicion.

"Thanks." Internally he seethed. *How am I going to deal with this guy without belting him? It's a long flight, and I don't want to fend him off the entire way.*

"You watch yourself," Rivers had said before he left Da Nang. "There's a lot of people pissed off because you're an officer, and more than a few will happily go out of their way to make your life miserable. Get in trouble of any kind and you'll end up with an Article 15 for conduct unbecoming."

As he fastened his seatbelt, a lovely brunette stewardess came up and asked if he would like a drink before takeoff. Jackson smiled. "Scotch, please. Chivas Black with soda on the side."

"You can change mine to the same," Jackson's seat companion added. Then he smiled at Jackson. "You're a Marine lieutenant, correct?"

"Yes," said Jackson shortly.

"I thought so. I'm on my way to Quantico to become one myself."

Jackson was astonished. "You're what?"

"I'm on my way to complete the second half of the Platoon Leader's Course."

Jackson's eyes expressed doubt. "What's the Platoon Leader's Course?"

"It's a program that allows students to complete their officer training while in college. All I have left is the six weeks of the final phase. I believe they call it Officer Candidates School."

"Congratulations," Jackson said sarcastically. *Who does this guy think he's kidding? I know the Corps lowered its recruiting standards, even accepts draftees into the enlisted ranks now, but I didn't think it was desperate enough to commission guys like this.* But the guy didn't talk like a homosexual, and his wrist wasn't limp. Of course, not all people of that persuasion were passive.

"Thank you," the man said, ignoring Jackson's sarcasm. "I'd like to talk about Officer Candidates School, if you don't mind."

Jackson's curiosity was aroused, and he was beginning to have doubts about his first impression. The guy's reaction to the female stewardess, whom he thoroughly undressed with his eyes, didn't seem right for a homosexual. "You're really going into the Corps?"

"Yes, I am." He stuck out his hand. "Bill Williams."

Jackson grasped the hand. It was firm and strong. "Paul Jackson."

The stewardess brought the drinks, and Jackson reached for his wallet. The gorgeous brunette flashed a smile seductive enough to melt chrome off a bumper hitch. "The drinks are complimentary, Lieutenant."

"Looks like you've made another conquest," Williams said. "Must be the uniform."

Jackson was able to relax into his seat now that the issue of the civilian's sexuality was settled. "What do you mean, another?"

"I heard the blonde who showed you to your seat. 'I'll be back to give you my address in case you'd like to see D.C.'s attractions,'" Williams parroted. "I bet what she wants to show you doesn't appear on any D.C. tour I've ever been on."

Jackson laughed, picked up the scotch, and contemplated the blonde's offer. Thinking about her reminded him of how long it had been.

Williams interrupted his reverie. "Can I ask the lieutenant a question?"

"On the condition you stop calling me 'lieutenant.' I'm Paul."

"Bill, and thanks."

"So what's your question, Bill? 'How'd a nice boy like you end up in uniform?'"

Williams smiled as if he understood Jackson's sarcasm. "Saw the protestors out front, did you?"

"I didn't see any at LAX, but there was a shitload of them at Norton."

"Norton? Isn't it where you land when you're coming back from Vietnam?"

"Yeah. Does it show?"

"Christ, no. You just look too young to be an officer, let alone one returning from Vietnam. Hell, no, it doesn't show."

"Good. I'd hate to have to belt one of those assholes if he gets too close. Now what's your question?"

Williams started out cautiously. "Well, I was going to ask how someone as young as you appear to be got to be an officer. I thought twenty-one was the minimum."

Jackson didn't go into his situation at all. "That's the general rule."

"It's just that you don't look old enough."

"Why? Does it bother you?"

"Not at all. I'm just curious."

Jackson looked closely at Bill, and what he saw wasn't disbelief but genuine curiosity. "I was commissioned in the field."

"A battlefield commission?"

"Some people call it that, yeah."

"I didn't think the Corps did that anymore." There was no hint of disbelief in Williams' voice, just a kind of wonder.

"They don't; at least not often."

Bill laughed. "Actually, when I first saw you in the bar I thought you were an actor, but your haircut ruled that out."

"Why?"

"This is 1968, Paul. Actors don't cut their hair that short except for really big parts, and I didn't see a film crew in the terminal. Besides, an actor who *had* cut his hair would've worn a wig into the airport."

Jackson nodded his understanding.

Williams changed the subject. "What's your MOS?"

"I'm a basic 0302 right now. I'll get my permanent MOS when I finish OCS."

"Now I'm confused. You're already an officer. Why would you have to go to OCS?"

Jackson didn't suffer fools easily. "Because the Corps said so," he said impatiently. "It's like that. They tell you what to do, and you do it. It's known as willful obedience to orders. If you're going to be an officer, you have one hell of a lot to learn."

Williams didn't like the condescending tone. "Hey, look, if you don't want to talk about it, then fine, but don't talk to me like I'm some kind of dumbass."

Jackson was set back a bit by the sharpness in Bill's response. *Maybe I pegged this guy wrong. He doesn't act like a candy-ass. Maybe he's even got some balls. At least he didn't have any trouble telling me where to get off.* "Perhaps we should start over again. My name's Paul," he said holding out his hand.

"Good. Like I said, I'm Bill." He took Jackson's hand and shook it firmly. "So why are you going to OCS?"

Jackson repeated his earlier response but left out the malice. "The people who commissioned me thought I would benefit by learning how to properly conduct myself. You know, which fork to use and when it's proper to say 'fuck' in the club; that sort of thing."

"Is there a lot of difference between being enlisted and an officer?"

"I guess so, but the truth is I haven't been a lieutenant long enough to know. Besides, where I was at, everyone looks pretty much the same. No one actually wears their rank."

Williams' face expressed doubt. "Why not? Where were you?"

Damn it, Jackson thought. *I didn't want to talk about 'Nam, and now that's all this guy's going to want to hear.* "I'd rather talk about something else."

Bill's disappointment showed in his voice. "Okay, such as?"

"What's D.C. like? I'm, or rather we, are going to be stationed near there, so if you know the city I'd rather talk about how to get laid."

"The best way I know of is with a woman."

Jackson looked at Bill for a second, then laughed out loud.

"If you tell me what Vietnam is like, Lieutenant Jackson, I'll give you instructions on getting laid in our capital city. Who knows, if we have any luck, those two stewardesses will help us get started."

Jackson caught the attention of the pretty brunette stewardess with the stimulating smile and ordered another drink. "I told my old skipper that I'd stay out of trouble, but if I keep drinking with you, I'm going to get drunk enough to get into a whole bunch. He isn't here, though, and I don't give a shit. You can get laid in Phu Bai for a pack of cigarettes. What does it cost in D.C.?"

"Like I said, this is 1968. Love is free."

Fuck it, Jackson thought. *I like this guy. Perhaps Rivers wouldn't mind if I did a little recon of the local talent.*

TWENTY-TWO

St. Paul Hotel, Washington, D.C.

0900, February 28, 1968

JACKSON AWOKE TO the sound of the shower. *What a night!* He rolled over to the spot where only a few hours ago the sexy blonde stewardess satisfied him as no other woman ever had. His morning wood reminded him of how hot the sex had been and just how much he wanted her . . . again. Just five days ago he had been sitting in the Stone Elephant alongside Rivers with no thoughts of, or prospects for, getting laid. Now, there was a beautiful—no, gorgeous—round-eyed woman in his bathroom cleaning every delicious curve of her insatiable body. *Eat your heart out, Rivers.*

"Where did you get that?" Karen had asked, staring slack-jawed at the scar on Jackson's head. She was freaked out by the story and very concerned about the injury. After that, she was all over him . . . all night long.

Jackson sat up, and his head started to swim. He wasn't sure if it was a hangover from the river of liquor he drank last night or his half-healed wound. He needed a drink of water desperately. The inside of his mouth felt like the entire North Vietnamese Army had marched through it. He walked into the bathroom and filled a glass from the tap. The water was so cold that it sweated up the glass and made his teeth ache.

The hotel bathroom was incredible. There were little bottles of shampoo and hair conditioner sitting neatly on the counter next to a pile of towels. There was a real commode—and a bidet. He looked in the mirror and backed up a step. His eyes were bloodshot and his body was covered with . . . *lipstick*. Everywhere. He reviewed the past night and remembered how the red marks had gotten where they were.

Christ, she was something. He could still feel the softness of her lips, the heat of her breath on his naked body. He sat on the toilet to relieve himself. It felt good to sit on porcelain. He'd forgotten how cold a toilet seat could get. Just five days ago he'd shared a plywood four-holer with three other guys. It smelled so bad they needed to hold their noses just to get inside the door.

Karen's reflected image appeared through the fog on the mirror; she was washing her hair. He turned to look through the etched-glass shower door and watched in wonder as she added more shampoo to the thick lather covering her head. She moved away from the door, and he leaned forward so he could watch her. Her body was perfect—slim and athletic with incredibly firm breasts; but it was her legs that blew him away.

When he shut his eyes he could still feel the velvety softness of her skin. His body started to respond. Carefully opening the shower door, he stood very still admiring what had been hidden. Her legs set off a terrific ass, and the light-colored patch of hair confirmed her status as a real blonde. He pinched himself to make sure he was really standing there.

"Hey, close the door," she said. "I'm cold."

"Perhaps we can work on that," he said as he stepped into the stream of hot water.

★

Much later, Paul sat on the bed and watched Karen dress and put on her makeup. "Why do you bother with cosmetics?" he asked. "You're beautiful without all that stuff."

She laughed and slipped on her shoes. "I'm sorry I can't stay, but my flight leaves at two."

"That is a damned shame. I could think of a thousand different ways to spend the rest of the day."

"I'll bet you could, and I'd like to help you, but not this trip. I'll be back next week with a five-day layover if you're interested."

"Oh, I'm interested. But I have to report in to Quantico by midnight, and I don't know if I'll have liberty while I'm in school."

"Well, I'll call you when I get in."

"I don't know where you can call. In fact, I doubt if they let students receive phone calls. Why don't you leave me a number and I'll call you."

A frown darkened her face. "Yeah. I've heard that one before."

"I'm not kidding. What I said is true, and I'd really like to see you again. If you leave the number, I'll call. You can count on it." He admired the woman standing before him, now dressed in the uniform of an American Airlines stewardess. "I enjoyed last night. You're damned right I'll call, and often."

Loud banging on the bedroom door interrupted the conversation, and Jackson pulled on his uniform pants just as the door burst open to reveal Williams and the brunette stewardess. "Debbie says they have to go."

Jackson nodded. "So I've heard." He helped Karen gather her suitcases and put them on the little pull cart airline crews used for their luggage, then pulled it out into the suite's living room for her. When he reached the door, she was standing right next to him and they embraced for a long time. Her kiss started out warm and sweet but quickly grew passionate. She left him breathless.

"That will remind you to call," she said and handed him a card with her name and a phone number. "That's my parents' home in Georgetown. If I'm in D.C., I'll be there. And I'll hope for that call." Looking over her shoulder, Karen blew a kiss and left the room with Debbie.

Williams turned to Jackson with a huge grin. "I've come to a conclusion, Lieutenant. You're an evil prick sent to lead me astray before I can rise to become an officer and a gentleman."

Jackson laughed. "You may become an officer, Mr. Williams, but I seriously doubt if you'll ever be a gentleman."

"I had a good time," Williams said.

Jackson whistled. "Christ, me too. Karen was fuckin' great."

"Literally, I'm sure."

Jackson didn't have a watch. "What time is it?"

"Just after ten. How about getting some breakfast after I finish dressing?"

"Sounds like a plan. What's the name of this dump, anyway, and what's this suite costing us? I wasn't too interested last night, but now it's different. This place looks like it's expensive as hell."

Williams laughed as he returned from the other bedroom fastening an expensive-looking watch to his wrist. "Not a problem, my military friend."

"I want to split the cost of this cathouse, Bill. I'm not into mooching off casual acquaintances."

"It's friends, Paul. Acquaintances don't lift skirts together. Nor do they drink all of the booze in Washington in one night. We're friends. Clear?"

"Yeah, whatever. How much for the joint?"

Williams just shrugged. This was a penthouse in one of the oldest and finest hotels in the capital. The cost would have stunned Jackson. "Don't sweat it, I'll sign the slip and they'll bill the company."

"What company?"

"My father's. He has a small firm in San Francisco specializing in screwing good people out of their hard-earned money. The old bastard can pay." Williams winked. "That's enough . . . subject closed."

Jackson led the way downstairs to breakfast. "What the hell? Let's eat this dump out of breakfast food. I'm thinking fresh-squeezed orange juice followed by an entourage of specialties."

Williams smiled. "I'm thinking about a three-egg omelet followed by hash browns, steak, toast, and a bowl of oatmeal with bananas. We can wash everything down with a couple of pots of coffee and a few bottles of German ale."

"Yeah. There's nothing like the hair of the dog."

When they were finished, Williams told the bell desk to pick up their bags and close the room's bill. Then they caught a cab to Quantico.

TWENTY-THREE

Marine Corps Base Quantico, Virginia

1542, February 28, 1968

THE MP AT THE GATE took one look at Jackson's gold bars, snapped to attention, and saluted. He looked suspiciously at the civilian in the cab as he bent over for the lieutenant's orders. "These say you're to report to the Officer Candidates School as a student. Is that right, sir?" the MP asked.

"That's it," the lieutenant said. "Both of us." He nodded in the direction of Williams, who handed the MP his single page of orders.

Taking the mimeographed paper, the MP said, "You, I can deal with. Wait for the OCS shuttle. Over there." He pointed to a wooden bench where several other civilians were sitting. Then he took both sets of orders and went into the guard shack to stamp the time and date of arrival on the front of each. When he returned, he handed Williams his orders and told him again to get over to the bench. His tone was contemptuous. "Fucking college boys."

Jackson said goodbye to Williams, then faced the MP. "Corporal, when I was an NCO I made it a practice to be real sure who I made derogatory comments around."

The MP took his first hard look at the lieutenant. His onceover took in gold bars old enough to shine almost silver, and he knew instantly that Jackson wasn't a recent graduate of the chickenshit factory. Then his eye fell on Jackson's ribbons: the badges of a rifle and pistol expert; just above those the Vietnam Campaign and Conflict ribbons, the Combat Infantryman's Ribbon, and the Vietnamese Cross of Gallantry. And above them the Purple Heart with two stars and the Bronze Star with V. The young officer also had a deep tan that suggested a great deal of time spent in the hot sun. The MP knew that was in 'Nam because they didn't put the combat V on end-of-tour awards. The MP pulled his eyes back to Jackson's face and stood taller when he spoke. "Excuse me, sir, I meant no offense."

Jackson graciously let the MP off the hook. "None taken. However, there are some chickenshit officers around who would delight in eatin' your ass."

"Yes, sir."

"Now, where do I go?"

"You, sir, are a problem."

Jackson raised his eyebrows.

"What I mean, sir, is your orders aren't standard. They say you're to report as a student for OCS, but that can't be right, sir."

Jackson enjoyed watching the wiseass NCO squirm through the explanation. "Why not, Corporal?"

"Well, sir, officers don't go to OCS. That's where civilians *become* lieutenants, sir, not a place someone goes after he's already commissioned."

The corporal squirmed a little more and Jackson let him off the hook again. "I assure you, Corporal, I'm going to be a student in OCS. I've been ordered here for that specific purpose."

The MP took a longer look at the orders and saw they were issued by the 3rd Marine Division; there was no mistaking the instructions they carried. Lieutenant Jackson was to report to OCS for duty as a student. "I'm going to have to call the OD for instructions, sir. Would the lieutenant mind waiting inside the guardhouse?"

"If you'll see to my bag."

"You," the MP yelled at one of the civilians on the bench. "Get over here and carry the lieutenant's bag into the guard shack."

Jackson watched the college boy struggle with the heavy valpak and then followed him inside. Within minutes a staff car pulled up in front of the guard shack and a first lieutenant wearing a red armband with the letters "JOD" embroidered on it got out. Jackson rose to his feet as the officer approached him. "Lieutenant Jackson, Paul A., reporting for duty, sir."

"Welcome aboard, Lieutenant." Jackson noted that the officer didn't extend his hand. "How can I be of service?" the officer continued.

Jackson stayed on his feet and assumed a relaxed version of parade rest when addressing his senior. "The corporal thinks there's a problem with my orders, sir."

"Can I see them?"

"Yes, sir." Jackson handed his orders to the officer and watched as the JOD read them.

The man looked up, his eyebrows mashed together in clear confusion. "These," the JOD began, "order you to OCS as a student."

"Yes, sir. If I could explain, sir."

"Certainly. This one I've got to hear."

Jackson told the JOD how he received his commission, why the general wanted him to go through OCS, and how his tour in 'Nam had been interrupted to accommodate his attendance. When he was done, he stiffened in preparation for the harangue he anticipated the JOD to deliver. When it didn't come, he relaxed.

"I will take you down to Schools Battalion," the JOD said. "They'll clear this up and decide what to do with you. Have the corporal fetch your bag and follow me."

The NCO hustled up another man to fetch Lieutenant Jackson's luggage. "Get your ass over here," the MP yelled. "Officers don't carry anything as long as there's a puke like you around."

At least not at Schools Command, Marine Corps Base, Quantico, thought Jackson, *the birthplace of Marine Corps–style chickenshit.*

TWENTY-FOUR

Schools Battalion, Marine Corps Base, Quantico, Virginia

1625, February 28, 1968

AS THEY ENTERED the building, Jackson examined the linoleum floor. It was the standard for all Corps office buildings, made shiny by well-buffed wax and the sweat of innumerable enlisted men. Even the door handles—brass knobs set into long push plates—shone from hours of polishing with cloth and Brasso.

Jackson couldn't believe the JOD walked down the center of the floor. No real Marine, regardless of his rank, did that. Jackson walked down the edge to make sure he didn't scuff the shine. When he looked up, he saw the ubiquitous red sign found on every Marine Corps office door: "Knock, Remove Headgear, and Wait for Permission to Enter."

The JOD ignored the warning and pushed on into the room.

Jackson checked his uniform to make sure his gig line was straight and he wasn't showing any wrinkles, then followed his senior inside. The office could have been the one outside Colonel MacDonald's in Phu Bai; the layout was identical. The first sergeant's desk sat next to the commanding officer's door, between him and the adjutant, who, as usual, was a pasty-faced REMF.

The burly first sergeant said, "What can I do for you gentlemen?"

"Top?" The JOD's use of the improper title drew a hard scowl from First Sergeant Mickelson.

Jackson bit back a laugh, remembering a lecture he'd received the only time he'd said something similarly stupid. "Top? Do I have a goddamned stick comin' out of my head? Do I look like a friggin' toy you push up and down?" Such outbursts were classic in the annals of senior enlisted Marines. Jackson knew the only reason the REMF first john didn't hear one now was because the first sergeant was professional enough to restrain himself in front of another officer.

"The lieutenant is reporting from the 3rd Division as an OCS student."

"You don't say." The first sergeant ignored the stack of orders the JOD held out and looked at Jackson. "You must be Lieutenant Jackson." Continuing to ignore the JOD, the venerable sergeant held out his hand to the younger officer.

"Yes, s—," Jackson bit back the mistake and rebuked himself silently. *Oh, that's just fuckin' beautiful. Start out by calling the first sergeant "sir." He'll love that. You're a dumbass, Jackson.* "Yes, First Sergeant."

"I'll take care of the lieutenant," the first sergeant told the JOD. "You may return to your duties." The instruction was clearly an order. The JOD wanted to remind the first sergeant that enlisted men don't dismiss officers but held back. He put Jackson's orders on the desk and stalked out.

"He's our resident Boat School grad," the first sergeant said. "Don't mean nothin'. His job is counting condoms for the commandant's cat. Thinks he's hot shit. You know the type, don't you, Jackson?" The first sergeant's tone wasn't disrespectful. To the contrary, he spoke as one would address an equal.

"Yes I do, First Sergeant."

"Lieutenant Colonel Paulon, that's our skipper, will be back shortly. He's expecting you. Got a MARS call from Colonel MacDonald, who said we were to treat you square when you reported in. Got any idea what he meant?"

"No, First Sergeant."

The first shirt liked the response. The officer wasn't trying to kiss ass by bullshitting about being a special case. He also liked that the lieutenant remained polite and recognized battalion first sergeants as important men. "When did they promote you?"

"Six days ago. Does it show?"

"You seem a bit out of your element. But I like the way you handled yourself around Mr. Touchdown. Man's been a pain in the ass since he reported in. Skipper's going to assign him to the mess hall if he screws up one more time."

Jackson was surprised and said so. "Jesus, who'd he piss off? Aren't Annapolis grads regulars?"

"Yes, and most first lieutenants command companies."

"I've never heard of one being a mess officer," Jackson said. "I thought such complex tasks were left for those considered less professional. You know, Reserve officers commissioned from OCS?"

The first sergeant actually smiled. "We get damned few, and when we do he's groomed for command immediately; but this guy makes Hogan's goat look like a precision machine. The Basic School assigned him to Headquarters Marine Corps instead of a platoon in 'Nam. That should tell you something, but it wouldn't be enough. Seems this gung-ho Superman wannabe pissed off General Toomey, who sent him to us. If we're contemplatin' the mess hall, you gotta see he's a total shitbird.

"He came here with a fitness report hot enough to fuck. At first, we thought they caught him bangin' somebody's wife, but that wasn't it. Seems he tried to fuck up an enlisted man and then make himself look good by submitting a false report. The Corps is filled with men who have few qualms about doin' someone's wife if she's willin', but if they're caught, there's little mercy, especially if the husband is enlisted. That's a ticket to a bad performance review and the pass over it'll bring. They tell you that once you're passed over for promotion there's little chance of being allowed to stay in, let alone receive a commission in the regulars?"

Jackson bit his tongue to keep from laughing. "No, they neglected that."

"Well, screwin' another man's wife is taboo, but it's minor shit compared to lying or submitting a false report. Got a good report about you, though. Colonel Paulon told me you were one of the only two survivors at Duc Lo. Musta been a real bitch." The old sergeant lifted his eyebrows and waited.

Jackson looked at the floor and waved his hand in dismissal. He didn't want to talk about Duc Lo.

The action told the first sergeant a lot about Jackson's character. It was easy to see why his regiment was eager to get him back. "Sit down, sir." He waved to an old leather couch placed next to a wall emblazoned with Marine Corps paraphernalia and pictures of the first sergeant in different combat situations. Some of them were taken in Vietnam, and Jackson thought he recognized a few of the locations. "How about some coffee?"

"That would be fine, First Sergeant."

The first sergeant raised his voice. "Dooly! A cup of joe for the lieutenant." First sergeants don't fetch coffee for anyone, not even colonels.

"You reporting in like this has really created a stir around here. There's been more head scratchin' than since Toby was a baby." Toby was an imaginary Marine, said to be the youngest member of the Old Corps. Senior noncoms liked to refer to him as a baby to let others know they were charter members of the Old Breed.

"I'm nothin' special, First Sergeant."

"The Corps is real small at my level, Lieutenant. Gossip travels fast, and the Zebra Club misses damned little. I didn't get all these stripes 'cause I resemble an African horse."

"I wouldn't think so, First Sergeant."

"Things like Duc Lo don't happen in the Corps—not ever. It's a disgrace, that's what it is. All those men lost 'cause of poor intel. It's a cryin' shame."

"I guess so." Jackson replied only because he thought a response was expected, not because he believed any of the crap being spouted. The first shirt should've had enough sense to keep his opinions to himself.

"You must've gotten along pretty well with your commanding officer."

Jackson's hackles went up. "How's that?" *I'm willing to accept certain comments from any first sergeant, but if he keeps this shit up I'm going to enlighten his tired old ass. There's a limit to what this shavetail is prepared to put up with. I didn't get my commission because I was a friend of the old man. I got it because I hauled my ass through the grass better than most.*

The first shirt quickly saw the tightness appear in Jackson's demeanor. "Relax, Lieutenant. I'm just voicing what will be said at every club in the Corps when word gets around that an eighteen-year-old was commissioned. I mean you no harm. In fact, I've served with Colonel Mac and I'm on a first-name basis with General Lew. They're exceptional officers, and from firsthand experience I know neither one gives anyone special consideration. If those two think you should be an officer, it's okay by me."

Just then the hall door flew open and a bald lieutenant colonel boiled into the room roaring, "Where is that jackass? I want that Boat School shitbird outta here this afternoon. You hear me, First Sergeant? Get him out today." The steamroller was the commanding officer of Schools Battalion, and he blew past the first sergeant and disappeared behind his office door.

The first shirt didn't flinch. "Dooly."

A tall lance corporal appeared instantly. "I'll have the orders typed in twenty minutes, First Sergeant."

"Whew," the first shirt whistled. "The old man's really pissed. Must've been classic this time. I haven't seen him this mad since . . . hell, last week." He laughed and opened the colonel's door. "Skipper, we got that second john from the 26th Marines out here. Mr. Touchdown brought him over from the main gate. Would the colonel like to see him now, sir?"

"Give me a minute, First Sergeant."

When Jackson was ushered inside the commanding officer's door, he was more than a little apprehensive. "Second Lieutenant Jackson reporting to the commanding officer as ordered, sir."

"I've known Reggie MacDonald for almost twenty years," the colonel began. "We spent our first tour of duty together with 1/5 in Korea. He'll see his star on the next promotion board. So if he commissioned you from the field, you must be very special. Welcome aboard, Lieutenant." With a wave of his hand the colonel indicated an old couch that was a twin to the one in the outer office. "Please sit down. Damned glad to have you here."

"Thank you, sir."

"Sorry about the outburst," he continued, "but I've got a real problem. The first sergeant said you rode up here with a first lieutenant name of Dudley. Is that right?"

"I rode up here with a first lieutenant, sir, but I wasn't offered his name."

"Figures he wouldn't name himself to a junior. Well, his name is Dudley, Peter R., and he just put you on report at Regiment for being out of uniform and conduct unbecoming."

"*What*? *Why*?" Jackson couldn't believe it. All he'd done was accept a ride with the lieutenant. Not once during the journey did the lieutenant express any displeasure with Jackson's uniform or with Jackson himself.

"Seems he doesn't believe you're an officer; and if you are, you don't rate the ribbons you're wearing. So the prick goes over my head to Regiment and puts you on report. Did you give him a set of your orders?"

"No, sir. He asked for them and I showed them to him, but I didn't offer him a copy, sir."

"Well, he had one," the colonel said. "He took it to Regiment and told the skipper he'd found an officer candidate wearing the insignia of a lieutenant and several illegal decorations. He asked the colonel to look into it because he didn't trust me to conduct a thorough investigation. Can you believe that shit?"

It's no wonder he's about ready to blow a gasket. He must have left a big piece of his ass at Regiment just now.

The colonel ranted on, his voice growing louder. "I hear, 'Why can't you control your junior officers, Colonel? Why do I have to listen to bullshit from a lieutenant under your command?'"

Ass-chewing sessions among officers were rarely conducted in loud tones, but they burned through the recipient just the same. The colonel, like every officer, was responsible for his men twenty-four hours a day. If someone screwed up, the person's senior was always accountable. And going over your CO's head with a story of mistrust was about the worst kind of fuckup imaginable.

The door swung open and the first sergeant appeared with coffee. "Perhaps the colonel needs a break. Let's pick a happier subject. How about the lieutenant telling us what's happening in 'Nam?"

The colonel stopped his tirade and burst out laughing. "Am I that bad, First Sergeant?"

"They can hear you in the barracks, sir." The first shirt wrapped his lip over the mug's edge. His eyes didn't meet the colonel's, so the rebuke fell flat on the floor.

Jackson remained on the couch frozen at attention when the old sergeant walked in and laid down the law. *This guy is some kind of a shit-hot Marine,* he thought. *He has real balls and a shitload of diplomacy to go with them. Oooh-rah.*

"I assume you have it under control, First Sergeant."

"Yes, sir. Just tell Daddy and all your troubles will go away."

The colonel broke up again. When his laughter subsided he sat on the couch next to the open-mouthed Jackson. "Relax, Paul, I'm entitled to a little outburst now and again. It's over, and I would consider it a personal favor if you didn't repeat what you've heard this morning."

Jackson began to breathe again. "Aye, aye, sir."

The colonel was genial now. "Colonel MacDonald tells me you're one hell of a Marine."

"Thank you, sir."

"We have to figure out how we're going to get you into OCS. We've been waiting for you so we could work out the details."

"I don't want to be a problem, sir."

"I realize that, but it doesn't solve our challenge. We've never done something like this before, and, frankly, it severely crimps a major element of the curriculum."

"Sir?"

"One of the most important parts of OCS is getting men to respond to orders. You'll remember how it was accomplished in recruit training."

"Here at OCS," the first sergeant interjected, "the belief is, if you can't follow orders, you shouldn't be giving them."

"There's the rub," Paulon continued. "You're an officer. We can't have our drill instructors treating you like a standard candidate, and if we put you in a normal platoon they'll never treat the other candidates the way they have to if they're to develop the obedience we're seeking. Follow me?"

"Not really, sir."

"What the colonel means," the first sergeant said, "is if you'd come here as a sergeant, we would've simply removed your chevrons and booted your ass into the fray." First sergeants generally have a colorful way with words and an uncanny ability to cut through bullshit. "The DIs would have treated you like shit because they would've seen you as another rank-hungry asshole trying to get ahead. Then we could've used you as a training objective. The other candidates would've seen how you conducted yourself under pressure and would've learned from it. Now we can't do that."

"Why not?"

"Because officers don't scrub heads or showers," the first sergeant threw back immediately. "And NCOs don't yell at officers, that's why."

The colonel laughed. "The last part is true everywhere except in this office, Lieutenant." He scowled at the old noncom and motioned for him to lower his voice.

"I see, sir. Things would've been easier for you if I were still a sergeant."

"That's right," said the colonel, "and frankly, the two of us have worn ourselves out trying to come up with a solution."

"May I offer a suggestion?"

"Why not? You're the dilemma. If you have something, I'd be happy to hear it."

"Does anyone else know I'm an officer?"

"I don't think so," the colonel responded. "First Sergeant?"

"No, sir. We've kept it between the two of us, at least until now. I guess we'll have to add Colonel Greene and Lieutenant Touchdown to the list, but they can be taken care of."

"Well, then," continued Jackson, "put me in a platoon as an enlisted man. I'll go through training as a sergeant going topside."

The colonel's forehead furrowed. "I don't know. That would break a dozen regulations I know of. Could get us all in some serious trouble. But it sure would straighten out the problem."

The first sergeant shook his head. "I don't know, sir. Candidates are allowed to voluntarily drop from the program. If the lieutenant ops out and we send him back to his unit as an officer, how's that gonna look?"

"I have no intention of dropping, First Sergeant."

"Not now, maybe, but when the going gets tough you might think otherwise." The old top kick was profoundly streetwise.

Jackson didn't back off. "It's my ass, and I'm not about to have a 'Dropped on Request' stamped in my OQR. One of those stamps and I'll never see another promotion." A DOR told everyone, everywhere, that the receiver was too much of a feather merchant to make it through training.

"Dooly," Colonel Paulon called.

"Yes, sir."

"Get Mr. Jackson a shirt with sergeant's chevrons on it. He's reporting for duty."

TWENTY-FIVE

Platoon 68-097, Schools Battalion, Quantico, Virginia

0800, February 29, 1968

THE EIGHTY-SIX OFFICER candidates who formed Platoon 68-097 stood in four lines facing the front door of the Armory, a Quonset hut distinguishable from the school's other buildings only by its sign.

"Candy-dates," the drill instructor yelled. "You will file through the door, and you will, by God, stay in line until you are done. Inside you will receive one rifle, caliber 7.62 mm, M14. This is an individual shoulder weapon of incredible power. It fires the 7.62 NATO round at 850 meters per second. It's deadly accurate to 500 meters, and in the hands of an expert rifleman, which none of you shitbirds are, it's capable of a maximum sustained rate of fire of 700 rounds per minute. The by-God Commandant believes it's the ultimate combat weapon."

This was their fourth stop of the morning. Since reveille at 0400 the men had been fed, shorn with the requisite buzz cut at the barbershop, and heard a welcome-to-training speech delivered by Lieutenant Colonel Paulon. Most of the candidates were still dressed in the civilian clothes they had worn to camp. Four, however, were wearing uniforms.

Jackson had asked for utilities back at Paulon's office because he didn't think they would call attention to his service in 'Nam. The challenge would come—of that he was certain—but not until later. When it did, he planned to play the role he had signed on for. He hoped it would be enough to keep the DIs off his back.

Shit, he thought when he looked down the line of men to his right. *That's Bill Williams.* Jackson didn't recognize his friend at first because the new haircut made a huge difference in his appearance. He was just another face Jackson had encountered somewhere and didn't know well enough to remember. Knowing Williams was in the platoon scared the shit out of Jackson.

"What the fuck are you looking at, asshole?" The platoon's drill instructor, Staff Sergeant Parish, saw Jackson staring at the other candidate and moved his face to within an inch of Jackson's nose.

"Sir, nothing, sir." Jackson responded loudly, his eyes fixed on a point over the DI's shoulder. He'd seen Parish coming toward him and braced himself for the onslaught.

"What's your name, candy-date?"

"*Sir,* Jackson, Paul A., *sir!*" Jackson knew he was in for it. Parish was going to make him an example.

"Jackson, you're one of the assholes who doesn't like being an NCO. Right?"

"*Sir,* yes, sir . . . 'er, no, *sir.*"

"Well which is it, asshole? Yes or no?" This was the opportunity Parish had been waiting for. There were four former NCOs in the platoon. If he showed the college boys he wasn't going to cut his former peers any slack, they wouldn't expect any for themselves. His job just became a lot easier.

"Sir, I liked being a sergeant just fine, sir."

"Well, why are you here, shithead?" Parish enjoyed landing on rank grabbers. Like thousands of other staff NCOs he thought of noncoms as the backbone of the Marine Corps.

"Sir, I was ordered here, sir." It was time for Jackson to get it out in the open. He knew the DIs would find out his story as soon as they read the entries in the phony records the first sergeant drew up yesterday.

Parish smiled. "What do you mean, you were ordered here?"

"Sir, the commanding general, 3rd Marine Division, ordered me here, sir." *Fuck this asshole. Giving trainees a hard time might be part of his job, but he shouldn't enjoy it.*

"The 3rd Division's in Vietnam, asshole. Don't fuckin' lie to me." Parish was now so close to Jackson that his "Smokey" pressed against the candidate's forehead.

"Sir, I was with the 26th Marines in Phu Bai."

"Yeah? Doin' what? You a REMF?" Parish was rocked back onto his heels at what he'd gotten into. This game wasn't playing out the way he needed it to. Every candidate was listening. He needed to discredit Jackson or risk making him the unofficial leader of the platoon.

"Sir, I was a sniper attached to a special long-range reconnaissance group." *Eat shit and die, asshole. You keep playing this game and you're the one who's going to end up looking bad.*

Parish wisely ended the exchange, but this was a long way from over. He would continue when a better opportunity presented itself. He turned, called the platoon to attention, and marched them toward the mess hall. "Double time."

What a prick, thought Jackson.

Parish saw Jackson raise his weapon to the position of "trail arms" and the rest of the platoon copy his movement. Now he was really pissed. "Lunch," Parish said, "for everyone except those of you I identified as fat bodies, will be roast beef and mashed potatoes, complete with salad, bread and butter, cut vegetables, and condiments. There's water, milk, and coffee to wash it down. Take all you want, but eat all you take. All fat bodies will eat only salad and drink black coffee or water."

Jackson sat next to the drink pitchers. He knew that those who weren't among the first to partake wouldn't get any. He poured himself a glass of water and a cup of coffee.

"What're you doing here?"

The whisper startled Jackson and took his attention from his food to the eyes of the candidate sitting across from him. It was Bill Williams. "What does it look like?"

"I thought you were already an officer."

"I am, but no one's supposed to know it. The colonel fixed it so I could be trained just like the rest of you. This way I won't interfere with your training."

"How would you interfere? I don't get it."

"You don't think Parish would've yelled at me if he knew I was an officer, do you?"

"I guess not."

"What he was doing was training the entire platoon through me. The exchange was meant for you to hear. He was telling you that not even a former NCO, which he believes me to be, is going to get a break, so don't you college boys expect one."

"Well, you're here, and I like the idea of having a friend around."

"That's a bad idea, Bill."

Williams' surprise showed. "Why?"

"Parish has singled me out to use as an example. When he has a look at my records he's going to know he made a mistake in doing that. He isn't the type who likes to make mistakes, so he's going to take his anger out on me and everyone around me. So we're not friends. Understand?"

"Well, screw you."

"Look. I'm only trying to keep you from becoming one of Parish's scapegoats. He'll be a lot harder on you if he thinks we're friends. It won't be long until we get some time off, then we'll head back up to D.C. and lift some more skirts."

The fact that his friendship wasn't being rejected pleased Williams. "Great."

After lunch, the platoon marched back to their quarters and learned how to disassemble and clean their weapons. Following the five-minute lecture Parish presented on cleaning the M14, the platoon got their buckets and sat on the road to clean rifles.

Moving to where Jackson was seated, Parish said, "Follow me, asshole."

When he got to the DI's hut, Jackson banged his fist on the door three times, centered himself in the open door frame, and yelled, "Sir. Candidate Jackson requests permission to enter the drill instructor's quarters, sir."

"Get in here, shitball."

When Jackson entered, Parish was sitting behind a large desk.

"Sir, Candidate Jackson reporting to the drill instructor as ordered, sir."

"Let's knock off the shit for a minute, Jackson. We need to talk before this goes any further."

Jackson didn't speak.

"There are four NCOs in the platoon," Parish said. "I wasn't sure which one you were until we left the Armory."

Jackson didn't reply.

"Are you going to give me trouble, Jackson?"

"That's not why I'm here."

"Just why are you here?" Parish persisted. "And save the 'I was ordered here' bullshit for someone who believes it."

"That's the truth. I was ordered here."

"You didn't volunteer?"

"I signed a volunteer slip after they asked me to, and I attended a screening board, but I *was* ordered here."

"Why did you give me a hard time this morning?"

"That wasn't my intention. I answered your questions honestly." *And you deserved what you got,* thought Jackson.

Parish thought a long time before accepting Jackson's statement. "The story I get is you were the only survivor at a firebase that was overrun."

"There was one more." Jackson's voice came across as far more severe than he intended.

"How'd *you* make it out?"

The question implied Jackson was a coward. *Truth time.* He told Parish about Duc Lo without slanting anything in his favor. The DI needed to make up his own mind.

"The other story is you have someone in a high place watching over you—a 'rabbi.' Every drill instructor in Quantico despises rabbis."

"I don't have anyone like that."

"Bullshit! I hate liars. Let me make things perfectly clear to you, Jackson. I don't need you making things difficult when I'm training this platoon. You stay out of my way, do what everybody else does, and you just might make it through. You step out of line, just once, and I'll land on you like a ton of bricks. Do I make myself clear?"

"Crystal."

"Good. Now get your ass outta here."

Jackson came to attention, completed a textbook about face, and marched back into the street.

TWENTY-SIX

Platoon 68-097 Quarters, Quantico, Virginia

0800, March 14, 1968

THE NEXT TWO WEEKS passed quickly. OCS included much of the same training Jackson had endured in boot camp in San Diego, but it also provided classes, physical demands, and demonstrations that were never part of recruit training. Out of Parish's earshot Jackson told candidates who complained about the long hours and strict discipline how survival in combat depended on teamwork. He worked with everyone until all understood why it was necessary to respond immediately and without question to every order. He also told them what would happen if anyone didn't: immediate punishment for everyone in the platoon.

"What more can we do?" Williams moaned. "I've had immediate response hammered into my head by hundreds of hours of close-order drill. Now, when I hear 'right face' my right foot automatically turns ninety degrees to my left."

"We've practiced so hard," Simmons, the 1st Squad leader, chimed in, "that the entire drill maneuver sounds like a single man is marching. Everyone's heels strike the pavement at the same instant. Not a single head moves when we shift our weapons from position to position, and our bodies move in a single fluid motion. Actually, it's kind of cool to hear one sharp *bang* instead of the *rat-a-tat-tat* we made when we first started."

"Having DIs move from candidate to candidate dishing out bullshit gripes my ass, though," Williams said bitterly. "They're a bunch of cold-hearted bastards."

"I suppose," Simmons said. "But it works. Look at us. In only two weeks we've come together as a unit. Christ, we eat together, shower together, and even, well . . . shit together. And in every action the DIs are reinforcing the importance of even the most basic action. Nothing's overlooked . . . nothing."

Jackson frowned. "You're right. I couldn't believe they'd do it here, but the first time we shit they made as big a production of it as the DIs did back in 'Dago."

Williams jumped in. "I couldn't, and still can't, believe the Crotch is worried about making sure everybody shits 'in a military manner.'"

Jackson laughed. "Here it doesn't mean much. We get six minutes a day to perform. But in combat, time can be damned critical. If you're in the bush, you have to get the job done quickly. It's not dignified for an officer to get shot with his pants down." He enjoyed being the teacher. "Just keep this in mind. The drill instructors are always on the lookout for anything they can use to drive home the importance of discipline. Fall out on a run and they'll make you carry your rifle at port arms and run your ass around and around the platoon until you pass out."

Williams pushed out a petulant lower lip. "The inspections are the worst. Parish looks for everything."

Jackson continued. "Inspections are damned important too. We all need to know how to clean our gear and arrange it properly. As an officer you'll be expected to anticipate action and make sure your men are prepared."

A candidate named Martin pushed his way into the group. "Parish is strictly by the book, ain't he? I'll bet he refers to the Platoon Leader's Manual before he mounts his old lady, just to make sure he performs in a precise military manner."

★

On a Saturday morning in early April, toward the end of the training period, the platoon was ready for the weekly personnel inspection when Parish yelled, "Attention on deck."

Out of the corner of his eye Jackson saw the inspecting officer, clad in well-tailored trops, carefully scrutinizing the line of candidates. As the inspection party finished with the candidate to his left and moved directly in front of him, Jackson snatched the M14 through the first half of the inspection arms maneuver and presented his rifle, bolt open, to 1st Lt. Peter R. Dudley, USMC.

"How are you, Jackson?" Dudley sneered. "Enjoying being an enlisted man again?"

"Yes, sir."

"You certainly look different than you did when we met before. No ribbons, no bars, no pretty medals."

"Yes, sir," Jackson said pensively. *The shit is about to hit the fan.*

The officer looked Jackson's weapon over once, and then again. "Did you know they transferred me the same day you arrived?"

"No, sir." *This is one of those moments when honesty isn't going to be the best policy. I need to cover my ass big-time.*

Dudley looked Jackson in the eye. "They did. And I think you're the reason."

"I don't know what the lieutenant's talking about, sir."

The lieutenant beckoned Parish with his hand. "The lieutenant's rifle is dirty and he needs a shave. Make sure you get that down, Staff Sergeant."

If looks could kill, both Jackson and Dudley would have dropped where they stood. There was silence in the barracks as the other candidates listened to the exchange.

Parish kept his face expressionless, but inside he was seething—and scared. It seemed Jackson hadn't told him the whole truth on the first day of OCS. And now this zero had stirred up a hornet's nest.

Dudley returned Jackson's rifle, turned on his heel, and immediately left the barracks, saying over his shoulder, "That'll be all, Sergeant."

Parish marched to the center of the Quonset hut before speaking. "Everyone without demerits is dismissed for the weekend. That means everybody . . . *except Jackson.* Put away your gear, mister, and report to the platoon office immediately."

As soon as Parish left, Bill Williams and several others pushed into Jackson's area.

Williams spoke first. "What was all that about?"

"It's better if we don't discuss it," Jackson said forcefully. "There's nothing you need to know." The other candidates backed away from the one man in the platoon they had all respected and listened to.

Williams persisted. "Why not?"

Another candidate stepped up behind Jackson. "We have a right to know."

Jackson turned around. "You don't have a right to know anything. Look. The shit's going to hit the fan, and I don't want any of you splattered."

Williams would not be put off. "If these assholes don't understand how much you've helped us . . . then fuck the Marine Corps."

Jackson touched his friend's arm to recognize the gesture. "Thanks, but it's because you're my friends that I don't want you involved. You've come too far. You're all going to make fine officers, so stay out of this—and away from me—until it gets worked out. That, in case you didn't recognize it, gentlemen, is an order."

"You can't order us to do shit," another candidate said.

Williams immediately supported Jackson. "Yes, he can. He *is* an officer, and he's been one all along. Yet he's never asked for special consideration, has always been ready to help us, and never made anyone feel inferior. Now it's our turn. We can best help Paul by minding our own business."

Jackson left the barrack feeling good about having friends like Bill Williams.

Parish was mad as hell. "Mr. Jackson, or is it going to be lieutenant now?"

"Whatever you say, Sergeant." Jackson didn't bother to respond like a normal trainee. He knew it wouldn't help.

Parish fairly shouted, "What the fuck's going on?"

"You tell me, Sergeant."

"Don't be a wiseass, Jackson. You're a fucking officer, and I demand you tell me what you're doing here."

Jackson's eyes grew cold. "That's enough. I *am* an officer, and I don't have to take this shit from any staff NCO, under any circumstances. Shut your mouth, Sergeant, before you say or do something you'll regret." Jackson's eyes were narrow slits, and the menace in his voice made it clear he was in charge. "Sit down and listen."

Parish sat down but couldn't contain the bluster. He swept his hand across the desk and knocked several training records to the floor.

Jackson assumed command. "Parish, you will sit there, with your mouth shut, and listen to me before this gets out of hand. There are other people involved, and if you stir the shit too high, they're going to get splattered. That wouldn't look good for them, or for you."

Getting a grip on himself, Parish said, "Just what are you doing here, Lieutenant? And I want the whole truth this time." He looked at Jackson with utter contempt, certain that the young lieutenant was here to undermine his performance as a drill instructor. "It's common practice to 'plant' officers to obtain firsthand evidence regarding the treatment of candidates. Is that why you're here?"

Jackson sat down and explained what Dudley had done that resulted in his transfer and why Jackson had been placed in the platoon as a regular candidate. "You can verify this by calling the first sergeant, but keep it to yourself until you have. A lot of people have worked damned hard to put me in this school, and I don't want any of them hurt because some asshole can't keep his mouth shut. Dudley's accusations are meaningless unless they're corroborated, and no one will or can do that except you. And keep this in mind, Parish. If you open your mouth and I wash out, I revert to a lieutenant. Once that happens, I'll make it my life's mission to fuck you so hard your head will spin."

Parish looked at Jackson warily. "Why should I believe you?"

"Because I don't have anything to gain. I came here as an officer, voluntarily entered training as a regular candidate, and have never asked for special treatment. The only thing I want to do is graduate and to return to my unit. I don't give a shit about you, and I'll forget all of the stupid crap you've pulled the instant I leave."

First Lieutenant Dudley stuck his head into the platoon office in time to hear Jackson's last words. "So, that's how you see it, Jackson. You're going to cover up what Paulon did to me."

"Colonel Paulon didn't do anything to you," Jackson said. "You did it to yourself. You went over his head and told Regiment he wasn't trustworthy. Who the hell do you think you are?"

Dudley yelled so loud spittle shot out of his mouth and ran down his chin. "I'm your superior officer, that's who I am."

Jackson wasn't buying in. "You're senior, all right, but I seriously doubt if you're superior to anything on two legs." He turned back to Parish. "Sergeant, you will telephone the first sergeant and explain what transpired here." The tone in his voice made it clear to Parish that this was an order to be accomplished without question.

Dudley countermanded Jackson's order. "You'll do no such thing." He was in a rage. His face was bright red, and sweat ran down his neck to darken the top of his shirt collar.

After a quick look at both officers, Parish made his decision.

Ten minutes later, a jeep pulled up outside the platoon office and disgorged the commanding officer of the Schools Battalion and his first sergeant. Both were wildly pissed off. They stormed into the building to find an unexpected scene. First Lieutenant Dudley was sitting in a chair holding a white handkerchief against his lower lip. The color of the linen clearly indicated that the officer had recently bled profusely. Candidate Jackson was nowhere to be seen.

"What's going on here, Lieutenant?" The colonel's tone was deathly calm. Paulon knew he couldn't let his rage show. "Are you trying to make trouble for me again?" The veiled anger made Sergeant Parish's asshole slam shut.

Dudley moved the rag away from his mouth, and the colonel could see the source of the blood. "Sir?"

"Who hit you, Lieutenant?"

"No one, sir."

"Do you think I'm stupid?" Paulon asked in a tone so menacing that Parish paled. "Someone hit you in the mouth. By the looks of it, damned hard. Your lip's busted, and there's blood everywhere. You aren't so stupid you don't understand a simple question, are you?"

A shocked Dudley barely responded. "No, sir."

The colonel asked Parish, "Where is Candidate Jackson?"

He was pleased to hear a calm, professional response from the sergeant. "He has returned to his duties, sir."

"Very good," the colonel said. "Whatever has been going on is obviously over. Tell me what that was."

"Begging the colonel's pardon, sir," Parish began, "the matter's been rectified, sir." He indicated the lieutenant and pointed to his own lip.

First Sergeant Mickelson spoke for the first time. "Are you sure?"

"Absolutely, sir."

The colonel looked at Parish's hands.

"Not on your life, Skipper," Parish said to the unspoken question, and the colonel knew instantly who did hit Dudley . . . Jackson.

Paulon's voice was viciously cold. "You better hope not. If you hit him, your ass is grass and I'm a lawnmower." He turned back to Dudley. "What happened to your lip, Lieutenant?"

"I fell and struck the edge of the desk, sir."

"You did what?"

Dudley repeated his answer.

The colonel turned to Parish. "Why'd you call us down here, Sergeant?"

"We thought there was a problem, sir, but Candidate Jackson was kind enough to clear the matter up." The statement did nothing to conceal the absolute joy he had experienced from seeing Jackson hit the stupid zero. In fact, he hit Dudley several times, but only one blow left a mark. The other two were delivered to soft parts of the body where they would make Dudley sore as hell but wouldn't leave bruises. The speed and intensity of the attack had startled Parish, and what Jackson said to Dudley as he lay on the floor still rang in his ears.

"If you so much as utter a single word about this to anyone, I'll fuck you up so bad you'll eat through a straw the rest of your miserable life. Do you understand me, you worthless cocksucker?" After he received the answer he wanted, Jackson kicked Dudley hard enough in the solar plexus to make him shit himself. Parish enjoyed that too. He led the first sergeant to a corner and related the entire incident, and his plans for keeping Jackson in the platoon.

Returning to the colonel, the first sergeant said, "Staff Sergeant Parish informs me he and Lieutenant Dudley have been discussing the lieutenant's desire to receive orders to WestPac, sir."

The colonel nodded and the two men departed, leaving Lieutenant Dudley to contemplate his future.

TWENTY-SEVEN

Regimental Headquarters, Marine Corps Base, Quantico, Virginia

1430, April 4, 1968

DUDLEY HAD BEEN SITTING in the sergeant major's office for more than an hour, and he was pissed. *The colonel's in. He walked right by me going into his office, but he ignored me. Why hasn't he seen me yet?*

After ten minutes more the sergeant major's voice barked his contempt. "The colonel will see you now."

Fuck you, you old bastard, Dudley mused. *You have no right to talk to me like that.* He entered the office and reported to the colonel like an Annapolis plebe. "First Lieutenant Dudley reporting to the commanding officer as ordered, sir." Colonel Greene didn't look up. *Why hasn't he given me ease? Even severe protocol would allow the position of parade rest. He should have asked me to sit down by now. Why is he upset?* "It's sure hot outside, sir."

Colonel Greene didn't trust himself to speak just yet. He was still steamed, and the cause of his anger was standing before him. After getting his ass reamed out by General Willobouy, Greene ripped Colonel Paulon and First Sergeant Mickelson new assholes for getting caught putting an officer into an OCS class. Up to now Greene had completely supported their little charade because he understood it was done for the good of the Corps. That, however, didn't change the fact they'd been caught at it. After a moment he said, "I don't recall giving you permission to speak, Lieutenant."

HQMC had recently notified Greene of his selection to brigadier general. He was marking time before being transferred overseas, where he hoped to be assigned as the assistant division commander. And he did not want to have to deal with this pissant of a lieutenant.

Dudley immediately snapped to attention. "I beg the colonel's pardon, sir."

Finally Colonel Greene began. "Lieutenant, you've been a source of difficulty since the day you reported. I've read your OQR and found it lacking. Let's start by you telling me how an Annapolis graduate could be so screwed up?"

"I don't understand, sir."

"How about the fitness report you received from General Toomey?"

Dudley brightened with unexpected enthusiasm. "Yes, sir. I've wanted to discuss his fitness report for quite some time, sir."

"I'll bet you have. I've read your rebuttal statement, so it's not necessary to cover those areas."

"Yes, sir. May I say that I believe the general erred when he wrote his evaluation, sir?"

"Are you saying a general officer didn't thoroughly evaluate the circumstances before he wrote a negative fitness report? Is that what I'm hearing, Lieutenant?"

"No, sir," Dudley said quickly. "Nothing like that, sir. But there are two sides to every story, and I don't think mine was adequately considered, sir." Dudley felt the office grow warm and pulled at the collar of his shirt.

"You are at attention, mister."

Dudley immediately snapped his right hand back along the seam of his trouser. "Yes, sir. It's just that it's hot in here, sir."

"That's your problem, Lieutenant. Orders good for other people aren't quite enough for you. Is that right? And how dare you question the integrity of a general officer? I've known General Toomey for many years, and I'm positive he wrote your fitness report only after a great deal of investigation."

"Yes, sir."

Greene stood up. "How did you screw yourself up so badly? I graduated from Annapolis, and I should have been proud to have you in my command."

"I don't know what to say, sir."

"I was more than willing to give you a chance to overcome the general's fitness report, but this recent fiasco is the proverbial last straw. If resignations of officers who haven't completed a tour in Vietnam weren't frozen, I would demand yours right now."

"Yes, sir."

"How dare you even suggest that Colonel Paulon would stoop to such an outrageous act? The idea that a highly decorated field-grade officer would subject a junior lieutenant to the humiliation of Officer Candidate School is reprehensible. I looked the other way when you accused Colonel Paulon of not being trustworthy, and for that I can only pray he will one day forgive me."

"Yes, sir."

"If you say 'sir' to me one more time, I'm going to forget I'm a gentleman and kick the livin' shit out of you. Just shut your mouth."

Lieutenant Dudley's sphincter muscle closed tightly around his throat as the colonel's threat hit home.

Greene knew Dudley's report to be the only one that remotely approached the truth. While the other four reports supported one another, each told a version concocted by First Sergeant Mickelson. "I have four other reports that are similar enough to make yours appear like a bald-faced lie. Still, I wouldn't have said anything if you hadn't submitted your report to General Willobouy. I suppose you think I should court-martial these four men, Dudley?"

Dudley stammered. "I don't know what to suggest, sir. I reported only what I know to be true."

"Shut your face, mister." Losing control again, Greene went behind his desk and sat on his hands. He waited until he was calm before continuing. "What I can do—what I *will* do—is see to it that you will not further complicate the orderly process of this command. I have secured orders for you to the 3rd Marine Division. I will write your performance review and include a statement that suggests you never be allowed to command men in the field. With two negative reports in your jacket, your chances of promotion are less than zero.

"You must understand what that means. But just in case you don't, let me spell it out. You'll arrive in Da Nang and your OQR will be reviewed before you're assigned. That will cause your orders to be modified to someplace like Special Services as the officer in charge of issuing snowshoes or some rear-echelon job reviewing reports and incidents that involved real men; if you're lucky you'll end up as an Intel pogue—they're all assholes. After your tour, perhaps you'll see the wisdom in resigning from the service."

Dudley's voice quavered. "Colonel Greene, there's obviously been a misunderstanding."

"There . . . is . . . no . . . misunderstanding, Lieutenant."

"Perhaps I could explain my report to General Willobouy."

Colonel Greene let the lieutenant's suggestion fall flat on the floor. He couldn't believe the bastard's effrontery, but he didn't say any more. Instead, he picked up his phone and asked to be connected to General Willobouy's aide. "Good morning, Jack. Colonel Greene for the general." When Willobouy came on the line Greene said, "I have Dudley in my office. He feels you will understand his report far better than I, sir."

After a slight pause to hear the general's response Greene flipped the phone's intercom switch and the general's voice filled the room. "Lieutenant, you pick up your orders and get on a plane this afternoon. If I have any reason to think you're on this base after 1600, I'll have you arrested. Do I make myself clear?"

Lieutenant Dudley's face went white.

The colonel thanked the general and hung up the phone. "You can pick up your orders from the adjutant on your way out. Dismissed."

TWENTY-EIGHT

Platoon 68-097, Schools Battalion, Quantico, Virginia

1600, April 10, 1968

WHEN OFFICER CANDIDATE Jackson returned to his barrack from Regiment he still didn't know his status. A notice was posted to the barrack door, and he read it carefully before he entered.

> This begins the last part of the training cycle. Starting tomorrow, training will be altered to allow every candidate to understand the reality facing him after he is commissioned. This "reality break" will be provided in the form of a ninety-six-hour pass for all candidates not subject to extra duty. Those subject individuals will spend the weekend working in the area or appearing in front of the Performance Review Board.
> —J. A. Parish, Staff Sergeant, USMC

Jackson closed the door behind him and spoke quietly to Williams. "If I'm boarded, I won't return and I won't go back to Recon. That isn't what I want, but I have no choice. Dudley's fiasco isn't over."

Having to face the board was a distinct possibility. Jackson had told Colonel Paulon that he struck Dudley, and Paulon had informed Colonel Greene. Such conduct was not acceptable between enlisted Marines; for officers, it was always considered conduct unbecoming and rarely forgiven. The best Jackson could hope for was to be returned to Phu Bai at the rank he held when he left, and then be asked to resign on the completion of his tour. The worst would see him assigned to the infantry as a platoon commander.

Jackson railed, "I should've killed the miserable shit!"

"Why *did* you hit him?" Williams asked.

Jackson shrugged. "He was out of control, and it seemed like the right thing to do."

When Colonel Paulon had appeared with First Sergeant Mickelson, Jackson knew he was dead meat. They had stopped on the pretense of providing a ride to headquarters so Jackson and Parish could file their reports, but when the two entered the car, Mickelson told them what they were to write in their "official" reports.

The first sergeant brooked no argument. "You will use your own words, but you will stay within the framework I provided. Any deviation will be dealt with severely."

Colonel Paulon reinforced the order. "Jackson, I expect your absolute obedience to those instructions. You will forget you struck Dudley. I will deal with you on that issue. After you submit your report you will return to your duties."

"Aye, aye, sir." Jackson had not deviated from Mickelson's framework on his official report of the incident. While writing a false report didn't please him, he wasn't prepared to go against the colonel. Orders were orders. When you were given one you said, "Aye-aye, sir," and followed it.

A despondent Jackson told Williams, "I figure they've got to drop me. I can't see how they can do anything else."

"You don't know that. Quit bitchin' and get with the program. What is it you're always saying? 'Worry about those things you can control.' You better get your head and ass wired together because Parish is conducting the pre-liberty inspection."

Jackson smiled. "It's a real pain in the ass to stand an inspection before being ordered to the Performance Board. And while I'm wallopin' pots in the mess hall, you pricks will be on liberty."

Williams surprised Jackson by grabbing him in the ribs.

"What did you do that for?"

"Hey, take it easy, buddy."

"For the last time, Bill, I'm *not* your buddy." Seeing the hurt in his friend's eyes, Jackson sighed and relented. "Do you know how the Corps defines the word?"

"Of course I do. A friend, someone you pal around with."

"No, I mean the Old Corps definition."

"No, but I'm sure you're gonna' enlighten this poor, ignorant soul."

"A buddy, in Old Corps terms, is a guy who goes to town, gets two blow jobs, then comes back and gives you one." Jackson laughed to take out the sting. In fact, he was touched by Williams' loyalty and support. "You're going to make a good officer, Bill. A little dumb, maybe, but you're definitely someone who tries to do what's right."

"What the hell does that mean?"

"When I was on the shit list, I told you to leave me alone because I was afraid you might be found guilty by association; birds of a feather and all that shit."

"Yeah, and I told you to piss off."

"That's what I mean. You haven't deviated an iota in our relationship, and that's why I know you'll be a good officer. You do the right thing. Now," he said, bringing the conversation back from the maudlin, "run another rag over your shoes and straighten your gig line. What kind of officer are you gonna be, anyway?"

"One smart enough not to get caught up in all of the shit you seem to land in."

Staff Sergeant Parish came into the barrack just then, and one of the candidates yelled, "Attention on deck."

"Attention to orders."

Jackson knew this was it. He was going to the Performance Board. There was no way of avoiding it; even worse, he knew he deserved it.

Parish raised his voice. "As you know, one candidate in this platoon will receive special recognition for his outstanding contribution. The determination of who he is comes from his training record, marksmanship scores, leadership qualities, and, to a very small degree, your votes."

Jackson wanted Parish to get it over with. He didn't want to wait all night for the inevitable.

"Class 68-097, greet your honor graduate, Paul Jackson."

The platoon pounded Jackson on the back and offered congratulations.

Parish let the celebration carry on for a minute, then reassumed control. "As you were. How the hell do you ever expect to command Marines if you behave like that?" He grinned as he voiced the insult and marched in front of Jackson. Holding out the platoon guidon, he offered his hand. "Congratulations, mister. If you can't find your way to the front of the platoon, I hear there are plenty of first lieutenants ready to assist."

Jackson took the outstretched guidon. "Thank you, Sergeant."

He marched to his new position in the front of the platoon as its officially recognized leader, held the guidon high above his head, and yelled, "68-097 . . . *Semper Fi!*"

He was immediately answered with the crashing echo of fifty-two other voices: "*Ooh-rah!*"

When the clamor died down, Parish spoke again.

"Attention to orders. The following men will report to the Performance Review Board at 0800 Friday." The list of three names did not include Officer Candidate Jackson. "There's one last thing," Parish said. "The selection of this platoon's honor graduate marks the first time since I've been a drill instructor that the recipient was elected unanimously. Congratulations, Mr. Jackson."

After the inspection, Officer Candidate Williams walked over to the newly appointed honor man. "I knew they wouldn't shit-can you. Who else are they going to find stupid enough to run around the boonies looking for dinks?"

Jackson's face shone with excitement. "Let's go find a telephone. I've got a girl to call."

"Great! Then we'll get the hell out of here."

"Now you're talking. I want to buy my uniforms in a special place. Ever heard of Saks or Brooks Brothers?"

Williams smiled. "They're in New York, my friend. I know them well."

TWENTY-NINE

Hotel Delmonico, New York City

0720, April 12, 1968

WHEN JACKSON CALLED the number Karen gave him after their night together, he got disappointing news. "She's in Los Angeles," he told Williams after hanging up the phone. "She's not coming back to Washington until two days *after* we return to Quantico. Shit," he added. "I've never been able to deal with female rejection."

"Yeah, right," Williams snickered, "and I suppose it happens all the time?"

"More'n you know, but not as frequently as you'd like to think."

Their luck didn't improve on the flight to Kennedy. The stewardesses on the Eastern Airlines commuter flight were too harried to pay any attention to the amorous advances of two horny Marines.

As they walked down the concourse and into the airport, Williams said, "Okay. New York's my town, so I'm in charge."

Jackson laughed derisively. "Sure."

"We'll take a cab to the Delmonico on Madison Avenue," Williams said firmly. "From there we'll be within walking distance of Brooks Brothers. The hotel's one of the classiest places in New York. We'll get a suite overlooking Central Park and have one of the best views in the city."

When their cab stopped in front of the elegant marquee, a doorman dressed like an eighteenth-century Russian tsar opened the door. One look at the passengers told him they were not the sort of people who could afford the Delmonico. He spoke haughtily in a nasal voice. "May I help you, *sir?* Are you sure you're in the *right place?*"

Williams smiled. "We'll be checking in, *boy.*"

"Do you have a reservation, *sir?*"

"No, but I can assure you the management will be happy we're here."

Williams got out of the cab and grabbed his valpak. Ripping off a twenty, he waved the tip into the cabby's hands, picked up the suitcase, and headed up the stairs, leaving nothing for the doorman to carry. Jackson followed with the would-be tsar in hot pursuit.

Williams moved confidently across the enormous lobby to the front desk, grabbed a registration card, and filled it out without receiving so much as a nod from the clerk.

When the desk clerk finally deigned to notice the two officer candidates, he took his time before moving in their direction. Pissed off, Williams flipped the registration card at the clerk, who watched as it skidded to the floor behind the registration desk.

After daintily retrieving the card, the clerk said, "May I help you, *gentlemen?*" He looked down his nose at them, one second away from having Security rid the lobby of the riffraff standing before him.

Again Williams picked up the ball. "We'd like a suite; a two-bedroom set, if you please."

"We have only the penthouse available, sir," responded the effeminate desk clerk, "and I rather doubt you can afford it."

"Don't you worry about it, sister," Williams said.

"Where the hell are we?" Jackson asked.

Williams smiled. "We, sir, are in the Delmonico, Manhattan's finest hotel. Look around; isn't it beautiful?"

Jackson panicked. "What's a place like this cost? I only brought enough money to buy uniforms and get laid. I can't afford this."

Williams grinned. "Don't you worry about it. Our man here is going to give us his best rate. Aren't you, *sweetheart?*" Williams flipped a gold American Express card to the now-seething desk clerk and gave him a phone number to call for verification.

As the clerk went to the telephone, Jackson once again cornered Williams.

"I'm not into mooching off my friends, Bill. I've told you that before."

"Oh, so we're friends now?"

"I'm serious. I don't want to rely on your generosity."

"I said not to sweat the small shit. Look, you've been shepherding me through the perils of Quantico for the past six weeks. Now I get to return the favor. Relax as I waltz you through the wonders of the West Side."

The desk clerk returned with the hotel manager in tow. The older man quickly took control of the situation. He introduced himself and offered his personal assistance. "We're very happy to have you with us, Mr. Williams," the fat man slobbered. "Had we known you were coming, sir, we would have prepared a special greeting. Will the penthouse suit your purposes, sir?"

Williams held back. "Yes. That will be fine. Please have someone see to our luggage and have a valet report to the room in thirty minutes with some civilian clothes. Size sixteen shirts, and trousers, say, size 32-32. We'll need matching shoes. Loafers will do, definitely nothing with shoestrings. Oh, and have room service bring up several bottles of your best Scotch. Chivas will do, but GlenDronach would be better." Williams smiled and gave the gaping desk clerk the finger.

"Yes, sir. Right away, sir," blubbered the manager as Williams turned grandly from the desk and made his way toward the elevators.

Jackson grabbed his arm. "Jesus, Bill, let's not get carried away. How are we going to pay for all of the stuff you just ordered?"

Williams stopped dead still in the middle of the lobby. "Look around you, Paul. What do you see?"

Jackson did a quick scan of the lobby. "The most expensive place I've ever been in."

"That's right, and it's mine."

"What the hell do you mean, *it's yours?*"

"The hotel. My father's firm owns the dump. I own 25 percent of the firm; therefore I own this hotel, or at least 25 percent of it."

"Jesus Christ. You're *that* rich? What the hell are you doin' hanging around with me? I don't have any money, let alone the kind that can afford this."

"I'm hanging around with you, you dumb son of a bitch, because I want to. I don't give a shit if you have money or not. I've got enough for both of us. What I don't have is balls, or at least I didn't until you showed me how to grow some. So knock off the poor-mouth routine and hang on. I'm going to show you the time of your life."

"What the hell," said Jackson. "Let 'er rip." Both men laughed hard enough to turn heads from all points in the lobby.

Jackson pushed open the door to the suite and sucked in his breath. He walked immediately to the huge floor-to-ceiling windows and then took a step back. It felt like he was standing on air. He had thought the hotel in Washington was amazing, but it was nothing compared with the Delmonico.

Williams spoke to the bellman. "We haven't eaten. Have the kitchen rustle up a couple of thick steaks with baked potatoes? Throw in some fresh salad and a green vegetable . . . steamed broccoli would be nice." He handed over a twenty-dollar bill and nodded toward the door, then sat on a plush sofa and picked up the phone.

Jackson left the windows to explore the suite. He was blown away. The place made him feel like a real hayseed. The luxury surrounding him was beyond anything he had ever dreamed. "Christ, Bill. Have you seen this place? There's a friggin' refrigerator completely stocked with champagne and things with names I can't pronounce. We're going to have some fun here, by God."

Williams merely waved his hand to indicate that he wanted something to drink and pointed in the direction of a large room service table laden with scotch bottles. He covered the mouthpiece and said, "Neat."

Jackson crossed the room to the table, guessing that "neat" meant no ice. He poured a liberal amount of GlenDronach into two glasses, brought one to Williams, and sat down with the other in an armchair opposite the sofa. "I'm having a hard time believing you own 25 percent of this," he said as soon as Williams hung up the phone.

Bill leaned back on the couch, drained his glass, and ignored the comment. "Aaah. I'd forgotten what good scotch tastes like. I swear to all the gods ever worshiped I'll never let that happen again."

Jackson laughed. "Goddamn if you're not a friggin' philosopher, too."

Williams' face turned glum. "I haven't had any luck finding locals with talent." He held up his empty glass, and Jackson walked back for the bottle. "So, we're going to have to go hunt up some willing young things on our own, and I have a few ideas about where to find them."

Jackson grew serious. "Bill, what's a place like this really cost?"

Williams jumped off the couch and headed for the bar. "Look, asshole, I told you not to sweat it. You just sit back and let old Bill shepherd you through the small shit."

Jackson didn't back off. "Come on."

"Look, goddamn it. This is the Delmonico. It, along with eighteen other hotels, is part of a trust fund I inherited from my grandfather and is now managed by my Dad's firm. Granddad was into oil with a guy named Rockefeller back in the twenties and made a bundle. He invested in real estate and put his earnings into a trust fund for his only grandchild: me." He emphasized the "me" by jabbing himself in the chest with his thumb.

Jackson's mouth fell open.

"You keep your mouth shut about this," Bill said fiercely. "It's not something I want known. I intend to do my thing in the Corps just like a normal officer. I don't want any special attention, ever."

"I don't get it," Jackson said. "Vietnam's a poor man's war. Everyone who can get away with it is in college somewhere or enjoying a deferment conveniently arranged with their draft board. Why does someone of your means want to be an officer?"

"For the fun, the travel, and . . . the babes. Mostly the babes."

"Bullshit. Money attracts women like a magnet. You don't need to be an officer for that."

Bill paused for a moment before speaking. "Look. I've had everything given to me since I was a kid. There's never been a shortage of people to make sure little Billy got what he wanted. I hate ass-kissers, and for once I want to do something on my own, without any help. Something I can take pride in before all the bloodsuckin' shitballs turn me into a pansy." His honesty was obvious; no one could fake the emotion he showed.

"That's why you thought you needed me?"

"Yeah. I didn't think I could do it without help, so I latched onto you."

Jackson saw the unhappiness his friend's admission caused. "Well, it doesn't look like I've been much help. You're still a shitbird, and you'll probably get shot in the ass by your own troops."

The look of relief that spread across Williams' face made Jackson look away and change the subject. "Come on. I want to eat my steak and then get laid." He grabbed his friend by the arm and pushed him toward the bedroom where the new civilian clothes from the hotel's clothing store awaited.

THIRTY

New York City

2130, April 12, 1968

THE TWO OFFICER CANDIDATES scoured the city looking for acceptable female companionship. Williams decreed, "Acceptable does not mean anything unattached and willing. I take pride in the company I keep, and we're going to be very selective in choosing who we spend time with."

Williams started their foraging in the Delmonico's bar, then led Jackson on a whirlwind tour of New York nightlife. Everywhere they went they ran into women who knew Bill and men who were not happy to have him around. Jackson enjoyed watching the nervous college boys keep a wary eye on their dates. Bill was quite a ladies' man, and Paul was certain the women preferred his company to that of their dates. Jackson kept pace but was out of his comfort zone. Bill's acquaintances talked about everything from Wall Street to which Harvard classmates were making a name for themselves, and he had nothing to add to those conversations.

One woman in particular caught Jackson's eye, but when he engaged her in conversation he came away badly bruised. Looking up at him through long lashes she softly asked, "Where did you matriculate?"

Jackson's response was classic Marine Corps. "Ma'am, I have no plan to matriculate as long as there are beautiful women available." When she finally got the joke she sniffed and walked away.

A friend in one of the clubs asked about their short haircuts. "What're you doing, Bill, trying to set a new trend?" Williams ignored the comment and led Jackson outside. Their next stop was a club called O'Malley's on the lower East Side that had a long line of partygoers waiting out front to get in. Williams ignored the line. He went directly to the doorman and greeted him warmly. "Good to see you again, old boy."

There was no sign of recognition in the doorman's eyes. "Who the fuck are you, asshole?"

"Bill Williams, shithead. Did you go blind or just stupid since we shared a room on the Common?"

The astonished doorman looked hard until recognition set in. "Well, I'll be dipped in shit. Get in there, and take whatever this is with you. You're stinking up the place."

Once inside, Williams walked past a crowd of people waiting for tables and up to a tuxedo-clad man standing behind a small pedestal. Bill handed him something, and the man led him and Jackson immediately to a booth near the stage.

"Who was that?" Jackson asked.

"The owner. I shared a room at Harvard with his son, the doorman, during my freshman and sophomore years. Nice family; you'd like them a lot."

After they had consumed several drinks and danced with a bevy of New York's most available women, Jackson was sure this would be the place where they got lucky. More than twenty women came up to their booth to chat, and everyone was interested in their plans for the evening. Williams, however, decided these women were not right. He rose and guided Jackson through the crowded lobby, past people still waiting to get in.

"What the hell's wrong with you?" Jackson asked when they were outside. "I could have spent the night—hell, the entire weekend—with any of those women. What are you looking for?"

"Patience, my friend. There are women, and then *there are women.*"

"What the hell are you talkin' about?"

"The women in there, my friend, come in two categories. Those who want your money and those who . . . well, want your money. I don't like either type. When I'm interested in a woman it's because she likes *me*, not the soft life she thinks I can provide. I've known bloodsuckers like those all my life, and I'm telling you, none of them is capable of or willing to perform the unspeakable things I intend to accomplish tonight."

"Okay," Jackson said with resignation. "Lead on. I've danced with more beautiful women in the past few hours than I have in my whole life, so I have no complaints."

Williams hailed a cab. "I know just the place to find who we're looking for. Get in." He threw a fifty on the seat and told the hack, "Twenty-One North Sixty-Fifth, and step on it. The night grows short." The driver wasn't rude, but he definitely wasn't friendly either. He pocketed the money and stepped on the gas.

The trip across town, as Williams referred to it, frightened Jackson more than anything he had experienced in 'Nam. He couldn't understand how the driver kept from hitting the parked vehicles they passed. Only inches of air separated the edge of his door and the bumpers of hundreds of cars as the cab weaved through Manhattan at high speed. "*Jesus H. Christ! Tell this guy to slow down!*"

Williams was completely in his element. "Relax. You're gonna make him nervous."

"Nervous? You're worried about *him* gettin' nervous? What about us? I have grander plans for my first night in New York than getting killed."

Williams laughed and sank deeper into the seat.

When the taxi finally stopped, Jackson jumped out and jerked Williams' door open. His eyes almost popped out of his head when Bill showed him a large sign on the rear of the taxi. In letters easily ten inches high it said: "Danger—Do Not Tailgate."

"That ain't no shit," wheezed Jackson.

Williams laughed so hard he almost cried. Pounding Paul on the back, he said, "First time in a gypsy cab, huh, hotshot?"

"Why, you son of a bitch. You asked him to do that."

"No. They always drive like that. I just knew what to expect and enjoyed the experience." He punched Jackson in the arm and motioned for him to follow by jerking his head toward a large brownstone.

When the two friends walked through the hand-carved oak doors, a black man standing six-foot-six who looked like he weighed more than three hundred pounds greeted them. Jackson didn't see an ounce of fat on the guy, just huge, treelike arms . . . one holding up a massive hand. "Ya'll betta stop right theah."

Jackson came to an immediate halt. "No argument here."

Williams, on the other hand, moved directly to the big man. "Hello, Mike," he said. "Nice to see you again. We heard there's a party upstairs."

Williams waved Jackson up to the desk, handed the big man his coat, and signaled for Jackson to do likewise.

"Well, I be dawged. Welcome back, Mr. Williams, suh. I hardly recognized you wit' dat buzz cut. Miz Masterson know you be home?"

Williams laughed. "She will in a few minutes. The ugly guy here is Paul Jackson. He's safe enough for Marjorie's parties."

"If you say so, suh."

Upstairs, an older woman in a maid's uniform greeted him with a kiss. "Oh, welcome home, Master Williams."

Williams gave her a hug and introduced her to Jackson. "This fine creature, Paul, is the great Mrs. Ing. And this," he said, indicating Jackson to her, "is a man of ill repute."

The woman's laughter did nothing to calm Jackson's nerves. "Well," she said, as she showed them into a large room, "you know the rules. There's food and plenty of ladies, but you watch your bad self, big fella." She jabbed Williams in the stomach and gave him another kiss before turning to greet the next guest.

Jackson saw more food laid out in the room than ever before in his life. A large table held a huge turkey, several trays of sliced ham, and a steamship round of beef. Spread in between were a large variety of salads, raw vegetables, condiments, and assorted breads. He started to get a little irritated. "I thought we were going to get laid," he said to Bill. "Food is *not* what I need."

"Relax. An old friend of my father owns this restaurant. This is the best place in town to meet women—at least it was during the years I was in college. Just enjoy the meal and we'll go home lucky. Trust me."

"You know, Williams. My old man had a definition for that phrase."

"Yeah, what was that?"

"He said 'trust me' comes from an ancient Hebrew idiom that loosely translates as 'I'm about to fuck you.'"

"I told you, don't sweat the small shit. New York is different, Paul. Here, people eat their evening meal late. We're here for the busiest part of the evening. Now, sit down."

"These people are too much like you," Jackson said good-naturedly. "Everyone's rich, and by the looks of them, no one really gives a shit about it one way or another. The only person in here I've got anything in common with is you, and that's only because you were stupid enough to join the Crotch."

"Well, this place is not your ordinary restaurant; it's a supper club. After the guests are seated, they alternate between eating and wandering around greeting people they know or wish to. Here, I'll show you."

Jackson watched as Williams got up and spoke to several people. Each time, he nodded his head toward where Paul was sitting.

While Williams was away on one of his visits, a young woman came to the booth and sat down next to him. Jackson thought she was the most beautiful woman he had ever seen. Her long, straight brown hair flowed like silk, and her huge brown eyes sparkled when she talked. Her skin was flawless. When he let his eyes trail down her face and past her lips, he noticed that her sweater and skirt lightly molded a petite body about five feet tall. *She's dressed conservatively, not like the other women in here, and her only jewelry is a simple gold necklace. She's my age and definitely out of place, just like me.*

She talked with an ease Jackson found intoxicating. "How do you know Bill? And what brought you to New York?"

Her closeness made Jackson profoundly uncomfortable. He found it difficult to answer her questions. "I met him in Quantico," he said. "And we came here to get, uh, . . . uniforms."

She gave him a "yeah, sure" look and excused herself.

Jackson immediately felt more alone than he could ever remember. The girl sat in a booth on the other side of the room, and Jackson thought she looked in his direction several times. Each time their eyes met, hers dropped to her plate as if to say, "Don't bother me."

Jackson felt dejected. *If she keeps looking over here, I'm never going to get laid. There's no one in the room who can hold a candle to her.*

"Don't be a jerk," Williams said when he told him that. "There are at least ten girls in this room better looking." He got a little pissed off when Jackson didn't pick up on any of the women who paraded by. "What the hell's wrong with you?"

"Nothing," replied Jackson. "I'm not feeling so good. Must be the rich food and the booze. I'm going back to the hotel."

Williams was dumbstruck. "That's just fuckin' wonderful. I'm knocking myself out to find somebody to get you off, and you tell me you have a stomachache? Well, take off if you must, but don't expect me to follow. I'm not going home alone."

Jackson left Williams in the company of two very attentive females who looked relieved at Jackson's departure. Each of them leaned on one of Bill's shoulders and smiled up at him as Jackson walked away. Williams called after him. "I'll see you sometime tomorrow; late in the morning. And don't go to Brooks Brothers without me."

When he got to the bottom of the stairs, Jackson saw the petite brunette talking to the huge doorman. As he waited for them to complete their conversation, he looked around the room, memorizing every detail to remember the experience.

The brunette turned and spoke to him in a soft voice. "Are you leaving too?"

"Yeah. I don't like the smoke. It reminds me of the base, and I don't want the smell in my nose all night."

"You looked like you were about to fall asleep up there."

"No. Actually, I'm not very tired."

She laughed nervously. "You could've fooled me."

The thin gold necklace made a small indentation in her sweater just above the rise of her breasts. Jackson caught his breath and laughed to get his composure back. "I was just thinking," he said.

"About what?"

"About how much I don't fit in upstairs."

"Why not?"

"Well, I'm not used to being around so many wealthy people, or eating such extravagant food."

The girl appeared confused. "I don't understand. You're here with Bill, aren't you?"

"I'm with him, but I'm not anything like him." The more he talked, the more nervous he became and the tighter his voice. She moved closer to hear him, and the scent of her perfume nearly overwhelmed his senses. He almost jumped out of his skin when she touched his forearm.

"What've you been doing, then?"

"I've recently returned from overseas."

"You've been to Vietnam?" She saw pain flash through his eyes and tentatively reached out her hand.

"Yes. Does that bother you?"

"Not in the slightest. You just look so young to have gone and returned. You haven't been hurt, have you?"

"Not badly."

"I'm sorry." Her response came quickly and was accompanied by a gentle touch to his arm.

"Why? Why would you care?" He sensed he'd hurt her and watched dejectedly as she moved toward the door. "I'm sorry," he said. "Since I returned, I've run into a lot of people who acted like they didn't want me back, and all of them asked questions similar to yours."

Her face looked genuinely sad. "Once again, I apologize." He saw something in her eyes he didn't understand, but the smile on her face warmed him to the bone.

"Look, you seem like a very nice person, and I'm very sorry I got testy. The last couple of months have been difficult. I hope you won't hold it against me."

"Okay, but only on the condition we start over again." Holding out her hand, she said, "My name is Susan."

When he took her hand, Jackson was nearly overcome by its softness. He looked into her big brown eyes and felt his knees weaken. His voice was as gentle as he could make it. "Hi, Susan. I'm Paul."

"What did you do in Vietnam?"

"I was a member of a special reconnaissance team." *Here we go. She won't want anything to do with me now. I should've kept my mouth shut.*

"Not regular infantry, then?"

Jackson was surprised she knew anything about the military.

She smiled. "Somehow I didn't *think* you ran in the same circles as Bill."

"I guess I really stick out."

Susan understood and laughed. "There's nothing wrong with being different from this crowd."

"Scuse me, young'uns," the doorman said, "but can y'all take your talkin' outside, or back upstairs? It's likely to get crowded in here real soon." Jackson and Susan jumped at the sound of the big man's voice. He had invaded their quiet moment and shocked them out of their thoughts of each other.

Jackson was the first to speak. "Upstairs is out for me." He turned to Susan. "It's been nice talking with you." He grabbed his coat from the back of the chair and started to put it on.

"What's your hurry?" she said. "I know a nice place nearby where we can grab a cup of coffee. If you're interested?"

"I'd like that very much." He took her coat and held it open for her.

THIRTY-ONE

New York City

0210, April 13, 1968

"WHERE ARE YOU TAKING ME?" Jackson kept his voice soft and his question polite.

Susan's smile was warm and inviting. "There's a little place a few blocks from here where they sell the best coffee in New York."

"And is also frequented by only the finest people?"

Susan's smile faded. "Look, I don't like the atmosphere in Marjorie's either, but most of the people there are my friends. I don't appreciate your derision."

Jackson felt the sting. "You're right. I'm not being critical; I just felt so out of place." *Good move, asshole. Keep bad-mouthing the place and she'll leave you standing here with your tongue hanging out.*

Instead, she tucked her arm inside his and smiled. "Let's walk. I like spring evenings."

"You sure you wouldn't prefer a cab?"

"A walk is nicer. We can window shop. Have you ever been to . . . no, of course not. I'll enjoy showing you." She watched his reaction to the different types of people they passed and felt safe with him. She squeezed his arm and marveled at the hardness of the muscles beneath the fabric.

He placed his hand over hers, and they walked arm-in-arm past brilliantly lit store windows.

★

Why did I invite him for coffee? Was it the uniform or the gentleness of the guy wearing it? I've never left Marjorie's with anyone before. Why him? She knew why her friends went there. To meet men like Bill Williams: rich, eligible bachelors they hoped would put a ring on their left hand. But in the years she'd frequented the place, not a single friend got that lucky. *Paul's different,* she thought. *But why?*

As they were standing in front of Macy's admiring the window display, a drunk staggered past and whistled lewdly at Susan. Immediately, she felt the muscles of Jackson's arm grow taut and saw something happen to his carriage. He raised himself fully erect and cast a cold glance toward the drunk with eyes filled with menace. He

[150]

frightened *her* more than he did the drunk. *My God. This guy is capable of doing serious harm.*

The young Marine's gaze wasn't lost on the drunk either, who stumbled out of harm's way when he saw the man's eyes narrow and fill with danger.

Paul's eyes stayed fixed on him until the drunk moved out of range, but when he turned toward her, the menace was gone and the eyes were filled with tenderness.

My God! That was unbelievable. "How'd you do that?" she asked.

"Do what?"

"Make the drunk understand you disapproved. You scared me a little." *He looked almost mad enough to kill him.* For an instant she was petrified. *I don't really know anything about him.*

"I'm really sorry," he said.

She drew a deep breath and let it out. *Wait a minute. There's nothing to be afraid of. In fact, I think he's afraid of me.* She took her arm out from under his, grabbed his hand, and marveled at how gently he held hers. "I have a temper, too," she said, "but it's mostly controlled."

"Oh, yeah? Are you sending me a message?"

"Only if you tease or lie to me."

He threw up his free hand in mock surrender. "I promise nothing but the truth, and I can assure you I've no intention of teasing."

She laughed easily. *I believe him. He hasn't even tried to touch me.*

"You're safe with me," he added.

"What if I don't want to be safe with you?" *God. What did I just say?*

His face reddened and he pulled away from her. They walked on, but he kept his distance and didn't allow her to retake his hand.

"This is the best place in Manhattan to eat," she said as they entered an old railroad car diner and she led him to an open booth. "Feel more comfortable here, Paul?"

"Yes. Much."

The diner was filled with people in all manner of dress. Those who looked up at all gave them glances that ran the gamut from disapproval to disinterest. New Yorkers didn't worry much about the virtue of any woman, but many disliked the appearance of anything military. Even though the only piece of uniform he wore was his overcoat, the short hair coupled with the green wool marked him clearly for what he was.

A gum-chewing waitress came up to the booth. "What can I getcha?" she asked rudely, smacking her gum in Jackson's ear. It was definitely a voice from Brooklyn.

Paul looked up and smiled. "A couple of menus would be good to start."

A couple of regulars sitting at the bar laughed. "Guess he's gotcha there, Rosy," one of them said.

The waitress glared at the loudmouth and retrieved the menus. "Shut up, Bob."

"Damn it," whispered Jackson, who didn't enjoy being the butt of their joke. He looked at Susan a little sheepishly. "Oh, sorry about that. I hope you'll remember that up to a few hours ago I've been living only with men for almost a year. Being near someone like you is almost a new experience."

"Don't worry about it. I grew up around the military, and I've heard men swear before. If it makes you feel better, cuss all you like."

"What do you mean you grew up around the military?"

"My father is a career Coastie."

"Excuse me?"

"A career Coast Guard officer."

"Oh. The shallow-water Navy."

"You'd better not let my father, or my brothers, hear you say that. All of them are serving officers in the Coast Guard."

He looked at her warmly and averted his eyes only when the waitress returned with the menus. She dropped them in front of the couple and said, "Well, what's it gonna be, hon?"

They hadn't even looked at the menus, but Jackson said quickly, "Two hamburgers with everything and coffee, black." Then he turned his eyes back to Susan. Their eyes remained locked as they waited for their food. Jackson sat with his hands resting on the top of the table. When Susan touched one, he flinched as if he had been burned.

Not about to give up, she let her foot find his under the table.

"What's it like?" she asked.

"What?"

"Vietnam?" She watched him bristle and quickly added, "I hear my brothers talking about it all of the time. Both of them are anxious to go and have volunteered for riverboat patrol. I'm not trying to pry. I'd just like to know from someone who's been there."

Sensing the honesty in her voice, Jackson relaxed. "It's hot."

"That's all? It's hot?"

"Well," he went on, finding her incredibly easy to talk to, "It's *damned* hot and very wet." With that both of them laughed away their last feelings of uneasiness and Jackson began to tell her what Vietnam was like. He didn't pull any punches; nor did he glamorize anything. He didn't go into any of the action he'd participated in, believing she wouldn't understand. If her brothers did go to 'Nam, she'd be better off not knowing anyway.

"You said you'd been hurt."

"I've been wounded, very slightly, three times."

"Where?"

His eyes almost begged her to change the subject.

"Where were you wounded?"

Jackson could see concern in her eyes, and it embarrassed him, so he touched his forehead where his hair met the hairline. She immediately saw the purple scar. She was horrified. "That's a fresh wound."

"How do you know that?"

"I'm a nursing major at NYU. I know recent suture scars and I can recognize healing tissue."

Jackson didn't answer and was relieved when the hamburgers and coffee arrived. They dug in with relish. It was his first real hamburger in months, and Susan couldn't remember the last time she'd been so hungry. They ate in silence and drank several cups of coffee. Both were scared . . . him of saying the wrong thing, and her of going home without him.

"I can't eat another bite," she said at last. "This is my second meal tonight, and I'll pay for it next time I weigh myself."

He sighed happily. "That was really good. I'd forgotten how a real hamburger tastes." As he rose to help her with her coat, his hand brushed the side of her breast and she gasped.

Shocked and embarrassed he stammered, "Oh, Christ, I'm sorry."

For some reason, both of them needed to hold the top of the counter to steady themselves while he paid the check.

Outside, she wanted to take a cab.

"Where are we going?"

She pushed her hand into the warmth of his coat pocket, bringing her breast up against his body. Both of them felt a shock race across their skin. "West Twelfth Street."

"Come upstairs," she said softly as the taxi pulled up in front of a small brownstone. "My apartment's small, but its comfortable."

Both were breathless after climbing the four flights of stairs to her apartment. Jackson had to lean against her door to regain his strength. He wondered what was wrong with him. Four flights of stairs shouldn't tax him at all.

Susan leaned on the door and looked through her handbag. *Why are my legs shaking? I climb those stairs several times a day and have never been out of breath before.* "Quick," she said. "Get inside, I've got nosy neighbors."

His eyes took in the entire apartment in a single sweep. When he brought them back to her, she was still leaning against the door. "Nice place," he said.

She pushed herself away from the door and walked toward the kitchen. "I'm glad you like it. It's only three rooms. This is the sitting room and kitchen. Down the hallway is the bathroom on the right and the bedroom on the left."

"I'm glad you aren't like the women Bill introduced me to."

"Oh?" she teased. "How am I different?"

"Well, you're not rich. That's the first thing. And you're not looking for a quick roll in the hay, for another."

"What makes you think I'm not interested in the second thing? After all, I invited you up to my apartment."

Their eyes met and held for a long time.

"I guess I'd better leave."

Susan's face flushed. "Why? I don't want you to . . . not yet." She was so close to him that her perfume filled his senses.

Why is he just standing there? He didn't try to kiss her, and she knew if she let the moment pass he wouldn't. She stood on her toes and kissed him very gently on the lips. He pulled her close with a gentle pressure. When their lips parted, he looked into her eyes, lifted her into his arms, and asked, "Which one's the bedroom again?"

THIRTY-TWO

American Airlines Flight 718 to Washington, D.C.

1715, April 15, 1968

BILL WILLIAMS SAT in the aisle seat. Paul Jackson sat on his right, gazing sightlessly out the window. Williams thought his friend looked like a sick puppy. "That's the last time I'm going on liberty with *you*. I thought we were going to lift skirts together, but after you left Marjorie's I hardly saw you."

"I told you. I met a girl. I wouldn't have come back at all if we didn't have to buy uniforms."

"Yeah, I enjoyed not knowing where you were," Williams said sarcastically.

"Don't get your panties in a knot."

Williams ignored the remark. "Well, where did this woman keep you?"

Jackson changed the subject. "Those uniforms at Brooks Brothers were really something. If I'd bought everything they showed me, I would've spent a fortune."

"Well," Williams asked acerbically. "What *did* you buy? I don't even know that. You were there and then gone again before I knew it."

"Just the minimum. Where I'm headed I won't need dress uniforms."

"Did you buy the whites and dress blues?"

"No. Those definitely aren't necessary. I'm going back to 'Nam after we graduate, and even class A uniforms aren't used there. Everybody wears ripstops."

"What the hell are they?"

"Camouflaged jungle utilities. It's two pieces: a blouse that falls over the top of trousers, both with huge pockets on the outside. The Army's been using them for years, but they're just now being issued to Marines."

Changing the subject to something that interested him, Williams said, "When we were being fitted, I thought you were going to punch the tailor."

"I damned near did. It was bad enough when the guy had his hands all over me pinning and marking my uniforms, but when he grabbed my dick, that was the last straw."

"The Corps likes its officers to look like poster boys," Williams laughed, "and he was just trying to find out how much of a 'boy' you were."

"Well, at least I didn't break the bank. How much did you spend?"

Williams blew off the question. "A little more than you, probably."

"Oh, come on, don't give me that shit. I spent the allowance and a couple of hundred more. You bought three times what I did."

"Okay, if it'll shut you up, I spent about three grand, but only because I bought extra shirts and trousers."

Jackson laughed. "*And* you bought the friggin' sword. Christ, that pig-sticker was over four hundred by itself. By the way, are you sure they'll have the uniforms in Quantico by next Friday?"

"Well, your tailor 'buddy' asked when we needed them and said he'd personally see to it that yours were there. Mine, he wasn't worried about."

Laughing, Jackson decided it was the right moment to bring up Williams' offer to pay for his uniforms. "Thanks again for offering to help, Bill, but I don't need your money. I've spent the last few months earning pay I couldn't spend, and I have more than enough." He couldn't quite keep the edge out of his voice.

For a brief moment Williams was really pissed off and let it show. "Relax. I was offering to help, not rubbing your nose in anything."

"Sorry. I've been on my own for a long time, and I kind of like it that way."

"Fine. I understand. But get one thing straight. I like having money and I'm not the least bit ashamed of it. I don't apologize for inheriting enough to keep myself comfortable, and I seldom offer any to anyone. You're the exception because you're the best friend I've ever had. But don't ever come at me again like I've committed the unforgivable sin. I can do without the poor-mouth routine. It doesn't become you."

"Okay, okay. I get it. Let's drop the subject and continue on as before."

"Roger that. Let's start as soon as we land. We can grab a big lunch and check out the local talent."

Jackson shook his head. "Lunch sounds great, but I'm not interested in the other."

"Wow. Who did you spend your time in New York with, Ann-Margret?"

"Susan Morrison," Jackson said more calmly than he felt. His knees got weak every time he thought about her.

"The one from Marjorie's? You were with her every day?"

"Yes, we both wanted to."

"Oh, I'll bet she wanted to," Williams said fervently. "Does she know you're a Marine and not loaded?"

"She knows, and it doesn't matter."

"I'll bet." After seeing the crushed look in his friend's eyes, Bill softened his voice. "Look, Paul. The women who go to Marjorie's are looking for rich husbands. They're not interested in anyone who works for a living. They want to be taken care of, not the other way around. Understand?"

"Susan isn't like that. Her father's career military, and both of her brothers are officers in the Coast Guard."

Williams raised his voice at his friend's stupidity. "Did you say *Coast Guard?*"

"What's wrong with that? At least they're not dodging the draft."

"The hell they're not. The Coast Guard's where all of the bright little rich boys hide when they can't get into the National Guard."

Jackson's jaw tightened threateningly. "What did you say?"

Not wishing to damage their relationship, or have his ass kicked, Williams lowered his voice. "Look, Paul, the Coast Guard is the service of choice for rich kids with low draft numbers. They know the closest they'll get to Vietnam is the West Coast, where they'll spend their time teaching water survival classes to chicks at the local YWCA. Their fathers bend some arms and get them in ahead of those who can't afford to buy influence. They figure if they have to serve, they can do so on their terms, not the government's. Understand?"

Jackson allowed his earlier resentment to escape. "Yeah. I'm not stupid. What you're saying is that a lot of rich guys are gutless."

Williams laughed. "That's about it. They call it being smart, but you're closer to the truth."

"Thanks for the warning, but I don't think it's necessary. Susan's nice. I like her a lot, and I don't give a shit why her father and brothers are in the Coast Guard. I'm sure it's not for the reasons you mention. They don't have enough money to buy influence."

"Well . . . good then. That's a load off of my mind. When do I meet her?"

"You don't. She knows all about you and doesn't want her family to get the idea she's running with your pack."

Williams hung his head in mock anguish. "Now I am crushed."

Jackson laughed and thanked Bill for caring. "Screw you."

Later, as Jackson dozed, Williams wondered why he couldn't meet a woman like Susan Morrison.

As Platoon 68-097 entered its last week of training at Quantico, the men started looking forward to graduation and moving on. Most wondered where they would be posted. "Almost all of you are going to head across the base to the Basic School," Parish told them. "Over there, they're gonna teach you advanced tactics and leadership. They'll take the fundamentals you've learned here and turn 'em into the skills you'll need to survive in combat as an infantry platoon commander—which nearly 90 percent of you will be."

Bill Williams defined the purpose of the Basic School better than anyone when he called it a "finishing school for savages."

They spent the last week of OCS attending classes on financial management, officers' club attendance and conduct, and the etiquette expected of an officer of Marines.

"Those skills aren't high on the list of things I'll use," Jackson told the others, "but you'll need 'em at the Basic School."

"Where are you're going?" Candidate Miller asked.

"Back to 'Nam. The Corps isn't about to turn me loose on an unsuspecting platoon of enlisted men. At least not until I've completed my tour. So while you're enjoying the soft summer sun here in Quantico, I'll be sweating in Phu Bai."

As graduation drew close with no sign yet of the Brooks Brothers uniforms, Jackson became anxious. "Where are they?" he asked Williams. "The uniform store made its delivery yesterday, but our stuff hasn't arrived yet and we graduate the day after tomorrow."

Williams merely laughed. "Relax, mon ami. They'll get here."

And indeed, in the early afternoon a truck pulled up and offloaded a mountainous stack of packages, shoe- and hatboxes, and bag after bag of shirts and trousers.

Jackson tried on his uniforms to make sure they fit and was amazed by the quality. "These things fit great, and the material is much better than what they sell at the uniform shop. Ours not only fit better, they look a hell of a lot sharper. Perhaps these things are worth what they cost after all. Shit, even you look like an officer, Williams."

"Attention on deck!"

"As you were," responded Parish as he handed each candidate a stack of orders that identified his next duty assignment. "Headquarters Marine Corps has issued two different paragraphs of a basic order. On top of the stack you'll see your name and a statement that says, 'You will comply with special order 68-1896, paragraph 1, for further assignment to the Basic School.' Everyone's orders except Jackson's read the same."

Jackson was covered by the same basic order, but his individual package was endorsed in paragraph 2, which read, "Subject officer will travel via commercial air to Norton Air Force Base, San Bernardino, California, for assignment to MAC flight 012 for further assignment to 3rdMarDiv, FMFPac, for duty with Third Force Recon Company. Travel by POV is not authorized. Delay en route is not authorized. Subject officer will proceed and report no later than 2400, June 16, 1968." Jackson threw the orders on his rack and nodded to Parish.

Williams read paragraph 2 and asked, "What the hell does all that mean?"

Jackson's tone had an edge, but he smiled when he spoke. "Just like I said, I'm going back to 'Nam. The Corps doesn't go to all of this trouble and then let anyone off the hook. Shit, I didn't care where they sent me until I met Susan."

Williams shook his head at his love-starved friend. "Are you in love?"

"I don't think so. But since I've met her, things seem different. I want to stay in the States and pursue our relationship. She feels like I do. Now I won't have enough time to even see her before I leave."

THIRTY-THREE

Quantico, Virginia

1100, June 14, 1968

1100 PRECISELY, PLATOON 68-097 fell in for the last time. The graduates wore the summer service C uniform of a second lieutenant of Marines: short-sleeved tropical uniform and the bicornered soft cover called a "piss-cutter," but no insignia of rank.

Staff Sergeant Parish marched them in front of a small reviewing stand crowded with civilians and other Marines and called his last order to the platoon. "Candidate Jackson, front and cennnnterrr."

Jackson marched to a position directly in front of his former nemesis. As soon as he stopped, Parish came to attention and saluted. "Take charge of the platoon, sir."

Jackson returned the salute. "Take your post, Sergeant."

The two Marines exchanged salutes a second time. Parish did an about face and marched to assume a new position behind the reviewing officers.

Lieutenant Colonel Paulon marched to within one pace of Jackson.

Jackson saluted smartly. "Sir, the parade is formed."

"Very good, Mr. Jackson."

Paulon sidestepped one pace to the left and administered the oath of allegiance to the platoon. When the oath was completed, Paulon ordered Jackson to follow him. Schools Battalion's first sergeant joined them, and they handed each man his commission papers. Finally, the colonel addressed the platoon. "Congratulations, and welcome to the officer corps of the United States Marines. It is the tradition of this school to recognize the most outstanding candidate in each platoon with the designation 'honor graduate.' He shall receive, as recognition of his achievement, an inscribed sword. It is my desire that he wear it with as much dignity as did the officer for whom the original was designed, Lieutenant Presley O'Bannon. Platoon 68-097 has selected for its honor graduate Lieutenant Paul Jackson."

The colonel turned to his left, and First Sergeant Mickelson handed him a brand-new sword with a smooth-faced pearl hilt and brushed-gold hand guard, complete with leather frog and belt. The sword was pulled partway out of its scabbard, and Jackson could see the words "Honor Graduate OCS Class 68-097" engraved on the blade, which glittered in the noonday sun.

"Congratulations, Lieutenant. I believe they've chosen well. You may dismiss these gentlemen."

"Aye, aye, sir." Jackson saluted and, after the colonel returned to the reviewing stand, did an about face. Holding his new sword, Lieutenant Jackson gave his first official order as a commissioned officer to junior men under his command. "Platoon 68-097 . . . dissssssmissssed."

The platoon stood in place for a few moments as if the new officers were unable to accept the fact that their ordeal was over. Finally, a tall, lanky individual from Louisiana let out a rebel yell, and the others shook hands and slapped each other on the back.

"Careful you don't cut yourself, Lieutenant," a voice said behind him.

Turning around, Lieutenant Jackson came face to face with Colonel Greene, the regimental commander. He popped to attention and saluted the senior officer with as much perfection as he knew.

The colonel returned the salute with equal respect. "That little matter with a certain officer has been resolved. Take care of yourself and give my respects to Colonel MacDonald when next you see him."

"Yes, sir. That will be very soon, sir," he added a bit glumly.

"What's the matter, Lieutenant? Don't like your orders?"

"Yes, sir, they're just fine, sir." Second lieutenants do not criticize the wisdom of Headquarters Marine Corps by complaining to their commanding officer.

"Then what is it, Paul?"

"Well, sir. I met this girl, and I was looking forward to saying goodbye to her, but I won't be able to."

"Why not?"

Jackson didn't know if he should, but he continued, "I've been ordered to report immediately, with no delay-in-route authorized."

"Sergeant Ma—" the colonel bellowed, stopping short when he noticed the older man standing just behind him. "Sergeant Major. Why would HQMC not authorize a man delay-in-route before transferring him overseas?"

"Urgency of need, sir."

"That's entirely inappropriate considering the circumstances. Perhaps you could call one of your Zebra Club cronies and modify Mr. Jackson's orders to include, shall we say, ten days delay-in-route, and travel by private vehicle? They give you extra days delay if you travel by car, Paul," he added to Jackson.

The old sergeant smiled. "I'd be happy to, sir. Ten days and POV. If the lieutenant will stop by headquarters before leaving, I'll have his modification on my desk."

The colonel smiled. "Very good, Sergeant Major. Is there anything else I can do for you, Lieutenant?"

Second Lt. Paul Jackson, USMCR, came to attention and saluted. "No, sir. Thank you, sir." His excitement at hearing he'd have a few days to spend with Susan was evident in the broad smile on his face.

"Very good, then. You may carry on, Lieutenant." The colonel returned the salute.

"Aye, aye, sir."

As he began to turn away, Greene stopped and said, "There is one more thing, Paul."

"Sir?"

The colonel simply stuck out his hand and shook the young officer's warmly. "I've not met many men who deserved their bars more than you. Don't disappoint the new assistant division commander of the 3rd Division."

"Sir, you mean they're replacing General Davis?"

"What's the matter, Lieutenant, worried about losing your rabbi?"

Jackson shook his head at the colonel's comment. "The general was never any man's rabbi, sir. Least of all mine. It's just that I think of him as a hell of a Marine and wanted to serve with him again."

"You will, Paul. He'll be around for a long time. But what you need to worry about is the new ADC."

"With respect, sir. I'm confident the ADC won't take notice of another brown-bar lieutenant checking into his command, sir."

The colonel grinned. "Oh, you're wrong, Lieutenant. Dead wrong. Because I sure as hell will."

After Colonel Greene dismissed him, Jackson walked toward the reviewing stand to find the regimental sergeant major. He wanted to respect Marine Corps traditions, and this specific thing he wanted to do right.

The Corps lives for its traditions, and the first one a newly minted lieutenant faces is providing a silver dollar to the first enlisted man he salutes. Jackson wanted that person to be someone special. He refused to give his dollar to Parish. If he did, he knew it would be squandered on a pitcher of beer at the staff NCO club and Parish would spend the night bragging about how he'd "screwed" another zero. He spotted the sergeant major by the bleachers. When he approached, the regiment's senior enlisted man came to attention and saluted the Corps' youngest officer. "Sergeant Major, I hope you'll do me the honor of accepting this small token of my esteem." Jackson held out the silver dollar in his left hand, and the sergeant major took it with a small nod, not trusting himself to speak.

They shook hands, and the old sergeant came to rigid attention. "Good luck to you, sir." The emotion in the older man's voice was palpable.

Jackson was equally moved. "Thank you, Sergeant Major." He returned the salute and turned away quickly. He didn't see the sergeant major place the silver dollar into his breast pocket and reverently tap the shirt.

When he turned, Jackson immediately confronted a grinning Lieutenant Williams with two civilians in tow. "I looked for you in the line in front of Parish but couldn't find you," Williams said.

Jackson scowled. "You didn't give him your dollar, did you?"

"Hell, no. I gave it to that first sergeant who helped you. I think Parish is a bona fide asshole."

"You're wising up, Lieutenant." Jackson punched his friend in the arm.

"I'd like you to meet my parents," Williams said. "They're here from San Francisco on a business trip."

Judging by the look of pride both displayed, Jackson suspected the real purpose of their visit was to watch their only son commissioned an officer of Marines.

Riley Williams, founder and senior partner of Williams, Fishbairn and Wilkes, Attorneys at Law, smiled and held out his hand. "It's a pleasure to meet you, Paul."

Paul admired the strength in Mr. Williams' handshake. "Yes, sir."

"A former enlisted man can always spot another," Mr. Williams continued.

"Sir?" Jackson was confused. He'd envisioned Williams' father as pasty faced and overweight—nothing at all like the rugged-looking individual standing in front of him.

Lieutenant Williams chuckled. "My father was enlisted in World War II. He never got over it."

The men laughed, and Jackson turned to be introduced to one of the most beautiful women he had ever seen. Bill's mother was elegantly clad in an unpretentious silk dress, open at the neck to show off a simple strand of what Paul imagined to be extremely expensive pearls.

"Paul, may I present my mother?"

Holding out her hand, Mrs. Williams said, "Thank you for helping Bill. He was concerned about how well he would do until he met you."

"He'll be just fine, ma'am. It worked both ways. We shared a lot. He's the best friend I've ever had."

"I can imagine what he shared with you. Was her name Joan or Margaret?"

"Neither, ma'am. Those he kept for himself."

All four shared the laughter of people who genuinely liked one other. Bill's parents took to Paul right off. Clearly he was a very positive influence on their son. The elder Williamses invited the two officers to dinner at the Washington Stratford, where a suite had been booked for them through the weekend.

"Dinner sounds great, sir, but Paul's got to catch a plane tonight."

Mrs. Williams seemed disappointed. "Where to?"

"He's got orders overseas," Bill answered.

"Why so soon?" the elder Mr. Williams asked.

"I was in Vietnam when I was ordered to OCS, sir, and I'm going back to complete my tour."

Mr. Williams didn't understand. "Certainly the Marine Corps isn't so short of second lieutenants that it can't give you a little leave before you go. What's your MOS?"

Jackson ignored the question about his military occupational specialty. "Well in this case, it appears so."

"Paul has a special job, Dad."

Jackson looked at his friend with narrowed eyes. "Shut up, Bill. He has no need to know."

Bill's parents burst out laughing. Mrs. Williams said, "Well, William. It looks like you've finally learned to obey someone."

Mr. Williams' grin was huge. "You will join us for dinner, though, won't you, Paul?"

"Yes, sir. Thank you. We'll catch the bus up this afternoon. We need to finish some things here before we leave."

"Good. Then we'll see you, say, around eight."

Both officers spoke at once. "Thank you, sir."

Jackson found himself greatly admiring the elder Williams, who was very different from his own father. Paul's dad was an automobile mechanic who lived in Phoenix now. He didn't have the education or style of Riley Williams, but he was still a man Paul admired greatly. He was the most honest person Paul knew, and that is how he described him to the very few people with whom he discussed his personal life. Not a man given to gentleness, he had been a hard taskmaster where Paul was concerned; but as the years passed, the son came to realize the quality of his sire and loved him deeply. His father had cried when Paul got on the bus for the ride to the enlistment center and boot camp.

After Mr. and Mrs. Williams departed, Jackson told his friend about the revised orders giving him time to visit Susan in New York. The two lieutenants picked up their gear and closed out their affairs in Quantico before leaving. "You're only traveling with me as far as D.C.," Paul said. "From there we're taking different routes."

"You sure you don't want me to come to New York with you?"

Jackson laughed. "You stay out of New York, stupid. And further, you stay away from Susan. If I so much as hear you've kissed her cheek, I'll come back, rip your head off, and shit down your neck."

When the two officers emerged from regimental headquarters, Jackson was all smiles. "You know, there is a God, and life is good."

Williams looked at his friend as if he'd gone off the deep end. "What do you mean?"

"I now have fourteen days to spend carvorting about New York City: ten delay-in-route days and four POV travel."

"That's great. How did the sergeant major swing it?"

"Who cares? Right now, I think we should get the hell out of Dodge before they change their minds. How about we go meet your parents in D.C. and then I catch the late shuttle to New York?"

"Sounds like a plan. Lead on, Mr. Jackson."

THIRTY-FOUR

St. Paul's Hotel, Washington, D.C.

2000, June 14, 1968

DINNER AT THE ST. PAUL'S elegant restaurant was low key. The men discussed politics and the Marine Corps while Mrs. Williams smiled politely and remained subdued. A couple of times Jackson caught her staring at her son as if she was afraid of forgetting what he looked like. It was the look of a mother who knows that her only son has finally become a man and she can no longer protect him from the evil in the world.

After dinner the foursome stopped in the hotel bar for a farewell cocktail. Bill and his father went to the men's room, leaving Jackson alone with his friend's mother. The mood was awkward, and Paul sipped at his drink to ease his tension.

"Is Bill going to have to go to Vietnam?"

There it is. The single thing that's been on her mind all night. How to answer that? "I don't know, ma'am. It depends on the job he's assigned and what the demands are for it in-country."

Tears welled in her eyes and her voice filled with desperation. "You can't give me a better answer than that? I'm going crazy with worry. I'm just about ready to lose it right now."

"I wish I could, ma'am." Her pain was palpable, but there was nothing Jackson could say to dispel her fears. *Best just to be straight with her.* "Bill's a serving officer who will go where he's ordered, just like the rest of us. He'll take the same risks, and he stands just as good a chance of being hurt. I can't hide those facts."

Mrs. Williams sobbed quietly into her handkerchief. "I wanted him to go into the Air Force. Why didn't he?"

Jackson spoke firmly. "Because he's better than that. Bill is one of the finest men I've ever known: capable, talented, and smart. He would've been miserable around those pasty-faced feather merchants."

"Oh, Christ, you men are all alike, every goddamned one of you. It wasn't enough for him to join the military; he had to be a Marine. If his father hadn't put all of those stupid ideas in his head, we wouldn't be here."

Paul shook his head. "Mrs. Williams. You're the mother of the closest friend I've ever had, and you are failing him. He deserves better from you. He'll be fine. You're dreaming things up to worry about. I've spent time in Vietnam, and while I won't lie and say it was enjoyable, I can tell you a great many men who aren't half as capable as your son have gone there, completed their tour, and returned home without so much as a scratch."

"I'm scared, Paul."

"Yes ma'am. You have every right to be. These are tough times, and your son has chosen a dangerous vocation. But the training he has received, and will continue to get, is the best in the world. That ensures him a much better chance of surviving Vietnam then he would have in any of the other services. He's a member of the finest group of men in the world, and he's the best of the best. I'd follow him into combat anytime; he's that good. You should be proud of him, Mrs. Williams, and show it by supporting his decision to do what he believes is right."

Mrs. Williams looked at the much younger man and marveled at his ability to understand. She was nearly thirty years his senior, and yet he was explaining life's realities to her. If all the men Bill served with were like Paul, he *would* be safe. She smiled and quietly dabbed at the tears in her eyes.

"There's just one more thing, Mrs. Williams."

"Yes?"

"Bill told me about how people with money often get their sons deferments or find places for them in the Reserves or the Coast Guard. He said you and your husband didn't believe in that sort of thing. That takes guts, ma'am. Your son has the same type of courage. The strength you instilled in him—he uses it to see things clearly. He'll be just fine. I really do believe that."

The woman whispered. "Thank you, Paul. Thank you."

Bill's voice came from behind his mother. "What's going on here? What has this filthy-mouthed Marine been telling you while we were gone, Mom?"

Mrs. Williams tried to look stern. "This very fine gentlemen has been telling me funny stories about how much trouble you were during training. I've been laughing so hard that I'm crying."

The two Marines looked at each other knowingly.

"Well, just as long as he didn't tell you how I spent my leisure time."

"He didn't have to tell me. I've known you a long time. I know about all of your conquests and how much you enjoy the fruits of the vine." The general laughter that followed Mrs. Williams' comments broke the melancholy that was beginning to engulf the evening.

Bill could see that Paul was extremely uncomfortable. "I'm sorry, folks, but we have to dash. My good friend the lieutenant here has to catch his flight, and I'm riding out to National with him."

Although disappointed not to spend more time with their son and his friend, Mr. and Mrs. Williams thanked both men politely and took turns hugging Paul. Mrs. Williams clung to the young officer longer than necessary, as if she were afraid she would never have the opportunity again. The two officers simply shook hands with Bill's father and said goodbye.

THIRTY-FIVE

302 West Twelfth Street, New York City

0630, June 28, 1968

JACKSON SAT QUIETLY in the easy chair and looked down at the tiny court-yard. He loved the garden's peacefulness and wished he could take it with him—or at least use it to calm himself before he confronted the inevitable. The sure beauty of the place helped him come to grips with his upcoming departure and the pain he knew Susan would feel.

"*Why does it have to be you?*"

Paul was shocked at the sharp tone and intensity of the question. He hadn't heard such hostility from Susan before—hadn't believed her capable of voicing it. He turned around, his breath catching in his throat when he saw her clad only in the long white T-shirt she slept in. He was stunned into silence as she paced the room.

Tears tumbled down her cheeks. "How can you just sit there saying nothing? Explain it to me! *Why* do you have to leave?" With the last question, she ran and buried her head in his shoulder. "Why you, again?"

Jackson felt his voice weakening, yearning. "Susan . . ."

"Just tell me, Paul. I want to understand. You've been there. You've been wounded, not once but *three* times. They even gave you a medal. Haven't you done enough? Haven't they asked enough?"

"Susan, I have to complete my tour, and that's it. When I get back, it'll be stateside duty until I get out."

"It doesn't matter. You're what has been missing from my life. Now that we've found each other, I don't want you to leave."

His voice hardened to cover the ache in his chest. "I'm a Marine Corps officer. I have no choice. You've known that all along. I haven't hidden anything from you." He tried to embrace her, but she shook herself free and walked toward the bedroom. *Jesus. Why does it hurt so much? Why can't she understand?*

When she turned to look at him, her tears had turned into an invitation. "Come over here, Mr. Jackson. I want you."

"Yes, ma'am." He walked over and scooped her up, and she nestled her head into his shoulder.

He didn't know how anyone's feelings could change so quickly, but right now he was okay with it. "God, you're beautiful." He closed his eyes as he held her, feeling the warmth and softness she offered. *I have to go. I can't change that. Rivers never made any bones about it. My assignment isn't totally voluntary. But even beyond my orders, there's something pulling me back. I don't seek the danger, but if I don't go I'll never be the man I want to be. Vietnam helped create the person I am by turning a boy into man. Hell, I want to go back. I believe in what we're doing. Besides, Bart, Colonel Greene, and General Lew are counting on me, and I owe them a lot. They would remind me that I just met Susan, that we aren't married and there are millions of available women out there. Yet, I feel a closeness to Susan I've never known with anyone else.* He nuzzled her hair, and she raised her face to receive the first of his kisses. She kissed him back, softly at first, and then more urgently as she willed him back to bed.

Their lovemaking wasn't urgent. It was slow . . . almost reverent. Gentle and pure, as if both of them wanted to imprint into their minds the special moments they were sharing. For her, it was as if she wanted it to last for the entire time he was away. Jackson was amazed at how she allowed her passion to run free. She explored and moved with utter abandon. When gasps and moans she drew him deep inside her, and when she rode him it was with complete abandon.

★

She drew her nails across his chest, and when she climaxed it was like she was standing outside herself. She never felt anything to match the feeling. *Oh, God, why does he have to go?* She collapsed onto his chest and lay there feeling the strong muscles of his torso, hard against her breasts. Her nipples tightened as he shifted his weight beneath her and she felt him grow hard again without having removed himself from inside her.

When they finally lay exhausted beside each other, she gently drew small circles on his chest and looked deep into his eyes. He lay back on the pillows and drifted, gently stroking her hair as he watched the light from the garden move into the bedroom.

He reminisced. "We've had fourteen wonderful days together, but the time I enjoyed most was when I showed up at your school on the first day."

"I remember," she said. "They got me out of my class and told me there was Marine officer asking for me. When I saw you in the office you looked like a little boy dressed up for a masquerade party, not the man I'm in love with."

"But you didn't even hesitate. You just threw your arms around my neck without thinking about what the teachers might be thinking. I can still feel that first kiss."

"You bet your ass. I was so happy to see you that I started crying, and then I knew I was in love."

"Yeah, well, you didn't act on it right away. You didn't bring me back to the apartment until after your last class."

"We made love the rest of the evening," she pointed out, "and I haven't attended any classes since then. We've spent every moment of your leave together." She was doing her best to remain cheerful and loving, especially physically, but as their time grew short she found herself wanting him more and more frequently.

They'd spent time walking around the city and even drove up to Connecticut to spend a night in a lake cottage near Redding. He enjoyed making love on the beach.

He didn't want to talk about Vietnam, and that was fine with her. But when the subject of leaving did come up, she could barely stand it. She knew he was trying to spare her when he referred to it as going overseas, not back to Vietnam. While she was filled with pride for him, she despised the idea of his leaving and was terrified by what that could mean.

As the sun began to brighten the bedroom, Paul drank in every inch of her beauty. He memorized the softness of her skin and the curve of her breast against his chest. *She's incredible. I want her body pressed against mine forever. I'll never forget the smell and freshness of her hair, her curves, the delicate features of her face. The sexy little mole beneath her right breast is my special secret—one I'll dream about often.*

Susan's head blocked out the sun's rays as she kissed him. "Hey, Lieutenant, are you there?"

Paul jumped back to full consciousness with a start. "Sorry, what did you say?"

"I said it's getting cold and I'd like a little breakfast before we drive out to Kennedy." She rose and reached out her hands for him, "Come on, Marine. No laziness today."

He got up and followed her into the shower. It may have been the warmth of the water cascading over them or her small hands lathering his body, but within seconds he was inside her again. They held each other as if they knew there would be no more tomorrow and made love for the final time with a tenderness found only by people who love each other deeply. Afterward, he followed her into the bedroom and put on his uniform.

He's very meticulous. I like that. Last night when I watched him put the ribbons and badges over his pocket and the gold bars on his shirt collar he looked like a little boy, vulnerable and fragile, nothing like the warrior he is. When he told me what each of the small ribbons stood for, all I could think about was that he'd soon be in danger again. Susan put her arms around his neck. "Where do you want to eat?"

Jackson kissed her tenderly, drinking in her beauty, storing it in his memory for the long months of separation to come. "Is Marjorie's open this early?"

"Yes, and she serves a wonderful brunch. I'll put on a dress while you finish your tie."

An early crowd of businessmen filled the restaurant, and they were lucky to get a seat without a reservation. Paul ate a three-egg omelet and washed it down with black coffee. Susan ate grapefruit and dry toast. They consumed an entire carafe of fresh orange juice and lingered over the deep warmth of espresso. She talked about nursing school. He simply listened and filled his heart with the sound of her voice.

★

Jackson presented his orders to the military liaison at Kennedy. "Your flight departs in two hours from Gate 2, Lieutenant."

"God," he said to Susan. "I feel haunted. I remember the first time I left for overseas. My father cried. It was only the second time I saw him show any kind of emotion."

"I'll bet your father is something special."

He smiled. "He is to me. He's a man's man who holds his feelings close. In fact, he never once told me he loved me before that day. I think I got the strength to board the airplane and leave because he said it."

Her smile lit her face. "And now it's me sitting beside you. But this time, it's you giving me strength. I'm frightened just sitting here, Paul. Let's go find a place to have coffee while we wait."

Again she amazed him. "Damn. How can anyone as small as you eat so much?"

"It's frightening, I know. But I didn't eat much at breakfast, and what's wrong with a couple of doughnuts with coffee?"

He pulled her close and kissed the powdered sugar off the end of her nose. "Are you okay?"

"Maybe a little scared and shaky. I think we made love once too often."

"Seems to me we did it just right."

The warmth of his smile stirred her emotions and she looked away so he wouldn't see her tears. He put his arm around her shoulders and she put her head on his chest. When Jackson saw people watching them he said, "Who cares what others think? I figure it's no one's business what we do. Besides, didn't you say most New Yorkers don't notice what happens around them?"

"I think I said, 'If they found two people making love on a Wall Street sidewalk, they'd just step around.'"

"I'll be back as soon as I complete the tour."

"You promise? You won't extend, or do anything stupid like volunteering for another assignment, will you?"

He shook his head. "I won't volunteer for anything." He'd never told her that his entire assignment was voluntary. If he hadn't told Rivers he would work with him, he wouldn't be in this situation now. But then, he wouldn't have been sent to Quantico and they would never have met.

Susan's eyes brimmed with tears, but she fought hard to keep them at bay. "Paul Jackson, I love you, and I'm going to miss you every moment of every day you're away."

Jackson touched her cheek and pushed away an escaping tear. His heart filled with more emotion than he'd thought himself capable of feeling. "I love you too. I'll carry you in my heart and think of you all of the time, but especially at sunrise."

"And I'll sit in the easy chair every morning and help the dawn send my love to you."

They sat in silence, with Jackson watching the big clock over her shoulder.

Susan touched his face the way a blind person might, imprinting every detail in her memory. *I have so much I want to say to him, but I just can't find the words. What is he feeling? I don't doubt him, but if he loves me, why does he want to go back? Why can't he just stay and let me love him?*

When the gate agent called last boarding for Jackson's flight, Susan watched him reluctantly pick up his gear, her face showing a mixture of pride and pain. Then she stood and placed her head against his chest and slowly traced his ribbons with a fingernail. When she came to the Bronze Star and Purple Heart, she stopped. "Nothing foolish, Paul. No more of these bullshit medals."

"It's time," he said as he tilted her head up and kissed her lightly.

Bullshit, buster, she thought as she closed her eyes and pushed her tongue between his teeth. *I want you to remember this kiss every day you're gone.*

Jackson felt himself stir in response and reddened with embarrassment. After a brief moment she pushed him away. "That, Lieutenant, was to remind you of how much I want you to come back."

Jackson smiled. "I'll be back. I love you."

"I love you, too."

He turned and walked through the gate.

THIRTY-SIX

Phu Bai

1715, July 1, 1968

JACKSON TALKED TO the crew chief as the Chinook's engines wound down. "Believe it or not, I'm actually glad we're here."

"Why's that, sir?"

"I've been in an airplane seat or a transit lounge for more hours than I can count. I'm tired, dirty, and done in."

The crew chief picked up Jackson's B4 bag. "What you need, sir, is a shower, shave, and about twelve hours' sleep. That'll get your shit together."

Jackson took his bag. "That's it, but I have to get the admin bullshit over with first. Thanks for the lift."

"You can grab a jeep in front of the tower," the crusty sergeant said. "Someone will take you to the Twenty-Sixth. It's right where you left it, sir."

And it was. His destination was distinguished by a roof covered with a triple layer of sandbags and a sign hanging over the door that read "26th Marine Regiment, 3rd Marine Division, III Marine Amphibious Force, R. F. MacDonald, Colonel— Commanding."

Jackson walked into the adjutant's office, dropped his luggage, and looked around. A corporal was running a mimeograph machine, and a rather bedraggled first lieutenant sat behind a desk poring over service record books.

The officer looked up as Jackson moved in front of his desk. "What is it?" The haughty attitude made him sound like Dudley.

Jackson didn't need any shit this late in the day. "Second Lieutenant Jackson reporting for duty, sir." He set his orders and OQR in the middle of the adjutant's desk, sending SRBs skidding to the floor.

The adjutant jumped up. "Just what the hell do you think you're doing, Lieutenant?"

"Like I said, *sir*, reporting for duty."

"Well, you look like shit. Who the hell told you to report in here looking like an unmade bed?"

"The commandant."

"Who?"

Jackson pegged the adjutant as a died-in-the-wool REMF. "Look, Lieutenant, I've been in the air for the better part of two days traveling on a five-A priority. My orders state I'm to report to the commanding officer of the 26th Marines immediately upon arrival. To me that means without delay, shave or no shave. I've done that, sir, and I'd appreciate it if you'd arrange for me to see the colonel."

Jackson's outburst had an immediate effect. "Jackson, you say?"

"That's right, *sir*. Paul A."

Searching through a pile of loose documents, the officer found what he was looking for and abruptly changed his tone and manner. "Just a minute, Lieutenant. I'll see if the colonel will see you now." He picked up Jackson's orders and OQR and hurried into the colonel's office. He was back in less than a minute. "The colonel will see you now, Lieutenant."

The sudden respect and courtesy rang strangely in Jackson's ears. Almost like a warning. He pulled himself erect and strode through the colonel's door. Inside, three Marines moved toward him, each with his right hand extended. He shook hands with Colonel MacDonald, Major Rivers, and Sergeant Major Jonas. He was home.

"Come in, Lieutenant," Colonel MacDonald said. "We've been waiting for you. How long have we been waiting, Bart? Seems like, what . . . ten, fifteen days?"

"That's about it, Skipper." Major Rivers kept his face void of emotion and didn't look Jackson in the eye.

"Mind telling us just where the hell you've been, Lieutenant?" MacDonald asked.

Jackson snapped to attention and managed to keep his mouth shut. He'd learned early in his career that when bird colonels asked rhetorical questions, every response would be wrong.

"I asked you a question, Lieutenant."

The look of horror on Jackson's face was too much, and the three fell into fits of laughter. They slapped him on the back and laughed until tears rolled down their cheeks. Finally, the colonel got hold of himself and told Jackson to sit down.

Jackson looked at *Major* Bart Rivers closely. "Well, I'll be damned." He extended his hand and congratulated his friend and mentor on the richly deserved promotion.

The sergeant major poured Jackson a cup of coffee and offered cigarettes all around.

Jackson smiled. "This coffee is good. It's real, not like that stale mess hall ink I've been drinking for the last few days."

"You, Lieutenant, look like shit." Colonel MacDonald's broad smile softened the reprimand, but it was clear just the same. "Didn't they instruct you on the proper way to report in before you left Quantico? Brand-new second johns are supposed to make a good first impression."

Jackson was undaunted. "I considered stopping to shave and shower before coming here, sir, but assumed that would've given someone reason to believe I hadn't reported in immediately. I therefore concluded it was better to make a poor impression than to get my butt thrown in the brig for disobeying my orders." He stood at rigid attention but bowed his head slightly at the end of his statement. The entire group laughed.

Jackson covertly examined the colonel and was once again impressed by what he saw. MacDonald was five-foot-eight but exuded an aura of energy that made him seem much taller. His hair was cut so short that his head looked shaved. The natural hairline receded well above a large forehead, and the square-jawed face expressed determination. He wore the sharpest-creased, most heavily starched ripstops Jackson had ever seen.

Major Rivers pulled a chair up close to his protégé and studied him carefully. Jackson wondered what he was looking for. Why was he being examined like a piece of meat? Rivers was making him nervous. Suddenly, the major sat up straight and started patting the left leg of his uniform. He pulled a small black cigar from a box he retrieved from his sock and rocked his chair back onto its rear legs. "Cigar, Lieutenant?"

The room once again filled with laughter. This time Jackson joined in. "No thank you, *Major*. I once saw a VD film that showed a Marine smoking one of those after he got laid by a two-dollar whore in Bangkok. I swore I'd never get the clap that way." Laughter pealed through the room in warm comradeship that made Jackson feel included and truly welcome.

"Paul—and I'm going to call you by your first name from now on," Colonel MacDonald said, "let us be the first to welcome you back into the belly of the beast. As you can see, we've long anticipated your arrival. If you'd gotten here when you were supposed to, and I use the word 'if' in place of a court-martial, we would've regaled you with dancing girls and real Kentucky liquor. But I'm sorry to report we've exhausted our entire reserve, so you'll have to settle for the first sergeant's mediocre coffee, C-ration cigarettes, or some of the major's now, shall we say, questionable cigars."

"These will do fine, sir." Jackson took one of the colonel's cigarettes.

"Okay, let's get down to business. I, unlike you three, have important matters pressing my schedule." The other three stopped clowning around and gave him 100 percent of their attention. "I don't need to tell you," he began, "that I'm a true believer in long-distance recon when it's conducted properly; that means when it develops the best intel possible."

"This war is far different from any the Corps has ever fought. For the first time we're being kept in the field for extended periods and we're not being asked to hold the real estate we take. We are also fighting a wily and incredibly competent enemy; one who seems to know our next move before we do. To conduct this war effectively, we have had to alter our traditional role greatly; therefore Headquarters Marine Corps is beginning to understand that we must also change our methods of gathering intelligence. But that doesn't mean everyone in HQMC believes change is necessary. In fact, many have voiced strong opposition to the creation of Force Recon. The opposition swears by the battalion recon concept, but then, most of those people have never heard a shot fired in anger."

The colonel paused and examined his cigarette, then looked directly at Rivers and Jackson, apparently expecting some type of response, so both officers said, "Yes, sir." The colonel beamed the smile of one who knows he has been understood by subordinates he respects. "We need to prove to the REMFs, and to the Corps in general, that Force Recon can be a major asset. I believe it may be the single thing that makes victory in this miserable war possible. We can start this shift by finding out how Charlie knows where to look for our LRRPS."

Jackson wondered why that problem hadn't already been solved, but nodded his head to indicate his agreement with the colonel's statements.

MacDonald put out his cigarette and immediately lit another. A cloud of toxic and foul-smelling smoke swirled around his head, and Jackson, remembering the lectures he'd received from Susan, decided he'd give serious consideration to breaking the habit.

"Having said all of that, I'll turn the matter of what I expect over to the excellent Major Rivers for further elaboration at a time when you're in better shape."

"Yes, sir."

The colonel studied the young lieutenant and was pleased by what he saw. Jackson, even in his disheveled state, looked like an officer. He had bright, inquisitive eyes, and his quiet, level-headed demeanor didn't quite reveal the very capable man that he was. He had the fortitude to speak his mind, even when it conflicted with a superior officer. The colonel stood and held out his hand. Jackson took it and returned the colonel's smile.

"Good God, Bart," the colonel said to Rivers. "Take this cherry and see to it he doesn't do himself harm. You know how second lieutenants are prone to screw up. Harden your men and turn them into razors who believe as we do, then go and find out what Charlie's secret is. Then the Twenty-Sixth will kick some ass. When we're finished, we'll report the truth back to the REMFs."

All three junior men came to attention, turned smartly, and left the colonel's office.

MacDonald is really shit hot, Jackson thought. *One of those rare men who can say turgid things in simple words and make you think they're more than basic bullshit.*

THIRTY-SEVEN

3rd Force Recon Officers' Quarters, Phu Bai

1810, July 1, 1968

"YOU TWO CAN USE the jeep. Corporal Ramirez will take you anywhere you need to go."

Jackson smiled. "Thanks, Sergeant Major. A shower and a bed is all I need."

Rivers chuckled. "That we can provide, Lieutenant."

The sergeant major envied the officers their easy camaraderie. "Ramirez is in the adjutant's office. I'll send him out."

The two officers returned the sergeant major's salute and waited for Ramirez and the jeep to pull up. When they were alone, Rivers opened up. "Welcome home, Paul."

Once again Jackson felt truly welcome, like a member of a close family happy to have him back home again.

"I wish I could say I was glad to be back, but it wouldn't be close to the truth."

"Well, at least you're still dumb enough to be painfully honest. Quantico didn't mess you up too bad?"

"No, but it was an experience I'm damned glad I won't have to repeat."

Rivers laughed. "All kidding aside, how does it feel to be back?"

"Jesus, Bart, I don't know. I feel like I'm dreamin'. Seeing you, the colonel, and the sergeant major again is surreal. By the way, congratulations again on the promotion. I don't need to tell you I think it's long overdue."

"Thanks. Look, I know I shanghaied you into this deal, and I've spoken with the colonel about it. If you want out, we understand."

Jackson snorted. "Thanks a hell of a lot. Just what would you and the colonel have me doing if I decided to un-volunteer? Leading a platoon of cherries?"

"No, nothing like that. MacDonald said he'd find a place for you here at headquarters. He knows how you feel about being a platoon leader."

Jackson's voice dripped sarcasm. "Well, my choices are so varied. I can be either a gung-ho idiot and chase your ass around the hills or a REMF no one has any use for because he's too chickenshit to volunteer. Thanks a hell of a lot."

Rivers stopped to examine the younger officer's face, as if he were having doubts about him. Then he saw the beginnings of a smile creep into Jackson's face. "Okay, wiseass. You're on board." He laughed and slammed his hand onto the younger man's back.

"When do I begin . . . *sir?*"

"An hour ago, but I needed to offer you a way out. Not that I expected you to take it."

"In for a penny, in for a pound, and all that."

"Look Paul, we have an unprecedented opportunity here. We can make this good duty and eliminate as much of the danger as possible by training hard. If we make this unit successful, it'll be good for all of us."

"How safe can that be? We have yet to solve the original problem of the dead LRRPs."

"Well, it hasn't been for lack of trying. I'm not going to bullshit anybody . . . there's no covering up the danger. We're fighting an unbelievably capable adversary—something you understand better than most. We *will* find out what Charles knows, but it will always be dangerous. Perhaps not as much as being a grunt, but bad enough."

Jackson stuck with his sarcasm. "No balls, no blue chips."

When the jeep reached the officers' club, Rivers got out. "I'm going to have a few beers and adjust my attitude. I have your Stoner and M40 in my locker, so you won't need a weapon, and Ramirez will organize the rest. I'll see you at 2100. We'll burn some steak, and you can meet the other officers."

Jackson got back into the jeep. Mention of sleep made him aware of his fatigue but could not kill his excitement.

Corporal Ramirez led Jackson to Officers' Quarters, 3rd Force Reconnaissance Company. "It's a standard officers' hooch, except for inside," Ramirez said. "This has only four areas and is as secure as it can be made. It's two rows away from the center of officers' country and six from the perimeter." The corporal dropped Jackson's bags next to the only vacant rack, then pulled a notebook from his pocket and wrote down Jackson's sizes. What kind of weapon do you want, sir? Forty-five or M16?"

"The major has my Stoner and M40, and I have a .357 broken down in my valpak." Jackson waited to see how the corporal would handle this violation of the weapons regulations.

The corporal looked at him with a little more respect. "Yes, sir. What's an officer doing with a sniper rifle, sir?"

"I haven't always been a zero, Ramirez. Eight weeks ago I was a buck sergeant attached to Rivers' recon team, and I still haven't shaken the bad luck."

The corporal's eyes widened and his mouth fell open. "You're *that* Jackson, sir?"

"Well, I don't really know what you mean by '*that Jackson*,' but I reckon I'm the only one stupid enough to serve with the major."

"Yes, sir. Its just there are a lot of stories about you and the Duc Lo incident, sir."

"All bad, I'll bet."

"Only some, sir." Ramirez thought Jackson was okay . . . for a zero. To begin with, he didn't act like some stupid cherry that was going to get men killed. "I'll draw bulk ammo for your Stoner, a couple hundred rounds for the M40, and several boxes of .357 shells if that's okay."

Jackson liked Ramirez right off. He didn't use ass-kissing comments like, "Glad to have you back, sir"; what he said was simple and straight to the point.

"What do they have you doing, Corporal, besides chauffeuring the sergeant major?"

"That's about it, sir, but I've asked Major Rivers if I could volunteer for this outfit."

"Not that it's any of my business, but can I ask why you'd like to work with that crazy son of a bitch?"

"I respect him, sir. He's no gung-ho college boy who's going to get my ass shot off, *sir.*"

"Well, I can agree with you there. There's no one better, and if you have to be here, et cetera."

Ramirez shot a hot look at Jackson. "That's not it, Lieutenant. I spent my six months with the 3rd Battalion, walking point for a bunch of cherries who didn't know their ass from a popcorn fart. One of them walked us into a gook ambush and I got hit. I don't want to work with FNGs . . . not ever again."

Jackson detected a little hostility coming his way. "Well, Corporal, if it puts us on friendlier terms, I know how you feel. I spent time with the grunts and walked my share at point. I didn't like it or the college boys either."

The corporal decided Jackson was telling the truth. Major Rivers and Colonel MacDonald treated him like an equal, and they wouldn't do that with a feather merchant.

"Tell you what," Jackson said. "I'll speak to the skipper for you."

"Thank you, sir."

"No sweat. Us point-walkers gotta stick together or the college boys will get us all."

Jackson did talk to Rivers. "What do you think about Ramirez?"

"I talked with him few weeks back. I liked him, but I wasn't sure I wanted someone that young in the outfit. If you're recommending him, though, my earlier opinion is confirmed." Because they shared similar opinions of Ramirez as steady, confident, and reliable, and because they needed corporals, Rivers agreed to his transfer.

Over dinner the major introduced Jackson to two other recently commissioned officers whom he'd recruited for Force Recon. "This one, he's the oldest, is Milt Severs. He was a staff sergeant with the 1st Battalion, 9th, at Khe Sanh. In fact, he took the second patrol out after the blockade was broken and has been recommended for the Navy Cross. He was hit in a particularly vicious firefight but managed to beat off an NVA charge. Following a second wound, he refused evacuation until all of his people were safe. But what really makes him a questionable asset is he actually volunteered for Recon."

Rivers pointed to the other officer. "This one is Jerry Robinson, also a former staff sergeant, who served with me during our first tour. He's led patrols into the Z on six different occasions and returned with his team intact every time. After Tet, he located two NVA battalions in the Au Shau Valley and kept his team in contact for a full day while a battalion of the Sixth was lifted in to engage. During the fight, he directed artillery and aircraft strikes until Charlie was contained. He's particularly interested in finding out Charlie's secrets." A large smile broke across Rivers' face. "But what makes him about the stupidest person I've ever met is, if you can believe it, after he was commissioned, this guy *voluntarily extended* his tour. I found him lounging around China Beach and recruited him after he told me his most important concern throughout the Au Shau Valley operation."

"And that was?" Jackson asked.

"Getting my team back in one piece," Robinson said.

Rivers pushed his plate aside. "We've been preparing for your arrival for the past fifteen days, Paul, and now that you've finally decided to grace us with your presence, we have our full complement of officers."

Jerry Robinson lifted his chin. "By the way, just where in the hell have you been? Bart's been crawlin' the walls thinkin' you went AWOL." The three men laughed and waited for an answer.

"I," Jackson said slowly, "have been exploring the feminine possibilities of the fine city of New York." He didn't elaborate. What he felt for Susan was very special, and he didn't want her to be the subject of boisterous gossip. He merely waved his hand in an exaggerated bow and let the subject slip back to the major.

Rivers regained the floor. "Okay, okay. We have the errant one back in the fold, and we'll write off his absence to amorous wanderings." After all four men had a good laugh the major grew serious. "Look, the fun's over. We've been assigned an important job, and we need to get on with it. Last week we lost another eight LRRPs, and I've just about run out of excuses."

Spreading a map of northern I Corps on top of the table, he quickly outlined their area of operation. "I've circled our area. It stretches from the Hai Van Pass north to the Z. That means, gentlemen, we get to browse through all of Quang Nam, Thua Thien, and Quang Tri Provinces . . . plus the entire DMZ. This is one hell of a big piece of real estate to be covered by just four recon teams, so I'll explain some things that'll help us get the job done."

The three lieutenants kept their eyes open and their mouths shut as the major continued.

"The first thing, and I'm sure all of you welcome this revelation," Rivers said, "is we won't walk to any of our AOs. All insertions will be by helicopter—Army Hueys, to be exact. We'll be supported by the 101st Airborne out of Camp Eagle. They're new to I Corps, but they have a lot of experience in the type of insertions we'll need. They're young, veteran pilots who know how to work around a hot LZ, and they won't ask us to do stupid things like 'pop smoke,' right Paul?"

Jackson laughed. "Christ, I hope not, sir."

The other officers let the private joke go over their heads. They knew the major had worked with Jackson on the initial setup of Force Recon, and it didn't bother them that the two men shared a special bond.

"Jerry, Milt, and I have developed a company training schedule," Rivers said. "We'll be leading the men, who will begin arriving tomorrow, through as rapidly as possible and training them as thoroughly as possible in the time we have. The emphasis is going to be in five major areas: rappelling, sniping, close air support, naval gun support, and what we're calling 'advanced' patrolling technique—or APT. In APT we'll teach the men to operate like VC. We'll eat only Vietnamese food, bathe with unscented soap, and wear clothes dried over buffalo shit. The idea is for us to smell and move like VC every minute we're outside the wire. During the next two days I want you three to get your heads together and fine-tune every facet of the program."

The three junior officers nodded, and Rivers was pleased to see initial camaraderie building. He'd been worried about the older men's acceptance of Jackson and was relieved at the absence of friction. That made his next job easier. "The last thing I want to cover is the chain of command. As long as I have no objections, and it pleases me to see none, I will command the circus and the executive officer will be Jackson. I realize Paul is junior and much younger than you two, and, technically speaking, less experienced; however, I'm convinced he's the man for the job." Detecting some concern in the faces of the older officers, Rivers continued, "I have good reasons for this selection, and I ask for some latitude before you jump to any conclusions."

The older officers had assessed Jackson earlier in the evening, and their initial evaluations were not good, so they were clearly surprised by the major's announcement. They thought Jackson was too inexperienced, and they were concerned about the many rumors surrounding Duc Lo, not all of which painted Jackson in a positive light. The prospect of having him as their immediate senior gave them pause.

Rivers didn't quibble. "I know you've heard the stories of his being yellow and hiding in the cave at Duc Lo to save his ass."

This was the first time Jackson had heard about that, and he bristled under the weight of the words.

Seeing his reaction, Rivers motioned for him to relax. Turning to the other two, he put steel in his voice. "I can assure you, there is absolutely no truth in that bullshit. I talked with Major Kruzak before they medevaced him and he told me what happened. I'll tell you only because I think you need to know, not because I feel Jackson, or my selection of him as XO, needs defending."

Jackson sat quietly and listened to Major Rivers relate the facts about Duc Lo to the two older officers. He didn't add to the conversation or comment after it was over.

The evening concluded with the two older lieutenants drifting off to talk things over.

Jackson wasn't happy about being appointed XO, but Rivers was adamant. The assignment was made; it was up to Jackson to win support.

"Why me, Bart?"

"Because you're the right man."

Jackson hesitated. "I don't know. I don't have as much experience as either Robinson or Severs."

"Look Paul, I realize that, but this is important work. You'll get the job done. I also trust you. I don't have that confidence in either Severs or Robinson—not yet, at least. They've both been told how I feel and why. Now it's up to them."

"What if they don't accept the decision?"

"Then I'll transfer them and look for two who will. I'm not going to change my mind, so get used to it."

"But, sir . . ."

Rivers had heard enough. "Lieutenant, when an officer is given an order, the proper response is 'aye, aye, sir.' You have been given an order, and the subject is not open to debate. You are the executive officer of this lash-up, and that's final. Do I make myself clear?"

"Aye, aye, sir."

THIRTY-EIGHT

3rd Force Recon, Phu Bai

0910, July 6, 1968

DURING THE DAYS following Jackson's assignment as XO, four staff NCOs, twelve enlisted Marines, and four Navy corpsmen arrived to bring Recon Company up to full strength. "These men complete the four teams we've been authorized," Rivers told Jackson. "Each team will contain an officer, a staff NCO, a corpsman, and three enlisted. Two-man teams weren't big enough; I was always scared. I want better than that for Force Recon."

"I agree," Jackson said. "Six-man teams provide enough firepower to get out of a scrap but are small enough to avoid detection. That is, if you're still planning to have every enlisted man carry a radio and every man to be sniper qualified."

In response, Rivers aped the commanding general of III MAF: "Your initial mission, Major, is to develop an elite force capable of conducting preassault and long-distant postassault reconnaissance." He continued, "Because we've been given a free hand, Paul, I've decided everyone will be trained as swimmers, boat handlers, forward observers, and parachutists as time and operational commitments allow. Only the best of the volunteers have been chosen, and I intend to work their butts off."

"Have you thought of a motto, Skipper?" Robinson asked.

"Now that you mention it, General Greene, the new ADC, talked about that yesterday and offered 'Celer, Silens, Mortalis.'"

"Excuse me, sir," Jackson said, "but for the sake of the ignorant, what the hell does that mean?"

"It's Latin for 'Swift, Silent, Deadly.' I think it fits."

Training began with Jackson delivering a speech. "Over the past year," he told the group, "LRRP losses have been horrendous. Charlie seems to know when they're coming and where they're going. Therefore, we've been ordered to create a new type of recon unit. Your training will be difficult and intensive . . . perhaps even brutal. The intent is to keep you alive. You may withdraw at any time without prejudice, but everyone here, including the skipper, will participate in every aspect of training. If you can't hack it, you will be transferred. There will be no exceptions."

Then Rivers took center stage. "Well, that concludes the welcome speech. The thing I want you to remember is *this no game*. We're up against an enemy that has only two goals: first, to seize all of Vietnam; and, second, to kill every American here. Enlisted, be back here at 1300. Officers and staff NCOs will conduct Force Recon's first officer's call in my office in fifteen minutes."

Jackson kicked the meeting off with a bottle of Chivas Black. "I don't normally condone this sort of thing," he said, "but this time it's appropriate. This command is special. We will work very closely together. There will be little formality, and those who claim rank and seniority will find little patience from the major or me. For example, I watched as you retrieved the liquor. What I saw was eight very disciplined officers who poured drinks in order of seniority; what I *need* is four well-coordinated teams. From this point forward, whenever we are alone, you will not segregate yourselves by rank. The skipper and I have been watching you together and have started to match you into two-man command teams."

"How did you do that, sir?" Staff Sergeant Jacobs asked.

"By identifying things that complement one other. For example, the skipper ain't all that good a shot, so he'll get the staff NCO with the best marksmanship skills." The comment drew a few guffaws and a couple of long faces, but otherwise the men accepted the concept, just as Jackson and Rivers had thought they would. "Take a few minutes and work out which one of you that might be. Our first assignment is to identify things about the LRRPs that help Charlie find them. I'll be back in about fifteen minutes. While I'm gone, identify what you think they're keying on."

★

Jackson returned to a vigorous conversation. "What have you identified?"

Staff Sergeant Halcro was the first to answer. "I think we smell different. It's our shaving cream, laundry soap, mouthwash, and aftershave. They simply can smell us, sir."

Jackson nodded. "We do smell different, and that will start to change today. From this time forward, gentlemen, we will bathe and eat like gooks and wear clothes dried over burning buffalo shit, and we won't use anything that produces an unnatural odor. Glad you're on board, Halcro."

Lieutenant Severs was next. "We talk too much, and our equipment makes too much noise."

Jackson smiled. "Agreed. Therefore, our rule will be no talking outside the wire. We will use hand and arm signals, and if we have to speak, it will be whispers directly into the ear. Finally, everyone will make sure his gear and that of each man in his team is noise-proofed. If they can't hear or smell us, we'll have a better chance of escaping detection."

Over the next half hour the command group continued to voice their thoughts. There was little duplication, and they came up with many ideas that Rivers and Jackson had not thought of.

At 1300 the entire unit came back together to be addressed by Major Rivers. "Our mission is to provide highly specialized reconnaissance in situations where it's either too dangerous or too difficult to use LRRPs. We'll accomplish this mission by being the most aggressive unit in the Corps."

"I don't mean to rain on your parade, Major," Gunnery Sergeant Williams said.

"But just how are you going to take a bunch of overweight noncoms and three junior officers and create such a force?"

Rivers smiled. "Good question, Gunny. First, you're all volunteers. I take that to mean you've given me permission to work you until you drop. We'll employ the most difficult physical training that can be devised and augment it with instruction in very specialized skills. We'll sleep on the ground instead of in racks. We'll eat, drink, and work like Vietnamese. In short, we'll become Charlie.

"Colonel MacDonald wants us to be the finest reconnaissance outfit that's ever existed in the Corps. *I* want you to live long enough to catch the freedom bird home. To make sure those things happen, I expect every man to maintain himself in a continual state of readiness and a positive state of mind. Nothing less than 100 percent will be tolerated. Unless we're discovered, we will operate independently. Therefore each man will develop sufficient skill to keep his unit alive long enough to complete the mission. We're assigned a difficult task, and this company will accomplish every assignment."

The guts of the major's talk came mostly from the unit's operational order, but the spirit in which he delivered it had all of the men screaming, "*Oooh-rah.*"

Lieutenant Severs followed the major. "I'm going to address our area of operations. It's big and damned rough. In fact, the topography covers just about every conceivable type of real estate in Vietnam, from dense jungle to open meadow. Elevations range from a hundred meters above sea level to well over a thousand."

"It's just I Corps, ain't it, LT?" Corporal Ramirez asked.

"Yeah, it's I Corps—but the worst parts of it, including the border with Laos. Some of the mountains reach more than a thousand meters, and the average slope is around forty degrees. In fact, in the Au Shau Valley it approaches vertical."

The room grew very quiet.

"We will be patrolling some of the densest jungle in the world, infested with NVA and what few VC are left. This is serious work for serious people. Therefore, teamwork will be absolute at all times. We must be cohesive if we're going to survive. Detection, gentlemen, means death."

"On that happy note," Jackson said, "you're dismissed. Assemble on the flight line at 0600 to commence rappelling instruction."

At first light, the company stood next to a large observation tower. Lieutenant Severs was on top. "I will demonstrate proper rappelling technique," he said, then pushed himself out and away from the wall and covered the fifteen-meter drop in less than three seconds. Then he climbed back to the top and acted as inspector and safety officer for the exercise.

"When you get to the edge of the tower," Severs said. "I'll check your equipment. After I've determined you're safe, move to the edge of the platform. With your back toward the ground and your heels hanging over the edge, push back and descend in three or four bounds."

Not all of the efforts were proficient. A corpsman who had never rappelled before found himself hanging upside down five meters from the ground.

Lieutenant Severs talked him down. "Focus on the tower roof. Then slowly let the slack out of the rope." The instructions turned a potentially deadly experience into a successful one as the corpsman bounced his way to the ground amid friendly laughter.

By the end of the day the company had progressed from simple rappels wearing only their utility uniforms to drops that included equipment and weapons. The feeling of joint accomplishment was the beginning of a special bond among the men. Working together created camaraderie.

★

The next element, conducted by Jackson, was the M40 sniper rifle. "When you fire, you will shoot to kill. The most effective place is the head, but that's difficult to hit over long distance. Therefore, aim your rounds at the chest, just below where the soft part of the neck joins the chest cavity." After a short period of instruction Jackson took the group to the firing range. He enjoyed demonstrating the weapon and was pleased with the men's enthusiasm.

"Wow," exclaimed Sergeant Martin, a radioman in Major Rivers' team. "The XO can really shoot. He may look like a kid, but anybody who can shoot like that is welcome on my team anytime. His entire shot count was covered with a single marker."

Major Rivers added to the XO's growing acceptance by letting it quietly slip that Jackson felled eleven NVA officers at Duc Lo from a distance of more than five hundred meters with a single shot to each of their foreheads—in the dark.

Jackson concluded the training session by talking about bullets. "We will use hollow-points, a soft lead projectile that possesses enormous stopping power. And we will make every round even more effective by filling the hollow point of each bullet with a drop of mercury and covering it with wax."

"The wax," Major Rivers added when he saw the dubious looks cross the men's faces, "will keep the mercury from spilling inside your weapon."

"How does that improve the stopping power?" Staff Sergeant Halcro asked. "The wax'll melt before the bullet exits the barrel."

Jackson nodded. "That's right, but the air resistance will keep the liquid inside the hollow until the bullet hits home. On impact, the mercury will splatter and add tremendous power to the projectile."

Rivers interrupted again. "When a standard hollow-point strikes a man's shoulder, it leaves a small entry hole and a larger exit wound. However, when mercury is added, it's impossible to determine where the bullet entered or exited because the impact will blow the man's shoulder and arm completely off his body."

Within hours each man had his own ammunition stash.

Lieutenant Robinson taught the knife as a silent killing weapon. "While it's our mission to remain undetected," he told the group, "that won't always be possible. There'll be stubborn gooks whose continued presence endangers the team. When left with no alternative, you will remove the obstacle quickly and silently. XO, can you help demonstrate the best technique?"

Robinson had Jackson take a position facing away from him. "Grab Charlie across his face and mouth and insert the knife under the soft tissue in the neck at the base of the skull like so." He put his hand over Jackson's mouth and jerked his head back roughly. "When you have him in this position, thrust your knife upward into the brain and twist the blade from side to side. This will kill instantly and without sound." Lieutenant Robinson deliberately manhandled Jackson during the demonstration, and everyone present noticed it.

Corporal Ramirez spoke to cover his discomfort. "Why not just cut the throat?"

Robinson pushed Jackson away and smirked as the XO rubbed his now very sore neck. "Only John Wayne uses that technique. Out here, if you bend someone over your shoulder and slash his throat, three things will happen. One, blood will soak your uniform and equipment; blood smells and draws attention. Two, it makes noise that can be heard by others. But most important, it's not an instant kill. It can take longer than you think for someone to bleed to death, and in that time he can kill you."

"Can you do me a favor and stay after we adjourn, Mr. Robinson?" Jackson said. "I'd like to go over this again."

"Sure."

Rivers lingered in the background and watched as Jackson again allowed himself to be the enemy. When Robinson placed his hand over Jackson's mouth, the "enemy" threw his hip into his attacker, knocked him to the ground, and kicked him in the stomach. "If you ever pull any bullshit like that again," Jackson said. "I'll kick your ass, then transfer you outta here so fast your fuckin' head will spin."

Rivers nodded and walked away.

The training continued with night ambush patrols and lectures on the effective use of terrain and camouflage. Each man was taught how to apply "cammie" paint to break up the sharpness of human features, and how to move through the jungle without making a sound.

At the end of the training period, Rivers called the full force together for a final meeting. "You've been trained to accomplish the mission by using your heads, practicing stealth, and applying your knowledge of the enemy," Rivers told them, "and we've practiced until you can perform automatically. As a result, the company is now a single, cohesive, listening force."

"Yes, sir," Corporal Ramirez said, "and we all smell like gooks."

Rivers chuckled and nodded his head in agreement. "I've told Colonel MacDonald we're ready. I'm proud of every man in this unit. You've crammed five months of intensive training into as many weeks, and as I look before me I can find no fault. We've been ordered to commence operations immediately, and I expect us to be under way within a few days. However, there's one final thing I need to cover, and that's how we'll report what we see."

He paused to emphasize the urgency of what was coming. When the men started to lean forward, their anticipation creating a physical reaction that built to unbearable tension, Rivers continued. "I'm reminded of the Gurkhas of Nepal who fought with the British during World War II. They were widely considered the finest soldiers of their time and had the complete trust of the British Army. One of the most important reasons for this confidence was . . . *they never lied*. If they saw a hundred enemy soldiers, that's what they reported. If they saw only one, he was the solitary enemy discussed."

The major's point was made: Third Force Recon would tell the truth.

THIRTY-NINE

Hai Van Pass

0620, August 18, 1968

THE SUN MELTED AWAY the fog as the helicopter flew across the jungle, its dark shadow clearly visible on the treetops below. Inside sat the second team, 3rd Force Recon, under the command of Lt. Paul Jackson. Their mission was to scout the Hai Van Pass, a major enemy stronghold in the south. The team was codenamed Con Voi, Vietnamese for "elephant." They felt it was symbolic because their "trunks" were fully exposed.

The sound of the Huey's rotor changed slightly as the pilot slowed the helicopter, the first indication the insertion point was near. Jackson yelled over the rotor wash, "Take positions."

"Look down, Skipper." Corporal Ramirez pointed to where two Cobra gunships made low passes over the intended LZ. "I don't see any green tracers." The Communists' automatic weapons used green tracers; Americans' weapons used red.

"Or any sign of movement," Staff Sergeant Halcro added.

"Doesn't mean they aren't down there," Jackson yelled. "Could be they're just not showing themselves."

Before the Huey's skids touched the ground, the team was out and pushing its way through the elephant grass toward the safety of the jungle. Using hand and arm signals Jackson said, "Follow me," and the team quickly moved out toward its initial observation post. As they moved, Jackson kept looking back toward the LZ and the helicopter.

"Why doesn't it get the hell outta here?" Halcro whispered.

"How should I know? It's going to draw a large crowd, though, and real soon."

Five minutes later, when the team reached the initial objective, the escorting Cobra gunships were still circling the LZ, keeping a close watch over the grounded Huey. This was not a good sign. Jackson turned to his radioman. "Ramirez, get the chopper on the horn and find out what the problem is."

"They've got a broken hydraulic line, Skipper," Ramirez reported. "The pilot said the crew chief's makin' the repair, and he doesn't like being on the ground any more than we like having him there."

"He gets an 'A' for smarts," Halcro said. "He knows he's about to become a huge target, but I don't think he gives a shit about us."

Minutes later the team heard the Huey apply power and watched as the helicopter lifted off safely. As they began the trek up the steep slopes, Halcro whispered. "Wouldn't you know it? Rain! By noon it'll be fallin' in sheets, and it'll be puddled ass deep to a tall giant by evening."

"Skipper, the rain's sticky, like thin juice," Ramirez said.

Jackson nodded. "Runoff from the trees; it'll make your skin itch. Think of it as nature's revenge for invading the jungle's solitude."

"Quiet," Halcro hissed. "It will also smother Charlie's noise if he's movin'. We're supposed to be silent, remember?"

The only signs they saw of the enemy were some flooded tunnel openings and two caches of rotting rice. By the end of the day, the team had climbed through the cloud cover and into the bright sunlight.

Halcro reported a problem. "Two men have a fungus on their skin."

"Already? How'd they get it?" Jackson asked.

"Probably brushed up against a tree."

"Yeah, well, the source of their misery is about to change. When the rain stops, the bugs come out."

Indeed, swarms of flies, gnats, mosquitoes, and midges combined with fat red spiders, snakes, and leeches to torment the men, who continually pulled parasites from their boots and from their shirt buttons. Corporal Harris stumbled and fell against the wet leaves of the hill. When he stood, three leeches, one as big as his thumb, clung to the side of his face.

"Tell Ramirez to take his antenna down," Jackson ordered. "It's sweeping red ants out of the trees and they're falling on the men behind him."

Halcro relayed the order. "Ramirez, get that friggin' antenna down. You're killing us." The ants bit fiercely and had to be pulled off one by one.

At 1600 the team reached a good harbor site. They laid out their PSIDs and claymores, then withdrew into a cave cut into a solid rock wall. Exhausted, they spread out their groundsheets, and all but the first watch fell asleep immediately. They slept in a semicircle, with each man's feet pointed toward the center and his head and shoulders toward the cave opening. The night passed uneventfully.

"We're move across the ridges today," Jackson told them as they ate a quick breakfast, "and, if the Intel weenies are correct, we should see plenty. Recheck your gear, and keep it down to whispers only. Let's not let them know we're here."

Jackson led the team back into the jungle before dawn dissipated the ground fog. "Leave any food you find untouched, but if we find weapons, remove the firing pins and detonators and fix explosive charges to go off when someone handles the weapon. That'll allow us to take out a few and remain undetected."

Halcro nodded agreement. "Good idea, Skipper. We'll be long gone and get some payback at no risk."

"That's it. Those left alive will blame the Chinese for shoddy workmanship."

By early afternoon their trek had taken them back down through the clouds and closer to the valley floor.

"We're about six klicks from the LZ, Skipper."

"Good. Let's find a place to run the mission from. I don't like the situation we're in. The cloud cover won't allow air support, and the valley walls are too steep for extraction by helicopter."

"Yeah, well that ain't the worst of it," Halcro said. "That canopy's several hundred feet over our heads. That means we're on our own."

"Let's get tucked away for the evening. Nightfall comes early in jungle this deep, and it'll be pitch dark before 1630."

After the team was secured, Jackson and Halcro withdrew to discuss their situation. Both men were nervous, and neither was hesitant in voicing his concern.

Jackson spoke directly into the ear of the staff NCO. "I'm not liking this."

"Agreed, Skipper."

"Why haven't we seen any gooks? Just a shitload of tracks that tells me Charlie's moving away from us, toward the far end of the valley." Jackson spread out a small map that showed the Hai Van Pass and four kilometers around it in each direction. With a finger he outlined the team's advance. "We've covered the area between the LZ and where G2 thinks the gooks are. Tomorrow we'll stick to the ridges. It will slow us down, but it'll be a lot safer."

Halcro agreed completely, somewhat to Jackson's surprise. *He's far more experienced than I am,* thought Jackson. *Why is he so willing to put his life in my hands?*

Halcro did bring up one concern. "Sir?"

"Yeah, Mike."

"I'm thinking air and artillery can't be precisely spotted where we're going."

"That's right."

"I've been trained to call it in from above the clouds. We'll have to have them follow the river and come into the zone from behind. When they're overhead, we'll call the strike using the sound of their engines."

"Are you out of your mind? Call five-hundred-pound frags through the trees aimed only by sound? What're you smokin'?"

Halcro smiled. "Relax, Skipper. I did it a dozen times when I was with 7th ANGLICO. We primarily used the technique for naval gun, but it works great with air and artillery too. I dropped some heavy shit at Khe Sanh, and I have an overlay we can use with your map to make sure the shit doesn't rain on us."

"Okay, Mike. If you say you can put bombs in Uncle Ho's soup in the middle of a state dinner, I won't doubt you. I'm damned glad you're teamed with me." He pointed to a spot on the map where the valley narrowed, about six kilometers beyond their present position. "Here's where I think we'll find Charles. The river turns and slows at this point, and the valley floor flattens out. This looks like a good place to hide a large force, and I think it'll be lousy with gooks. So tomorrow, we climb up the slope again. Agreed?"

Halcro nodded, and they broke off the conference, returned to their sleeping positions, and curled up to await their watch. Jackson fell into a nervous doze. *I should have told Halcro I think we're in real trouble. I have a feeling the valley will be filled with thousands of NVA, not just the few skinny VC the Intel pogues talked about. A normal LRRP would report only size, morale, and condition, but we're being asked to do a lot more.*

Major Rivers had discussed the mission with him over dinner the night before their departure. "We need to prove what we're doing here is a sound concept, Paul. We need to find the enemy and get out of Dodge safely every time we head into the bush. If we can provide quality intelligence, Division will destroy them." The patrol couldn't simply guess at the enemy's strength; it had to know for sure. And the closer they got to Charlie, the greater their chance of being discovered. Jackson made a mental note to have Halcro train him on the "sound trajectory" technique when they got back to camp, and then slept until it was his time for watch.

★

The next morning they broke from the harbor and climbed back up the pass. The cliff walls extended 150 meters straight up, and below them the jungle steamed its humidity into the air. Without rain to keep them away, the insects returned to feast.

When Jackson looked up, he couldn't see the tops of the slopes. If Charlie was up there, he couldn't see the team either. Stopping briefly, Jackson whispered to Halcro. "Look down there."

"Where down there?"

"The river. Look at how it's overrunning its banks."

"Yeah, so what?" the gruff sergeant responded, wondering where the LT was going with this. "Yesterday's rain was heavy enough."

Jackson ignored let the sergeant's frustration. "Look where the valley narrows as it approaches that big turn. The river is deep and swift at that point, and effectively cuts off the left side of the valley."

Halcro kicked himself for missing it. "Good catch, Skipper. The jungle cover looks too thin. I see more than a few rice paddies with rice high enough to require weeding and transplanting—"

Jackson interrupted, "So where are the farmers?"

The team continued moving. About 0900, Corporal Ramirez spotted the first gook and signaled, "*Freeze!*"

"Looks like a young kid," he reported. "He keeps turning around as if he's looking for someone."

They looked where Ramirez pointed, and Jackson whispered, "I see him. He moves about fifty meters, then turns and looks back into the jungle."

Halcro nodded. "He's a trail walker. If Charlie's using a kid for bait, he knows—or at least suspects—somebody's watchin'. I'll bet that goddamned Huey yesterday piqued his interest. I knew it would."

"The NVA always use local VC to walk point," Jackson added for Ramirez's benefit. "We'll watch him and look for booby traps. We don't go down the path unless we're absolutely sure it's safe."

The next time the signal to freeze was given Halcro was on point. The team was well above the trail and surrounded by excellent cover. Whispering directly into Jackson's ear, Halcro said, "Look downriver, where the large boulders break the stream into small rapids."

Jackson saw a point where the rapids were no more than ten feet wide.

Halcro pointed at several large rocks in the middle of the river. "The noise the water makes as it passes over those boulders could mask the movement of a hundred gooks. Let's wait and watch."

Jackson nodded. "Fine with me. Ramirez saw the kid before he heard him, and that scared the hell outta me."

As they stood frozen in their positions, each man observed a different part of the trail. Jackson, fourth in the line of march, looked down into the valley where the ground rose slightly to reveal an old hut in a poor state of repair. Large pieces of the roof's thatch lay on the ground as if they'd been blown off by the wind. He touched Halcro on the shoulder and pointed at the building. "There's something about the roof that ain't right. I smell a rat."

He trained his binoculars on the entrance to the small building, and what he saw in front of the door made his blood run cold. He quickly waved the team away from the edge.

Halcro saw the lieutenant stiffen. "What is it?"

"The sand," Jackson handed the binoculars to Halcro. "There's two trails down there, and both are worn enough to have been traveled by thousands."

Sliding carefully to the edge of the trail, Halcro slipped the tips of the field glasses through the vines. Seconds later he was back at Jackson's side. "You're right. That hut ain't what it appears to be. Looks like an opening to a tunnel complex to me. That roof is made with green rushes. I could see fresh cuts in the wood."

As the VC trail walker started to climb to the hut, soldiers appeared at the doorway and beckoned to him.

Jackson whispered while Halcro wrote furiously in his notebook. "NVA. Dark green shirts, tan trousers, sandals, and sun helmets. Each holding an AK. Wait. Someone's different. Brown uniform; leather boots, not sandals; and a hat with a red band. Armed with a pistol. His friggin' skin's white . . . must be a Russian."

The young VC joined the three soldiers at the mouth of the hut. They talked for several minutes, then the Vietnamese went inside and didn't return. The European remained outside the entrance and was soon joined by three more, *all of them Caucasian.*

"Well, Skipper," Halcro whispered. "We found them, but how many, what are they doing, and why?"

"Those Soviets bother me. That Intel REMF didn't say anything about Europeans being here."

The enemy remained within easy killing range of the M40s, and the sights of three were fixed on the Caucasians' foreheads. The team could have dropped all three, but Jackson remained silent. Their mission was to observe. Turning to Halcro, he whispered, "When those three go inside, let's move back along the valley wall. I want to talk to Rivers."

Ramirez whispered into the radio. "Alpha X-Ray Delta, this is Con Voi Four, over."

The radio squawked and everyone jumped. "Con Voi Four, this is Alpha X-Ray Delta." Ramirez handed the mike to Jackson.

"Alpha X-Ray, this is Con Voi Actual. I have a sitrep." He reported the presence of the Russians and pressed the receive button.

"Con Voi Actual, is it possible to grab one?"

Jackson shook his head as if the guy in Phu Bai could see him. "No. Forget it." The possibility of grabbing an adviser this far out in the jungle and returning him to base seemed too remote to consider.

Afterward, Sergeant Halcro wanted to talk about it. "Why don't we try to grab one of those Russians, sir?"

"I'm not sure we should risk it," Jackson said. "We're a long way out, and if we have to shoot, it's a long run back to an LZ."

"I saw a place where we can do a snatch and run. We could grab one and didi without being discovered."

"Let me think about it," Jackson said. *My primary job is to get us back in one piece. Rivers doesn't want to start Force Recon's official record with a busted patrol and KIAs.*

Jackson took the radio handset from Ramirez and whispered, "Whiskey Alpha, this is Con Voi Actual, over."

Within seconds Phu Bai was on the line. "Roger, Con Voi Actual. This is Whiskey Alpha, over."

"Whiskey Alpha, need to talk with Whiskey Alpha Actual." Jackson turned to Halcro. "You're right. The chance to grab a Russian doesn't present itself often, and it could yield valuable information. It might be worth the risk, but I want to verify the potential with the major."

"Con Voi Actual, this is Whiskey Alpha Actual."

Rivers' voice had a calming effect on Jackson. "Roger, Actual. Have uncovered major base camp. Looks like thousands of possibles, with Russian advisers. Possible snatch and run, but I want some advice before we set it up. We could get our ass in a serious jam."

Rivers threw the decision right back at Jackson. "Con Voi Actual, I can't measure the risk. If you think it can be done, then do it. Snatching a Bear would be damned nice, but only attempt if you feel you can escape. I want you back, and that's my only priority."

Jackson didn't like it but understood. "Roger, Actual. Con Voi clear." After he dropped the mike, Jackson moved up the line to find Halcro. "Can we snatch a Russian and get clear, Mike?"

"I think so, Skipper. It'll be dicey, but I've done it before."

Jackson picked up the older man's confidence. "Okay. Let's break for the noon meal. We can eat and discuss it."

"What we need," Halcro said as he opened a can of peaches, "is a place where the trail narrows and makes a hard turn. I saw one where the path climbs away from the valley floor."

"That's more than five hundred meters from the tunnel," Jackson said.

"And well within range of our M40s. If needed, we can keep the gooks pinned inside while the snatch is done."

"Okay, that's it. But, we'll sit in ambush for only one night. If no Russians show, we didi. Three men will look down the long axis of the trail, directly into the tunnel entrance. The rest will be at the bend, where they can cover the opposite direction."

Halcro approved. "Sounds good. The snatch guy has to be Ramirez. He's the biggest we got."

Jackson smiled. "Okay, but tell him to subdue the Bear, not kill him. Use whatever force necessary, but kill only to prevent escape or if his life is threatened."

"Do you understand?" Halcro asked the corporal after issuing the instructions.

Ramirez was excited. "Can I fuck him up a little?"

Halcro ignored that and continued, "You'll be on the opposite side of the trail, unarmed. If a Bear does come by, and providing his escort isn't too large, you'll dive across the trail, tackle the bastard, and push him toward our side of the path."

Jackson agreed with the plan. "Okay. As soon as the snatch guy moves, we kill the escort party. The M40s won't fire unless help comes out of the tunnel. If that occurs, we kill everyone before they get free of the doorway."

The team was in position before sundown.

Jackson was nervous. "We don't want to be ambushed ourselves. Have one man approach each side. If it's clear, they can signal us up."

Nightfall brought a hard rain that pelted the men as they huddled along the trail. The team ran over the signals they would use if things went bad. The normal signal for "freeze," a raised clenched fist, would be used to call off the operation.

Jackson looked hard at each man. "Questions?"

"What about the bodies?"

"Leave 'em where they fall," Halcro said. "We need to get out of the area fast. Don't worry about them. We'll be gone before anybody finds them."

The men felt confident.

Jackson whispered to Halcro. "The weather's on our side. The gooks will have their heads bent low to keep rain out of their eyes, and the noise will mask any sounds we make. Have the men keep their gear close in case we have to didi."

Halcro nodded and the ambush was set. All they needed now was a Bear to come down the trail. Two hours passed agonizingly slowly.

Jackson was the first to sight movement. "Look at the tunnel. Men are starting up the path. Four NVA in the lead, with their heads down and no one paying attention to the jungle."

Charlie was too damned confident.

FORTY

Ambush Site, Au Shau Valley, Quang Tri Province

0200, August 21, 1968

HALCRO BREATHED A LOW WHISTLE. "Damn! There's three Bears in the file, and the escort is carrying AKs."

Jackson watched carefully as the patrol moved closer. *The middle Russian's paying close attention. He only came to the front when the others encouraged him. They must want to get out of the weather.*

Halcro also watched the gook patrol and a terrible thought jumped into his head. *We never thought there'd be more than one Bear.*

Just as the first Russian turned and followed the patrol up the trail, Ramirez drove him into the jungle. Immediately, the Marines stood up and killed the remaining enemy. There were no words for the fear, apprehension, and, yes, excitement that ran through the team. Afterward, none of them could move or find the strength to talk until Jackson stepped onto the path and kicked a downed Russian major in the balls. "Make sure they're dead." He looked at the dead major and saw where his Stoner had laid a three-round stitch across the side of his head and blown off his face. The open skull shone an eerie white as the rain washed away the blood.

Doc Williams moved to the next body. "This one's not dead, but he ain't gonna make it. Most of his throat's shot away."

"Use your knife," Halcro said.

The two team members who'd taken down the lead part of the patrol checked the bodies at the far end of the trail.

Hearing some rustling in the jungle, Jackson pulled his eyes right and saw Ramirez step onto the path. He held a stocky Russian colonel by the collar.

The Bear started to speak, but Sergeant Halcro made things clear. "If you say a word, shitbird, I'll blow your fuckin' head off."

The Russian's eyes grew as big as silver dollars when Doc Williams stuck a sock in his mouth and wrapped duct tape tightly around his head. When he pulled the Russian's hands behind his back, the corpsman saw the whiteness of an ulna bone sticking out of the man's arm. The corpsman chuckled. "Damn, Ramirez, we said tackle him, not kill him. You broke his friggin' arm." When Williams pulled straight down on the Russian's wrist and covered the hole with a sterile dressing, the colonel's eyes rolled white.

Jackson spoke quietly. "Let's get the hell out of here. Ramirez, you take point and get us back on the trail as fast as possible. Move toward last night's harbor. This place is going to be alive with gooks, and I want to be as far away from here as possible before they get here."

The heavy rain continued to fall, and the team didn't worry about stealth. They simply ran as fast as they could into the safety of the jungle. After fifteen minutes alternating between a rapid walk and an all-out run, Jackson called a halt and the men gathered in a group.

Corporal Ramirez whispered, "Skipper, I shit myself the moment you started firing."

Not a single member of the team laughed.

Jackson nodded. "I'd rather have you alive with your pants full than dead back down the trail. Good job back there."

"Alpha X-Ray Delta, this is Con Voi Actual."

"Go ahead, Actual. This is Whiskey Delta Actual."

"Roger. Require extraction. Suggest coordinates 12-58-36 by 7-15-29. Have one prisoner, over."

"Roger, Con Voi; 12-58-36 by 7-15-29 with one captive."

Jackson found Halcro and talked as they walked. "Rivers says Division wants us out of here as soon as possible."

Halcro smiled. "Well, for once I agree."

Jackson held his response and looked for his radio. "Ramirez, you're to give a two-click check every ten minutes."

"Sir? If they're listenin' that'll give the gooks a straight line to follow."

Jackson's eyes flashed. "I don't like it either, but get it done."

Throughout the night the team climbed across the face of the cliffs. As the first streaks of daylight broke through the cloud cover they reached the top of the ridge: six extremely weary Marines and one terrified Russian colonel.

Jackson spoke to Halcro. "Mike, let's finish this up. That tunnel complex was lousy with gooks."

"No shit, and I still can't get the smell of rotten fish outta my nose. They must've been feeding thousands. I say we give 'em a wakeup call." Halcro grinned, and as he threaded his way through the jungle he talked with 7th ANGLICO. "Papa John Delta, this is Con Voi Two.

"Con Voi Two, this is Papa John Delta Actual."

Halcro almost dropped the mike when his old skipper came on the line.

"Papa John Delta, request Arc Light for the front door of the coordinates we gave you last night."

"Roger, Con Voi," the radio squawked. "Consider it done."

At 0900 the patrol reached the far side of the clearing and called the evac bird.

"Roger, Con Voi. Pickup as soon as area has been cleared."

Jackson tapped Halcro on the shoulder and pointed into the sky. "That OV-10 lookin' for something?"

"You bet. He's been swinging back and forth for the last five minutes. He has to be searching for something, or someone." All at once the "Bronco" pulled up in a near vertical climb and hauled ass.

"Here it comes," Jackson yelled. "Everybody down! BUFF's here. Grab as much real estate as you can."

The team heard heavy bombs falling into the valley as a flight of four B-52s dropped their payloads on the coordinates Halcro provided. For more than two minutes 500-pound bombs struck the valley floor. Even far above the impact area Con Voi felt the shock.

The PRC 77 crackled into life. "Con Voi, Con Voi, this is Dog Food Five Seven, over." The OV-10 was up on the team's frequency. "Con Voi, do you see any triple A, over."

"Negative, Dog Food. No triple A seen."

The pilot's relief was audible. "Roger. Recommend you run like hell. There's a shitload of NVA movin' into the clearing at your rear. If you haul ass, there's a small river about three hundred yards forward of your current position. Don't worry about Charlie hearing you; looks like he knows where you're at."

"Move out," Jackson yelled as he started running through the jungle. They were moving too fast to look up and see the Bronco, but they heard it overhead on two occasions before they reached the river. When they were across, the pilot was once again on their frequency.

"Con Voi," called the pilot. "No response necessary. I will fire two Willie Peter rockets to mark the enemy's position. Keep your heads down."

Jackson signaled the team and moved to a position where he could watch. He needed to send corrections to the OV-10 pilot, who would relay them to the inbound aircraft. The first to arrive were Navy A-7s that raced across the white phosphorus markings left by OV-10 and dropped high-explosive (HE) bombs into the clearing.

"On target, Dog Food," Jackson yelled as the HE detonated. "Have your next flight come right ninety degrees and drop on the same coordinates."

A second flight flew across the axis of the first and dropped large canisters that erupted in huge fireballs. The napalm's heat was so intense that Jackson coughed and gagged from lack of oxygen.

"Con Voi," radioed the OV-10. "Gooks haulin' ass. All that's left are back over the lip of the pass. All movement to your rear has ceased."

"Roger, Dog Food. We owe you."

Jackson was all business. "Get the evac bird down here, and the rest of you, saddle up." He led them toward the LZ, where two Army Hueys lowered into the clearing.

"The extraction was completed without further incident and we were home by noon," Jackson told Rivers when the team was safely back in Phu Bai. "I was relieved as hell."

Jackson was working up his formal patrol report a few days later when Rivers came in. "You don't need to include anything about the size or disposition of the enemy, Paul. Just before we sent him down to MACV, that Russian colonel gave the Intel weenies a complete breakdown on the disposition, morale, equipment, and number of NVA and VC operating within the AO. He also told us how Charlie knew when our patrols were in the bush. They did smell us, but they also have been using portable thermal energy units to track our helicopters into and out of landing zones, so they knew exactly when and our teams were dropped off and how many men were in the teams. According to the Bear, they shadowed our patrols and set up ambush sites near sensitive areas. If we got close, they killed the team.

A week later, elements of the 26th and 9th Marine Regiments conducted a large-scale sweep in the pass and uncovered huge caches of weapons, food, and medical supplies right where the Bear colonel said they would be. But the Marines weren't alone.

FORTY-ONE

Headquarters 3rd Force Recon, Phu Bai

1420, August 23, 1968

RIVERS' AFTER-ACTION REPORT shed little light on the overall success of the mission because he drafted it as a statement of fact, not discovery.

From: Commanding Officer, 3rd Force Recon Company
To: Commanding General, 3rd Marine Division
Subject: After Action Report 0010868

The patrol through the Hai Van Pass by the second recon team of this command, codename Con Voi, provided realistic intelligence regarding the placement, size, capabilities, and morale of NVA and VC forces.

The conduct of the men was brilliant and, in every respect, reflective of the highest standards of the Marine Corps and the U.S. Navy. As to the significance of the action, the Con Voi patrol led directly to the destruction of at least two NVA battalions and produced valuable intelligence regarding how the enemy detected LRRP units in the field.

Success was achieved with help from Navy units supporting our withdrawal with close air support. Marine aircraft from VMO-6 and VMFA-212, and Army helicopters from the 101st Airborne Division led to the final extraction.

The mission represents classic use of small-team reconnaissance as a major contributing factor to the overall success of Marine infantry. The capture of a Russian officer led directly to the gathering of more information concerning the order of march and offensive capability of the enemy than has been collected by any one single mission in the past five years and is significant in the annals of Marine Corps history.

Signed,
Bartholomew J. Rivers
Major, USMC

FIRST ENDORSEMENT

From: Commanding General, 3rd Marine Division
To: Commanding General, III Marine Amphibious Force

There is little to add regarding the conduct of the Recon team codenamed Con Voi, other than to strongly reinforce that its conduct reflects the highest traditions of the U.S. Marine Corps and the naval service.

As to the significance of the ground forces action of August 1–7, 1968, I submit the destruction of a regimental-size force of the North Vietnamese Army, its Viet Cong supporting forces, and a large base camp must be held as a major success. That the mission resulted in no new territory being held is in keeping with current III MAF policy; i.e., seek and destroy. This was accomplished—utterly.

In the original intelligence summary, Major Rivers did not elaborate on the extraordinary accomplishments of the Con Voi recon patrol, commanded by Lt. Paul Jackson, USMCR. However, their use of enemy terrain and stealth resulted in the capture of a senior Soviet officer in the midst of an overwhelmingly superior enemy force, and that was noteworthy.

The leadership, command presence, and focus on safety displayed by Lieutenant Jackson are reflective of an officer far superior in rank and experience. His actions led to the safe extraction of the recon team and the uncovering of intelligence sought for more than six months. This officer's willingness to lead his team back into the Hai Van Pass to scout and to provide forward aircraft and naval gun observation is truly indicative of the special spirit and leadership we strive to develop in company grade officers.

As to the ground action, it is important to note the excellent performance of the North Vietnamese Army in the field. The enemy concentrated enough firepower on Alpha Company, 1st Battalion, 9th Marine Regiment, to nearly eliminate it as an effective fighting force.

The failure of this command to anticipate such ability was due to the poor planning provided by the III MAF's G2 section, which failed to utilize newly acquired information regarding the NVA presence in the area of operation.

The enemy concealed artillery on the surrounding ridges and above normal cloud cover. This was brought to bear between the point unit (A/1/9) and the central body of advance. This prevented the strengthening, or withdrawal, of the lead elements.

The resulting action produced heavy casualties not in proportion to those suffered by the enemy, whose counted (and verified) losses exceeded our total casualties by a margin of fourteen to one, but the largest suffered by a single Marine unit since World War II.

The losses in company and field grade officers were particularly grave. The Division mourns the loss of Lt. Col. Russell Browning, USMC, commanding officer of the 1st Battalion, 9th Marine Regiment; Maj. Miller Brandon; Capt. Marlin C. Braddock; Lt. G. J. Miller; Lt. T. C. Johns; and Lt. K. P. Miles. A full

list of recommendations for decorations will be forwarded via separate corre-
spondence; however, special mention is made of two officers whose actions
contributed significantly and without whose valor the losses suffered by this
division would have been significantly greater: 1st Lt. Paul C. Molet, USMC,
who assumed command of Alpha Company 1/9 following the death of his
commanding officer and continued to lead his men under extraordinary circumstances until relieved; and 2nd Lt. Paul A. Jackson, who led the initial recon
patrol and returned to the pass to provide forward observation during the
engagement. He guided air and artillery support to within twenty meters of the
forward elements of A/1/9, thereby keeping it from being overrun.

W. C. Smith

Major General, Commanding

"Mike, I've decided the men can have R&R at China Beach. I think they've earned it."

The sarcasm in Halcro's reply was diluted by a big smile. "What you mean, *sir*, is
we've been ordered off the line for the foreseeable future."

Jackson laughed. "That too."

Halcro upended his beer. "That'll make the men feel guilty, Skipper, but the R&R
the lieutenant has so graciously provided is richly deserved."

Both men collapsed in peals of drunken laughter and hugged each other hard with
a level of emotion only men who owe each other their lives can understand. Neither
thought about what took them back to the pass in the first place.

"I volunteered the team to return to the pass to spot artillery and air for the regiment.
We have firsthand knowledge of the valley that'll be indispensable to the operation."

Halcro was really and truly pissed. "What did Rivers say?"

"He liked the idea. He arranged for Headquarters Company, 1/9, to provide our
security."

"Oh, lucky fucking us. One Nine? Do you know what their nickname is,
Lieutenant?" Not waiting for an answer, he roared, 'The Walking Dead.' They're called
that, *sir*, 'cause, they've had more of their people killed than the rest of the friggin'
division combined. Thanks a hell of a lot."

"Saddle up, Mike."

FORTY-TWO

Hai Van Pass

1420, August 24, 1968

THE RAIN STOPPED on the second day, and the jungle steamed its heat into the Marines searching the jungle. Dark, ominous clouds roiled overhead and shrouded the hilltops above six hundred meters. Captain Braddock, commanding Alpha Company of the 1st Battalion, 9th Marine Regiment (A/1/9), peered at the river. "The banks are swollen, but there's plenty of fords."

First Lt. Paul Molet, the company XO, nodded. "I don't like it, sir. I'm concerned by how the pass narrows near the big turn in the river. The hut Recon identified as the tunnel entrance is just past that point. We're too exposed."

"If we get hit," the colonel said, "we can hunker down in the bomb craters."

Molet wouldn't be deterred. "When we passed those rice paddies, didn't you think it odd there weren't any farmers or buffalo?"

Braddock didn't like having his decisions questioned. "No, goddamn it, I didn't. Lieutenant Dudley from Division G2 said he personally knows the Recon officer who filed the report. He said the guy is an immature kid and is prone to exaggeration, so all estimates were cut back." Those were the last words Braddock ever spoke. The bullet entered just below his left eye, the first round in an attack that followed like a violent thunderstorm.

Molet yelled into his handset. "We're receiving heavy automatic fire on our left flank. We're in the bomb craters with rockets and mortar falling all around us."

From the far side of the river the battalion commander yelled encouragement. "Hang on, Molet. Where's Captain Braddock?"

"Dead."

"How?"

Molet snorted in disbelief. "I don't know. Who the fuck cares? He's dead. I'm in command, and I'm organizing our defensive position around the machine guns. I've got most of them firing into the hillside to the left. There's a shitload of gooks massing over there for what looks like the main attack."

"What other heavy weapons do you have?"

"That's it; the rest ate it in the first barrage." Molet was calmer now. "We've still got heavy incoming. Mortars are coming from the backside of the forward cliff."

Colonel Brandt was having difficulty comprehending the situation. "Artillery and rockets are falling in the river behind you. You're cut off. Hang in there and we'll come get you."

Molet's radioman saw it clearer. "Battalion's full of shit, Skipper. They can't even help themselves."

★

Inside regimental headquarters, about half a kilometer behind Molet, the staff huddled in an old bomb crater. They rapidly collected information from the unit commanders, built a picture of the attack, and prepared a response to break free. Colonel McManus, the 9th Marine Regiment's CO, took a moment to marvel at the beautiful operation of his team: every movement purposeful and conservative, like a choreographed ballet. Radio traffic was heavy, but the voices were cool and calm. He knew his regiment would be fine.

Exuding confidence with every word and movement, the colonel picked out his operations and intelligence officers. "Okay. Two and three, talk to me." The S2 was Major Carlson, son of the founder of the World War II Marine Raiders, Col. Evans Carlson. The S3 was the first of his family to wear a Marine Corps uniform, Lieutenant Colonel Ribek. He spoke first.

"Alpha Company's pinned down and separated by heavy rocket and artillery fire. Colonel Brandt is using rifle fire only against the slopes to avoid hitting Alpha. He says rocket fire is intermixed with 90-mm and 60-mm mortar, and it's falling at the rate of twenty rounds per minute."

McManus nodded. "Bravo Company?"

"It's covering Charlie Company's flank."

"Colonel Brandt is very solid," McManus said. "What does he want?"

"He can't do anything until the rockets and artillery are stopped. He expects Alpha Company to be hit from the ridges to their front. Bravo is mortaring those positions now. Brandt says Alpha will have to beat off the charge before help can be brought up."

"What about the rocket and artillery fire? Where's it coming from?"

"Brandt can't tell. One of his platoon commanders, a Lieutenant Broderick, believes it's coming from the reverse slope of the cliff at the face of the pass . . . from above the clouds. Colonel Brandt wants those positions knocked out before making any attempt to reach Alpha."

"What's artillery think?"

"They can't hit anything behind the hill. The ridges are too high and the angle too steep. Alpha Company reports our rounds falling well below the enemy positions and doing little, if any, damage."

"Air?"

"Lieutenant Jackson recommends we lay in some HE on top of the cliff and along its facing, front and back."

"Tell him to get it done. What about the 2nd and 3rd Battalions?"

"Third Battalion is heavily engaged. They can see what's shaping up in the valley, but he can't get down there. Right now, he's pulled his heavy weapons back below the crest of the hill to deal with the heavy fire he's receiving," Major Carlson said.

"What kind of fire?"

"B40 rockets, mortar, and recoilless rifle, sir."

"And he can't take it out?" McManus heard impatience in his own voice. "We have to get this thing under control . . . *now*."

"He's delivering as much fire as he can, sir, but he can't shoot straight down the side of the cliff. He can't maneuver along its side either because of the near-vertical facing, so he's extremely limited in what he can bring to bear. He says he'll go over the side if he has to, but he doesn't want to lose men if he can get to the gook positions any other way."

Colonel McManus started to pace back and forth. "So?"

Just for a moment Major Carlson was stunned by the question. "So . . . he's trying to flank the positions using .50-caliber machine guns and, if they can get close enough, flame throwers."

"What's happening with 2nd Battalion?" The colonel shifted his train of thought to the battalion moving along the right side of the ridgeline.

"Colonel Martin says they haven't experienced anything in strength, sir. He's also faced with the cliffs and can't get over the edge. He says he'll have to reverse his line and return to a more gradual descent."

"Tell him to have one of his companies double-time back to where they can get down the slope." McManus slowed his pacing and stroked the stubble of his day-old beard. "I need your opinions, gentlemen."

Colonel Ribek said, "This was planned by a professional, sir. Not some rice farmer turned guerrilla."

McManus' voice was chilling. "What do you mean . . . 'professional'?"

"I think this is the work of the Russian that Recon captured."

McManus swore. "This was a trap. How could we have been so blind? If you're right, I'll personally see that bastard dies from a .45-caliber headache."

Lance Corporal McGuire, the radio operator monitoring the command net for Alpha Company, spoke up. "Sir?"

"Yes?"

"Sir, Lieutenant Molet says the mortars have stopped but there's a shitload of gooks massing to his front."

"What do you mean by 'shitload'?"

"The lieutenant's words, sir. I don't know."

The colonel's exasperation spilled over. "Well, ask him."

After a pause McGuire said, "Molet says he doesn't know . . . " McGuire's voice dropped off, and the colonel motioned for the remaining part of the message.

"Sir, he said, 'If McManus wants to count 'em, he can drag his fat ass down here and do so,' . . . *sir*."

McManus roared with laughter. "That does it, by God. We've got to save that kid. Ya gotta love a guy like that." He also knew that if he didn't get them some help, Molet would be starting his "whites of their eyes" speech very soon. "Okay, here it is. Have Khe Sanh concentrate their guns to the front of Molet's position. Tell them it's 'danger close' and walk the rounds back to the cliff facing. When the arty arrives, I want 2nd and 3rd Battalions to clear the gooks from the cliff. Get Bravo and Charlie Companies across the creek; and finally, get Recon on the phone and dial up some air and naval gun.

★

Today Jackson's unit fought with radios. Before the detachment left Phu Bai, Major Rivers had told Jackson to maintain two radios—one in contact with 3rd Recon Company and the other with ANGLICO—and to keep all frequencies open continually.

"Ramirez," Jackson yelled. "You're on me. Martin and Watkins, you watch Ramirez and switch your radio frequencies so you will always be on the nets I'm not. Mike, you and Miller are backup. Stay far enough away so one round won't kill us both, but close enough to compare notes. Third Platoon will give us one fire team for security. Keep their .50-caliber focused, will ya, Mike?"

Halcro plotted lines and distances from the team's location to every part of the valley.

Jackson told Ramirez to switch to the spot net and checked his call sign. "Alpha Delta, this is Sierra Delta Green Six."

Assignment control in Da Nang answered immediately. "Alpha Delta, roger."

"We have priority one to break up attacking heavy ground forces, artillery, and rocket launchers on the reverse slope of a hilltop."

"Target coordinates."

Ramirez handed Jackson a worksheet drawn by Halcro earlier and read out the coordinates.

"Coordinates of the closest friendlies."

Jackson read off the location, and the fire control center asked for the clear-of-target line, the danger-close lines on the various elements of the regiment, and the local weather conditions.

"Sierra Delta Green, we need to drop through the clouds. It's light and broken at two thousand feet. Your call."

Because the aircraft couldn't fly between the narrow, vertical cliffs, they would have to release their weapons above the cloud cover. "Your call" told Jackson it was his decision to approve the condition. "Roger, Alpha Delta."

"I'm giving you two flights. Black Sheep now and Diamonds in four minutes."

Jackson spoke slowly. "Roger, Alpha Delta. Black Sheep and Diamonds. Thank you."

"We will remain on line."

Jackson switched radio frequencies and picked up the inbound aircraft. "Black Sheep, Sierra Delta Green Six."

"You got the Black Sheep, partner. We're on your line and overhead in thirty seconds." Casual radio conversation was typical of aviation units, and especially VMFA-214, which traced its lineage to the early days of World War II when Pappy Boyington's squadron gained notoriety as the bad boys of Marine Corps aviation. Traditions die hard in the Corps.

"Types and payload?" Jackson shot back.

"Phantoms. Rockets, HE, and napalm."

"We will call you down by sound. Conditions are danger close. We cannot use the rockets."

"Roger. We'll pickle 'em off anyway. Everything counts now-a-days, boy."

Jackson ignored the comment. "Altitude and airspeed."

"Two-five hundred and four-niner-zero knots."

"Roger, Black Sheep. Confirming two-five hundred and four-niner-zero. I will need you in pairs."

"Roger that. Will drop on your hack. Overhead in less than ten seconds."

Jackson put the speed and latitude on his worksheet and looked at the distant hillside to judge its distance from his position. He added that and performed some basic math. *Thank God Halcro and I worked hard on this procedure. No room for error now.* Jackson yelled to Halcro, "Tell Khe Sanh to hold the arty. First run in ten seconds, and I don't want those F-4s flying into a friendly shell."

Jackson ignored the firefight and concentrated on the inbound aircraft. When he heard the high-pitched scream of jet engines, he punched his stopwatch. Two seconds later, the jets roared overhead. As soon as his stopwatch read eighteen seconds, he pressed the microphone and said, "Hack."

In the lead F-4, switches released high-explosive bombs and napalm canisters. As soon as the weapons were away, the aircraft gained altitude and moved away from the trajectory of the bombs. To the departing aircraft's rear, nearly 40,000 pounds of high explosives and 8 napalm canisters disappeared into the clouds.

"On its way, Six."

Jackson yelled, "Can Alpha give us a spot?"

Halcro spoke briefly into the handset. "Negative. They can hear the impact but can't see where they landed."

"Shit," Jackson swore. "Diamonds, Sierra Delta Green Six."

"Roger, Six. This is Diamond Lead."

"Use the same axis but come in on line; all aircraft at once. Fifty-meter intervals left and right of Black Sheep's line and on my hack."

Four Navy A-6 Intruders roared overhead.

"Hack." Jackson watched the ordnance fall into the clouds.

Halcro started jumping up and down. "Alpha says they can see flame and heavy smoke inside the clouds, and can hear multiple secondary explosions. He thinks we got the guns, and the incoming has stopped."

In the command trailer, Colonel McManus heard the report. "Get those companies over the side and get Alpha some relief. Get my chopper; I want to get up there. Come on, gentlemen, get the lead out."

FORTY-THREE

Hai Van Pass

1500, August 24, 1968

SECOND PLATOON, DELTA COMPANY, rolled over the ridge and moved into the pass. Lieutenant Miller said, "Keep half the men looking left and the rest forward."

"What about the right, LT?" the company gunny asked.

"Don't worry about the right, it's a sheer cliff, straight up. Get moving; people are dying down there."

The platoon hustled down a hard-packed road approximately ten feet wide that was clearly built to carry heavy vehicles. Miller told his radioman, "I'll bet the shit that's giving our guys hell was brought in on this friggin' road."

The platoon sergeant shouted orders. "Advance in fire team rushes, each in twenty-yard sprints. Machine guns up. Get your fire to the front and left of our advance." As the company moved, the M60s fired long bursts into the trees.

Delta Company's commander stressed speed. "Get the company down there, Gunny. First Platoon reported a safe advance." The captain thumbed the switch on his PRC 77's microphone. "Yankee Oscar Orange, this is Yankee Tango Actual. There's a large cave in the rock wall forward of your position about fifty feet over your head. Looks like a great place to hide an ambush. I suggest you put some LAWS into it fast."

The platoon leader disagreed. "LAWS are worthless. They'll just bounce around inside the cave."

"They're better than nothing. Maybe you'll get lucky."

"Yes, sir."

Second Platoon spread out across the road, and eight rockets entered the cave. Secondary explosions engulfed the cliffside, and pieces of NVA rained down on the roadbed. A fireball nearly a hundred feet high burned from the cave's mouth.

"Get some," yelled the company gunny.

Down in the valley, Alpha Company watched what looked like half of the North Vietnamese Army advance on its position.

"We got massed infantry to the front," Lieutenant Molet reported. "Looks like a regiment spread out over five hundred meters. Fire being received from all sides, and we're running low on belted ammo."

The two American companies descending the ridge found the way blocked by minefields. The gravel roadbed erupted violently when the point Marine stepped on a Bouncing Betty. As engineers located and tried to disarm the mines, NVA snipers methodically picked them off.

"Get some more LAWS and M79s up here and lace the sides of that goddamned cliff," the company gunny yelled. "Then throw some C4 on the road." Small white blocks of C4 rained down on the road surface. After it was blown, the Marines leapfrogged from hole to hole.

★

McManus was mad as hell. "Carlson, what's happening on the ridge? Have Second and Third begun their descent?"

"Yes, sir. Each has a company over the side, but they've run into minefields protected by sniper fire. They're advancing as fast as they can, but they're taking high casualties."

McManus wasn't placated. "Goddamn it. Somebody really underestimated what we were gonna find in here."

Lieutenant Colonel Ribek knew what might have been found. "Division didn't say anything about these conditions, sir, but I attended the briefing given by a kid lieutenant from Force Recon, and he stressed the potential difficulty and the number of troops we would encounter. But just after the Recon officer left, a first john from Division G2—Dudley, I think his name was—told us to forget those estimates because the kid was full of shit."

McManus' face went pale. "Are you shittin' me? Somebody knew this could happen and you didn't pay attention. *Why not?*"

"The REMF G2 lieutenant seemed to dislike the lieutenant, sir. He claimed he'd kissed General Lew's ass to get his commission after Duc Lo was overrun. They said he was sent to OCS to keep him away from reporters until the incident cooled down."

"What was the Recon officer's name?"

"Jackson, sir. He's spotting air and Navy gun."

"From Bart Rivers' group?"

"Yes, sir," Ribek said. "And if the stories about him hiding in a cave at Duc Lo are true, he could be a major liability. Then again, that was a hell of a piece of work taking out those rocket and artillery positions."

The hair on McManus' neck rose. "Jackson, you say? Young kid, about nineteen, twenty? Survived the ground attack at Duc Lo?"

"That's the guy. Like I said, the G2 said he was full of shit, so I discounted his report when I developed the ops order."

McManus lost it. "Well you fucked up, Colonel. I led the relief force into Duc Lo, and let me tell you how it happened, you chair-warmin' son of a bitch. That kid, that 'chickenshit glory hunter,' held off an NVA force of over a thousand men all by himself and called in artillery and napalm on his own position—not once, but several times. Through it all, his only concern was saving the life of the battalion commander he pulled from the ruined command post."

"Sir?" Ribek was stunned at the violence of the colonel's response. *Why is McManus so upset over a second lieutenant?*

"Listen to me you Boat School fuckup," McManus hissed. "That kid's got more guts than anyone I've ever met. He's the executive officer of Force Recon and has been recommended for the Medal of Honor for his actions at Duc Lo, and I'll be damned surprised if he doesn't get it. You discounted what he said? Goddamn you! You are relieved, Colonel. I'll not have a fuckup on my staff. No, by God."

"Sir . . . I . . . I don't know what to say." The light colonel sat down and shook his head from side to side when he realized the gravity of his mistake.

His agony increased a hundredfold when McManus said, "You could have prevented this."

The radio operator held a microphone toward McManus and jolted him back to the urgent situation. He'd deal with his former S3 later. Right now he needed to get the hell out of this trap.

"Sir."

"What is it?"

"It's Molet, sir. He wants an air strike. Says he can't hold the gooks off much longer. He reports they're massing in regimental strength in front of his position."

"Where's Colonel Browning?"

"Dead, sir," a young major said.

McManus grabbed a headset and spoke calmly. "Mustang leader, this is Six. Say again your situation."

"Receiving horrendous fire from three sides, sir. We can't hold."

"Stay calm, Lieutenant," McManus said "Two companies are on their way to you now."

"They aren't going to make it in time, sir. They're pinned down on the hillside."

McManus was pissed. "Molet, get Sierra Delta Green on the command net. Name's Jackson. He'll get you what you need."

★

Jackson turned his attention back to ANGLICO the moment the second flight of aircraft dropped their ordnance; two more flights were circling overhead. "Sierra Delta Green, this is Mustang Two Six," Molet's voice screeched. "Require danger-close support to eliminate massing infantry."

Jackson held his breath and signaled Halcro to the command net. "Two Six, we can't see the valley floor, or the aircraft. We can't deliver pinpoint—only area."

"Jackson, goddamn it! We're getting murdered down here. Give me a goddamned strike—now!" The desperation in Molet's voice was apparent to everyone on the command frequency.

"Molet, for Christ's sake, you have no idea what you're asking."

"Look, damn it. My people are dying. I've lost 40 percent of the company, and we're out of M60 ammo. We can't hold. If I get the air strike maybe we can save a few. Without it we'll all be dead in minutes. *We're being overrun!*"

Jackson remembered what he'd felt like at Duc Lo and knew what Molet was going through. He hoped he had sounded as brave when it was him on the other end of the wire. He turned to his sergeant. "Get over here and double-check my figures."

Halcro's face showed his reservations, but he clenched his teeth and moved beside the lieutenant.

Jackson pinched his handset. "Molet, it's too close, and we're too far back."

"Sierra Delta, this is Actual." In a low and very calm voice McManus said, "Jackson. I remember you from Duc Lo. You know, and I know, there's nothing that can't be done. Do it carefully, but get it done."

Switching back to the tactical net, Jackson's hands shook as he keyed the mike to talk to the inbound aircraft. "Wild Bird Leader, Sierra Delta Green Six. Danger close. Repeat, danger close. Heavy infantry concentration advancing on our lead elements. Will call your drop by sound. I need accurate responses only."

The flight leader's voice crackled into Jackson' headset. "Roger, Sierra Delta. You damn sure better know what you're doin', grunt. We have napalm and five-hundred-pound frags. They'll make a hell of a mess out of our men if we miss."

Unaffected by the pilot's warning, Jackson delivered the attack order. "Spread abreast, fifty meters' separation and abeam of one another."

"Roger, turning into formation now. We can drop to fifteen hundred but would like another twenty knots of forward airspeed to maintain flight level."

"Roger, three-one-zero knots."

Both Jackson and Halcro worked computations on their kneeboards.

"Drop on my hack," Jackson said. He compared his solution with Halcro's and saw they matched perfectly.

The command pilot's voice sounded cold and distant. "How close are the friendlies?"

"Danger close," Jackson said. "I repeat, danger close. Give us the napalm first, delay one second, and then give me the frags."

The voice of the pilot screeched over the com net. "Are you saying we're going to drop close enough that our bombs could blow napalm back onto our own men?"

"That's it. Friendlies are being overrun. Say again, overrun. There is no other option."

"Okay. It's your call. We're on line. It'll be the napalm on your hack and frags one second thereafter. We are thirty seconds out."

"Roger, flight." Jackson dropped the handset. "Ramirez, tell McManus and Molet we're dropping now."

Overhead, the tone of the jet engines rose to a screaming pitch. When they were directly overhead, Jackson punched his stopwatch. He closed his eyes. "Hack."

The entire Force Recon team heard the whoosh of the napalm as it detonated on the valley floor, followed immediately by the roar of the fragmentation bombs as they ripped the place apart.

"I've got flames jumping through the cloud cover," yelled Halcro. He peered over the edge of the cliff, and the blast wave from the bombs hit his face like a giant slap. "Goddamn!"

Jackson strained his eyes and waited for the radio report. "Come on, Molet. You have to make it. Please, God, let him make it."

"Sierra Delta Green, this is Molet," the radio sang. Jackson could hear the sharp crack of flames in the background, and his heart leapt.

McManus cut in. "Give me a sitrep, Molet."

"I can't describe it, sir."

Molet was crying into the mike, and his sobs made McManus' heart sink. "My men are singed. We've lost some hair and quite a few are suffering some minor cuts from the frags, but the gooks . . . well, sir, they're gone."

Colonel McManus' voice boomed. "There's no sign of further activity?"

"The smoke and flames are blocking our view, but the enemy's gone. There's no one to our front."

"Okay, Lieutenant. Well done."

"What do I do now, sir?"

"Stay put and tend to your wounded. Reinforcements are on their way. Improve your position and we'll come get you." McManus' voice broke as he handed the microphone back to the operator.

"Sir," the operator called after him immediately.

The colonel took the microphone again. "Actual," he said softly.

"Jackson, sir. How's Molet?"

"I'm right here, Jackson," the point commander said. "We're fine. Thank you. Oh, God. Thank you."

"Get off the net, you two." Colonel McManus spoke softly into the microphone, his voice too choked by emotion to enforce his order.

McManus wrote his final report on the action four days later.

> The battle continued for another three days. We chased Charlie toward Laos where the 26th Marines waited as a blocking force along the border. We caught the gooks between our positions and completely destroyed an overwhelmingly superior force.
>
> Our final estimates place Marine dead at 261. Most of which were lost in the lead company within minutes of the initial attack. Enemy dead has been estimated at 6,000, with 4,721 bodies counted. Higher numbers are based on blood trails and recovered equipment.

McManus told General Greene. "That small hut was the entrance to a fortification large enough to house thousands. It contained a surgical hospital with two hundred beds, over ten thousand pounds of rice, nearly two thousand AK-47s, and enough ammunition to supply a division in constant combat for a week."

On returning to the command post after the action, McManus found Jackson sitting on a cot in a medical tent, a large bandage covering a cut in his forearm. He touched the young officer's shoulder and sat down. "It's Paul, isn't it?"

"Yes, sir."

"This battle has proven Force Recon, Lieutenant."

"I don't understand, sir."

"This whole thing wouldn't have happened if the REMFs in Da Nang had listened to your briefing."

"*What?*"

"My S3 told me—right before I fired him—that G2 didn't take your briefing seriously, and he reflected that attitude when he drafted our ops order. If they had done their job properly, we would've come better prepared."

"That's a damned shame, Colonel."

"Yes it is. Will you do me a favor?"

"Yes, sir."

"Have a drink with me. I like drinking with people I respect." The colonel pulled a flask of Jack Daniels from his pocket and offered it Jackson.

"Thank you, sir."

The two men passed the flask back and forth until it was empty. Neither spoke another word.

FORTY-FOUR

Headquarters 3rd Force Recon, Phu Bai

September–October 1968

THE WEEKS AND MONTHS passed uneventfully after the Hai Van Pass engagement. While Division kept 3rd Recon patrolling aggressively, no more large-scale enemy movements were uncovered.

Jackson didn't let down his vigilance. After one long patrol he told Rivers, "Just because we don't see 'em, doesn't mean they aren't there."

Rivers laughed. "Schedule a routine to keep four teams on patrol and two in reserve. Our TO&E has been increased to six teams."

More time passed, and Major Rivers rotated back to the States to create a Force Recon Company within the 2nd Marine Division at Camp Lejeune. He was replaced by a lieutenant colonel named Michaels, who brought the blessings of Headquarters Marine Corps with him. Recon was now drawing the attention of officers looking to build a name for themselves.

Jackson was replaced as exec by a captain named Wainwright and spent his time leading patrols. Orders arrived transferring him to Headquarters Marine Corps. When he asked the new XO what kind of assignment he was likely to draw, the captain just shook his head.

"Hell, Paul, a second lieutenant assigned to HQMC is like pissing your pants in a dark suit. You get a warm sensation, but no one notices."

Jackson counted the days, and as he grew short he didn't venture far from his hooch. Finally it was his turn to take the freedom bird. On his last night in-country Jackson decided to break his rule and go to the officers' club for dinner. "Tonight's different, by God," he told his roommate, Lieutenant Mickelson. "There are a few people at the club I'd like to say goodbye to."

Mickelson chuckled. "Shit, Paul, I heard you hate officers."

"Only those like you, John," Jackson said with a laugh. "But I figure you'll be okay. Sooner or later Mike Halcro will straighten your ass out. You're right," he added. "I don't have a lot of respect for officers in general, but there are a few exceptions, and I want to see them one more time before I leave."

The air in the club was cold and stale. Jackson found a table in the dining room and took the menu from its holder.

"This seat taken?"

Looking up, Jackson saw Colonel McManus. He immediately started to rise.

"Sit down, Paul, and answer my question."

"No, sir, of course not."

"Good. I hate drinking alone, and it doesn't look like there's anybody in here except REMFs." Both men laughed. They had grown close after the Hai Van Pass, and both disliked the noncombatants who populated the club.

"So you're going home."

"Yes, sir. Tomorrow." Jackson raised his beer and took a long pull.

"You don't seem all that happy about it. Most of the people in this room would kill for your orders. I would expect you to be over telling those cherries how it feels to be short."

"Not tonight, Skipper."

"Why not?"

McManus didn't like the look on Jackson's face. He'd seen it too many times on the battlefield to be mistaken. It was fear.

"I don't know, sir," Jackson said looking at the group of boisterous officers. "Those people depress the shit out of me."

"Bullshit."

Jackson cocked an eye and eased himself down into the seat. He looked carefully at the colonel and saw much more than 220 pounds of muscle on a 6-foot-2-inch frame. He saw someone who understood, someone who had been in the middle of it and survived—a line Marine who measured high on Jackson's very short list of truly outstanding people.

"I guess I'm scared, Skipper."

"You? Of what?"

"Of going home. Of not knowing what comes next."

The colonel lifted his glass, touched the edge of Jackson's beer, and said, "To missing comrades."

"Missing comrades," Jackson said and swallowed his beer. He held up his hand and the waiter brought another round.

Jackson focused into his bottle. "I thought 'Nam would be really hard; and it was, but it's been something very special too. I've met incredible people, and now I'm afraid to leave."

"You want to talk about it?"

Jackson kept his gaze focused into the bottle. "I don't know how to say what I feel, sir."

"A lot of people in here think you're one fierce son of a bitch," the colonel said lightly. "They talk about you at night, like you're some kind of magician. Most of them haven't heard a shot fired in anger, but they all tell stories about you to keep the bogeyman away. Did you know that?"

"No, sir. I thought the only stories they told about me were 'he's too young to be an officer' and 'he was commissioned because he kissed General Davis' ass.'" The two men laughed and remembered when they last shared that little piece of information inside a first-aid tent in the Hai Van Pass.

McManus gradually got Jackson to talk.

First they talked about Bart Rivers—his calmness, his presence under fire, and his high-quality leadership. They laughed about Rivers' lack of a sense of humor. From his pocket the colonel pulled a letter he'd just received from Rivers and read it aloud.

Dear Skipper,

I'm back in the land of the big PX and it's surreal. They gave me a few empty Quonset huts bordering the ocean and told me to turn it into something. That will take awhile. Men are starting to report in, and as I watch them gather I'm reminded of the really great ones we served with. I haven't found anyone like Jackson yet, but someone with a big mouth and wild eyes will drift in, of that I'm sure. I just hope he's as tough as Paul.

I'm trying to teach my men that the enemy is a tough, smart, and savvy warrior, and not the bucktoothed, rice-burning weakling the newspapers make him out to be. If it's true the measure of a man is taken in the enemies he bests, then Charles is indeed a formidable opponent. If Hai Van didn't prove the NVA's quality to Washington, nothing will.

What I want to say is how much I miss it all. You know, we can't wait to come home, but once we're here it's as if we left the best part of ourselves back there. I miss the camaraderie of extraordinary men and the companionship of those who didn't make it back. I hope you will find Jackson and let him know I miss him most of all. We have to take care of men like him, because his kind are the lifeblood of our Corps.

What I don't miss are the REMFs. I guess Chesty Puller was right when he said that "there's two kinds of Marine officers, the line officer who does the bleedin' and the dying, and the chair-warmin' REMF who does the sittin' and the meddlin'." When you have time, hoist one for me and toast those line guys, will you?

I wish I could put into words what it means to me to have served with men like you and Paul Jackson, but I'll leave that for when we meet again.

With fondest regards,
Bart

Held together by Rivers' letter, the two men talked and drank far into the night in a friendship as natural and unforced as the passing of time. Each man felt and drew comfort from the other.

"Paul, we've talked about all the men we know except one."

"I don't know any others, sir."

"Sure you do." The colonel motioned to the waiter. "Lieutenant Paul Jackson." He waited patiently for Jackson to start.

Slowly, reluctantly, Jackson began to talk about himself. First in the context of the men the two knew, but then truly about himself. "I was always scared when I was out there," he admitted.

The colonel understood. "I suppose it's natural to fear combat. I sure as hell understand the emotion."

"But mostly I was afraid I wouldn't be able to perform well enough to protect my men."

"Well, there's something you never need worry about, Paul. Your leadership under fire is without peer. If I had five more like you I could win this dirty little war."

Jackson didn't respond. He turned away slightly so his friend couldn't see the water in his eyes, then changed the subject to his time in Quantico. With a faraway look Jackson said, "I met a girl when I was there. We fell in love our first night together."

The colonel smiled. "Congratulations. I'm glad you've found someone to share your life. When I met Gale I learned how the love of a woman has a strange way of making a man feel whole again after a bad experience."

By midnight Jackson was drained. He'd exposed himself completely to a very patient man. He'd shared every hurtful experience, every loss, and the colonel's quiet encouragement kept him talking. While the conversation didn't remove the pain, it did help him find a way to live with the ghosts. As the night grew late, Jackson was able to talk about the past months without developing tightness in his throat or stinging in his eyes. He once again felt in control and ready for something new.

"You remember back in Hai Van, Paul, how we sat on that sickbay cot, and drank from my flask?"

"Yes, sir." The image came rushing back into Jackson's head. He could picture them passing the flask back and forth, and he could feel the harsh liquid burning his throat.

"After those few moments, I've never been quite the same."

"Sir?"

"After we drank, I haven't carried my ghosts around anymore. Before, when I would try to sleep, my mind would fill up with the spirits of the men I've sent to die, and they always kept me awake."

"I know their presence, sir, and the vividness of their attack."

"I sleep peacefully now, Paul, and I owe you for that."

"Why, sir, I didn't do anything but sit there and drink your whiskey."

"You gave me quiet. You had enough sense to keep your thoughts to yourself, and I felt you understood. When I got off the cot, I knew there was another who understood the pain. It helped me deal with mine. I'm glad I met you, son."

"Thank you, sir."

McManus stood up. "No, thank you. I have to get up early in the morning, so I better drag my ass to the rack. You get on your flight and don't be afraid. You did good here, mister, and you'll be just fine in Washington." McManus held out his hand, and Jackson stood up to say goodbye. "Piece of advice, Lieutenant?"

"Yes, sir?"

"Forget what you can and what you should, but cherish the rest."

The two men shook hands again and held each other's eyes for a long moment.

"I'll try, sir. I think I can do that now. When I came in here, I wasn't so sure."

The colonel beamed and pulled the younger officer into a bear hug. "You go home to your young woman, Lieutenant, as quickly as you can. That'll help."

"Thank you, sir. You don't know how much you've helped me."

"You're a damned good man, Jackson; just like Rivers told everybody you were. I know, more than anyone, how you wanted to bring all your men home, and I know you tried, right to the end. No one could have done more. I'll finish with this. You've brought much to many and in a big way. You're a damned good officer, and I'm proud to call you my friend."

Jackson's throat was tight as he watched the colonel move toward the door, and the feeling was good, not painful. He picked up his beer, drained it, and followed his friend out the door.

GLOSSARY

I Corps	"One" Corps—northernmost of five operational regions in Vietnam; pronounced "eye-kor"
302	Military occupational specialty (MOS) number for basic infantry officer
782 gear	Field equipment, such as helmet, knife, haversack, and flak jacket
AAA	Antiaircraft artillery; referred to as "triple A"
AK-47	Assault rifle, designed in Russia, that was the favorite rifle of the NVA
Arc Light	Flight of B-52 bombers
Article 15	Fifteenth article in the Uniform Code of Military Justice that deals with nonjudicial punishment; i.e., punishment administered by a commanding officer in lieu of a court-martial
ARVN	Army of the Republic of Vietnam; soldiers of that army
As you were	Order to remain in position or doing the things one was doing
At ease, position of	Position allowing limited movement; opposite of "attention"
Attention, position of	Standing with back straight, eyes ahead, heels together, feet at a 45-degree angle, and thumbs pressed against outside trouser seam
AWOL	Absent without official leave; failure to be at the appointed place of duty at the time required
Blouse	Uniform jacket for camouflaged utilities and dress uniforms
Boat School	U.S. Naval Academy
Bottle of Jack	Fifth of Jack Daniels whiskey
Bouncing Betty	Antipersonnel landmine that when stepped on springs into the air before detonating
Brasso	Polish used to shine brass
Bronze Star	Fourth highest U.S. decoration for valor in combat
BUFF	Big, ugly, fat fella; affectionate name for B-52
Cammie paint	Camouflage skin paint, usually in shades of green; also "cammo"

CH-47	Army Chinook helicopter with twin rotors
Charlie	Viet Cong or Viet Cong soldier; also known as Charles, Victor Charlie, Luke, zipperhead, and gook
Cherry	Someone with more time to serve in Vietnam than another
Chu Hoi	"I surrender!" An operation to lure VC and NVA to surrender
Claymore	An antipersonnel mine used by U.S. forces
CO	Commanding officer
Commandant	The senior officer in the Marine Corps, a four-star general
Company gunny	The senior enlisted man in an infantry company—if filled by a gunnery sergeant or staff sergeant
Conduct unbecoming	The performance of an act considered unworthy of a military officer
Cover	Any hat worn by Marines; a place to hide
C ration (C-rat)	Canned food; best was peaches, worst was lima beans with ham
Crotch	A derogatory term for the Marine Corps
Cut and run	Drop everything and run away
'Dago	San Diego Marine Corps Recruit Training Depot
Didi	From Vietnamese for "leave"; also didi mau, "leave quickly"
Dink	Derogatory term for Vietnamese people
DMZ	The Demilitarized Zone between North Vietnam and South Vietnam
Doggie	Member of the U.S. Army
Dust-off	Medical evacuation flight, or medevac
F4	F4 Phantom II all-weather fighter/attack aircraft
Feather merchant	A lightweight; someone with more bravado than fortitude
Fire team	The basic four-man unit in a Marine Corps infantry platoon
First shirt	Senior enlisted Marine or first sergeant in a company or larger unit
Five A priority	Flight priority assigned only to critically essential people
Fly guys	Nickname for the U.S. Air Force or members of it
FNG	Acronym for "fucking new guy" (see cherry)—someone with one more day than another Marine to serve on his tour
Foo gas	Mixture of explosives and napalm usually set in a fifty-five-gallon drum
Frag	Fragmentation grenade
Frog	Frenchman; member of the French army
FUBAR	Acronym for "fucked up beyond all recognition"
Gig line	The imaginary line created by lining up the edge of the uniform shirt, the right edge of the belt buckle, and the trouser fly

Golden Fleece	A series of operations conducted in I Corps from 1965 to 1967 to protect locally produced rice from theft by VC
Gook	Derogatory term for a Vietnamese person
Grunt	Marine infantryman; also "mud Marine"
Guidon	A small, triangular red flag with the unit's number stenciled on it
Gunny	Gunnery sergeant, E-7
Hack	Slang for "on your command"
Harassment fire	Artillery fired at no specific target in order to disrupt normal enemy activity; used by both sides in the Vietnam War
Hell-box	A plunger-activated electrical detonator
Hogan's goat	A mythical pet that represents everything that is screwed up, filthy, or unprofessional
Hooch	A barrack or quarters on a REMF base
HQMC	Headquarters Marine Corps at 8th and I Streets in Washington, D.C.; often referred to as "Eighth and I"
Immediate-action drills	Training designed to provide swift action initiated with minimum commands
In-country	Stationed or assigned to a unit operating in Vietnam
Intel	Abbreviation for "Intelligence" or the S2/G2 Intelligence offices
JOD	Junior officer of the day
Klick	Slang term for kilometer
LAWS	The M72 LAW or Light Antitank Weapon; a portable, disposable, one-shot, 66-mm weapon used as a replacement for the bazooka
LAX	Los Angeles International Airport
Limited-duty officer (LDO)	Commissioned officer in grades second lieutenant through lieutenant colonel who is restricted to performing in only one MOS
LRRP	Long-range reconnaissance patrol or the men who perform them; pronounced "lurp"
LT	Spoken abbreviation for "lieutenant"; pronounced "ell-tee"
Luke	Viet Cong; as in "Luke the gook"
LZ	Landing zone
M14	Heavy large-caliber rifle that served as U.S. infantrymen's primary weapon between the era of the M1 and the M16
M60	Standard Lightweight Machine Gun; fires belted 7.62-mm cartridges
M79	Single shot, shoulder-fired, break-action, 40-mm grenade launcher; sometimes called the "blooper" because of its distinctive sound
Marking time	Standing or marching in place; waiting
MARS	Military Access Relay System—a shortwave radio system used to call home
Matched weapon	A carefully worked rifle built for accuracy in competition

Medal of Honor	The highest American decoration for bravery
MOS	Military Occupational Specialty—a four-digit number assigned to each specific job in the military service
MPC	Military Payment Certificate
Napalm	An incendiary weapon composed of petroleum mixed with a thickening agent made from naphthenic acid and palmitic acid
NCO	Noncommissioned officer
OCS	Officer Candidates School
Old Breed	A member of the "Old Corps"
Old Corps	Fictional organization claimed by those having seniority/ longevity that conjures up visions of what life was like in the "bad old days"
OQR	Officer's Qualification Record—a file that catalogs an officer's service, awards, punishments, and achievements
OV-10	Fixed-wing, twin-engine turboprop aircraft used for reconnaissance
Parade rest	Modified position of attention in which legs are open to shoulder width, hands are locked behind the back, and eyes are permitted only slight movement
Pass over	A dubious celebration "honoring" someone not selected for promotion
PFC	Private first class—the second-lowest enlisted rank
P.I.	The Philippine Islands
Pogue	Person; usually referring to a REMF
PRC 77	Standard radio set used by Marines in Vietnam
Punji stick	A sharpened bamboo stake, usually covered with human feces, planted in pathways
Rack	Bed
R&R	Rest and recuperation—a short period spent outside Vietnam
RAPS unit	Remote Activated Position Signal—a device used to mark specific positions for later bombing by aircraft
REMF	Acronym for "rear-echelon mother fucker"; someone without combat experience
Ripstops	U.S. Army term for camouflaged working uniform; usually called "utilities" or "jungle utilities" by Marines
Rock and roll	Rifle fire on full automatic
S2	Command section responsible for gathering intelligence— G2 at Division level
S3	Command section responsible for training and operations—G3 at Division level
S4	Command section responsible for supply and logistics— G4 at Division level
Saddle up	Slang for "get ready"

Sapper	A highly trained and motivated NVA or VC infiltration specialist
Scuttlebutt	Rumor or gossip; unverified information
Sergeant Major Daly	A legendary Marine NCO who was awarded two Medals of Honor and is famous for uttering the phrase, "Come on Marines, do you want to live forever?"
Shavetail	A brand-new second lieutenant
Short-timer	Someone with less than thirty days left on his or her tour
Sitrep	Situation report—a verbal expression of one's situation
Six	Your posterior
Six-by	A heavy truck with three axles, ten tires, and two-and-one-half-ton capacity
Skipper	Nickname for a respected officer or commander
SKS	SKS-45—a Soviet semiautomatic rifle, chambered for the 7.62-by-39-mm round, designed in 1943 by Sergei Gavrilovich Simonov
SMEAC	Acronym for the five-paragraph order: Situation, Mission, Execution, Admin/Logistics, and Command/Signal
Snake eaters	Members of U.S. Army Special Forces; sometimes applied to LRRPs
SOP	Standard operating procedure
Squid	Anyone in the U.S. Navy
SRB	Service Record Book—personnel file that documented an enlisted Marine's achievements and punishments
Starlight scope	A night-vision device that gathers images using low-emission starlight and shows objects in green light
Stars and Stripes	A military newspaper notorious for its biased reporting in favor of MACV
Stoner	Original name of the M16; named for its designer, Eugene Stoner
Straight skinny	The truth
TO&E	Table of Organization and Equipment—the authorized structure of a Marine unit
Top	A nickname for master sergeants and master gunnery sergeants; not to be used with first sergeants and sergeants major
Transient pukes	REMFs working in temporary assignments
Trops	Abbreviation for "tropical worsted"—the light brown uniform shirt and trousers worn during the summer months
Utilities	Battle or work uniform
Valpak	Officers' issue suitcase; also called a B-4 bag
Ville	Village
Warrant	Enlisted Marine's promotion document
Warrant officer	An officer rank that falls in between enlisted and commissioned ranks: senior to a sergeant major but junior to a second lieutenant

Weather bird	A specially equipped helicopter capable of flying in any weather
Well turned out	Appearing neat, well groomed, and in possession of professional bearing
WESTPAC	Western Pacific theater of operations; i.e., Vietnam
Whites and dress blues	Officer's dress uniforms
XO	Executive officer
Zebra Club	Unofficial group of very senior enlisted men
Zero	Name used by enlisted men to refer to officers that originates from their pay grade scale, 0–1 through 0–10

ABOUT THE AUTHOR

JAMES HAWKINS spent more than eleven years as a United States Marine, and is a veteran of the Vietnam War. Since returning to civilian life, he has become an international educator, author, and business executive whose career has spanned more than three decades and has brought cutting-edge training technology to more than 100 international countries. His professional career highlights include: U. S. Marine Corps Officer; Financial Executive, and, today, he is the Chairman and Chief Executive Officer of The Autumn Group, LLC, a humanitarian and ecologically-sensitive land development company.